10649897

AGASSIZ

AGASSIZ

A Novel in Stories

by

Sandra Birdsell

MILKWEED EDITIONS

AGASSIZ: A Novel in Stories

© 1991, Text by Sandra Birdsell
© 1991, Designs by R.W. Scholes

Printed in the United States of America
Published in 1991 by Milkweed Editions
by arrangement with Turnstone Press.
Originally published in Canada by Turnstone Press as *Agassiz Stories*.

Milkweed Editions
Post Office Box 3226
Minneapolis, Minnesota 55403
Books may be ordered from the above address.

ISBN: 0–915943–61–1

94 93 92 91   4 3 2 1

Publication of this book is made possible by grant support from the
Literature Program of the National Endowment for the Arts, the Cowles
Media / Star Tribune Foundation, the Dayton Hudson Foundation for
Dayton's and Target Stores, the First Bank System Foundation, the General
Mills Foundation, the I.A. O'Shaughnessy Foundation, the Jerome
Foundation, the Minnesota State Arts Board through an appropriation by
the Minnesota Legislature, the Northwest Area Foundation, and by the
support of generous individuals.

Library of Congress Cataloging-in-Publication Data

Birdsell, Sandra, 1942–
    Agassiz : a novel in stories / by Sandra Birdsell ; graphics by
R.W. Scholes
        p. cm.
    ISBN 0–915943–61–1 : $18.95
    I. Title.
PR9199.3.B4385A35   1991
813'.54—dc20   90–22663
                                                                    CIP

The paper used in this publication meets the minimum requirements of
American National Standard for Information Sciences—Permanence of
Paper for Printed Library Materials. ANSI Z39.48-1984.

Agassiz: A Novel in Stories

AGASSIZ

A Novel in Stories

1 / The Flood

Maurice Lafreniere stood on the fire escape on the south side of the hotel and looked with awe at the litter-strewn lake which spread out where the town had been only two weeks ago.

"My God," he said, because he needed to hear the sound of his own voice. He felt abandoned, as though he were the only remaining human on earth.

Across the street, a chunk of dirt-riddled ice battered against the Bank of Montreal. The wind had swept the ice into town during the night. He'd lain shivering in bed, listening to that ice crashing like a battering ram against everything that was his. And his thoughts had run together, had overflowed: his submerged business, the barber chairs bolted to the floor, one hundred years old, at least. Brought up from St. Paul on a steamboat, bequeathed to him by Henry Roy who had been like a father to him and who had also taught him his barbering trade. Mika, in Choritza, awaiting the birth of their sixth child. His other five children, cut off, wood chips floating about until the flood would subside. And his mother. When exhaustion had overcome the noise of the ice, he'd dreamed of his mother who was not dead, but alive in his dream, standing beside the river. She was gathering willow branches for her baskets. She'd looked up suddenly and she was not as he'd remembered, defeated and broken, eyes turned inward. Her broad face was strong and serious, her black eyes demanding his attention. If you have a large family, she said, you will need a bigger boat.

He thought of his boat moored below and smiled. They didn't come any smaller than his rowboat. He pulled his tweed cap tighter on his head and made his way carefully down the ice-coated fire escape. One slip and he'd be gone. Two minutes was all a person could hope for in the icy water even if he could get the hipwaders off. And then the little woman would be a widow, his children fatherless. The town would rush in for a woman like Mika. The town thought Mika had taken him in hand and with her clean habits and Mennonite ways had made him what he was today.

His boat rose and fell with the waves, its wood squeaking and protesting against the piece of wooden sidewalk he'd lashed to the bottom of the fire escape to serve as a dock. Water, as far as the eye could see. Who would have thought that their tired, narrow river could have come to this? He told himself that he was anxious to see how the men at the courthouse had endured the ice. Damned fools, he called them, for letting a few rats in the hotel frighten them from sleeping safely as he did. But he knew his real anxiety. It had surfaced during the night and he needed to reassure himself that this flood had happened gradually, others knew about it too. It was not something that had happened overnight to him alone. He was not the only human being left in the world.

He crouched, moved low in the boat and seated himself in the center of it. No one accused him of being a careless person anymore. He still took chances, certainly, but not until he was sure everything was shipshape first. He untied the knot which moored his boat to the fire escape. He pushed off from the sidewalk with the oar and sliced deeply through the ice slush floating on the surface as he headed out toward the center of Main Street. He wondered what condition the courthouse basement would be in. It was not what you'd call shipshape. No matter what Bill Livingston said, he would try and persuade the others to move into the hotel before it was too late.

Up and down the wide street, there wasn't another boat to be seen, no human sounds, just the wind and water rushing against the buildings. He stopped rowing, let the oars sink deep into the water and stared for a moment at the bottom of

the boat where his boots had crushed through the film of
muddy ice. He felt the oar scrape against one of the drowned
vehicles that had been parked on Main Street and he
shuddered. It was like disturbing the dead, bumping into
submerged things. He began rowing against the current which
swept down from the mouth of the Agassiz River, across the
cemetery and into town. The bottom of the hotel sign bobbed
in the water. The sign had been sheared off by the ice during
the night, one of the sounds that had kept him awake. He'd
been kept awake all spring by the sounds of the ice cracking
and groaning like a woman about to give birth. What are you
up to? he'd asked the river. Gather up your skirts, it's time, he
said, fancying the sound of his thoughts, the idea that the
river was a pregnant woman. But its deep complaining rumble
made him uneasy. Then, when the weather turned on them,
becoming bitterly cold with freezing rain and snowstorms, he
sent his children away and only he and Mika remained.
They'd been prepared. The flood hadn't taken him by surprise.
The last of the townspeople had been evacuated only three
days ago, taken like cattle in boats with the few things they
had time to pack and loaded onto railcars at the CN line.
Evacuees, flood victims, the *Winnipeg Free Press* called them.

Agassiz evacuation climaxes grim saga, the headline read.
The saga of the rivers. The Agassiz and the Red meeting
headlong in the north end of town, each carrying full loads
into the late-melting tributaries. The pincer-like movement
caused the waters near the mouth of the Agassiz to back up in
twenty-four hours and run across Main Street at Agassiz
Bridge. The saga of the government engineer's stupidity: "We
expect nothing this year to approach the '48 flood."

"Expect?" Maurice had said and smacked the report in the
newspaper with the back of his hand. "How can anyone
expect things from the river? You listen and watch and you
can feel what's going to happen. You don't go by charts and
expect. It's unpredictable."

The barbershop had become the meeting place for the

daily discussions about the possibilities of the river's flooding. Maurice, standing at the barber chair cutting hair, had remained silent until now. He was surprised by his outburst, to find himself throwing aside the need to be agreeable and to keep the peace with all around him at any cost. But if he knew anything well, it was the river. The knowledge was hidden inside him and flowed out naturally when he put his mind to it. The conversation which had centered around Bill Livingston, Agassiz's mayor, trailed away. The men stared at Maurice.

He was standing on an edge. His word on the line. "I'm telling you. If you know what's good for you, then get ready for a doozer of a flood."

In the same tone of voice Bill Livingston had used thirty odd years ago when he'd pulled the blanket up over Maurice's mother's face and said to those present, "Now that's drunk. Dead drunk. But what can you expect?" he got up from the bench, walked over to the barber chair and stuck his red face into Maurice's. "Horse shit," he said. "You'll have everyone running for the hills."

Maurice caught sight of his own reflection in the mirror above the bench where the men had gathered. He moved around the chair gracefully, he was light on his feet. He wore his thick black hair swept back, it made him look taller. He saw the slender back of himself, the blue birthmark on his neck, while in the plate glass mirror above his marble sinks, he could see the front of himself. Mika fed him well. He had the beginning of a double chin and a slight paunch. He saw himself begin to gesture expansively, his hand extended, palm up in a sweeping motion. Look here, he was going to say to Livingston, I'm an agreeable man. He dropped his arm quickly.

"Use your head. Forget what they're saying in Winnipeg. Those dumbbells can't forecast a flood until they're up to their asses in water. I predict that it'll be the worst flood ever."

Maurice's breath came faster now as he rowed against a

small side current where the water swept between two buildings. He'd said it. His word had stood and one by one the men had begun to trust his knowledge and come to him for advice. He passed by the barbershop. He passed by the movie theater. The sign on the marquee, THE LADY TAKES A SAILOR, used to make him laugh, but because of the ferocity of the flood, now seemed to him to have been a portent filled with meaning.

Freed of the metal graveyard of drowned vehicles that had been parked down Main Street, Maurice stopped rowing. He started up the small outboard motor that Flood Control had issued him. Engine straining, he moved out faster into the current, the bow whacking against the choppy water. And then he saw the lights of the courthouse beaming out at him from the tall narrow windows. So, the basement, she'd held. The courthouse had been built up on its foundation. It was entrenched behind sandbags, but water lapped inches from the top of the dike. He heard the sound of another motor and tension fled from his muscles. He wasn't alone. A boat moved out from behind the courthouse, its hull cutting a deep V down into the water. It veered suddenly in his direction. He shut down his motor and waited. There were three men in the boat, two of them farmers from the area, and Woods, a young RCMP officer whose cap appeared to be held in place by his ears.

"What's up?" Maurice asked.

Stevens, the younger one of the farmers, motioned wearily to the west. All three men looked alike, unshaven, complexions gray from too much coffee and too little sleep. Maurice saw the rifles on the floor of their boat.

"He's got fifty head of Herefords," Woods said. His voice rose to an excited screech. "They're stranded. Haven't been able to get feed into them. Not sure they'll even be there now, not after this ice."

"That was some night," Maurice said. "Have you checked the basement?"

"It's tighter than a drum," Woods said, echoing a Livingston pronouncement.

That was the whole damned trouble. It was too tight. There was too much pressure on the walls. They should flood the basement or the whole thing would pop inward. Damned farmers. The closest they'd been to water before the flood was the dugouts they'd led their cows down to and Woods was still wet behind his big flapping ears.

"What's the situation with the livestock?" he asked.

Stevens lifted one of the rifles and laid it across his knees.

"Plain damned shame. Something should be done," Maurice said. He'd told Stevens, ship 'em out. If you don't, may as well shoot them now. "We're all in the same condition," he said. "My shop, your cattle. We'll have to start over, that's all." He was surprised by his own sudden optimism. It was what Henry Roy would have said. He'd dispensed good will like pills when the going got tough.

"Sure we will," the farmer said. "With what? The money I'll get from this year's crop?"

Maurice said, "Wait and see, the government will come through in the end."

The farmer spat. "Laurent doesn't even know where Agassiz is," he said. "And all they care about on Broadway is making sure the houses on Wellington Crescent don't get wet."

"Watch, watch," Maurice called out suddenly as a sharp piece of ice swept close to their boats. He angled his craft away into the waves. The ice slid inches from the hull of the other boat and then was gone. The three men watched it pass by. Maurice could tell they were unaware of the danger. It was a wonder there hadn't been a serious accident, what with the mayor heading up the flood control committee. He had a bulldozer for a brain. Ran over people who didn't agree with him. Sent people running off half-cocked to do what they damned well should have done a month ago.

"If that one had hit, you'd have been able to drive a grain

truck through the hole," Maurice said. He felt strong, in control. "Keep your eyes open out there. An aluminum boat is no damned good in this stuff." Old Man River. That was the name they'd given to him since his prediction of the flood had come true. Maurice Lafreniere reads the river like it was a newspaper. When the going gets tough, the tough get going, he told himself. And he'd proven himself. Why do you have to stay, now of all times, Mika had asked. And he couldn't explain to her that for once he didn't want to be on the outside, left out, but dead center. Because Mika didn't know otherwise. He was the one who went out each morning to check the waters' rising, measured on a pole at Agassiz Bridge, and took the reading to the courthouse where the police radioed it into Winnipeg.

"Why don't you come with us?" Woods asked.

Hold your hand, you mean. "I'm going to take the reading and then cruise around a bit, see what damage I can do. Was there any breakfast? Could eat a horse."

"We'll bring you one," Stevens said.

Maurice chuckled at the bad joke. His spirits rose. He watched the three men head out across the open field. It was just a case of numbers to Ottawa: 28:1. If they could get the real story. Drop Laurent down in the middle of this hell, get his feet wet and he wouldn't say, "No aid for the flood victims."

He tied the boat to the railing on the bridge. He didn't dare venture into the river channel, it was choked with debris. He took the binoculars from beneath the seat and lifted them. The water rose and fell at the level of 29:3 on the pole. He predicted that the crest was days away. Three more feet of water and even the tops of the trees, the only remaining indication of where the river's bank used to be, would be under. They were like scrawny black fingers now, pointing out the sweep and curve of the shoreline where he'd spent that terrible summer hiding from the priest who would take him to be with his brothers in the convent in the city.

The memory caught at him suddenly like a camouflaged barb hooking an unsuspecting fish.

He turned the glasses toward the cemetery. His hands shook with the cold. All the grave stones had vanished, had been tumbled by the waves or cut down by the ice and scattered like broken teeth at the bottom of the lake. He lowered the glasses. His eyes stung. His mother and father were there. They were side by side, locked into their early middle years behind the frozen ground. First his father; a railroad accident. And there had been no town clamoring to rescue that widow. She'd been ignored. Left alone to feed three kids with the money she made sewing and from her baskets. And a month later, they buried her. Dead drunk. Lying on her back in the center of the bed, her head in a pool of gray vomit. Perspiration ran down between his shoulder blades.

Hey, boy, do you want to keep these? Livingston had asked, holding up his mother's beaded moccasins. He'd come with a number of other men, now forgotten, to help carry her away and to poke around through the remains of his family. The wind rose and the icy blast of it seemed to bore straight through his skull. He wished suddenly that he'd been able to find one place for his children instead of shipping them off, piece by piece, to live out the flood among strangers. The ice slush was like crushed glass as it slid swiftly beneath and around his boat. He rowed steadily. His arms began to ache. The sound of a shrill whistle jarred him. He turned quickly and saw the huge white hull of a fishing vessel bearing down on him. It was the *Apex*, bringing supplies to Agassiz.

They plucked Maurice from his rowboat and towed his boat back to town. They took him back to the courthouse, unloaded the supplies, had something to eat, and then Maurice, by virtue of his title, Old Man River, was invited to come along on a cruise about the town to show a newspaper reporter who had come to see for himself what damage had been done.

"This is incredible," the man said. His name was Charles Medlake. The tall thin man spoke to them as though they hadn't already known that the flood was incredible, devastating, all the fancy words he used to describe what had happened to their town. "I've never seen anything like this," he kept saying.

He thinks he pays us a compliment, Maurice thought. Being ten feet under is a great accomplishment. He stood at the railing on the stern of the *Apex* with Bill Livingston and the reporter, listening to their conversation with growing impatience.

"I bloody well hope that we never do again, either," said Bill Livingston, but there was a strange tone of pride in his booming voice. "But according to an Indian legend, this happens every hundred years."

Medlake's hands shook as he cupped them and lit another cigarette. He drew deeply on it and expelled shreds of blue smoke which were snatched by the wind. "Have many people left the area for good?" he asked.

"Hell no. We're tough chickens."

Maurice shifted from one foot to another as the reporter asked the mayor many questions. According to an Indian legend? That was the first he'd heard of it. What Indian? Outwardly, he appeared solid and calm. His parka was unzipped, revealing his green curling sweater with the white rearing bucks on it. Mika's mother had knit it for him. He chewed thoughtfully on a toothpick, moving it from one side of his mouth to the other.

"This isn't the worst of it," the mayor said. "We haven't been east of town yet. The ice took out three or four houses."

"I've seen enough for now," the man said. He flicked his half-smoked cigarette over the stern. "Listen, the luckiest house in Agassiz is the worst hit in Winnipeg. I never saw anything this bad in the city."

"Really?" the mayor said.

It was what Maurice had suspected. Once they'd figured it

out, that the same river that was flooding Agassiz would eventually flood Winnipeg, they screamed bloody murder. Squeaky wheel gets the grease.

"I'd like to get back to the courthouse and call the paper to send out a photographer. This should be recorded."

Livingston called out directions to the pilot. The fishing boat began a slow wide turn.

"The feds have got to open their eyes to this," Livingston said. "Pictures would help. We estimate that property damage alone will be close to five million dollars. Then there's the months of lost revenue to consider." He turned suddenly to Maurice. "How long has it been since you've earned a cent, Maurie?"

"Eh?" He was jolted loose from his tumbling thoughts.

"I said, how are you going to manage to feed the kiddies when they get home? Let alone afford the lumber to rebuild the house and buy new furniture?"

"Well, I . . . ," Maurice began and stopped. I was prepared. My furniture is high and dry. We took what was left of the preserves to Mika's sister's place. But there was something in Livingston's tone of voice that kept him quiet. He sensed that there was more here than an innocent question.

Livingston didn't wait for his reply. "We must be compensated. We're going to need money and lots of it. Interest-free money for the business community to replace their inventory. I've lost my entire stock of hardware. The farmers, their seed and fertilizer. And people like Maurie, here, they'll need money to feed and clothe the family. He's got six kids."

"Five," Maurice said. "I've got five." He was stung. Money for people like Maurie, here. How are you going to feed your family? A straightforward question. But it rankled. It was intended to remind him that at one time he'd swept their floors, carried out their shit pails and shoveled clean the barns. He'd fallen down drunk in the street. He'd been looked upon with pity or scorn. And that he had risen only so far in twenty years that his main concern would be how to feed six mouths, nothing more. He sees me as being another flood victim, same as all the others. Maurice freed his hands from his parka pockets and cut the air in front of the two men in an impatient motion.

"Compensation, to be sure," he said.

"What was that?" Charles Medlake spoke directly to him for the first time.

"Compensation, to be sure. By all means." His was the quiet reasonable voice of Henry Roy, his mentor. He hoped it was the voice of someone who would listen for so long to the clamor of others and then, with a few chosen words, bring clarity to their ramblings so as to make them look ridiculous. "But look here, compensation and interest-free loans are only a small part of the whole picture," he continued.

The newsman moved in closer. He began to make notes on a tablet. "Just what do you think should be done?"

"Many things. Certainly, I could use a hand just as everyone else in this town could use a hand. I'm a businessman too. I've lost more than furniture." He avoided Livingston's eyes. "But I personally wouldn't care if I didn't get a penny from the government if we could take steps to make certain that this here flood will never happen again."

Livingston laughed outright and turned away.

"But how is that possible?" Medlake asked.

Maurice was unsettled by the laughter. He shoved his hands back into his pockets. They were heading back toward the courthouse. They had circled the town and approached the stone building from behind, moving slowly down Elm Avenue. The trees were bare, bark black with orange rusty-looking growths in the crooks of limbs. A chair was caught in the lower branches of one tree. Maurice cleared his throat to speak. Build a sewage treatment plant so we no longer shit and piss on the river. We didn't have floods like this one until we got the running water. My God, the river, she doesn't pretend to be beautiful, but some honor is due, eh? Lure the goldeye and pickerel back with clean water. Forget the Indian legend that says we have no say in the matter. We should remember the river. She gave this region its life. But he knew they saw the river with different eyes. To them it was heavy, sluggish and ugly, a breeding ground for mosquitoes and eels.

"It's impossible to prevent flooding," Livingston said. He took Medlake by the elbow and attempted to steer him away by pointing out some particular damage.

"Wait, let him finish," Medlake said.

"We need to look to the future," Maurice said.

"How?"

"With all our minds, we should be able to come up with something instead of just saying it happens every hundred years. We should think about building a permanent dike around the town, for instance, or dig drainage ditches in the country to let the spring run-off enter into the Red further downstream."

"Winnipeg would never go for that," Livingston interrupted. "Because it would mean more water for them."

He speaks as though he has just bit into a lemon, Maurice thought.

"There must be a way around it," Medlake said.

The boat nudged slowly into the courthouse yard toward a large oak tree in the center of it. The pilot cut the engine and Maurice was jolted forward as the craft met bark with a hollow thud. The *Apex* whistled its arrival. Dark shapes appeared at the window and then the back door swung open. Woods and Stevens stepped out on the stairs. They climbed into Maurice's rowboat and began rowing toward them. Woods cupped his hands to his mouth. "Survivors," he shouted. "We found two women and a child stranded on the roof of a granary."

"Listen," Medlake said to Maurice. "I'd like to talk to you later on. What you say makes good sense."

Maurice felt the careful attentive posture of Livingston's large body. "Suits me," he said, trying to sound casual.

"Where can I find you?"

"If I'm not here—"

"He's over at the hotel," the mayor finished. "Maurie here doesn't like our company. He's always been what you might call a lone wolf."

Maurice's face grew warm. "Shoot, it's not that," he said. He felt as though his mouth was full of marbles. He juggled words in his mind. "It's not that. It's the basement. She's going to cave in."

"What?" Medlake asked. "And you're taking me in there?"

"He doesn't know what he's talking about," Livingston said. "The walls are two feet thick. This place is built like a brick shithouse."

The rowboat came alongside and they got into it. Maurice sat between the two men, slouched down into his parka, his fists curled tightly inside his pockets. Blow, goddammit, he urged as they approached the courthouse. Now. He imagined walls crumbling.

They removed their hipwaders in the basement. Maurice sat on the cot in the jail cell and leaned against the rough Tyndalstone wall and closed his eyes.

"Well, Maurie," Livingston said and laughed. "Drainage ditches, eh? It looks as though the wrong one ran for mayor."

Maurice didn't answer. He could see his parents' fresh graves, a mixture of yellow clay and topsoil. This room carried the memory. The priest had found him beside the river, trying to build a raft so that he could float downstream to his mother's people. And had agreed, Maurice could stay. He didn't have to join his brothers in the convent in the city. He'd sat in this very cell, tracing the outlines of strange creatures locked in the stone without knowing what they were while the men of the town decided his fate. Send for his mother's people, the priest advised. And so he waited it out in this room for a full week. They didn't want me? he asked.

Henry Roy winked. You wouldn't have wanted them, he said. I never sent the message. And he took Maurice in and gave him work in the hotel. It would have turned out well if it hadn't been that it took too long for a town to forget a person who would die suffocating on their own vomit. Dead drunk.

"Come on, Old Man River," Livingston said and clapped him on the shoulder. "Let's go on up and meet those survivors."

Maurice followed him into the main hall. Two women and the child huddled beneath blankets within the circle of men. The men parted to let Maurice and Livingston through. The women and child were of mixed blood, Maurice realized instantly. Mongrels. The women had identical expressions, wide smiles, like fools, displaying their rotting teeth. Don't let anyone tell you different, Henry Roy had said, mongrels don't make better dogs. But the child studied Maurice with the same serious black eyes as his mother had in his dream last night. If you're going to have a large family, she said, you will need a bigger boat. These people didn't even have a boat. Not even a small one. The men seemed to be waiting for him to do something.

"Do you speak French?" Maurice asked the women.

They laughed and covered the gaping holes in their teeth with hands that looked to be tinged by wood smoke.

Maurice felt the floor move.

"No, no, not French," Livingston said. "You never know. You could be related. Say something to them in Indian."

"In a pig's ass," Maurice said, his anger breaking loose in upraised fists. The floor tilted. And then there was a sound, like thunder, beneath them. Relief flooded every part of his body and his knees suddenly felt weak. He felt like laughing hysterically.

Stevens ran into the room. "Clear out," he yelled. "The basement just went."

The reporter scrambled for his parka. Maurice led the women and child to the back door. They were calm. They

pulled their blankets about themselves and walked slowly, as
though they were accustomed to calamities. Bill Livingston
ran to the tables, gathered papers to his chest, set them back
down again. Maurice heard the roar of the water filling the
basement, flooding the little room. He lifted the child quickly
and handed her to Stevens. When she saw the boat, she clung
to Maurice's sweater and began to cry. He peeled her loose
and handed her down. I was right, he told himself. Once
again, I was right. He felt like laughing and he felt like crying.
Thank God, the *Apex* was big enough, it would hold them all.
It would carry the whole damned works of them to the hills.

2 / Boundary Lines

"Howdy Doody," Maurice said as a customer sat down in his barber chair. The greeting was intended to disarm, one he reserved for strangers. With a flourish, he swept the striped barber cloth around the man's wide shoulders and fastened it with a clip at his sunburned neck.

SCISSORS SHARPENED WHILE YOU WAIT: 25 CENTS.
DRESSMAKERS TAKE NOTE: 3 FOR $1.00!!

His sign, intended as a joke, blared from one corner of the plate glass mirror and above it:

WE NEED YOUR HEAD IN OUR BUSINESS

Head number twenty-nine. And judging from the smell, this head hadn't been washed in a week. Maurice made a note to dip the comb into disinfectant when he'd finished with this one.

"Want me to lower your ears a bit, eh?"

The man laughed, settled back and crossed his legs. His work boots were caked with yellow clay. Maurice recognized him as one of the Franklin brothers the council had hired from a neighboring municipality to help construct the ring dike around the town. All day, the incessant rumbling of the heavy machinery could be heard as earth around Agassiz was scraped flat in preparation for the dike. In the north end of town, truck-loads of dirt were already being dumped into place.

"She's one hot day," the man said.

"You betcha." Maurice in his crisp white barber shirt, its collar like a priest's collar, appeared to be cool. The high neck and heavily starched shirt would prevent splinters of hair from becoming imbedded in his skin, but it also kept his body heat in. He raised his arms and winced with the pain that shot into his cramped muscles. Along the far wall, sitting on a bench, three men waited their turn. Behind the half-wall partition, all six pool tables were in use and thick smoke curled in the lights above the tables.

Maurice parted the man's sandy-colored hair, combed it into place. He reached for the scissors. "So, how's the work going on the dike?" he asked. "Everything going according to Hoyle?"

The man's hair was coarse and flew from the tips of his scissors, spraying the front of his shirt. Maurice only half-listened while the man talked, nodding occasionally and saying, "Oh, I see."

The smell of smoke mixed with hair tonic and the heavy odor that came from the pile of multi-colored hair on the floor made his stomach churn. It had become his smell. It lingered in all of his clothing, in his leather tool kit, so that when he took the kit home with him to cut his children's hair, the smell was there in the house as well. He'd been looking forward to getting away from it, had anticipated the weekend and fishing with his brothers. Now, he didn't know what he'd do. He'd have to telephone them and make up some excuse. He couldn't say, my wife doesn't want you in the house.

"How long since your last haircut?" Maurice asked. He would know from the man's reply, his preference, how much to cut off. Then he listened while the man recited the list of complaints, machinery breakdowns, about the houses that still had to be moved inside the dike's boundaries.

When Maurice had come to work that morning, it had been with Mika's "over my dead body" echoing in his ears. Smoke from forest fires had blown in over the town during the night and hung low, turning the sun red. The effect was like Mika's anger, tinging all with a faint golden hue, making him feel uneasy, strange, as though his feet were not touching the ground completely. "Over your dead body, eh? Well, that could be arranged," he'd retorted. She'd reminded him of his brothers' last visit. How Alphonse had gotten drunk and puked on the kitchen floor. But the worst of it, she said, standing there at the door with her hands on her hips, was that they'd spoken French the whole time.

"Maurice Ovide Lafreniere?" a voice said behind him, sending his thoughts scattering. The voice was low, husky, as though the person had a cold.

"Yes?" Maurice stopped snipping, stood poised with the scissors suspended in mid-air.

"You are the person responsible for the digging?"

Maurice turned slowly to face an old man. "I beg your pardon? I think you confuse me with someone else."

"Are you Maurice Lafreniere?" His face was a ripple of corrugated wrinkles from squinting into the sun and the wind. Mucus, like yellow pearls, had congealed in the corners of his black eyes. He was shorter than Maurice and of slight build. He raised his hand and Maurice saw that it was smooth and strong looking, the cords in his wrist sinewy ropes beneath his brown skin.

"Absolutely," Maurice said. The smell of the man made his eyes burn. It was the same smell that still clung to the corners of the furnace room. It was the sour smell of the flood. Why didn't these people stay on the reservation where they belonged? As long as there were people like Mika who would buy their braided door mats, invite them in for bread and jam, they would continue to come traipsing in looking for handouts.

"And you? I haven't had the pleasure."

"Norbert Desmarais, your uncle," the man said. "You should know who I am."

Maurice dropped the scissors. He bent to retrieve them. Where the man had walked, wet smudges trailed across the clean tile floor. The old man's feet were thickly caked with Red River gumbo and he was splattered to the knees with hardened mud the shape of clams which clung to the wool fabric of his pants. When Maurice stood up, his heart thrashed against his rib cage.

"Well," Maurice said. "Long time, no see. What's bringing you here to Agassiz?"

"The digging," Desmarais said. "I heard you're the person who made the digging happen."

Franklin shifted impatiently beneath the barber cloth. "We're the ones doing the digging. What's it to you?"

Maurice moved slowly, his actions a cover for his confusion. He began cutting hair once again. "If you're speaking of the dike, then it was my idea, to be sure. But it was put before the town and voted on in a fair manner."

"And you know where they're bringing the earth from?"

"Well, I'm not certain, but the municipality owns several—"

"It's yours."

"Mine?"

"They're bringing the earth from Grande Pointe. Land that belonged to your family. Something should be done about it."

Maurice grew aware of the silence in the barbershop. Keen interest was being taken in this conversation. "I've never lived at Grande Pointe," he said quietly. Maurice Lafreniere has a good head, it was often said. He kept everything going straight in this crooked place. He was calm now, and had the situation in control. "I believe my mother's relations once lived in Grande Pointe, but that was years ago."

"Trees," the old man said. He jerked his arm up to the window where cars and trucks parked at an angle against the sidewalk. The glare of the red sun made the windshields look solid, like a sheet of hot metal. A truck engine revved suddenly as another load of heavy earth slid into place on the dike.

"Eh?"

"From here to the river. Trees. Do you remember?"

"Absolutely," Maurice said and laughed. He scanned the

bench where the men sat waiting. Above their heads was a sign which read: WORK LIKE HELEN B. HAPPY. In two seconds, he'd ask the man to leave.

"Same as Grande Pointe. Trees, from here to the river. All gone. They cut the trees and haul away the dirt so that they can pile it up around the town of Agassiz."

"Well Uncle, I don't know about any land. But even if what you say is the case, then that was well before my time. There are no records. The land belongs to the municipality now. What can I do?"

"And your tongue? That too was taken away long ago?"

"My tongue is rusty, to be sure. But it's there when I need it."

"Speak to me then," the old man said in French.

Maurice glanced about. "It's not polite," he said.

"When you're in Rome, you do what the Romans do," Franklin said.

"Absolutely," Maurice agreed.

Desmarais ignored the comment. "And your children? What about them? They are also too polite to speak French?"

"There's no need to," Maurice said. "What this gentleman says is true."

"Ah. You think no further than the end of your thick nose. There's no need. There's no need for you to come and take back your land either. You have all this," he said. He moved in a circle as his black eyes took in the whole room for the first time and came to rest on the buffalo head. Maurice had rescued it from behind the curling rink after flood clean-up and had mounted it above the plate glass mirror. He used it to hang his hat on. The old man smiled and then began to laugh. His shoulders shook violently and he leaned against the barber chair to support himself.

The customers' interest in the man had changed to wariness. Maurice sensed it. Desmarais began coughing. His high narrow chest heaved beneath his plaid shirt.

"Calm yourself," Maurice said. He steeled himself against

the man's odor and taking him by the elbow, steered him over to a chair beneath the window, well away from the waiting customers.

"That's you," the old man whispered and pointed at the buffalo head. "You're useless. You allow people to hang their hats on you. They take away your land and it was your idea."

Maurice was stung. "It's necessary to build the dike," he said. "Where would we be without one? This town could never survive another flood like the last one. And I for one don't wish to go through that again." Like a knife, he comes through the bush sideways, his mother had said. He remembered this uncle only dimly as being a kind of vagabond. He would appear suddenly as in a dream at their door with a rabbit or a string of fish. Stay well away from that one, she'd warned him. He's more Indian than French.

"And you think a hill of dirt will stop the river?"

"But of course. It will be higher than the river will ever come."

"Then I've wasted my time. You're a foolish man. You will never have what is yours."

"You can't change history," Maurice said in an attempt to lighten the atmosphere. Now go. Go and leave me be.

As though reading his thoughts, the old man got up from the chair. "You know nothing of history," he said. "Did you know that your grandfather was a river man?"

Because his parents had died when he was a child, Maurice knew little about his relatives. He knew that his mother's people had come long before the settlers to the area that was now Grande Pointe. That they had been both hunters and farmers along the river, squatting on a large piece of land north of Agassiz about thirty miles. La Grande Pointe de la Saline, it was called for a time and then shortened to Grande Pointe when a town formed. His father's people had come from Quebec.

"Is that so?"

"It was during the time of the blue herons. Some say he rode those giant birds to the lake and back."

Maurice hid his smile. "You don't say? Rode the birds, eh?"

"And your great grandmother, she came from Buffalo Lake with ten children and a sick man. When he died, she kept herself and three families alive that winter with her snares."

Maurice swatted at an imaginary fly. "Ancient history," he said. "That has nothing whatsoever to do with me."

The men on the bench looked up from their newspapers as Desmarais walked over to the door. "We'll talk later," he said. "I'll wait for you at your house."

Oh God. No. "Wait," Maurice said. He could just see Mika's expression. He'd never told her about his mother. He'd let her think that both his parents were French. He put his hand on the man's arm. "I could get you a room here at the hotel," he said. "If you want to stay."

The old man stared at him for several moments. "You are saying I'm not welcome in your house?"

"Oh, it's not that. It's the little woman, she's busy with the children."

"You're like a raven caught in a thorn bush," Desmarais said. "I don't expect that anything will ever come from you. Much flapping of wings and that is all." He turned and left the barbershop as quietly as he'd come.

Maurice felt stricken, cut adrift. He wanted to follow the man, to explain. But his responsibilities kept him there. A newspaper crackled. Franklin cleared his throat impatiently. Maurice apologized for the delay. He picked up the clippers and went back to work.

The screen door opened suddenly.

"Hey Franklin, you'll never guess what we've found this time," a workman said. "Come and see."

Maurice followed along as the men ran down Main Street towards Agassiz Bridge and the ring dike. A group of them gathered on top of the unfinished dike in a circle, looking down at the ground. They were strange silhouettes against the red sky, motionless like granite headstones on a mound of black earth. Maurice didn't scramble and hurry with them. He felt that he knew what it was that they'd found. There had been many strange things, artifacts, pieces of pottery, arrowheads. He stepped into the circle of men. On the ground before them, partially buried, was the remains of a human.

"I called the RCMP, the workman said.

Maurice bent and examined the skull. It was porous and tinged brown from the earth. He felt sick. It could be the remains of one of his mother's people. One of his own people. "This is old," he said. "I guess these things happen when you're working that close to the cemetery. There are many lost markers, old grave sites that we don't know about." He stood up and wiped his hands on his pants. "But it's a good thing you called the police. Once they come, we can get on and bury it." He wished he knew something, anything, of his mother's people. He felt his loss in his fingertips; something important had slipped away from him like water through fingers, and he would never get it back.

Later that night, Maurice stood on the fire escape of the Scratching Chicken Hotel and leaned with his elbows against the railing. He was a little too drunk to go home yet. From his station, he could look out across the roofs of the houses, the skeletal frames of fresh lumber of the new ones, the bright yellow boards piercing together the older houses and grain elevators beyond them and far beyond the grain elevators, trees that were just faint brush strokes against the purple sky.

A sudden clinking noise in the alleyway below jolted him. He grasped the metal railing tightly. "Who's there?"

Since the flood, he scared easily. He often dreamed of drowning. Laurence Anderson emerged from the dark alleyway carrying two cartons of empty Coca-Cola bottles. He looked one way and then the other, failed to see Maurice above him, and ran down the street.

Maurice chuckled. It was just Johanna's boy; the mongrel was stealing cigarette money again. The boy was about fourteen years, he guessed, and had that clumsy knock-kneed gait of the half-grown. Because he had in the past slept with Johanna, he looked for his own features in the boy's face. But Laurence could be the kid of any one of dozens, he told himself. Maurice seemed to come upon him often in such out of the way places as the nuisance grounds, along the river, in the cemetery; and he was always alone, poking and turning things over. It was this roaming that reminded Maurice of himself.

Below him a fan churned out the smoky voices of the men in the parlor. There wasn't one distinguishable voice, the sounds were all mixed together, churning. The hotel had a new sign, it was a blinking neon chicken that had given the hotel its name, "Scratching Chicken." The chicken hunted and pecked out the words, EAT HERE, EAT HERE, EAT HERE. The sign, along with all the voices below him, mixed together as one, was to him a sign of progress. The town was booming. And he was part of it. He was accepted by the merchants along Main Street and it didn't help him one damned bit when people like Desmarais appeared on the scene like a scruffy spring rabbit.

Your worship, he said to himself, his mood swinging abruptly, as a member of this here town council, I would like to say that I think the flood had its benefits. Yessiree. On behalf of the children, old ladies and dogs, I propose that we install traffic lights at the corner. Slow those city buggers down when they come whipping through on the highway. He unzipped his fly. He laughed aloud. Your worship, as a member of the council, and in the interests of the people, I wish to bring to your attention the fact that people are pissing from the fire escape at the back of the hotel. Plain damned shame. Something should be done about it. Give everyone an umbrella.

Below him, the fan ceased moving. Closing time. Time to go home to the old lady. She'd be asleep, curled like a fist under the blankets on her side of the bed. He swayed unsteadily as he made his way down the fire escape. Hang on, or you're a goner, he told himself. When he got home, he'd peel himself free from his barber shirt, search for stray hairs in his neck and go to bed. And then, yessiree, by God, whether she was sleeping or not, he'd tell her about old man Desmarais and about his mother.

The following morning, with a vague memory of his dreams of strange-looking blue birds sweeping low on water, Maurice got up, pushed aside the curtains in the bedroom and looked down into the garden. The winds had dispersed the smoke and the sunlight was not red anymore. But the squealing and rumbling of machinery continued. As he drew on his pants, the smell of lovemaking rose from his crotch like the smell of a catfish left lying on the riverbank. He would leave early, get a key for one of the rooms at the hotel and bathe. If he didn't, his customers would know for sure what he'd been into last night. He knew Mika would be angry this morning. He wondered: to go straight down and apologize or let her think he didn't remember what had happened? He chose to delay facing Mika. He would instead go into the basement and search for his boots. He'd been meaning to have new clickers put on them.

As Maurice searched the corners of the basement for his boots, he heard Mika's feet slapping against the floor above his head and instantly he felt justified for his behavior. The sound of her feet was as angry and unyielding as she'd been. She didn't keep herself the way other women did either. No rouge or powder, not even to please him. In better moments he could admit that he actually preferred her unpolished face, but not this morning. He stood debating, get it over with. Go on up there. Or pretend it didn't happen. He'd let himself get out of hand, to be sure. But part of it had been the beer, the other had been the old man coming to town. He heard the sounds of his children coming from every corner of the house. Too late. He'd have to wait.

"Well, how should I know where it is, you look for it."

Mika's voice was raised suddenly, shattering the peacefulness of the basement.

"I did look for it," Lureen answered.

"Must I come?" It was a threat.

Lureen's tone matched her mother's. "I said I looked and so I did. I'm not lying."

"Alright then, I'll come," Mika said and Maurice heard her feet slap angrily across the kitchen floor. "But I'm warning you, if I find that shoe of yours, I'll give you such a smack for not looking for it properly. You have to get down on your knees when you look. You searched high and low, eh? We'll see about that."

She's still angry, Maurice thought. If apologizing would make life easier for her, he would do it. He was not one to mind going out of his way for another. It would make life easier for the children as well.

"Okay, okay. I'll look again," Lureen said and the rooms were calm once again as though a gust of wind had passed through them and gone. Then there was a soft murmur like dry leaves; Truda's voice, a halting search for words.

"I don't know what could have happened to your crayons," Mika said. Her voice was softer when she spoke to Truda. "Who would take them, a mouse?"

Peter the baby began to squall for attention. The remainder of their conversation was lost. Mika hurried across the kitchen. The cupboard door was opened, then closed. Maurice imagined her sprinkling puffed-wheat kernels across the tray for the baby to eat.

"Peter, Peter, pumpkin eater, had a wife and couldn't keep her," Mika said in a sing-song voice. The uneven legs of the highchair knocked against the floor as Mika jiggled it in time to her rhyme. "How are you this morning?" she asked the baby. "Eh? How is your little pumpkin, empty?"

Sharp rapid steps came from the corner of the dining room into the kitchen. Particles of dust floated downwards from the ceiling onto Maurice's neck. He rummaged about behind the furnace, searching for his army boots.

"Didn't I tell you?" Mika said, her voice harsh once again. "Get down on your hands and knees and you'll find your shoe. You kids. Now sit and eat."

It is only with the babies that she seems capable of gentleness, Maurice thought with sadness.

There were sounds of steps on the stairway as Betty came down from the top floor. "There you are, finally," Mika said. "You're always the last one. Today of all days to be late. Just when I've got so much to do. It's the Wednesday Circle today and it's my turn to have them here and you're late. Eat, while I braid your hair."

"I'm not hungry."

Mika sighed and it was felt all the way down Maurice's spine. Mika sighed when she kneaded bread at the table, she sighed when it rained, she sighed when the sun shone. When he had come home last night, she'd sighed as she stood before the mirror in their bedroom, unwinding her dark hair. When he curled against her back beneath the blankets and searched for words to tell her, my mother was an Indian, she'd mistaken his intentions. She sighed and said, no. Leave me be. Not until you install the kitchen window. And the anger had come rushing, thick and violent. He'd wanted to smash into her breasts with his fists but instead, he'd taken her with force, without using precautions, with a grinding punishing force that he felt in his own muscles this morning. His heartbeat rose. He shook a cigarette loose from his package, struck his match against the basement wall. Today, he'd buy the lumber for the goddamned window and he would give her the morning sun.

"Have some cereal, even if you aren't hungry. You're the oldest. You set the example," Mika said. "If you go off to school without eating, then they'll want to, too."

"I'm your example to the whole world," Betty said.

Maurice heard spoons clanking against bowls, saw mouths opening and closing, chewing, swallowing. He heard Sharon's dry cough echo in the furnace pipes and Rudy, who leaned against the door at the top of the basement stairs, bumping his head against it, signaling his need to use the toilet. He saw his boots hanging from a nail behind the furnace. He heard chairs scrape against the floor as the children gathered up their books and got up to leave for school. He dusted the boots off and slung them over his shoulder. It was time to go up there. He climbed the stairs slowly, dreading the initial contact with Mika's accusing eyes. If she had cried, anything, he would have been able to know how to approach her. This cold silence was another thing. He met Rudy on the stairs and ruffled his blond head playfully. "Don't let the spiders get you, fella," he said.

Mika stood at the kitchen cupboard with her back to him. She balanced the baby on one hip. She hadn't rolled her hair up and it hung uncombed on her shoulders. He wanted to reach out and touch it. He liked seeing it hanging loose instead of rolled into that tight sausage ring at the back of her head. The first time she'd lain beside him, her head cradled into his shoulder like a small child, he thought that he'd never touched anything so fine and so soft as her hair. He took his sweater down from the wall behind the door. She heard the noise and turned. He steadied himself against her bitter tongue.

There were pouches of color beneath her hazel eyes, like two bruises, but her face was calm. "On Saturday," she said, "the children are going to begin German lessons." She jostled the baby lightly.

German lessons? What now? "Is that so?"

"Yes. So, you don't mind, then? My father said he would take them on if I wanted. But he thought I should ask you first."

"Suit yourself." He was relieved. They were going to

pretend it hadn't happened. "But what's the reasoning? I can count on one hand the number of people who speak German in this town."

She licked her fingers and began making a curl stand up on the baby's head. He saw a certain cunning in her expression. "It's not that. It's part of their background. I think they should have it while my father is still able to do it."

And suddenly he was angry. She'd denied him the presence of his brothers in his own home. She was going to teach the children to speak German. "Fine. And what should we teach them of my background?"

Her tightly contained anger broke loose. Her eyes became pinpoints of hostility. "What would you teach them?" she asked, spitting the words at him overtop the baby's head. "How to drink?"

"Listen here, my grandfather was a river man."

"I thought you said he came from Quebec."

"On my mother's side, I mean."

"That must have been before I came," she said. She dismissed anything that had happened before she'd come to Canada as being unimportant, not affecting her in any way. She shifted the baby to the other hip and brushed hair from her face. "Anyway," she said, ending their conversation, "anyway, it was the wrong time. It was the wrong time for you to forget yourself. I could get pregnant."

He was momentarily stunned. She always surprised him like this. She was more concerned about being pregnant than by what he'd done. He thought about the possibility. Seven kids. That would be embarrassing. People were beginning to make crude jokes about Mika's yearly swelling and popping of babies. "I didn't know. I'm sorry," he said.

"That won't do any good," she said.

He'd offered his hand and been bitten. "Don't bother with my breakfast," he said. "I can always get a bite to eat at the hotel." He had always been able to use Mika's strong jealousy as an effective means of retaliation. Johanna cooked at the hotel.

He thought she was going to throw the baby at him. "So go and eat, I don't care."

But he saw the fear in her eyes. He was not a heartless man. "By the way," he said, as he buttoned up his sweater, "send one of the girls to the shop after school. I'm going to need a hand carrying the lumber home." This talk of land, this mooning over old bones. Desmarais was far away and should stay there. You live what you know, he told himself, and what you don't, well, you can't be held accountable for that. He could feel Mika's attitude towards him change. Her features softened. She set the baby into the highchair.

"What for?" she asked. "Lumber for what?"

He told her what she wanted to hear. "For the window. I've been meaning to get at it for some time now."

She looked up at the clock above the sink. "There's still time," she said. "Let me poach you an egg."

He smiled and reached for her. He put his face into her soft hair. "If it's a girl," he said, "we'll name her Tina, after your aunt."

She struggled free. "Heaven forbid," she said. "If it's a baby, I'll jump off the roof." But she wasn't angry anymore. She drew in her bottom lip, sucked at it, as though she'd only just remembered. "Did you telephone your brothers yet?"

"No, but I will today."

"What will you tell them?" she asked.

"I'll tell them there's a fly in the ointment."

She looked at him, puzzled. "I'll think of something," he said.

He watched as she prepared his food. She was strong and efficient and moved incredibly fast as she worked, and still she appeared to be small and often had the appearance of being lost, defenseless. It had taken him only one month to realize that she was as defenseless as a badger. His brothers had their wives and he had his and that was all any of them really had. He was joined together with her in the present. She was what he could put his hands on and touch. But he knew, for some reason, it would never be enough.

3 / Truda

"It's time to do something about all your drawings," Mika said to Truda. She knelt on the floor searching the bottom of the bedroom closet for plastic raincoats and hats. "Cloudy, possible showers this morning, some sunny patches in the southern regions, above normal temperatures," the announcer said. The radio in Mika's bedroom was turned up loud. Mika backed from the closet with a roll of Truda's drawings in her hand.

"Look at this mess, will you? You can't keep these drawings forever. The wax in the crayons will attract mice."

Mice had moved into the house during the flood, taking over the top floor, eating all of Mika's plants down to the earth in the pots and burrowing inside to get at the roots. Mice had chewed holes in their curtains, pulled strips of wallpaper loose from around the baseboards, gnawed at the plaster beneath, leaving behind hollows lined with delicate grooves like veins in a leaf. The mice had also left behind a furry smell, a gray moldy odor that Mika scrubbed free with Lysol. Mika had worked diligently, had reclaimed the house from the flood waters, and the mice had been banished, nothing of them remained except for the imagined fine whiskers twitching in the corners, the soft scurrying in the dust beneath the bed at night.

"I don't think mice like wax," Truda said.

"Mice or no mice, you can't keep all these drawings. It's getting out of hand. That's all you do, day and night, and it's not good for your eyes."

Truda was the only Lafreniere to wear glasses. Her mother couldn't understand it. Lack of carrots, her father said. Not only do carrots give you good eyesight, they also give you hair on your chest. Look at me, Maurice said, living proof. Swallow a fruit pit and a tree will grow inside, bee stings are really smooches for sweet children. Truda doubted it. She knew the reason for her poor eyesight. At one time, she'd cried too much.

Mika unrolled the drawings and spread them across the floor. "Where did you ever get all the paper?" she asked. She was practical, wondered more about the gathering of paper rather than why or what was in the drawings.

Truda couldn't decide whether or not to answer. She ran her tongue across her top teeth to keep the words inside. It was still easier for her to remain silent than it was to speak. When she sat at the washstand on her stool facing the window drawing pictures, she could go the whole day without speaking to anyone.

"From the bakeshop. The girl gave it to me."

"You crossed the highway alone?"

Caught. Truda felt sweat on her palms. Words were traps. "Betty came with me."

"That's neither here nor there. You can't keep every single drawing. Pick out the best ones and throw the rest out."

"I can't."

"There's no such word as can't."

Then why did you just use it yourself, Truda wondered.

"I didn't say to get rid of all of them. Just some, okay? Where would I be if everyone collected junk? Snowed under." Mika began shuffling through the drawings as though looking for some redeemable quality that might justify keeping them. She looked for genius and saw crude shapes of houses, barns, farm machinery, gardens, chickens. She picked out a drawing, pointed to the figure of a young girl. "Is this you?" she asked. "Have you drawn yourself into the pictures? Is that why you want to keep them?"

Of course it's not me. How could she be so ridiculous? The girl had black curly hair, she didn't wear glasses. "No, that's not me."

The pictures were drawings of the farm where she'd stayed during the flood. The girl was the one who'd been in the photograph on the piano with her eyes closed, a circle of flowers in her hair. Truda gathered the drawings together quickly. But Mika's attention had already begun to wander. "Where did I put those raincoats?" she asked herself. She got up from the floor and stepped over Truda. "Well, do what you want. But if you spent as much energy running and playing as you do on these drawings, then you wouldn't be so fat."

Truda didn't mind. She knew her mother's comment was punishment for not being agreeable, but she was able to keep the drawings. She listened as Mika went downstairs. She heard Lureen talking in the kitchen below. That was the way she liked the house to be. She preferred to be alone and still have people moving about, talking to each other. If she stayed in her room drawing and suddenly it grew silent beneath her, she went looking until she found them. She rolled up the drawings. She would need to find a safe place for them somewhere against any tampering that could later be blamed on a mouse, in the same way silence could be blamed on a cat.

"Oh good, you're here, finally," Mika said as Truda entered the kitchen. "Have some cereal."

Truda ate the cold breakfast cereal without tasting the blue-tinged powdered milk or the dry papery flavor of the puffed wheat kernels. She closed out the voices of her brothers and sisters and planned her next drawing. Everything about the farm had been backwards. When you came in the door there were latches on the wall in the porch. Latches that held brooms and mops firmly snapped into place. In one corner had been the cream separator with a checkered cloth draped over the bowl and in the other corner, a blue metal pie plate on the floor and cats feeding around it, wild frightened cats that zig-zagged out of her path when she entered the porch.

"I've got a job for you to do today," Mika said to Truda.

"I was going to ask if Truda could come with me after school when I go for the eggs," Betty said.

"Afraid to go alone?" Lureen's voice was strident. "What a suck."

"Well, sorry, but Truda can't go with you. I need her to pull weeds in the garden."

"How come?" Lureen asked. "Why do I have to stay in after school and wash sealers in the basement while Truda gets to do the garden? It's not fair. I always do the garden."

Their voices jabbed against Truda like a fork stabbing peas on a plate. There had been a window above the cats' feeding dish. And dried-up flies cradled in a spider's web. When you entered the farmhouse, instead of the kitchen there was a large dining room filled with dark furniture. Then to the left, sliding doors, a cramped parlor, a piano with a photograph of a young girl in a coffin. Stop: before that, the yard. She needed to remember the yard. She needed to reconstruct all parts of the farm because although she'd lived there almost six months, it was as though it had been a dream. She looked up at the refrigerator where she kept the bucket of crayons, out of reach of the little ones who would color the walls or eat the crayons, Mika said. They were gone.

"My crayons," Truda said. Had Mika discovered the way to stop the drawings?

"Look here," Mika said to Lureen. "If you'd done a better job weeding the garden last time, you'd be doing it now. Besides, it won't hurt Truda to get some fresh air."

"My crayons are missing."

"If Truda can come with me to get the eggs, I'll help her do the garden," Betty said.

"Well, I'm not sitting in this dumb house all day washing jars. What about my fresh air, eh? I could die down there. Why is it only Truda who needs fresh air?"

"You'll do as I tell you."

A spoon clattered to the floor. "And where are you off to?" Mika asked Truda. Truda was halfway across the kitchen.

"To look for my crayons. They're gone. Someone took them."

Truda

"Who would take them, a mouse?" Mika asked. "You don't need your crayons this very minute. Come and sit down. Don't slow things down; I've got so much to do." She turned to Betty. "Alright, I don't care. Truda can go with you just as long as everything gets done."

My crayons, my crayons, Truda thought. She's taken them. Mika reached for the Bible resting on top of the radio. She set the Bible down on the table with a thump and opened it to the place where a bay leaf had been stuck between the pages as a marker.

Thou shalt not steal, Truda thought. The delicate scent of the bay leaf was released as Mika began to read.

After school Truda and Betty walked along the highway to the small yellow cottage where Betty would pick up three dozen eggs. "I know it was her," Truda said. "I know she took my crayons." They had walked two blocks and then the houses dwindled and gave way to open fields. Their running shoes and legs were covered in a yellow dust from the fresh gravel on the shoulder of the road. Truda walked with her head down. She'd once seen a boy at school catch the sun in a glass and beneath the glass, paper smouldered and burned. The same thing would happen to her eyes if she looked at the sun. She disliked the clicking sounds that the grasshoppers made in the ditch along the highway. At the farm, she'd had an insect jump down the front of her dress. They'd laughed, teased her, took her dress off in the middle of the field. It wasn't pleasant laughter, but nevertheless it had been laughter which was scarce on the farm where everyone had their job to do and did it as though tomorrow wouldn't come if they didn't. In the small cramped parlor, the photograph of the little girl, and also on top of the piano, the mantle clock, striking the hour as she entered the house. Each time it bonged, the sound froze her mind. The sound of it was an old yellowing wooden sound and a lemon polish, warm milk and silverware cleaner sound. Beyond the kitchen, stairs to the attic had black rubber treads with grooves in them that made her think, black licorice; but

they weren't that, they tasted bitter when she put her tongue
on them.

> I'm coming up one step—dropping buns
> I'm coming up two steps—dropping buns
> I'm coming up three steps—dropping buns
> I'm coming up fourteen steps—dropping buns
> And there I met a horse who was—dropping buns.

The attic: along one wall, a chest with an embroidered
cloth on top of it. A fold-down cot with a crochet spread
beside a mangle iron.

"She doesn't want me to draw and so she took away my
crayons," Truda said.

Betty squeezed Truda's hand. "She only put them away for
the summer. Wait and see."

"I want to go home." And look for them.

"Well you can't. And there's a lot to see outside of your
room if you'd only look." Betty nudged Truda's chin upwards.

"Look, what do you see?"

She saw nothing. Fields, the sky. At the farm, a strange
humming sound had risen up out of the fields and the people
on the fields were like specks of dust moving across the
horizon into the midst of the humming. And then she saw
something else, like water, running overtop the highway. It
sparkled and jumped beneath the sun. It was glassy blue and
spilled off the highway into the fields. "A lake," she said. "I see
a lake."

Betty laughed. "That's what I thought too when I first saw
it. But it isn't a lake. I've been out there and you know, it gets
further away, you can never reach it."

"I see waves," Truda said. She was excited. They thought
she was still blind. They forgot, she could see now, even the
leaves on the trees. And she could see the lake. It wasn't the
yellowish brown of the river either, creeping up step by step
until they'd had to climb into a boat and paddle away from
town. The lake was like Betty's eyes, it was glassy blue.

Truda

"What you see are heat waves rising off the highway. I don't know how it happens. It just does." They crossed the highway and approached the cottage where Betty would get the eggs.

"But it looks real, like a lake."

Betty led Truda down into the shallow ditch beside the highway. A car shot past and Truda watched as the car met the lake on the highway, cut through and vanished. "Come," Betty said. "We'll sit for a while and rest our legs." She set the cartons down and flopped back into the grass. Truda lay down beside her. She heard the humming sound coming up from the fields. She heard the cry of the Franklin gulls and shaded her eyes to find them.

She had sat on the cot in the attic room at the farm and listened to the birds circling above the fields. The farm woman was awkward, thought Truda couldn't dress herself and complained as she forced Truda's arms into the armholes of a cotton blouse she'd ironed on the mangle. The cotton squeaked as the buttons were pushed through holes which were too small. The blouse was the color of goldenrod. It belonged to the dead girl on the piano. Draw: birds, gray with some blue shining in the gray wings. Their beaks made funny *kapoka* sounds on the gravel. They muttered and complained and once she thought she'd heard her name mentioned. She stood still, heart pumping blood wildly, fearful that they would smell her and fly away. The people were all on the fields. They were the specks in the dust coming to the house when they had breakdowns or for the prepared food. It made it easier to keep her vow not to speak when there was no one to talk to, except for the birds. She scooped chicken feed from the sack and scattered it around the yard. She moved among the birds slowly, speaking the sad soft cooing call of the male, and they rose up quickly, their wings fanning the air. She followed them, wheeling over the blue spruce, the willows at the far end of the pond, across the fields spread out below, golden patches on a huge quilt of green and blue, to Agassiz. To her home and her family.

Truda raised her arm and followed a single bird's flight with a finger, guided it down towards the lake but at the last moment, it veered away. She thought she could hear waves and the sound of it reminded her of the flood. She felt as though she carried her own Franklin gull sound inside her chest, overwhelming her with its terrible lonely cry. It was how she'd felt when she'd been at the farm, awake in the attic, waiting and waiting for the flood to be finished.

"Guess what, Truda? You have a new baby brother. I've named him Peter. Isn't that wonderful?" Static on the telephone wire, it was the sparrows bouncing on the wire outside the window, making Mika's words break into fragments . . . guess . . . baby . . . wonder. . . .

I said. I said. I said. I said. The sparrows one after another fluttered from the wire. It shivered, a silver arc, then it straightened and dissolved into the sky. Silence.

I said, don't leave me here. When are you coming to get me?

"Have you got nothing to say? Cat's got your tongue?"

"Don't worry, it's a little thing," the farm woman said. "Once you come she'll find her tongue again. We didn't want to worry you. It's a little thing and you have your hands full with the new baby."

After that, the rain began falling, making everything blurred around the edges and so she missed seeing her mother's face at the car window. She had stood crying in the house, looking out across the yard at the road through a rain-spattered window and it was the flood. That's what made everything so wet. That and her crying. The rain came and the road past the house dissolved and oozed black dirt into deep waterfilled gulleys on each side. A man pushed the car down the road away from the farm. They couldn't stop and come for her because of the new baby, the slippery road, the rain, the flood, her crying. Even though it was her seventh

Truda

birthday, and they'd promised to come, they didn't stop. And so she didn't get to see her mother's white moonshaped face at the car window. Look, look, she's waving, someone said. But Truda doubted it. See, there's your mother, girl. Stop crying for once. Don't you know, water attracts water? But she couldn't stop crying and so her two weeks' stay turned into three months and then another three months. Crying made everything worse. She'd ruined her eyes.

Ooowee, oowee, the gull inside her chest cried. *Ooowee.*

"Did you know that this land was once all under water?" Betty asked. "Once upon a time it was a large lake."

Happy Birthday to you, crying made everything worse. But she'd discovered that crayons and paper made it better. Drawing was a bird moving against a clean sky the way you wanted it to.

"Hey, you sleeping?"

"Next time, take me with you," Truda said. "I don't want to go to the farm. I'll run away if they make me stay there. Next time—"

Betty laughed and slid her arm beneath Truda's neck, pulling her head onto her shoulder. "What's this next time business? We probably won't have another flood. And even if we do, we have the dikes now. So forget about the flood once and for all and listen. Thousands of years ago, this was all lake. Lake Agassiz." Betty sat up and pointed across the fields. "A hundred miles away is the nearest shoreline. In the Pembina Hills. Miss Janzen showed us on a map at school."

"Will it ever come back?" Like the flood, a trickle first across the basement floor and later, a rushing waterfall and sealers bobbing about in the muddy water.

Betty gathered the egg cartons up and got to her feet. "No, it won't come back. Not in a million years. We've got nothing to worry about." She pulled Truda's ear. They crossed planks that led across the ditch to the yellow cottage. They stopped outside the gate.

"Like it out here?" Betty asked.

"Yes." The sun didn't hurt her eyes the way she thought it would.

"Good. Wait until the flax is blooming. It looks just like a lake too."

"There is a lake out there. I can hear waves."

"It's all in your head, believe me," Betty said. "Now wait right here. I won't be long."

Truda waited. She leaned into the fence and looked at the lake. It jumped forward and channels of water tipped down the highway towards her. It was all in her head but she could smell fish and see shells and sand. The gulls flew low, crossing and crisscrossing each other's flight paths. She could see their black feet tucked up against white-gray bottoms. She looked down and saw milky water receding before her feet, leaving wet crescent marks on the ends of her navy sneakers. Beige sand, dappled with curious flat gray pebbles, rounded perfectly smooth, was left in the water's wake. She stooped, picked several pebbles and dropped them into her pocket before the white frothy water rushed back up, cold, overtop her shoes and then up around her ankles. She lifted her eyes to the lake. The gulls cried with joy and bounced their solid bodies against its surface. It was like nothing she had ever drawn. Her own gull rose. She felt the cold water around her calves, at her knees and then it swirled about her thighs. She took a deep breath and dove under. The farm was gone and her imagination was a tree growing inside and green leaves unfolding one by one.

4 / The Wednesday Circle

Betty crosses the double planks that span the ditch in front of Joys' yard. Most people have only one plank. But Mrs. Joy needs two. Mrs. Joy is a possible candidate for the circus. Like sleeping with an elephant, Betty's father says often. But Mr. and Mrs. Joy, the egg people, don't sleep together. Betty knows this even though she's never gone further than inside their stale smelling kitchen.

The highway is a smeltering strip of gunmetal gray at her back. It leads to another town like the one she lives in. If you kept on going south, you would get to a place called Pembina in the States and a small dark tavern where a woman will serve under-age kids beer. Laurence, Betty's friend, knows about this. But if you turn from the highway and go west, there are dozens of villages and then the Pembina Hills which Betty has seen on one occasion, a school trip to the man-made lake at Morden. Home of the rich and the godly, Betty's father calls these villages. Wish the godly would stay home. Can't get a seat in the parlor on Friday nights.

Beyond her lies a field in summer fallow and a dirt road rising to a slight incline and then falling as it meets the highway. Before her is the Joys' crumbling yellow cottage, flanked on all sides by graying bales of straw which have swollen and broken free from their bindings and are scattered about the yard. Behind the cottage is the machine shed. Behind the machine shed and bumping up against the prairie is the chicken coop.

Because Mika, Betty's mother, sends her for the eggs instead of having them delivered by Mr. Joy, she gets them cheaper.

Betty balances the egg cartons beneath her chin and pushes open the gate. It shrieks on its rusty hinges. The noise

doesn't affect her as it usually does. Usually, the noise is like a
door opening into a dark room and she is filled with dread.
Today, she is prepared for it. Today is the day for the
Wednesday Circle. The church ladies are meeting at her
home. Even now, they're there in the dining room, sitting in a
circle with their Bibles in their laps. It's like women and
children in the center. And arrows flying. Wagons are going
up in flames and smoke. The goodness and matronly wisdom
of the Wednesday Circle is a newly discovered thing. She
belongs with them now. They can reach out to protect her
even here, by just being what they are. And although she
wants nothing to happen today, she is prepared for the worst.

"Come on in," Mrs. Joy calls from the kitchen.

Betty sets the egg cartons down on the steps and enters
the house. Mrs. Joy's kitchen resembles a Woolworth store.
There are porcelain dogs and cats in every corner on knick-
knack shelves. Once upon a time, she used to love looking at
those figurines but now she thinks they're ugly.

The woman sits in her specially made chair which is two
chairs wired together. Her legs are stretched out in front
resting up on another chair. Out of habit, Betty's heart
constricts because she knows the signs. Mrs. Joy is not up to
walking back to the chicken coop with her. And that's how it
all began.

"Lo, I am with you always even unto the end of the
world," her mind recites.

These verses rise unbidden. She has memorized one
hundred of them and won a trip to a summer Bible camp at
Lake Winnipeg. She has for the first time seen the ocean on
the prairie and tried to walk on water. The waves have lifted
and pulled her out where her feet couldn't touch the sandy
bottom and she has been swept beneath that mighty sea and
heard the roaring of the waves in her head and felt the sting
of fish water in her nostrils. Like a bubble of froth she is swept
beneath the water, back and forth by the motion of the
waves. She is drowning. What happens is just as she's heard.

Her whole life flashes by. Her head becomes a movie screen playing back every lie and swearing, malicious and unkind deeds, thoughts, words. There is not one thing that makes her look justified for having done or said them. And then her foot touches a rock and she pushes herself forward in desperation, hoping it's the right direction.

Miraculously, it is. She bounces forward from the depths to where she can tiptoe to safety, keeping her nose above the waves. She runs panting with fear to her cabin. She pulls the blankets over her. She tells no one. But that evening in the chapel during devotions, the rustling wind in the poplars against the screen causes her to think of God. When they all sing, "Love Lifted Me," the sunset parts the clouds above the water so there is a crack of gold where angels hover, watching. So she goes forward to the altar with several others and has her name written in the Book of Life. They tell her the angels are clapping and she thinks she can hear them there at that crack of gold which is the door to heaven. She confesses every sin she's been shown in the water except for one. For some reason, it wasn't there in the movie. And they are such gentle, smiling nice people who have never done what she's done. So she can't bring herself to tell them that Mr. Joy puts his hands in her pants.

"Rainin' today, ain't it child?" Mrs. Joy asks.

"No, not yet," Betty says. "It's very muggy."

"Don't I know it," she says.

"Are your legs sore?" Betty asks.

"Oh Lord, yes, how they ache," Mrs. Joy says and rolls her eyes back into her head. Her jersey dress is a tent stretched across her knees. She cradles a cookie tin in her lap.

"That's too bad," Betty says.

A chuckle comes from deep inside her mammoth chest. "You sound just like your mother," she says. "And you're looking more and more like her each time I see you. You're just like an opal, always changing."

God's precious jewels, Mrs. Joy calls them when she visits

Mika. She lines them up verbally, Betty and her sisters and brothers, comparing chins, noses. This one here, she says about Betty, she's an opal. You oughta keep a watch over that one. Always changing. But it just goes to show, His mysteries does He perform. Not one of them the same.

"Thank you," Betty says, but she hates being told she looks like her mother. Mika has hazel eyes and brown hair. She is blond and blue-eyed like her Aunt Elizabeth.

"Well, you know where the egg pail is," Mrs. Joy says, dismissing her with a flutter of her pudgy hand.

"Aren't you coming?" Betty asks.

"Not today, girl. It aches me so to walk. You collect the eggs and then you jest find Mr. Joy and you pay him. He gets it in the end anyhow."

Betty looks around the kitchen. His jacket is missing from its hook on the wall. She goes over to the corner by the window and feigns interest in the porcelain figures. She picks one up, sets it down. His truck is not in the yard.

"Where is he?"

"Went to town for something," Mrs. Joy says. "But I thought he'd be back by now. Doesn't matter though, jest leave the money in the back porch."

The egg pail thumps against her leg as she crosses the yard to the chicken coop. She walks towards the cluttered wire enclosure, past the machine shed. The doors are open wide. The hens scratch and dip their heads in her direction as she approaches. Hope rises like an erratic kite as she passes the shed and there are no sounds coming from it. She stamps her feet and the hens scatter before her, then circle around and approach her from behind, silently. She quickly gathers three dozen of the warm, straw-flecked eggs, and then steps free of the stifling smelly coop out into the fresh moist air. She is almost home-free. She won't have to face anything today. It has begun to rain. Large spatters spot her white blouse, feel cool on her back. She sets the pail down on the ground beside the egg cartons and begins to transfer the eggs.

"Here, you don't have to do that outside." His sudden voice, as she fills the egg cartons, brings blood to her face, threatens to pitch her forward over the pail.

He strides across the yard from the shed. "Haven't got enough sense to come in out of the rain," he says. "Don't you know you'll melt? Be nothing left of you but a puddle."

He carries the pail, she carries the cartons. He has told her: Mrs. Joy is fat and lazy, you are my sunshine, my only sunshine. I would like six little ones running around my place too, but Mrs. Joy is fat and lazy. His thin hand has gone from patting her on the head with affection, to playfully slapping her on the behind, graduated then to tickling her armpits and ribs and twice now, his hands have been inside her underpants.

"Be not afraid," a verse leaps into her head. "For I am with you." She will put her plan into action. The Wednesday Circle women are strong and mighty. She knows them all, they're her mother's friends. She'll just go to them and say, Mr. Joy feels me up, and that will be the end of it.

She walks behind him, her heart pounding. He has an oil rag hanging from his back pocket and his boots are caked with clay, adding inches to his height.

"I'm waiting for my parts," he says over his shoulder. "Can't do anything until I get that truck fixed." Sometimes he talks to her as though she were an adult. Sometimes as though she were ten again and just coming for the eggs for the first time. How old are you, he'd asked the last time and was surprised when she said, fourteen. My sunshine has grown up.

They enter the machine shed and he slides the doors closed behind them, first one and then the other, leaving a sliver of daylight beaming through where the doors join. A single light bulb dangles from a wire, shedding a circle of weak yellow light above the truck, not enough to clear the darkness from the corners.

"Okay-dokey," he says and puts the pail of eggs on the

workbench. "You can work here. I've got things to do." He goes over to the truck, disappears beneath its raised hood.

Then he's back at the workbench, searching through his tool-box. "Seen you with your boyfriend the other day," he says. "That Anderson boy."

"He's not my boyfriend," she says.

"I saw you," he says. His usual bantering tone is missing. "The two of you were in the coulee." Then his breath is warm on the side of her face as he reaches across her. His arm knocks against her breast, sending pain shooting through her chest. I need a bra, she has told Mika. Whatever for? Wear an undershirt if you think you really need to.

"Do you think it's a good idea to hang around in the coulee with your boyfriend?"

"He's not my boyfriend," she says. "I told you."

He sees her flushed cheeks, senses her discomfort. "Aha," he says. "So he is. You can't fool me."

She moves away from him. Begins to stack the cartons up against her chest, protection against his nudgings. Why is it that everyone but her own mother notices that she has breasts now?

"Don't rush off," he says. "Wait until the rain passes." The sound of it on the tin roof is like small pebbles being dropped one by one.

He takes the cartons from her and sets them back on the workbench. He smiles and she can see that perfect decayed circle between his front teeth. His hair is completely gray even though he's not as old as her father. He starts to walk past her, back towards the truck and then suddenly he grasps her about the waist and begins to tickle her ribs. She is slammed up against him and gasping for breath. His whiskers prickle against her neck. She tastes the bitterness of his flannel shirt.

She pushes away. "Stop."

He holds her tighter. "You're so pretty," he says. "No

wonder the boys are chasing you. When I'm working in here, know what I'm thinking all the time?"

"Let me go." She continues to push against his bony arms.

"I'm thinking about all the things I could do to you."

Against her will, she has been curious to know. She feels desire rising when he speaks of what he would like to do. He has drawn vivid word-pictures that she likes to reconstruct until her face burns. Only it isn't Mr. Joy in the pictures, it's Laurence. It's what made her pull aside her underpants so he could fumble inside her moist crevice with his grease-stained fingers.

"Show me your tits," he whispers into her neck. "I'll give you a dollar if you do."

She knows the only way out of this is to tell. When the whole thing is laid out before the Wednesday Circle, she will become whiter than snow. "No," she says.

"What do you mean, no," he says, jabbing her in the ribs once again.

"I'm going to tell," she says. "You can't make me do anything anymore because I'm going to tell on you." She feels as though a rock has been taken from her stomach. He is ugly. He is like a salamander dropping from the sky after a rainstorm into a mincemeat pail. She doesn't know how she could ever have liked him.

"Make you?" he says. "Make you? Listen here, girlie, I've only done what you wanted me to do."

She knows this to be true and not true. She isn't certain how she has come to accept and even expect his fondling. It has happened over a course of four years, gradually, like growing.

She walks to the double doors where the light shines through. "Open them, please," she says.

"Open them yourself," he says. She can feel the presence of the Wednesday Circle. The promise of their womanly strength is like a lamp unto her feet. They will surround her and protect her. Freedom from his word-pictures will make her a new person.

"You say anything," he says. "You say one thing and I'll have some pretty stories to tell about you. You betcha."

"That woman," Mika is saying to the Wednesday Circle as Betty enters the dining room. "That woman. She has absolutely no knowledge of the scriptures. She takes everything out of context." Mika is standing at the buffet with a china teacup in her hand. Betty steps into the circle of chairs and sits down in Mika's empty one. Mika stops talking, throws her a look of surprise and question. The other women greet her with smiles, nods.

"Did you get the eggs?" Mika asks.

Betty feels her mouth stretching, moving of its own accord into a silly smile. She knows the smile irritates Mika but she can't help it. At times like these, her face moves on its own. She can hear her own heartbeat in her ears, like the ocean, roaring.

"What now?" Mika asks, worried.

"What do you mean, she takes everything out of context?" Mrs. Brawn asks, ignoring Betty. It's her circle. She started it off, arranging for the church women to meet in each other's homes twice a month to read scripture and sew things which they send to a place in the city where they are distributed to the poor. The women are like the smell of coffee to Betty and at the same time, they are like the cool opaque squares of Mika's lemon slice which is arranged on bread and butter plates on the table. They are also like the sturdy varnished chairs they sit on. To be with them now is the same as when she was a child and thought that if you could always be near an adult when you were ill, you wouldn't die.

"My, my," Mika mimics someone to demonstrate to Mrs. Brawn what she means. She places her free hand against her chest in a dramatic gesture. "They are different, ain't they? God's precious jewels. Just goes to show, His mysteries does He perform."

Betty realizes with a sudden shock that her mother is imitating Mrs. Joy.

Mrs. Brawn takes in Mika's pose with a stern expression and immediately Mika looks guilty, drops her hand from her breast and begins to fill cups with coffee.

"I suppose that we really can't expect much from Mrs. Joy," Mika says with her back to them. Betty hears the slight mocking tone in her voice that passes them by.

Heads bent over needlework nod their understanding. The women's stitches form thumbs, forest-green fingers; except for the woman who sits beside Betty. With a hook she shapes intricate spidery patterns to lay across varnished surfaces, the backs of chairs. What the poor would want with those, I'll never know, Mika has said privately. But they include the doilies in their parcels anyway because they have an understanding. They whisper that this white-haired woman has known suffering.

She works swiftly. It seems to Betty as though the threads come from the ends of her fingers, white strings with a spot of red every few inches. It looks as though she's cut her finger and secretly bleeds the color into the lacy scallops. The women all unravel and knit and check closely for evenness of tension.

Mika enters the circle of chairs then, carrying the tray of coffee, and begins to make her way around it. She continues to speak of Mrs. Joy.

"Are you looking forward to school?" the white-haired woman asks Betty. Her voice is almost a whisper, a knife peeling skin from a taut apple. Betty senses that it has been difficult for her to speak, feels privileged that she has.

"Yes, I miss school."

The woman blinks as she examines a knot in her yarn. She scrapes at it with her large square thumbnail which is flecked oddly with white fish-hook-shaped marks. "Your mother tells us you were at camp," she says. "What did you do there?"

Mika approaches them with the tray of coffee. "I just wish she hadn't picked me out, that's all," Mika says. "She insists on coming over here in the morning and it's impossible to work with her here. And Mr. Joy is just as bad. I send Betty for the eggs now because he used to keep me at the door talking."

Mr. Joy is just as bad. Mr. Joy makes me ashamed of myself and I let him do it. The woman shakes loose the doily; it unfolds into the shape of a star as she holds it up.

"You like it?" the white-haired woman asks Betty.

"It's pretty."

"Maybe I give it to you."

"Ah, Mika," a woman across the circle says, "she just knows where she can find the best baking in town."

Then they all laugh; even the quiet woman beside Betty has a dry chuckle over the comment, only Mrs. Brawn doesn't smile. She stirs her coffee with more force than necessary and sets the spoon alongside it with a clang.

"Obesity is no laughing matter," she says. "Mrs. Joy is a glutton and that's to be pitied. We don't laugh at sin, the wages of sin is death."

"But the gift of God is eternal life through Jesus Christ our Lord," the woman says so softly, the words are nail filings dropping into her lap. If Betty hadn't seen her lips moving, she wouldn't have heard it. "God forgives," the woman says then, louder. She is an odd combination of young and old. Her voice and breasts are young but her hair is white.

Mika stands before them with the tray of coffee. "Not always," Mika says. "There's the unpardonable sin, don't forget about that." She seems pleased to have remembered this.

"Which is?" the woman asks.

"Well, suicide," Mika says. "It has to be, because when you think of it, it's something you can't repent of once the deed is done." Mika smiles around the circle as if to say to them, see, I'm being patient with this woman who has known suffering.

"Perhaps there is no need to repent," the woman says.

"Pardon?"

"In Russia," the woman begins and then stops to set her thread down into her lap. She folds her hands one on top of the other and closes her eyes. The others, sensing a story, fall silent.

"During the revolution in Russia, there was once a young girl who was caught by nine soldiers and was their prisoner for two weeks. She was only thirteen. These men had their way with her many times, each one taking their turn, every single night. In the end, she shot herself. What about her?"

"I've never heard of such a case," Mika says. She sounds as though she resents hearing of it now.

"There are always such cases," the woman says. "If God knows the falling of a single sparrow, He is also merciful. He knows we're only human."

Mrs. Brawn sets her knitting down on the floor in front of her chair, leans forward slightly. "Oh, He knows," she says. "But He never gives us more than we can bear. When temptation arises, He gives us the strength to resist." She closes her statement with her hands, like a conductor pinching closed the last sound.

Betty watches as the white-haired woman twists and untwists her yarn into a tight ring around her finger. "I don't believe for one moment," she says finally, "that God would condemn such a person to hell. Jesus walked the earth and so He knows."

"No, no," Mika says from the buffet. "He doesn't condemn us, don't you see? That's where you're wrong. We condemn ourselves. We make that choice."

"And what choice did that young girl have?" the woman asks. "It was her means of escape. God provided the gun."

Mika holds the tray of lemon squares up before her as though she were offering them to the sun. She looks stricken. Deep lines cut a sharp V above her nose. "You don't mean that," she says. "Suicide is unpardonable. I'm sure of it. Knowing that keeps me going. Otherwise, I would have done it myself long ago."

There is shocked silence and a rapid exchange of glances around the circle, at Betty, to see if she's heard.

"You shouldn't say such things," Mrs. Brawn says quietly. "For shame. You have no reason to say that."

The white-haired woman speaks with a gaunt smile. "Occasionally," she says, "in this room, someone dares to speak the truth."

"What do you mean?" asks Mrs. Brawn.

"Look at us," the woman says. "We're like filthy rags to Him in our self-righteousness. We obey because we fear punishment, not because we love."

Betty sees the grease spot on her blouse where his arm has brushed against her breast. Her whole body is covered in handprints. The stone is back in her stomach. She feels betrayed. For a moment the women are lost inside their own thoughts and they don't notice as she rises from her chair and sidles over to the door. Then, as if on some signal, their conversation resumes its usual level, each one waiting impatiently for the other to be finished so they can speak their words. Their laughter and goodwill have a feeling of urgency, of desperation. Betty stands at the door; a backward glance and she sees the white-haired woman bending over her work once again, eyes blinking rapidly, her fingers moving swiftly and the doily, its flecked pattern spreading like a web across her lap.

5 / Stones

Mother made a new apron the day after she and Father quarreled and he slammed the door and went walking. She didn't come away from the kitchen window for a long time, and I tiptoed around the house feeling nervous because she hadn't noticed that it was past my bedtime.

She was wearing the apron when she met the doctor's wife, Mrs. Hallman, out by the clothes-line, only you couldn't see it for the pouch of clothespegs tied around her thick waist. Mrs. Hallman stood tall and slim, her red toenails sticking out the end of her white sandals and she smelled like the sweet william that grew in a patch beside the back porch. I hung around like a sticky fly in August and listened while they talked. Mother played with the pegs in the pouch and made little squares in the dirt with her foot while Mrs. Hallman said how pleased she was to be living in the country instead of the city, so much nicer for the children, didn't she think? Then she asked which one I was and Mother told her, Lureen the second of five and one was coming.

Mrs. Hallman said, "Oh how nice," her Jane Russell lips forming a raspberry circle and I wished suddenly that Mother would take off the pouch so the ricrac on the apron would show. Mrs. Hallman patted her flat stomach and told Mother that it sure was good to be slim again and that was *it* for her. Then she laughed and her voice went high and tinkly like a wind chime. Mother laughed too, and her laughter was like rubbing two stones together.

At supper Mother said to Father that the kids were terrible. And how could she invite Mrs. Hallman in? He hadn't built the cage he'd promised now for a month and Rudy let Jeepers loose again in the kitchen and Sharon wouldn't come down from the kitchen table. She'd offered

Mrs. Hallman some tomatoes, but they're allergic to tomatoes, and it was too bad, but she couldn't play bridge with Mrs. Hallman because she had better things to do with her time.

When Mrs. Hallman came for coffee, Mother would send me to the cellar for a jar of jelly and spread a clean tablecloth. Then she would sit drawing circles with her finger, smiling and nodding while Mrs. Hallman rattled her charm bracelet and talked about Toronto and Minneapolis and "my husband the doctor." I would sit listening to her wind chime laughter, unable to move when told to go out and play with the others.

When Mrs. Hallman left, Mother would bang pots and pans on the stove or put on Father's fishing hat and chop weeds in the garden, making chunks of earth fly up around her feet.

The oldest daughter, Emily, and I became friends. She played store with real groceries and let me watch. She had bubble gum and pop whenever she wanted and sometimes gave me sips. She had her own bicycle and she wouldn't let me ride it. I gave up my perch in the maple tree where I'd spent the summer building a tree-house and began moping about the kitchen complaining of having nothing to do. When I asked Mother why we didn't have one measly bike, she slammed the oven door hard and said stoves were more important than bicycles and if we ever got anything new around this house it would be a stove that works right.

Then Rudy tried fly-casting at the telephone wires and caught a fishhook in his finger. Mother sent me to the Hallmans' and the doctor said he'd come over and then stayed to have a slice of fresh bread, his eyes never leaving the cupboard where Mother had piled her batches of bread and buns. And when he asked if it was really true, did she really make that delicious bread, she smiled at him the way she smiles at Father when he pulls the little curl on the back of her neck and says she's keeping her girlish figure.

The doctor stood in the door with two loaves of our bread

under his arm and asked if they could have the recipe. He said some more and Mother laughed high and tinkly like the wind chimes and said she'd always wanted to play bridge, she'd just never had anyone offer to teach her and yes, she'd be glad to give him the recipe.

She sent me the next day with the recipe which I put under a stone for a moment while I helped Rudy untangle Father's fishing reel, which was tied to a kite. We couldn't fix it, so we buried the reel in the garden and when I got back, I stood and watched the wind flip the paper under the stone. Then I saw Emily's bicycle lying in her driveway and I lifted the stone and let the recipe blow away. I told Mother the doctor's wife said she didn't have time to bake bread.

When Father came home for supper, Mother was banging pots on the stove and said that she wouldn't bother with bridge after all, she had too much to do. Father said there was no rest for the wicked and Mother laughed, and her laughter was like rubbing two stones together.

6 / The Rock Garden

I was one of four children who stood beneath the maple tree early one morning. We were on our way to school. Mika, our mother, had spit and licked and polished and we were fresh and as clean as was the day which smelled to me of lilacs. Above us, leaf buds, tight like babies' fists, began uncurling fingers one by one to the sun. It wasn't a day to argue. We stood beneath the tree looking down at a rock. The rock had appeared mysteriously overnight and we, like curious animals, sniffed and poked at it.

"I wonder where it came from," I said.

Truda, the third eldest, spoke. "It could have been a dog. A dog carried it in its mouth and dropped it."

Betty laughed at Truda and tickled the top of her head. "Silly."

I nudged the rock with my foot. It wouldn't budge and I was relieved, seeing in my mind the possibility of a garter snake curled beneath it, or thick slugs kissing the damp bottom of the rock with their sucky mouths.

I was the only black-haired child of the six Lafreniere children. My skin didn't blister and peel in the sun, but tanned to the color of a netted gem potato, dusty and dry looking. My hair, straight and black, resembled Maurice's, my father's hair. I was the only child in our family who looked like a Lafreniere should look, fine-boned, tiny feet and hands, small black eyes. I was conscious of being different, and felt cocky and self-assured in this difference. "It looks like a rock," I said. "But it could be something else, you know. It could, for instance, be a fossilized dinosaur egg. It was dug up when they made the ring dike."

"Yes, it could be an egg," said the myopic Truda.

I could tell that Betty was stung by Truda's disloyalty;

usually they were a team. "We'll be late for school," Betty said. "And then I'll get the blame for it. I'm the example." She gathered her books up from the grass and headed down the cinder-strewn driveway.

"If it's a dinosaur egg," Rudy said, always wanting to get to the truth of the matter, "then it might hatch, won't it? I think it will. And then it'll eat us up."

"It can't hatch," I told him. "It hasn't been fertilized." Put that in your pipe and smoke it, as my father would say. I took Truda and Rudy by the hand and led them down the dirt road where we traced our own footprints in the bottom of the deep ruts. Betty followed along behind us, neat and proper, never galloping, our perfect example.

After a time, we left the road and entered the coulee, a grassy dish of marshland that filled each spring with water which receded quickly, leaving behind twitch grass that grew waist-high, and spotted toads that leapt up before our feet.

"I am thee Count," a voice said in Draculan tones. "Let me bite your neck. Heh, heh, heh." Laurence Anderson's brown curly head parted the grasses as he stood up and came towards us. He carried a paper sack and wiped his palms against his white T-shirt, leaving behind gray smudges of something he'd been into.

"It's puke-face himself."

"Lureen!"

I knew Betty would tell Mother. Lureen swore, she'd say, her blue eyes wide with a pretended innocence. Lureen said: shit, piss and God. Exaggerating, because reciting the words was the only way Betty had the courage to do it too. And Mother would believe her because Betty was her favorite child. Betty had memorized one hundred Bible verses and won a trip to church summer camp. Our mother respected those who could do what she couldn't.

Girls don't swear, she often said.

But they do on Father's side of the family, I argued.

Well, I guess. What can you expect, she said. There are

no ladies in your father's family. None that I know of. They're coarse and hard. They paint their nails. They walk around in their war paint looking as though they've dipped their fingers in someone's blood. You want to be like that? I knew nothing of my father's family except what my mother told me. But, yes, that sounded exciting.

Why don't girls swear? Because, Mother said when she didn't want to talk to us, just because. Because I say so. And then, exasperated, it gives boys the wrong impression, you know. That you aren't to be respected. That you're Fair Game. Like a female dog in heat.

What is Fair Game? I wondered, and imagined a prairie chicken flapping up from the grass in the coulee. I was twelve years old, I knew what the spring dance of the dogs meant and I thought that she was coarse and hard for referring to it. But what was Fair Game?

Sometimes my mother would say, men, who needs them? In the same derogatory way she discussed my uncles' wives. She would say, Lureen, you would be "wery vise" to forget about boys until you have an education.

By education, Mother meant grade twelve, which, to me, seemed a preposterous length of time to wait for boys, an indication of her being so out of touch with reality, that her opinion couldn't be trusted. A person whose English was so faulty that they said, "wery vise," lost their credibility. Piss, shit and God are nothing to get excited about, my father would say with a laugh.

I began to hum because I knew it annoyed Laurence. "Twit," he said, not looking at me directly. He fell into step with Betty. "Wait until you see what I found," he said to her.

I wanted to fling mud at him. A solid blow to his shaggy head. Wham! It made me angry the way he followed Betty around when it was so obvious to me that I was better-looking. I watched as Laurence held open the paper bag and Betty looked inside it. Since Betty's new breasts, Mother's objections to their friendship had grown stronger. If I went to her and told her that they had met in the coulee, that would be that. But I wouldn't do that because I was beginning to use Betty's sins against her, to realize that there was something to my mother's admonition that sisters should be friends.

"What is it?" There was fear in Betty's voice. "Where did you find that awful thing?"

Laurence closed the bag quickly at the word "awful" and clutched it against his chest.

"I found it where they're digging," he said. "It's mine now. I'm going to keep it."

Betty looked frail and meek against the tall, sharp-bladed grasses. Her hair was wound about her head in a golden crown of tight braids which made her neck look thin, too thin to support so large a head. "But why would you want to?" she asked. "It looks real, like a real person's—"

"It is," said Laurence. "It's a human skull."

"But it must be wrong, you should get rid of it, bury it or something."

Let me look, I wanted to say, but they had joined themselves against me, turned their backs and were lost in their own conversation. I wanted to look inside the bag, force myself to touch, hold in my hands, whatever it was that frightened Betty, to show Laurence that he'd made a mistake in choosing Betty over me.

Weeks later, the lilacs had finished blooming and were just rust-colored flecks on the ground, and now there were seven buff-colored, pumpkin-sized rocks on the ground beneath the maple tree. Truda had wised up by then, and decided that the rocks weren't dinosaur eggs. "Maybe Mother laid them, like a chicken," she said once. That morning, when another stone had been added by mysterious circumstances to the growing mound of them beneath the rope swing, Truda called me over to examine the new rock and said, "Look at that, she laid another egg."

Rudy was there too. He was pumping fruitlessly on the rope swing, trying to gain some height, but his feet kept

The Rock Garden 71

glancing off the stones, making the swing careen wildly, bringing his shins too close to the rough bark of the maple tree. "Damn," Rudy said. "I don't think it's fair that we can't use the swing."

"Do something," Truda pleaded, her heavy thick glasses slipping down her nose and her myopic gray eyes clouded and pleading.

I decided to do something about the stones. I marched into the house and faced my father who had his day off from the barbershop and was sprawled in the maroon easy chair with his bare feet propped up on the hassock. He hid behind a magazine so he wouldn't have to take note of the multi-colored and malodorous piles of dirty laundry Mother sorted in the living and dining room every Monday.

Why do you have to do the laundry on my day off for God's sake, he complained. And I agreed fully, it was inconsiderate.

Because, she said. Just because I have to. Monday is wash-day. I can't help it if it also happens to be your day off.

Father looked at me overtop his *Game and Fish* magazine. "How should I know where the rocks came from? I'm not the chief cook and bottle-washer around here." He tried to tease me from my seriousness. "Serious, serious," he'd say. "That's your mother's department." His small black eyes reflected light in a curious way, making him look as though he were about to burst into tears or laughter. I could never tell which.

"Why don't you ask your mother where the rocks came from? She should know."

Everything in the yard and the two-story frame house belonged absolutely to us, the children. Mother had always arranged everything according to the patterns of our play. So the rocks were encroaching on our territory. I went to the kitchen where she folded diapers at the table. The washing machine sloshed and chugged another load clean in the back porch. There were two stacks of diapers, Peter's and Sharon's, white unspotted flannel, smelling of the reedy wind that blew in from the coulee.

"What rocks?" Mother asked.

"You know. Under the swing. Those rocks."

"They're mine." Her voice snapped the sentence shut the same way her strong white teeth nipped at knots in laces. You could ask Father anything and get an interesting, amusing answer, but not Mother. She was as serious as a mousetrap.

"What are they for? We can't use the swing anymore."

"Swing, fling. You're too old anyway. And you don't really care about the others, you just want to stir up trouble. I know you." She flicked a diaper and folded it into the shape of a kite, triple folds for Peter, because a boy pees the front. "Anyway, you have the rest of the yard to do what you want."

"It's our yard."

"I beg your pardon?"

"You should give us a reason, at least. You should tell us what the rocks are for."

"I don't have to tell you anything, missy," she said. "You only want reasons so that you can argue."

The sun moved behind the clouds for a moment and the yellow kitchen walls lost their sheen as the shadow came and fell on Mother's face, making her deeply set hazel eyes sink even further back into their bony sockets.

"Oh Lord," she said. "Please don't let it rain today."

"Why not?" I asked, grateful that she had been diverted from the tone of 'I beg your pardon.'

"You think I like mud from one end of this house to the other?"

The cloud passed and the room shone once again, but it seemed to me that pieces of the shadow lingered in her eyes. A creeping uneasiness made me close the screen door behind me gently.

That same evening as the garden arose silently from the black earth behind the chicken wire fence, I awoke to the sound of the latch on the screen door. I thought it was Father coming home from the hotel. But instead of my father's heavy step in the kitchen, there were light footsteps on the sidewalk at the side of the house and then silence. I looked out across the coulee and imagined Laurence crouching in the tall weeds, like a prairie chicken about to spring up. The moon was a silver disk, licked and pressed onto a black broadcloth sky. The night breezes fanned the tops of the grass in the coulee and sounded like the whispering of a single voice.

Let me bite your neck.

Mother stepped out from beneath the maple tree and crossed the yard to the driveway. She left the yard and walked down the center of the road, head bent into the darkness. The moon revealed the fish-white muscles in her calves. Mother's knotted tanned arms, her strong back, the muscles in her legs made her look chunky and shorter than she really was. She could carry a hundred-pound sack of flour in her arms. A dog barked in the distance and Mother vanished into the inky darkness. I knelt beside the window to wait.

When I awoke, my knees were stiff from kneeling. The wind had fallen. From Main Street came the insistent toot of a car horn. At the end of the street there was another sound. The sound was a needle-thin one, yet musical, like a violin being plucked instead of bowed. A blotted figure emerged from the darkness and gradually came to the light. The plucking sound was Mother's voice raised softly in a song. She came to the light. Her hair was unwound and flowed in a brown cascade of ripples across her shoulders. She carried a rock in her arms. She turned in at the driveway beneath the window. Still singing lightly, she strode across the yard and laid the stone gently down among the others.

Weeks later, the sweet peas had climbed to their glory on the chicken wire fence surrounding the garden and the bees droned above the profusion of pea blossoms. I was behind the sweet peas, hoeing the potato patch. I was unhappy. Laurence had put his hand on Betty's breast in the coulee. They thought I hadn't seen. I hadn't told anyone although I was burning up with the desire to do so. I heard a noise and looked up. Laurence was there, behind the tree out of sight, should anyone look out the window. He played with his knife. He held the blade at the end and then flung it, making the blade turn once in mid-air before it cut into the tree.

"That's easy," I said. "I can do that." I'd dropped the hoe, come to watch.

"You think you're so tough," Laurence said.

"I don't think. I know I am."

"God, you make me sick." He bent to pick up the knife which had bounced off the bark and stuck into the ground.

I beat him to it, grabbed the knife before he'd had the chance to reach for it.

"Give it to me."

"Make me."

His hand was strong on my wrist, chapped and raw-looking like his mouth; it felt like sandpaper as he twisted my skin red. I felt tears forming. They were going to squirt forward onto my cheeks in a second and betray me if I didn't do something. I made a fist with my free hand, punched him hard in the middle of his dirty T-shirt. Woof, he said, sounding like a dog, and let go of me.

"Here's your stupid knife." I threw it onto the rock pile. My wrist ached. I walked away from him rapidly and entered the house. I could hear Mother moving about in the rooms upstairs.

"If you've got nothing better to do, you could give me a hand," she said.

I sat cross-legged on the floor beside the bed as Mother changed the linens. I let my head drop so that my hair fell forward and hid my face. The effect I hoped to achieve was a look of despair or dejection.

"What is it?"

I sighed deeply.

"Well, out with it."

"I don't know—it's just that he follows her around. As

though she were a bitch in heat. We can never go anywhere without him."

"What did you say?"

"I said, I'm fed up. Everywhere we go, there he is. It's like we're Fair Game."

The color fled from Mother's cheeks. "Who's following you around?"

"Laurence. He's here again. And yesterday, when I went to school I saw him and Betty. He—they were necking."

Mother's shoulders sagged. She dropped a sheet and rushed over to the bedroom window. "Oh, this is no good," she said. "I don't like the sound of this at all."

She clattered down the stairs and then the front door rattled on its hinges. I got up from the floor and went over to the window and stood looking down at Laurence and Betty. I saw Mother run across the yard toward them. She hopped from foot to foot when she reached the pile of rocks.

"But Mother," Betty protested. "He's just fixing the swing. He's moving the ropes up so the little ones can use it."

"I'll fix him. Just you let him come around again and I'll fix him." Mother turned to Betty and shook her finger. "Really, you'd think you'd have more pride." She sputtered and glanced up at the bedroom window where I watched. "Don't you want more than that for yourself?"

I parted the curtains and smiled at the sight of Laurence retreating, edging backwards from the yard.

"Wait," Mother said and held out her hand. "Give me your knife."

Laurence removed it from its leather sheath. The blade shone as it crossed the space between them. She grabbed it from him and, teetering up the stony mound of rocks beneath the tree, she cut through the ropes of the swing with saw-like motions. Betty ran into the house with her hands covering her face.

I saw the tanned V at Mother's throat rising and falling rapidly as she stood looking down the road where Laurence had gone and then back at the house. And then, as though she had come to some decision, she strode over to the icehouse and returned moments later pushing the wheelbarrow, which held a pail of whitewash and a paintbrush. Betty rushed into the bedroom and threw herself onto the bed, crying loudly.

Mother stood beneath the maple tree with her hands on her hips. "All right," she said loudly. "All right, okay. You can't change a thing. No amount of harping will change anything. They'll do what they want to do in the end anyway. I'm butting my head against a stone wall." She pried open the pail of whitewash. "Don't take my advice. See what you get in the end." She stirred the thick paint and then dipped the brush into it. "Life is too short to butt your head against a stone wall." She began to paint a large rock a brilliant white. "And what do you get for it? Let them learn the hard way." She continued to complain bitterly as she finished painting the rock and set it aside. She rolled another stone down from the pile and began to paint it also.

An hour passed. Betty came to the window to watch what was happening below. We heard Peter the baby down in the kitchen banging impatiently on the tray of the highchair and the clatter of pots as Sharon amused herself in the cupboards. Mother continued to paint rock after rock and to place them into a large circle. I sent Truda and Rudy outside to make polite restrained overtures at conversation in order to jar Mother from her strange behavior, but her sour expression sent them scurrying back into the house.

At a quarter to twelve, Father came walking up the sidewalk for his lunch. He stood waiting as Mother wheeled a load of dirt through the garden towards him.

"It's a funny time to start that job," he said, glancing at his watch.

"It's now or never."

Father shrugged. "Suits me. But what's for lunch?"

Mother looked up angrily. "Why don't you have a look?"

The Rock Garden   77

He came back out minutes later. "There's nothing prepared," he said, sounding injured and puzzled.

"I know."

"Why not?"

"Because," she said quietly and then once again, louder, "because. Just because. I don't know why. I'm tired of answering stupid questions. Make your own lunch."

"Listen here," Father said, his voice rising above its accustomed gentle tone. "The babies are in there alone. Their diapers are dripping."

"And does that bother you?"

"Of course, what do you think? Something could happen to them."

Mother grunted as the wheelbarrow tilted suddenly from her grasp and fell onto its side. "Well, change them then," she said. "They're your babies too."

"What's the matter?" he asked, lowering his voice. "Is it— are you in the family way?"

Mother stopped shoveling and looked him straight in the eye. "Yes. I'm always in the family way. And I'm tired. I'm tired of being a mother."

What? Tired of being a mother? It was an astounding thought. In the same way I grew tired of playing 7-up against the house, or sick of my best friend, so that I picked a fight in order to cut myself off from her, Mother was tired of us, her children?

Father turned from her in disgust. "Is that all?" he said. "Who doesn't get tired? What if I should say the same thing, eh? Where would you be?"

Absolutely, I agreed, where would you be without him? Where would any of us be?

"I would change places with you in a flash. You stay home, I'll go to work."

Father edged away from her. I had to do something. I knocked on the windowpane. "We're hungry," I said, reminding them both of their parental duties. He looked up, startled. "What do you expect me to do about it?"

"Peter needs a bottle."

"I don't know what's going on here," Father said. "But I do know that I've got five heads waiting to be cut. So I'm going to grab a bite to eat at the hotel and then I'm going to get back to work. Somebody's got to work around here," he said loudly, for Mother's benefit.

"Oh, you're useless," she said. "You can go to the hotel. You couldn't look after a dog."

Father stared at her, shocked, and then retreated quickly.

"That's not fair," I said to my sister, "she's always so bloody unfair to him." Father had all the money. In case of marital breakdown, I wanted to be where the money was. So my sympathies in any of their arguments rested with him.

"I wouldn't know what's fair," Betty said. "Someone has to look after the kids today and I guess that leaves me." She went downstairs.

The sun passed center sky and the birds stopped singing. I nibbled at the sandwich Betty had brought to me, but my stomach was tight and the food tasted flat. So, Mother was tired of being a mother, eh? The idea was like a thunderstorm. I was unsettled by the sound of it. I didn't know how she could be so selfish.

Wet stains spread across my mother's back and from beneath her armpits, as she began to form a smaller circle of rocks on top of the larger one. Her hair was pasted in strands against her white neck. She looked to me like a sweaty, irritable child. Back and forth she went, scooping up the black dirt, wheeling it across the yard to the tree, dumping it, shoveling it into place, raking it smooth, back and forth, with a bulldog determination. And then, on one of her trips, she stumbled, broke her stride and fell beneath the weight of the dirt in the wheelbarrow. She landed flat on her back. She looked like a beetle squirming to right itself. The more she floundered, the more exposed she became. Her blue cotton

The Rock Garden

shift worked upwards, baring her thighs and then the white cotton V of her crotch.

My breath caught in my throat at the sight of my mother sprawled on the ground, at the sight of her vulnerability, that cotton mound between her legs.

She struggled upright, brushed dirt from her legs, her dress. I urged her to come inside. I wanted her to give up this silly project, wash her hands, or take up the broom and become a mother again. But she didn't. When she'd finished brushing herself off, she took up the handles of the wheelbarrow and began to fill in the second circle with earth.

She was forming the last, smallest circle when the sun began its falling behind the house, casting long pale shadows across the grass. Betty stood in the doorway of the bedroom with diaper pins in her mouth and a towel draped over her shoulder.

"I need a hand," she said.

"It's not our job," I said. "It's her job. Let her come and do it. She doesn't care if we starve, she only cares about herself." But my heart wasn't in it.

Betty threw the towel at me. "There's enough babies around here already without you becoming one too. Help me get them washed and into bed."

Together we bathed the children and put them into bed. We took turns reading stories to them to take their minds off their mother who wouldn't come inside and be a mother.

I listened to Betty's flat monotone voice reading, wooing the babies to sleep. Part of what happened was my fault. If I hadn't told on my sister, none of this would have happened. I would make tea, arrange a tray of food and lure her back inside. I might even begin to help around the house. Maybe finish changing the linens on the bed. Might not complain when asked to wipe the dishes.

I heard the door of the icehouse being closed. I crept to the window, looked down to see Mother scraping her shoes on the footscraper. I beckoned Truda and Rudy from the bed.

They tiptoed to the window. I instructed them to say goodnight. I arranged them side by side. They cleared their throats. One, two, three—now.

"Goodnight Mother."

She'd have to answer. She'd say, "Don't let the bed bugs bite." And then they would reply, "Oh no, we'll hit them black and blue with our shoes." We waited. No answer. I nudged them again. "Goodnight," they called once more. Their voices, clear in the moisture-laden air, were fruity and sweet.

Still no answer.

The screen door flapped shut. There was a long silent time. Then we heard the kitchen chair creaking beneath her weight and then the sound of her shoes dropping one after the other to the floor.

I'll memorize Bible verses, I vowed silently. I'll follow Betty's example. Then I stopped breathing, listened, as there came another sound from below. It was the dry swishing sound of the broom being swept briskly across the kitchen floor.

I began to breathe once again. "She's back. Listen, she's sweeping the floor." I sat down beside Betty who had gathered her knees up and rocked back and forth in the center of the bed.

My body felt weak, overpowered by the flooding of relief. The crisis was over. "I'll make tea," I said, "if you help me get together a plate of food for her."

"Are you crazy?" Betty said. "After what she did to Laurence? You go ahead and do that if you want to, but I couldn't care less."

I went back to the window to think about this new development. The rock garden glowed strangely in the falling light. Beside it on the ground were the ropes from our swing, curled like two large question marks. The rocks' pink glow dimmed slowly to a violet and then at last, a dull gray. My resolutions faded gently. Oh well, I told myself, she's used to making her own tea anyway. If I offered to make it, the shock would kill her.

"I know what you mean," I said. "What she did to Laurence was awful. I almost died. And it wasn't fair, either. He was only trying to help. She's so unfair."

"She's a witch," Betty, my example, said, "a frigging witch."

The first of the whispering sounds swept in from the coulee, gently puffing the curtains in and out like a frog's throat. I felt a slight chill. The sounds brought with them mystery, uncertainty.

Let me bite your neck.

I knew my mother had some of the answers to the mysteries. But the pull of an alliance between sisters was stronger. It was better than being on your own with a person who could suddenly grow tired of being your mother.

"Piss, shit and God," I said. "A mean witch." I stepped out and away from my mother. Suddenly, I was afraid.

7 / Night Travelers

"When a woman has intercourse," Mika told herself, "she thinks of what might happen." She climbed in the night the hill that led away from the river and James. She traveled in a black and white landscape because it was void of details that would have demanded her attention. And the night was also a cover. Above, the starlit summer sky served only to make God seem more remote, withdrawn. As she walked, she took comfort in the sound of the frogs in the moist ditches on either side of the road, the call of an owl hunting in the park below.

Men, she was certain, thinking of both James and Maurice, didn't think of such things as a seed piercing another seed and a baby growing instantly, latching itself fast to the sides of her life. Men were inside themselves when they shot their juices. It was just another trick that God played, to keep the babies coming. Replenish the earth. Well—she was doing her job.

She reached the top of the hill and then she stooped slightly, giving in to the weight of a stone which she cradled close to her breasts. If Maurice should ever think to ask, she would be able to say, "I was out gathering rocks for my rock garden. It's the only time I can go, when the children are sleeping." And she would still be telling the truth.

She stopped to catch her breath and turned to look back at the park beside the river. Lot's wife looking back with longing towards a forbidden city. But unlike Lot's wife, she did not become a pillar of salt. From among the trees in the park, light shone out from the tiny window in James's bunkhouse. He had turned on the lantern. Pride made her wish that he would have stood for a few decent moments and watched while she climbed the hill. For this reason she'd kept her back straight until she was certain he couldn't see her anymore. But already, he was stretched out, lost in one of the many books he kept on the floor beside the cot. What did she expect? That had been their agreement, not to look for anything from each other. She had Maurice and the children. He had his dream of voyages in a sailboat.

At the top of the hill, the road stretched broad and straight, one half mile to the center of town. She could see lights as cars on Main Street headed in and swiftly out of town. She passed by the grove of fruit trees that surrounded her parents' garden. The scent of ripe fruit carried across the road and she thought of the apples her mother had given to her, baskets of them, in the bottom of the cupboard. Her parents' white cottage stood beyond the garden in the darkness. I'm sorry, she said. I forgot about the apples. But with the children my hands are already full. She thought of the children, round cheeked and flushed with their dreams and her step quickened.

Beyond the ditch, there was a sudden rustling sound, like an animal rising up quickly. Mika, startled, stood still and listened. A dark figure stepped from the cover of the fruit trees onto the path that joined the cottage to the road.

"Who's there?" She heard movement, fabric rubbing against fabric. A dry cough. "Papa, is that you?"

Her father came forward in the darkness. Relief made her knees weak.

"Liebe, Mika. I was hoping, but I knew in my heart it was you."

Knew it was me, what? What did he know? "What are you doing up so late?" she asked instead. "The night air isn't good for your lungs."

"When one of my children is in trouble, I don't worry about such things."

"What's this, trouble?" she asked. She felt her heart jump against the stone she clutched tightly to her breast. As he turned towards her, he was illuminated by the moon and she saw that he'd pulled his pants on over his night clothes. His shirt lay open, exposing the onion-like skin on his chest to the cool breeze. She saw concern for her in the deep lines in his face. If only he would use anger, it would be easier to oppose him.

"Nah, you know of what I speak. I've seen your coming and going. I've seen him. I'm ashamed for you."

"What you've seen is me gathering rocks for a rock garden." She held up the stone. "I gather them from beneath the bridge."

"Mika." There was sorrow in his voice.

It was the same tone of voice he'd used on her all her life. It made her change her course of action because she didn't want to be responsible for his sorrow. It was the same thing with Maurice. Peace at all costs. Maurice had forced himself on her and she'd forgiven him because of an offer to build a new window in the kitchen. She hated that about herself.

"So, you've seen my coming and going and you're ashamed for me. I'm not."

He blocked her path. "Come to the house. We should talk and—"

She pushed around him and began to walk away. Talk? Talk about Maurice and his black night moods? About another baby coming in a house full of babies? No, we will talk about my responsibilities instead.

"Have you traveled that far then," she heard him call after her, "that you can now make excuses for your behavior? What am I to tell the elders at church?"

Before her, silhouetted against the sky, the flutter of wedge-shaped wings, two bats feeding on insects. They would become entangled in her hair. She heard his light step on the road and then he walked beside her. "Why should you tell them anything?" she asked. "It's none of their concern. What I do is my own business."

"We're a community," he said. "People united by our

belief, like a family. When one member hurts, the whole family suffers."

"A family. I'm not part of that family," Mika said. "I don't belong anywhere."

"How can you say that? The women welcome you into their homes. They pray for you."

"Oh, they welcome me, alright. I'm to be pitied, prayed for. It gives them something to do."

They walked for a few moments without speaking. He pulled at his thick white mustache, the way he did when he was deep in thought. She stopped, turned to him. "Look, Papa. You know they don't accept Maurice. Even if he wanted to go, they don't invite him into their homes. They don't really accept me, either. So, if you feel it's important to tell the elders, tell them. I don't care."

The bats—their flight was a dance, a sudden dipping, a flutter, a smooth glide and they swerved back in among the trees. Gone. She walked faster. "The children are alone," she said.

"Oh, so you think of the children at least?" he said.

"Of course I think of them. But I need something for myself too."

He put his large cool hand on her arm and drew her to the side of the road. His sun-tinged complexion had paled and there was fear in his eyes. "But not this," he said. "Not this. What are you saying? You need to ask God to forgive you. The wages of sin is death."

Always, Bible verses, given in love but becoming brick walls, erected swiftly in her path. The hair on her arms and neck prickled. "Papa," she said. "It's my sin and it's my death. Leave me be." She lifted the stone up and away from her breast and slammed it into the ground. She turned from him quickly and ran with her hands pressed against her stomach.

She undressed quickly, her heart still pounding, and listened to their sounds, the children, breathing all through the house. She'd stood first in one doorway, listening for them, then in another, and finally she'd bent over the baby in the crib at the foot of her bed. She'd felt for him in the dark, found a moist lump beneath the blankets. She'd changed his diaper without awaking him. Maurice was not home. He was still at the hotel. She waited for her heart to be still so that she could sleep. She rubbed her stomach gently. What would it be, she wondered, this one that she carried with her to James? Would it be touched or bent in any way by her anger? Below, a door opened. She stiffened, then rolled over and faced the wall as Maurice came up the stairs.

"What are you thinking?" James asked.

Mika swung her legs over the side of the cot and sat up. Her feet rested in a trapezoid of moonlight which shone through the small window of the bunkhouse. She'd been half-listening to James telling her about some one person he knew who had never let him down. His voice rose and fell in its strange British accent and she was able to think above it. Through the other small window at the end of the bunkhouse, she could see her parents' cottage, a white sentinel on a hill. It was in darkness once again, but she was certain her father's white face looked out from behind the lace curtains.

"Oh, I'm not thinking about any one thing in particular." But all day she'd been wondering, how could you be forgiven by God for something you'd done if you weren't sorry you'd done it?

He rose up on his elbow and ran his hand along her arm. The smell of the bunkhouse was his smell, faintly like nutmeg, the warmth of sun trapped in weathered gray planks and it was also the smell of the other men who had slept there; the men who had come to town as James had after the flood to help clean and rebuild it. She put her hand overtop his.

"God, you're beautiful," he said.

"Don't say that."

"What, not say you're beautiful?" He laughed and sat up

beside her. He reached for his cigarettes on the windowsill.
"You're a strange one."

He was tired of listening to himself talk and had drawn
her in by saying, "You're beautiful." In the beginning, he'd
pranced around her, so obviously delighted that he'd charmed
her into coming away from the river bank with him, through
the park to this bunkhouse. He'd followed her about, picking
up the clothing she'd shed, hanging it over a chair so she
wouldn't look rumpled when she left. He was a meticulous
love-maker. He began by kissing the bottoms of her feet, the
backs of her knees, her belly, causing the swing of the
pendulum inside her to pause for several seconds at midpoint,
so that she was neither being repelled nor attracted but
suspended and still.

"Why don't you want me to tell you that you're beautiful?"
James asked.

Because she didn't think she was beautiful. There was
nothing beautiful about a person who would come home
swollen and moist from love-making into the bed of another
man. But what Maurice had done was not beautiful either.
Two wrongs don't make a right, she'd instruct her own
children.

"No, what I meant was, don't say God. Don't bring God
into this."

Their thighs touched as they sat on the edge of the cot
and she was amazed at how quickly she had become
accustomed to the touch and smell of another man. The flare
of his match revealed his exquisitely ugly nose. It was a fleshy
hook pitted with blackheads. His chin and the skin around his
mouth were deeply scarred by acne. You're so ugly, she'd once
told him. She'd watched for evidence of injury, a faltering of
his tremendous self-confidence. He'd laughed at her attempt,
seen through it. She saw him daily as he walked past the
house and he was always in a hurry, loose-jointed and thin,
moving towards some vision he had of himself and his future.

He held the lit cigarette up to his watch. "Shouldn't you think about heading back? It's almost twelve."

"I've still got time."

He got up from the cot and his tanned chest moved into the trapezoid of light and then his buttocks, pinched together, muscular as he walked to the table beneath the window. He gathered up her hairpins and dropped them into her lap. He never forgot. He made certain each time that she left exactly as she'd come. She scooped the pins up and put them into the pocket of her dress.

"Don't you think you should fix your hair?"

"It's alright. Maurice is never home before I am."

He leaned over her, kissed her forehead. He slipped his hand inside her unbuttoned dress and fondled her. "I love your breasts. I think that's what I'll miss the most about Canada, your beautiful sexy breasts."

She put her arms about his neck and drew him down on top of her. "Once I'm gone," he said into her neck, "if we ever meet again, it will be chance. You know that, don't you?"

"Yes." In another month he wouldn't want her anyway. Already she could feel the baby between them. She listened to the sound of his heart pushing against her chest. The wind had fallen and the silence in the park was complete, the river still. The moment passed. She fingered the hairpins in her pocket. She pulled them loose and scattered them into the folds of his blanket. He'd find them tomorrow. When he was making his bed, tight corners, planning his day, his mind leaping forward to the next event, he'd find her pins and he'd think of her for one second. She knew he wouldn't think of her longer than that, or wonder what she might be doing at that moment or try and recall her features as she did his; she even longed for the sight of his lanky body, his brown trousers flapping loosely about his ankles, the funny way he walked, arms swinging, leading with his ugly nose. I thought of you today, he'd said once. And I got this enormous stiff prick. I think of you too. She couldn't say, I love you.

"You'd better go," he said. "Before I change my mind and keep you here with me all night."

She pushed him from her, sat up and buttoned her dress. She used his comb and began combing her hair which was tangled and damp with sweat. The comb seemed to contain some residue of his energy, a reminder of the range of feelings she'd experienced only thirty minutes before. James got up, walked to the door and she followed him. He stood naked on the step. She gave him the comb. He plucked her dark hairs from its teeth and let the breeze catch them away. Above them, the stars were brilliant and clear. "Will you come tomorrow?" he asked.

"I don't know. If I can, I will."

"Try." He took her hand in his. He pressed the hairpins into her hand. "You've forgotten these."

Mika walked up the hill away from the park, the river, James. She heard nothing of the sounds of the night, the singing of insects, the owl hunting, nor did she see the phosphorous glow of fireflies among the tall grasses in the ditch. She was listening to the sound of her feet on the road, her heart beating, her breath laboring slightly as she climbed the hill and her thoughts. How could she be forgiven by God and brought to a state of serenity and continue to see James at the same time?

When she reached the top of the hill, her father waited on the path, pacing back and forth, swishing mosquitoes from his arms with a switch of leaves. Mika walked faster so that he would know she had no intention of stopping. He ceased pacing. She lifted her head and strode by him. She felt the sting of leaves on her legs. She stopped suddenly, her breath caught in her throat, and fought back anger. He threw the switch aside.

"Where is the stone you've been searching for tonight?" he asked.

"I have nothing to say. You can't make me argue with you. If you want to argue, then do it with yourself." Her voice did not betray her anger. She still felt the biting edge of the leaves on her skin. She walked away swiftly, and then faster until she was running from him. Her breath became tight and then a spot of fire burned in her center. But she wouldn't stop running until she was home, safe, behind the door.

She sat at the kitchen table and pressed her face against the cool arborite. To be alone for once, just to be left alone. She listened to a fly buzzing against a window. The wind in the kitchen curtain swept against the potted plant. Water dripped into the sink. Something sticky against her arms—she sat up and frowned as her hand met toast crumbs and smears of jam left behind by one of the children. Her legs felt weak as she went over to the sink to stop the dripping of water and to get a cloth to wash the table. She reached to turn the light on above the sink and saw through the window her father entering the yard. She stood with her hands pressed to her face and waited. She wouldn't answer the door and he might think that she was upstairs, sleeping.

His light touch on the door, a gentle knock and—silence. Above her, the sound of electricity in the clock. He coughed twice. She could see him fumbling for his pocket, to spit his blood-flecked mucus into a handkerchief.

"Mika, I know you're there. Mika, open the door."

It wasn't locked, but she knew he wouldn't come in unless she opened it.

"You're causing much sorrow," he said. "Your mother has been crying most of the day."

Crying over children is a waste of time, Mika thought. In the end, they do what they want.

"She says for me to tell you, think of eternity."

The anger erupted. She stepped towards the closed door. "Eternity? Eternity? Papa, I've spent all my life preparing for eternity. No one tells me how to live each day. Right here, where I am."

She heard him sigh. "But when you think of it, we're here

for such a little time when you consider all of eternity," he said.

"Yes, and it's my little time. Mine. Not yours."

He didn't speak for a few moments. She held her breath. She waited for him to leave. She sensed his wretched disappointment in her, his fading spirit. I can't help that, she told herself.

"Mika, one thing," he said. His voice was barely more than a whisper. "There's something wrong with your thinking. If we could just talk. I'm not well. I need to know before I—" He broke off and began to cough.

Before I die. She finished the sentence for him. She turned her back to the door and pressed her knuckles into her teeth and bit into them. Anger rose and grew until her fists were free and raised up. That he would try to use his illness against her. It's my life, she told herself. It's my life.

"Go away," she cried. She faced the door once again and stamped her foot. "Go away." She would tear the curtains from the windows, upset chairs, bring all the children running to stare at her anger. She would let them see what had been done to her, she would tell them, it's my life. She would—she gasped. A sharp kick in her belly, then a fluttering of a limb against her walls. Another movement, a sliding downward, a memory drawing her inside instantly like a flick of a knuckle against her temple. The baby. Like all the others asleep in the rooms upstairs, it traveled with her.

"Mika, please. I care for you."

She opened the door and stood before him, head bent and arms hanging by her sides. They faced each other. His shoulders sagged beneath his thin shirt. "Come in," she said. "I'll lend you one of Maurice's sweaters." She began to cry.

He stepped inside quickly and put his hand on her shoulder. "Yes, yes," he said. "That's it. You must cry over what you've done. It's the beginning of healing. God loves a meek and contrite heart."

She leaned into him, felt the sharpness of his rib-cage

beneath her arms. I cry because I can't have what I want. He's going away soon. I am meek and contrite because he doesn't want anything more than just a fleeting small part of what I am. I am filled with sorrow because I know myself too well. If I could have him, I wouldn't want him.

"It's over," he said. "You won't go and see that man again."

She heard the rasping sound of fluids in his chest. She loved him.

"No, I won't see him anymore."

She turned her face against his chest and stared into the night beyond him. She felt empty, barren, but at peace. In the garden, a bright glow flared suddenly and she thought, it's a cigarette. But the glow rose and fell among the vegetation and then became bead-shaped, blue, brighter, her desire riding the night up and up in a wide arc, soaring across the garden into the branches of thick trees. A firefly, Mika thought. And she watched it until it vanished.

8 / Flowers for Weddings and Funerals

My Omah supplies flowers for weddings and funerals. In
winter, the flowers come from the greenhouse she keeps warm
with a woodstove as long as she can; and then the potted
begonias and asters are moved to the house and line the
shelves in front of the large triple-pane window she had
installed when Opah died so that she could carry on the
tradition of flowers for weddings and for funerals. She has no
telephone. Telephones are the devil's temptation to gossip and
God admonishes widows to beware of that exact thing.

And so I am the messenger. I bring requests to her, riding
my bicycle along the dirt road to her cottage that stands
watermarked beneath its whitewash because it so foolishly
nestles too close to the Red River.

A dozen or two glads please, the note says. The bride has
chosen coral for the color of her wedding and Omah adds a
few white ones because she says that white is important at a
wedding. She does not charge for this service. It is
unthinkable to her to ask for money to do this thing which
she loves.

She has studied carefully the long rows of blossoms to find
perfect ones with just the correct number of buds near the
top, and laid them gently on newspaper. She straightens and
absently brushes perspiration from her brow. She frowns at the
plum tree in the corner of the garden where the flies hover in
the heat waves. Their buzzing sounds and the thick humid air
make me feel lazy. But she never seems to notice the heat,
and works tirelessly.

"In Russia," she says as she once more bends to her task,
"we made jam. Wild plum jam to put into fruit pockets and
platz." Her hands, brown and earth-stained, feel for the proper
place to cut into the last gladiolus stalk.

She gathers the stalks into the crook of her arm, coral and white gladioli, large icy-looking petals that are beaded with tears. Babies' tears, she told me long ago. Each convex drop holds a perfectly shaped baby. The children of the world who cry out to be born are the dew of the earth.

For a long time afterward, I imagined I could hear the garden crying and when I told her this, she said it was true. All of creation cries and groans, you just cannot hear it. But God does.

Poor God. I squint at the sun because she has also said He is Light and I have grown accustomed to the thought that the sun is His eye. To have to face that every day. To have to look down and see a perpetually twisting, writhing, crying creation. The trees have arms uplifted, beseeching. Today I am not sure I can believe it, the way everything hangs limp and silent in the heat.

I follow her back to the house, thinking that perhaps tonight, after the wedding, there will be one less dewdrop in the morning.

"What now is a plum tree but a blessing to the red ants and flies only?" She mutters to herself and shakes dust from her feet before she enters the house. When she speaks her own language, her voice rises and falls like a butterfly on the wind as she smooths over the gutteral sounds. Unlike my mother, who does not grow gladioli or speak the language of her youth freely, but with square, harsh sounds, Omah makes a sonatina.

While I wait for her to come from the house, I search the ground beneath the tree to try to find out what offends her so greatly. I can see red ants crawling over sticky, pink pulp, studying the dynamics of moving one rotting plum.

"In Russia, we ate gophers and some people ate babies." I recall her words as I pedal back towards the town. The glads are in a pail of water inside my wire basket. Cool spikelets of flowers seemingly spread across my chest. Here I come. Here

comes the bride, big, fat and wide. Where is the groom?
Home washing diapers because the baby came too soon.

Laurence's version of that song reminds me that he is
waiting for me at the river.

"Jesus Christ, wild plums, that's just what I need,"
Laurence says and begins pacing up and down across the
baked river bank. His feet lift clay tiles as he paces and I squat
waiting, feeling the nylon line between my fingers, waiting for
something other than the river's current to tug there at the
end of it.

I am intrigued by the patterns the sun has baked into the
river bank. Octagonal shapes spread down to the willows.
How this happens, I don't know. But it reminds me of a
picture I have seen in Omah's Bible or geography book,
something old and ancient like the tile floor in a pharaoh's
garden. It is recreated here by the sun on the banks of the
Red River.

"What do you need plums for?"

"Can't you see," he says. "Wild plums are perfect to make
wine."

I wonder at the tone of his voice when it is just the two
of us fishing. He has told me two bobbers today instead of one
and the depth of the stick must be screwed down into the
muck just so. Only he can do it. And I never question as I
would want to because I am grateful to him for the world he
has opened up to me. If anyone should come and join us here,
Laurence would silently gather his line in, wind it around the
stick with precise movements that are meant to show his
annoyance, but really are a cover for his sense of not
belonging. He would move further down the bank or walk up
the hill to the road and his bike. He would turn his back on
me, the only friend he has.

I have loved you since grade three, my eyes keep telling
him. You, with your lice crawling about your thickly matted
hair. My father, being the town's barber, would know,
Laurence. But I defied him and played with you anyway.

It is of no consequence to Laurence that daily our friendship drives wedges into my life. He stops pacing and stands in front of me, hands raised up like a preacher's hands.

"Wild plums make damned good wine. My old man has a recipe."

I turn over a clay tile and watch an earthworm scramble to bury itself, so that my smile will not show and twist down inside him.

Laurence's father works up north cutting timber. He would know about wild plum wine. Laurence's mother cooks at the hotel because his father seldom sends money home. Laurence's brother is in the navy and has a tattoo on his arm. I envy Laurence for the way he can take his time rolling cigarettes, never having to worry about someone who might sneak up and look over his shoulder. I find it hard to understand his kind of freedom. He will have the space and time to make his wine at leisure.

"Come with me." I give him my hand.

Omah bends over in the garden. Her only concession to the summer's heat has been to roll her nylon stockings to her ankles. They circle her legs in neat coils. Her instep is swollen, mottled blue with broken blood vessels. She gathers tomatoes in her apron.

Laurence hesitates. He stands away from us with his arms folded across his chest as though he were bracing himself against extreme cold.

"His mother could use the plums," I tell Omah. Her eyes brighten and her tanned wrinkles spread outwards from her smile. She half-runs like a goose to her house with her apron bulging red fruit.

"See," I say to Laurence, "I told you she wouldn't mind."

When Omah returns with pails for picking, Laurence's arms hang down by his sides.

"You tell your Mama," she says to Laurence, "that it takes one cup of sugar to one cup of juice for the jelly." Her English is broken and she looks like any peasant standing in her

Flowers for Weddings and Funerals

bedroom slippers. She has hidden her beautiful white hair beneath a kerchief.

She's not what you think, I want to tell Laurence and erase that slight bit of derision from his mouth. Did you know that in their village they were once very wealthy? My grandfather was a teacher. Not just a teacher, but he could have been a professor here at a university.

But our heads are different. Laurence would not be impressed. He has never asked me about myself. We are friends on his territory only.

I beg Laurence silently not to swear in front of her. Her freckled hands pluck fruit joyfully.

"In the old country, we didn't waste fruit. Not like here where people let it fall to the ground and then go to the store and buy what they could have made for themselves. And much better too."

Laurence has sniffed out my uneasiness. "I like homemade jelly," he says. "My mother makes good crabapple jelly."

She studies him with renewed interest. When we each have a pail full of the dust-covered fruit, she tops it with a cabbage and several of the largest unblemished tomatoes I have ever seen.

"Give my regards to your Mama," she says, as though some bond has been established because this woman makes her own jelly.

We leave her standing at the edge of the road shielding her eyes against the setting sun. She waves and I am so proud that I want to tell Laurence about the apple that is named for her. She had experimented with crabapple trees for years and in recognition of her work, the experimental farm has given a new apple tree her name.

"What does she mean, give her regards?" Laurence asks and my intentions are lost in the explanation.

When we are well down the road and the pails begin to get heavy, we stop to rest. I sit beside the road and chew the tender end of a foxtail.

Laurence chooses the largest of the tomatoes carefully, and then, his arm a wide arc, he smashes it against a telephone pole.

I watch red juice dripping against the splintered gray wood. The sun is dying. It paints the water tower shades of gold. The killdeers call to each other as they pass as silhouettes above the road. The crickets in the ditch speak to me of Omah's greenhouse where they hide behind earthenware pots.

What does Laurence know of hauling pails of water from the river, bending and trailing moisture, row upon row? What does he know of coaxing seedlings to grow or babies crying from dewdrops beneath the eye of God?

I turn from him and walk with my face reflecting the fired sky and my dust-coated bare feet raising puffs of anger in the fine warm silt.

"Hey, where are you going?" Laurence calls to my retreating back. "Wait a minute. What did I do?"

The fleeing birds fill the silence with their cries and the night breezes begin to swoop down onto our heads.

She sits across from me, Bible open on the gray arborite, cleaning her wire-framed glasses with a tiny linen handkerchief that she has prettied with blue cross-stitch flowers. She places them back on her nose and continues to read while I dunk pastry in tea and suck noisily to keep from concentrating.

"And so," she concludes, "God called His people to be separated from the heathen."

I can see children from the window, three of them, scooting down the hill to the river and I try not to think of Laurence. I haven't been with him since the day on the road, but I've seen him. He is not alone anymore. He has friends now, kids who are strange to me. They are the same ones who make me feel stupid about the way I run at recess so that I can be pitcher when we play scrub. I envy the easy way they can laugh at everything.

"Well, if it isn't Sparky," he said, giving me a new name and I liked it. Then he also gave me a showy kiss for them to see and laugh. I pushed against his chest and smelled something sticky like jam, but faintly sour at the same time. He was wearing a new jacket and had hammered silver studs into the back of it that spelled his name out across his shoulders. Gone is the mousy step of my Laurence.

Omah closes the book. The sun reflects off her glasses into my eyes. "And so," she says, "it is very clear. When God calls us to be separate, we must respond. With adulthood comes a responsibility."

There is so much blood and death in what she says that I feel as though I am choking. I can smell sulphur from smoking mountains and dust rising from feet that circle a golden calf. With the teaching of these stories, changing from pleasant fairy tales of faraway lands to this joyless search for meaning, her house has become a snare.

She pushes sugar cubes into my pocket. "You are a fine child," she says, "to visit your Omah. God will reward you in heaven."

The following Saturday, I walk a different way to her house, the way that brings me past the hotel, and I can see them as I pass by the window, pressed together all in one booth. They greet me as though they knew I would come. I squeeze in beside Laurence and listen with amazement to their fast-moving conversation. The jukebox swells with forbidden music. I can feel its beat in Laurence's thigh.

I laugh at things I don't understand and try not to think of my Omah who will have weak tea and sugar cookies set out on her white cloth. Her stained fingers will turn pages, contemplating what lesson to point out.

"I'm glad you're here," Laurence says, his lips speaking the old way to me. When he joins the conversation that leaps and jumps without direction from one person to another, his voice is changed. But he has taken my hand in his and covered it beneath the table. He laughs and spreads his plum breath across my face.

I can see Omah bending in the garden cutting flowers for weddings and funerals. I can see her rising to search the way I take and she will not find me there.

9 / Judgment

It was early morning when Mr. Thiessen died, and wreaths of mist still hovered above the river in pockets, trapped by the shadows of overhanging willow branches. His corpse lay in the porch of a small white cottage. The cottage sat on the edge of a town beside a road that led over a hill and down the other side of it and came to an end in the river.

The expression frozen into the dead man's face was one of determination. His nostrils were packed with wads of cotton, making his nose his salient feature. When he'd been alive, his predominating feature had been his eyes, blue as snow when the sun has just dipped into the winter horizon. He always seemed to be looking beyond into something that was invisible to others. Even at the hotel in town, where he once walked late at night to sweep rubble from the parlor floor, his blue eyes contemplated a scene beyond the smoke-filled parlor, something amusing to make him stop sweeping and chuckle suddenly, or something somber and dark which he would take to the cottage with him to think about while he puttered in his flower garden. But his pale eyes no longer looked into the ridiculous or the profane. They were opened, staring up at the rafters which were strung with bundles of dried basil and sage leaves and spirals of flypaper thickly coated with the husks of insects.

Outside the cottage, an old woman sat on a bench and leaned against the narrow slats of the porch. The back of her head was almost level with his where he lay inside on the couch beneath the screened windows. She looked like a lizard sunning itself in the early morning on a moss-covered rock. She didn't wear her dentures and so her caved-in mouth made her nose jut forward from her face and her chin recede into her neck. She sat shapeless and colorless with her sun-spotted hands idle in her lap. The narrow slats of the porch wall pressed into the woman's fleshy back but she didn't notice. She was listening to the wind passing through the screens in the windows above her kerchiefed head. She thought that the sound of it was not a hopeless sound. It was the same sound as the river rushing along its course to its irrevocable end in a larger body of water. The wind had come early that morning, before the sun, and had drowned out the fluttering sound of her husband's breath struggling to free itself of the liquids in his lungs. She blinked rapidly and folded one pudgy, spotty hand overtop the other.

She scratched at her ankle with her slippered foot. The town was so still that she could hear the humming of electricity in the wires along the road and the sound of blood rushing in her veins. Birds cried as they circled the air above the river. Get up, she told herself. Put on your workboots and go into the back garden and pull the potatoes. All summer she had plucked beetles from the leaves and squashed them between her fingers. She had banked the plants with mounds of black dirt. Now is the time to pull the potatoes, she thought and then she caught herself. What am I doing? My husband is dead and I think of potatoes. But the idea of work to be done was restful. Instead of jumping up and running to the potting shed to take the bushel baskets down from the wall, she would rest. There was still time to sit. The town hadn't begun to stir and the doctor had yet to come and administer the six o'clock injection of morphine. She had this time of grace before she needed to accept the finality of her husband's stiffening blue-white features.

She bent down and picked at a loose thread on her plaid slipper and watched with fascination as the chain stitching unraveled. She looked about for a place to put the unraveled thread. She gathered it between her fingers and rolled it into a ball. She leaned back against the porch and through the slits of her half-closed eyes, she watched the sun rise. It was a fireball that swept from north to south above the trees that lined the river bank below. Back and forth it wheeled. She sighed and ran her tongue across her shrunken gums to erase a sour taste that nestled there like the orange sprinkles of beetles' eggs on the underside of a potato leaf. If only Eve hadn't sinned, she thought. Then there would have been no beetles to squash between her fingers or weeds to be hacked away. Because of Eve, each time her monthly bleeding had stopped and she'd been pregnant, she'd faced that nine months with dread, longing for a way around the curse. But there was no path around the pain of childbirth. You had to go through it before you could experience relief. It was all part of the curse, she told herself, beetles attaching themselves to her potatoes, childbirth and the silence in the porch.

She stared unblinking at the fireball above the trees and rolled the thread between her thick fingers until it was moist. Then she let it drop to the ground. She bent over, searched the other slipper for a loose thread, found one and pulled. What was worse for her now, she wondered? Loose threads or twenty-eight jars of watermelon pickles?

She saw them suddenly, the jars lined up on the shelves in the cellar, side by side, shining with the inner glow of the pale pink fruit, jewel-like and perfect. Of all the times he had to choose to die, it would be this time when the cellar was full of preserves. Yesterday he'd asked her for a dill pickle and she'd refused because they weren't sour enough. What did it matter whether the pickles were sour enough or not? What did it matter? Watermelon pickles or not watermelon pickles? What does anything matter now, she asked, but felt saddened by the look of her slippers. The tongues had been loosened when she'd pulled at the threads. They made things too cheaply. She forced her plucking hands to lie still in her lap. What am I to do now? she asked herself. What am I going to do with twenty-eight jars of watermelon pickles? She recited them:

two dozen peaches in heavy syrup
three dozen quarts crabs
two and a half pints pears
fourteen jars plum jam with wax seals, seven with tops
one dozen two-quart sealers dills

And I couldn't even give him one.

The fireball climbed higher in the sky. The sound of the wind changed. It carried within it another sound. It was the sound of dried corn stalks when her skirts brushed against them. It was the sound of a man's hoarse whisper, urgent.

"Anna."

"Yes, what is it?" she asked. She had always promised herself that if an angel should speak, she would say, here am I, Lord.

"Water. Please. I want a drink."

She rose from the bench slowly. She climbed the three stairs. She entered the porch and passed by the bed of the dead man without looking at him. She went over to the treadle sewing machine where there was a tumbler and a jug of water. She tried to lift the jug. Her hands were two spotted stones dangling uselessly from the ends of her arms. She knew her husband was dead. She'd pulled the plaid blanket up around his chin and felt the unyielding heaviness of his cold arms when she'd placed them beneath the blanket. Could it be grief that caused her to hear voices where there should be none?

"I can't lift the jug. You don't really need water, do you?" Dried leaves stirred on the windowsill where his potted plants were lined, now just brown stalks in hard earth, neglected because of his illness. It was as though her words had lifted the leaves into motion.

"Ahh," his voice was expelled slowly. "Why would I ask you for water if I didn't need it? I'm so very hot."

The snake of fear uncoiled in her chest. Hot. He was hot? "Where are you?" she asked. She had warned him and warned him. All through the long night she had read the Bible, first the Psalms and then the New Testament, and had come to the parable of Lazarus and the rich man, when the sun first sat upon the trees. Send Lazarus to touch the tip of my tongue, she had read. The flames torment me. For those who didn't believe in a real hell, this was the place they should look, she was going to tell him and then noticed the absence of his rattling breath. She'd set the Bible aside, gotten up swiftly and knelt beside him and listened. His nose had stopped bleeding and the cotton wads in his nostrils were stiff with dried blood.

All night long he'd plucked at the cotton with his nicotine fingers and his sin had glared in the early morning light as she knelt beside his cooling body. His stained fingers were evidence of his sin, his habit of slipping into the potting shed every hour to roll a cigarette. The indelible yellow stains were proof of his imperfection. Where are you, God had asked Adam and Adam had answered, I hid because I was afraid; and that was what he'd done too, shutting himself away inside the potting shed to smoke his cigarettes, as though God couldn't see. She'd knelt and prayed that God could overlook this one thing, but she doubted that He would. She saw her husband's nosebleeds, his coughing and spitting of blood as judgment of guilt. She'd warned him every single day for sixty-two years that this could happen.

"Where I am is not your concern," he said.

"Just so. Don't blame me if you're hot. What more could I do? I bathed you every hour. Now tell me, what else before I go? The potatoes are ready for pulling."

He looked past her with his steady contemplative blue gaze. He looked into each far corner of the porch and then up at the dangling spirals of flypaper. "What else? A smoke. Mother, make me a cigarette."

She was beyond anger. There was an immense sadness flooding into every part of her large body. "The body is the temple of the Holy Spirit. You would defile it with nicotine, even now?"

He sighed. He closed his eyes. His mouth was cracked from his fever. He ran his tongue across his chapped lips. She wondered if she should dip a hanky into the jug and moisten his lips for him and then she remembered that he was dead and she was standing there talking to a dead man and he was answering her, which was as far as she was willing to go, because he was not an angel.

"I never told you this," he said after a short time.

She stopped breathing.

"Never mind. It doesn't really matter."

"What? What?"

"It's nothing. I was going to say something about the way you look. But it doesn't matter."

She looked at herself. There was nothing wrong with her appearance. She felt comfortable in the shapeless dress. She dressed in the manner fitting for an older Christian woman. Nothing between mid-calf and the neck was revealed. She even wore heavy cotton stockings during the summer.

He was casting stones at her to draw attention away from his own wrongdoing. "I'm running here and I'm running there," she said. "You make yourself sick, I have the running around. I wonder what you would look like if you followed me through the day? And what else? I stayed up and prayed for you all night. The girls come every day and I do the cooking. I haven't had time to fix my hair for three days and so I wear the scarf."

"I didn't mean that."

"What then?"

"It doesn't matter."

"Say it."

"I meant that—oh, I don't know if after sixty years it helps to say anything about it, but—you're too fat."

"I?"

He nodded his silver head.

She slammed the porch door behind her. Her slippers smacked loudly against the stairs. She suddenly hated the color green. He'd painted the bench she'd sat on and the platform that held the rain barrel on the south corner of the house facing the potting shed and the three steps leading into the porch, the same vivid green as the fruit trees. He had never asked her, what do you think of green? Do you think green would be a fair color? He'd never asked her whether she thought fruit trees across the back of the garden were a good thing. The first thing she would do would be to walk into town to the hardware store and buy a can of paint. Gray or brown, or something the color of a potato beetle. And who would have to bring in his glad bulbs for winter storage? She would. Even though her vegetable garden had been placed in the back field farthest from the rain barrel and beneath the fruit trees (wood ticks in spring and three part rows of corn lost to the shade of the fruit trees) and even though his flowers had gradually taken over half of the vegetable garden, she'd never complained. A continual dropping on a very rainy day and a contentious woman were alike, the Bible said, and that was not her sin, being quarrelsome. Not that it would have helped to complain. Complaining would have just sent him into his faraway expression more often or into the potting shed. She would bring his glad bulbs in and she would also bring in the potatoes.

She sat back down on the bench and let her hands fall into her lap. She half closed her eyes once again, lulled by the sound of the wind in the screens. Even so, she told herself. Watermelon pickles or not watermelon pickles, what does it matter? Once more she viewed the sun through half-closed eyes. It became a fireball that jiggled and darted off to the right. She felt the warmth of it in her broad cheeks. It filled up all of her eyes. If she could turn her head right around, the fireball would make a full circle around her. She turned her head as far as it would go. The fireball followed. She turned her head the other way and heard the clatter of clay pots knocking against each other in the potting shed.

"And listen here, Father," she said. "And not only that. I

told you and told you it wasn't a good thing to feed that cat. It's back here again. It's knocking over your plants. And who's going to have to clean up that mess, I wonder?" Hah, let the cat reach above the door where he hid his papers and the tin of tobacco and let the cat form a cigarette for him. That was what tobacco was good for. It was good for animals only. Poison for stray cats. She searched about in her dress pocket and found a peppermint candy. She rolled it about her mouth. She felt some of the tension begin to leave her body as its sweetness was released and slid down the back of her throat.

"Mother. Oh Mother. Are you still there?"

"I am here."

"Make me a cigarette, Mother. Just this once."

"Never. I won't be a part of you willfully harming your body."

"But you do it yourself. You're harming your body with food."

She withdrew the diminished peppermint from her mouth and examined it closely. "That's foolishness," she said and put the candy back into her mouth. "God gave us food. If we didn't eat, we'd die."

"You refuse to make me a cigarette?"

"I refuse." She wouldn't have that on her conscience. She'd never made it easy for him. She hadn't permitted him to smoke his weed in the house. She was positive that he had her to thank for his eighty-one years. I have fought the fight, she told herself, I have won the race.

"In this case, I must obey God rather than man," she said and smiled gently, a toothless innocent smile. She waited for him to reply but heard instead the sound of a car moving slowly up the road. Six o'clock already. The fireball danced crazily. She arranged her skirt to cover her knees. The doctor's car entered the lane slowly and came to a halt. He got out of the car and walked across the yard and stood in front of her.

"Look," she said, and pointed to her feet. "My slippers are

coming apart. They make everything too cheaply in this country."

"Nothing lasts forever," the doctor said. "Tell me, did Mr. Thiessen have a good night?"

"A good night, yes."

He was short and squat, wide enough to block out her view of the sun. She didn't like this man because even though she had never seen him smoke a cigarette, or smelled tobacco on his clothing, she suspected that he did smoke because he'd never reprimanded her husband for smoking or advised him to stop.

"And how about you?" he asked. "How did it go yesterday? Did your daughters come over and help out?"

"They come over every day," she said. "It's a little extra work cooking meals for them. But I don't mind."

"It's unfortunate at a time like this, but we do have to eat, don't we?"

"That's what I told him. God intended that we should eat."

He shifted his black bag from one hand to the other. "Some more than others." Then he set the bag down on the bench beside her, opened it and took out the stethoscope. "I may as well have a look at you too, while I'm here."

"There's nothing the matter with me."

"Give me your arm, please."

She held up her arm. He felt for her pulse. He frowned. He placed the stethoscope against the pulse in the crook of her arm, listened for a few moments and put the instrument back into his bag. "I'm not fussy about the sound of that," he said. She caught a fleeting glimpse of the syringe of painkiller that he'd come to inject into her husband's thin veins.

"Well," the doctor said. "Tell you what. It might be a good idea to have one of your daughters bring you into the office for a check-up. Do you think you could arrange that?"

"The potatoes are ready for pulling."

"The potatoes. I suppose so. But couldn't you get someone to do it for you this year?"

She stared at him.

"Well, never mind. We can talk about it later. I'll just have a look in on Mr. Thiessen right now."

"He's in the porch."

She heard the sound of his feet as he walked up the three green stairs. She heard the porch door squeak as it opened and closed. Her time of grace was over. She got up from the bench to follow the doctor. She heard the sound of pottery breaking in the potting shed.

That cat. She would have to go and chase that animal away before it broke every last one of her husband's pots. Why didn't he think of those things? He fed the cat and left her to take care of the consequences. She took the broom down from its clasp on the wall beside the rain barrel. It was the outside broom, used to sweep dust and snow from shoes and for chasing animals. She raised the broom and walked lightly along the pathway to the potting shed. She was looking at the bottom of the door for the cat to come scooting out and then she would lower the broom. She saw her husband's shoes first. He was wearing his brown walking boots. Then her eyes travelled up the length of him until his blue eyes looked straight into her own.

"You! I thought it was a cat."

He'd pulled the cotton wads from his nostrils and his nose was back to its normal size. He wore his tweed cap low onto his forehead and his black serge jacket, the one he wore when he went to work at the hotel, was buttoned neatly. He clutched two earthenware pots, one inside the other, to his chest.

"Don't worry," he said finally. "I cleaned up the mess."

She lowered the broom and stepped to one side as he pushed past her on the narrow path. She caught a glimpse of a flash of yellow inside the pot which he held to his chest. It was his tobacco tin. He'd hidden his tobacco and papers down inside the earthenware pot.

"What are you doing? Where are you going with that?"

He walked away quickly, looking straight ahead. He passed by the green bench, strode jauntily down the lane to the dirt road.

"Father, wait. Leave the tobacco behind. Someone might see you." She followed him but the distance between them widened. She began to trot. What would people think if they saw him? She panted with the effort to keep up. The sound of her running pounded thickly inside her head. He was leaving her behind. "Wait for me. I want to come," she called one last time. But she knew it was useless. Once he'd made up his mind, there was no use talking. She sat down heavily on the bench and wiped perspiration from her forehead. He walked swiftly down the road to the bottom of the hill where the road flattened out towards the river.

He hesitated at the edge of the river and then turned around. He shielded his eyes with his hands. "Look here," he called to her. "I'm not coming back, so don't think that I am, because I'm not."

Tears burst and ran across her tanned broad cheeks. "And who is going to bring in your glad bulbs for winter?" she asked, hoping wildly to sway him with his beloved flowers. "I can't. The doctor says that maybe I should get someone to pull the potatoes."

He waved her question away. "Where I'm going there are enough flowers to go around and I will have my own mansion, white, with a flat roof like the houses in Mexico." He turned his back to her, faced the river and vanished. In the shadowy pockets along the river bank, the wreaths of mist uncurled and evaporated in the sun. A crayfish scuttled along the muddy river bottom sending a swirl of yellow bubbles to break at the surface.

She felt the seconds fleeing from her. She had to do something, but what? What to do now that she was a widow?

What would she do with ruined slippers and twenty-eight jars of watermelon pickles? She heard footsteps as the doctor descended the three stairs.

"He's dead, I'm sorry," the doctor said. "You should have sent someone to get me. I would have come."

She got up from the bench and wrung her plump hands and began to pace up and down. Father, oh Father, she said to herself, you should have let me come with you for once. What am I to do without you? She searched quickly through one pocket and then another until she found a peppermint. She popped the candy into her mouth and rolled it about her tender gums. She felt the relief of its sweetness meeting her stomach. Then she felt the doctor's warm hands, leading her back to the bench.

Her breasts jiggled as she sat down. What could she do? A man always did that. They always left women with the consequences. He made the decisions, she was left with the mess. And all because of Eve.

The doctor sat down beside her and stroked her arm. "I would have come," he said once again.

She shrugged free of his touch. "And what difference would it make to call you? You couldn't have stopped him. He wanted to go and so he went."

"I suppose you're right," the doctor said.

"And to think of it, one dozen two-quart sealers dills," she said. "And I couldn't even give him one."

She watched as far above her the fireball wavered and began to lose its shape. Then the top of it sank to meet the bottom and the sides of it spilled out into the morning sky.

10 / The Wild Plum Tree

Mr. Malcolm, English 100
Betty Lafreniere

ESSAY
The Wild Plum Tree

It is more than a shrub but not a tree, bark is smooth when young. Inside, white sapwood, porous bark splits with age and leaves narrow tipped, fruit slightly reddish with blood flowers showy white gracing southern end of Manitoba and other provinces, of no commercial value.

Mr. Malcolm is English 100. He is also Betty's mathematics teacher, history teacher and language arts teacher. He is straight from Jamaica and looks to pregnant wayward girls and delinquents to teach him all they know about Manitoba.

"Now surely," he says, "you must know more about this subject. It was your free choice."

Betty shrugs, feigns indifference. The essay is the best she can do under the circumstances. The reference books in the classroom are *The Book of Knowledge* and *Weeds, Trees and Wildflowers in Canada*. Some of the girls have taken a bus down to the public library on William Avenue. But not her. What she doesn't know, she will make up. That's life, she tells herself.

"But you see, I asked for six pages, at least," he says. He wears pastel colors. Pale green polyester pants, a pinkish tie against a coral-colored shirt. She ignores him, looks out the dusty window down into the city. The rapid darting of traffic intrigues her. Where are all these people going to, coming from? And why? It seems pointless. She saw shadows in the graveyard last night. She'd sat on the radiator in her room looking out and thought, how appropriate: a graveyard in the back yard of the home for wayward girls. They were all burying things, their past, their present, the things that came out of them. And she saw shadows down there, lithe phantoms sprinting from tree to tree, leaping up from the hard granite stones. Today, several of the tombstones are toppled into the grass. The praying virgin with her blind eyes and reverent posture, hands held up in frozen supplication, lies on one side.

"Did you not understand my instructions then?" the teacher asks.

"Yes, Mr. Malcolm, I understood your instructions." She wants only to be left alone.

"Mr. Jackson."

"Yes, Mr. Jackson." His name is Malcolm P. Jackson. You have never heard the sound of a mob, he has told them. He'd sat on the desk in front of them, swinging his knees in and out, like a young child needing to urinate. I was a boy when I once heard such a mob. It was like the sound of a swarm of angry bees growing louder and louder. Let me tell you, it was not a pleasant sound. Angry people. A mob rushing along the street. I was very young but I learned quickly to be afraid of the mob.

"Well then, if you knew the instructions, why have you handed me this?" He holds up the single sheet of paper. The classroom has grown quiet. The girls stop talking to listen.

"Because I felt like it."

Several of the girls titter. Betty has not said this for their benefit. She only needs, wants, to be left on her own. A detention is a way to accomplish this end. Mr. Jackson sets the paper down, takes a piece of yellow chalk from his shirt pocket and rolls it from hand to hand.

"My dear girl. Listen. In my country, education is a privilege. Only the cleverest people go beyond grade school. Our parents made great sacrifices for us. We're grateful. With us, it is never a question, whether we feel like it or not; we do it."

"If you're so smart," someone says, "then why are you here with us?"

He pretends he hasn't heard, but the muscles in his jaw contract suddenly as though he just bit into a stone.

Betty wants no part of their taunting. She wants to be away from them all, to be able to sift through all the information she has gathered, to make some order of it.

"Surely you could do better than this," he persists. "There must be more you could write about the wild plum tree."

Even now, she smells the fruit of it. The tart flavor, taut skin splitting in her mouth, the slippery membrane of its meat, a piece of slime at the bottom of a quart sealer jar of homemade wine coming suddenly into her mouth like a great clot of blood. There is too much to say about the wild plum tree. The assignment has paralyzed her.

"Yes, Chocolate Drop. I'm sure there is." She uses the girls' private name for Mr. Jackson.

His nostrils flare. The room grows silent. Then laughter erupts, spills over. "Chocolate Drop," a girl says and then they all say, "Chocolate Drop."

His eyes dart about the room. Betty continues to stand before the window, toying with the frayed cord on the venetian blind. Thousands of girls have stood at this very same window and played with this cord. It's marked with their anguish, their boredom and frustrations.

"Well um," Mr. Jackson says, bouncing the chalk from palm to palm. "Well um." The palms of his hands are tinged pink. The skin has been worn away. It's from masturbating, flogging his meat, the girls say. He clutches at his crotch frequently in the classroom. Adjusts his testicles before he sits down on the edge of the desk to confront them.

"Who needs you, Chocolate Drop?" a girl asks.

"Well, Miss," Mr. Jackson says to Betty, "you see what you

have instigated? You may call me what you like. What can one expect from Satan's daughter?"

Betty yanks the frayed cord. It snaps free and falls to the floor. Several of the girls leave their desks. Mr. Jackson turns and faces them quickly. "Well um," he says. "That will be ten pages now. You seem to think she is a humorous person. Do you think ten pages is also funny?"

They groan. "You can't make us do ten pages," a tall girl with angry gray eyes says.

He strides to his desk, pulls open a drawer and takes out a wooden ruler. "Ten pages, I said." He bangs the ruler against his desk.

"Fuck off," the tall girl says.

He walks swiftly to her and whacks her across the face with the ruler. Smiles fade, all movement is suspended. A red welt rises on the girl's cheek. "And who else wishes to express themselves in such a manner?" he asks. The girls one by one return to their desks.

"You heard her," Betty says. "Go fuck yourself in Jamaica and leave us alone." A flood of tension is released suddenly. She feels the teacher's wooden ruler bounce off her shoulder blade. The girls laugh and call out their individual hate names for Mr. Jackson. An eraser bounces off the wall beside his head. He backs slowly over to the classroom door and stands with one hand on the knob. His lips are flecked with spittle. "Ten pages, you naughty spoiled children. When you can control yourselves, we will continue this class," he says and flees.

Control yourselves. Is it lack of control then, that has brought them all to this place? The windowpane is cool against Betty's forehead as she looks down into the street. A young man cuts through the cemetery, hands plunged deep into his pockets; he walks with his shoulders hunched up, a cigarette hangs from his mouth. He glances up at the window where she stands and is gone.

The Wild Plum Tree

Notes for essay on wild plum tree
Mr. Malcolm, English 100

the beginning

*Suddenly you face across the street where once there was only a
coulee with bullrushes, twitch grass four feet high, God and Indian
arrowheads, a brand new house.*

*But first, machines squashed frogs and garter snakes and a pen
once lost and never found and then plowed them beneath tons of
landfill from a field where they also discovered the skeletons part of
which Laurence brought to school.*
(the skull)

*Then, when the four-and-a-half member family move into that new
house, the dark-haired woman has a bump in front so she is
probably pregnant (being the oldest of six teaches you to watch for
those things); the beginning ends.*

through yellowing lace curtains
I have always watched
the games of others
hiding and seeking the waning sun
shadows the mourning dove's
spotted gray
bird sounds temper the shrill play
sounds
that strike my note
of sorrow
I have not found anything good
in tomorrow

notes   *before the beginning*

Leaves (somewhat hairy) of the dog mustard plant, which, like the

mother of seven, originated in Europe and was first found in
Canada at Emerson in 1922, tickle bare legs when walking in the
coulee. And their flower, clusters of pale yellow stain white
organdy, which also scratches bare legs when walking, sitting,
standing, period. When you wander with Laurence in the coulee, he
carries your shoes and you can feel the spongy ground and make it
squeeze up between your toes and then he shows you his hidden
pool

and in the deep pool
melted snow yellows
bright all the dead grasses
pink granite stones and your face
rising and falling as feet dipped clean
drip the surface and make you wrinkle

Russian pigweed stands as high as you because you are eight, but
Laurence's head is a little above it. The plant is like the two of you,
one plant and two different kinds of flowers, male and female.

And God is also in the coulee, moving before you. You can feel
His breath on your body, coming through the organdy you have
worn especially for Him because it is Sunday.

And Laurence, even though he does not go to any church, is of the
same plant that nods in the same breath. But for some reason, the
mother of seven doesn't think so which is why you walk among the
Russian pigweed, so she can't see you and get angry and send you
down the road to your grandfather's house to get a lesson in the
Bible.

God you were
there inside
my knees and elbows
scratched raw
crawling from imaginary

The Wild Plum Tree

Indians
would take my yellow hair
make a belt or something, God
your voice
fades faster than games
of Indians don't last
forever

"Betty uses foul language and shows disrespect for the property of the institution," the social worker says. She reads from the teacher's report. She wears black cat's-eyes-shaped glasses and adjusts them before she speaks again. Betty can feel her father's shyness of this woman, his eagerness to appease and have everyone agree quickly that everything will be fine so that he can go home and report to Mika with a clear conscience that he's done his best. He sits on a chair beside Betty. They face the social worker's desk beneath the window. The room is a basement room. The window is at street level and Betty watches and counts the feet of people who pass by on the sidewalk.

"If you won't adhere to the rules of this institution, what choice will we have, but to ask you to leave it?"

"Certainly, she's going to follow the rules and regulations," Maurice says. "There's no maybe about it."

He plays with the brim of his hat and looks down at the floor. He's put on his suit and tie and taken the bus in from the country especially for this meeting. He's deeply embarrassed. He cannot bring himself to say the words "pregnant" and "social worker."

The woman writes something on her pad. Betty wonders if she is writing "Father is co-operative," or "Supportive father." With whom and of whom?

"What about rules regarding hitting students with rulers?" Betty asks.

"Listen here," Maurice says, suddenly irritated. "What

makes you think you can ask that, eh? You're not in any position here to ask questions."

"And what position am I in?"

Maurice is flustered. He twirls the hat between his thick brown fingers, clears his throat several times.

The social worker gets up quickly. "I think the two of you need to talk alone. It's important that we reach an understanding today." The door closes behind her. Maurice relaxes. He wipes his brow, sits up straighter and looks about the room for the first time. The walls are cement block, unpainted. There are no pictures. "This here place is not so bad," he says. "I don't know what you're griping about."

A black mongrel zig-zags across the boulevard and sidewalk. It stops and looks down into the room, sniffs and then continues on its way.

"You don't have to live here. I hate it."

"Well now, that wasn't our doing, was it?" Maurice says. It's the closest he's come to mentioning her pregnancy. "Anyway, it's a darn sight better than being out on the street because, believe you me, that's where you're headed if you don't shape up."

Betty stifles the urge to laugh. Shape up. She is rapidly shaping up. She knows that her parents' number one concern is her shape. They're afraid that she might be expelled from the home and shame them with her bulging presence in the community. It's the only reason for his trip into the city. She knows she's been cut off, that she can't look to either of her parents for anything.

"It's okay," she says. "I'll be okay now. It's just been hard to adjust."

Maurice brightens. He looks at her with a wide smile, his eyes uneasy though, carefully avoiding looking at her stomach. "Adjust, absolutely. I can understand that. Certainly it takes time to get used to new situations."

"Losing your home is a new situation all right."

"Eh?" His hands stop in mid-air.

"I feel as though I have no home." For one second she wants to fling herself at him, bury her face into his shoulder and hold on.

Maurice works furiously as he flicks nonexistent lint from his hat.

"Well, that's not quite so," he says. "You've still got a home. You're only here for a few more months, that's all. Once it's over, it's over." He stands up and puts his hat on, adjusts the brim. "You've learned."

I am learning to control myself, no more fucking. "In a few more months, I'll have my baby." She wants him to think about this.

"On that score your mother and I agree. You can't bring the bastard home." He takes his wallet from his pocket. "Just in case you need something," he says and hands her several bills. His hands are shaking. She takes the money from him. Everything is okay, taken care of, he'll tell Mika. You know, it's not easy, it takes time to adjust to these things. All she needed was a little talk and a little time. He's in a hurry, anxious to be away.

"I have to go," she says.

The door closes behind him. She waits. She sees his feet pass by on the sidewalk along with the feet of another person, strangers passing by.

notes for the essay   *Bible lessons at Opah's*

Opah means Grandfather. Omah means Grandmother. (This is for the benefit of Mr. Malcolm, English 100, the Chocolate Drop who came directly from Jamaica and wants to know everything he can about Canada.)

The lesson for today, Opah says, is: HOW GOD LED HIS PEOPLE OUT OF THE LAND OF EGYPT. But then he forgets and his sky-blue eyes melt into the horizon and he speaks of

*hundreds of people gathering around twenty-eight train cars in
Russia. They are coming, these people, like the dog mustard, only a
year later, to spread out across the fields of southern Manitoba.
Faith is the Victory, Faith is the Victory, Opah hums, wiping tears
from his face and Omah comes out from the pantry wiping hands
of flour onto her apron. There is a boy in the garden, she says.
When she goes to call him in, he runs away, she explains, worried.
They still dream of thieves and Bolshevik murderers. Laurence is
waiting for the lesson to be finished so that there will be someone to
go fishing with. He has only one friend because he is on welfare.*

*First you learn, Opah says, no longer can you get into heaven free
because of your parents or grandparents. When you're twelve,
you're on your own with God.*

*He makes you learn the ten commandments even though you know
Emily, who lives across the road, whose father is a doctor and
drives a Lincoln and with his money has built the gingerbread house
that now has a patio and one more child added, which looks out
over another row of houses where the coulee once was, this girl,
whose father's building also destroyed an Indian burial ground, will
not hesitate to walk across the friendship and go fishing with
Laurence.*

*—round-leaved mallow is different from common mallow and is a
nuisance only in the prairie provinces where it nudges aside
Kentucky Blue and Shady Nook grass but that doesn't matter
because you can't really eat cultured lawn the way you can the
nutlets of round mallow an after school treat not double bubble
gum or fudgsicles but a prairie weed that stayed behind to live in
town to color green your teeth you forgot to brush today but ants
don't brush do they or for that matter neither do grasshoppers they
squirt tobacco—*

too bad   Emily can't eat round-leaved mallow

The Wild Plum Tree   123

too bad   she has to eat juicy fruit cracker jack and all
              that crap
too bad   she isn't a grasshopper or an ant

I would press her lightly with my toe and scare the shit out of her.
Emily is a stinking willie.
She is poisonous inside.
To her, fishing with Laurence is an opportunity to practise lying.
She is like a plum rotting in the grass.

I lost Laurence one summer
didn't last and he was gone
I looked: in the garden
              in the poolroom
              bowling alley
              cafe
              fair grounds
no Laurence

Look—he has waited long enough for you to go fishing.
It's your fault you learned the ten commandments.

And now, Emily wears his arrowhead around her neck. Your
arrowheads gather dust in a cigarette box in the rafters of the
icehouse while she, whose back yard has a patio surrounded by
stinking willie, wears his arrowhead because plum wine is strong
enough inside Laurence that no longer does he care that
occasionally he is on welfare or that at ten he had lice.

The small lamp in the corner on the table spreads a pink
glow in the room. There are six girls in various stages of
pregnancy dressed in bathrobes, feet tucked up beneath them,
one lies flat on her back, she is only in her third month.
"When I get out of this place I'm going to slash the bugger's
tires, all four of them," the girl with the angry gray eyes says.
They have been telling 'how I lost my virginity' stories. Betty

listens, she has not contributed and she knows they expect her to soon. She thinks that only this tall girl has been honest.

"I used to tell my parents I was staying at a friend's house," one of the girls says. "They never checked, usually they never checked, that is. Then one time, wouldn't you know it, my girlfriend's father answered the phone before she could get to it? And made her tell my Dad where I was? God, I almost died. There I was, Rick was doing it to me, you get what I mean? He didn't even knock—"

"Doing what?"

"Aw, come on, you know—"

"Was it big, small, did it hurt? You've got to tell a better story than that."

"I opened my eyes and saw my father. He just stood there staring and didn't say anything. It gave me the creeps. Like, for a minute, I didn't know what he was going to do. Then he went and waited for me in the car. When I came out he was sitting there crying. I felt like a piece of shit."

The girls moan sympathetically. They stare at their feet, at the space in front of them. They are all getting into shape, out of control, Betty thinks. Sometimes one of their boyfriends visits and then the rest of them slouch in corners, snapping gum, dissatisfied until he leaves. Where's your boyfriend, they've asked Betty, sixty-five girls who have eaten too many sweets, superior because they have visitors, more righteous for a time, than her.

They turn to her. They wait now for her story to begin. I was fourteen. He was an old man. At first he just used his finger. I screwed sixteen men this year and have written their names down in a scribbler.

"His name is Frank," she says. "We're in love. He wants to marry me."

The tall gray-eyed girl rises first and the others follow her one by one and file out of the lounge. Woolworth diamonds sparkle on their fingers. Now, at last, she can be alone.

The Wild Plum Tree

Laurence's anger moves in circles, his teeth on edge against an unnamed foe burned off in the sound of his motorcycle held into place by centrifugal force around and around. His anger spent, the dust settling, he stops moving, stands beside you and finally you are once again behind him, your arms about his narrow leather waist climbing the yellow fields, cutting a swath through black-headed cattails (fire torches, good for eating) in the ditches beside the highway, up and down Main Street. He doesn't speak, but only with others does he need to, you never cared, his silence was like a lady slipper growing beside a swampy marsh. He takes the old skull from his saddle bag, lines it up on Main Street, takes a run at it and shatters the old bone like pieces of coconut shell skittering curses across a table top. Don't do it, you think, but it's his skull, he can do what he wants. You ride and drink until the sun is down behind old weathered caved-in barns and he pukes plum wine, purple and violent in the grass at your feet. He lies you down and you are surprised at his fumbling, thought he would know how to do it better and so you help him with his clothing and guide him. (Was it big, was it fat or small, did it hurt? Come on, you've got to tell a better story than that.)

His nostril in your eye and when he turns his head you notice: hair in his ear, dirty. Emily, Emily, he says, not your name, but hers and his nostrils puff out warm plum air and his mouth, not gentle, smells of sour jam as he pins you to the earth but the worst is that after, he pulls grass from your hair, says he's sorry and treats you like a friend.

you are—

Listening until the sound of the engine is a distant whine on the highway, an angry wasp, a wavering line of sound straightening, becoming threadlike, thin, and then it snaps and—

Betty switches off the lamp. The traffic below in the city street is a ribbon connecting people together. The gravestones sheltered beneath the trees seem to move in the light filtering down between the tree branches. She hears a sharp whistle like a signal, and the figures rise up from among the stones, gather beneath the streetlight and plan their night errands. She watches and waits for tomorrow.

11 / The Day My Grandfather Died

I remember the day I bought a small bottle of Evening in Paris cologne. I was on my way home from school at lunch-time and took the long way home, going down Main Street and past the drugstore instead of cutting through the coulee as I usually did, because I wanted to see the display of cologne in the window. My friend Claudette Gagnon had seen it earlier and told me about it. Claudette wore a cardigan sweater that had poodles and pom-poms on it and a black "Frederick's of Hollywood" type brassiere beneath her sweater which gathered her breasts up into swollen jiggling shelves of jelly. She also shaved off her eyebrows and painted them back on in a thin coquettish black arch. Wherever I went with her a residue of attention, like dandruff, fell on me. But for me, the attraction of Claudette was more than that. Claudette was French, as was my father. I had even picked up her accent and went out of my way to say things such as, "The car, she is parked in the driveway," and, "H'it's going to rain."

"For Pete's sake," Mika, my mother, would say, "your English is worse than mine. You sound as bad as the Lafrenieres." Which made me smile because to be like the Lafrenieres, my father's people, would make my rebellion complete and finally take me out and away from the rest of the family.

"From Bourjois of Paris and Montreal," the display card in the drugstore read. Blue bottles the shape of uteruses nestled down inside the blue satin-lined boxes. I unscrewed the cap from the sample bottle. The smell of cologne was like almonds. It made me ache in "that place" and I would have liked to have touched and gentled myself until the bud flowered. But the warning I'd received from Mika was profound and clear. "Play with yourself and you'll never want

a man," she said. And I knew that I wanted a man,
eventually. At that time, I was still like a dog chasing a car,
barking and nipping at boys' heels, not knowing what I'd do if
I ever caught one.

I stood there in the drugstore, getting off, as they say, on
the smell of Evening in Paris cologne. It reminded me of a
mystery novel I'd once read. It was a story about a short bald
man who murdered beautiful but cruel women who laughed at
him. The women were either blond and cold or brunette and
very shallow. They all had long hair and wore skin-tight black
sheath dresses and rhinestone jewelery. They smoked
cigarettes using a holder. I liked the bald man. He had
impeccable manners and manicured fingernails. I thought that
killing people for laughing at you was justifiable homicide.
According to the novel, he would smile a sinister smile as he
took a silver box from his pocket and flicked open the lid.
The woman continued to laugh heartlessly through a curl of
cigarette smoke while he offered her a deadly candied almond.
Then it was his turn to laugh as death came slowly and the
victim's contorted features made her ugly in the end.

The smell of the cologne reminded me of my mother
walking to the corner to catch the Greyhound into Winnipeg.
She carried a shopping bag on her arm. She wore her navy
suit which displayed her trim figure, a pink frilly blouse and a
navy pillbox hat. I carried a box for her, filled with mittens
and scarves which her women's church group had made. All
winter they'd met weekly in each other's homes. I despised
their fervent good works and their complete lack of
adornment. It made them seem unnatural and grimly severe.
They seldom smiled. My mother had been elected to take the
results of their labors into the city and deliver them to a
mission. I swung the box up into the baggage department.

"She's one 'eavy box," I complained. My mother stared at
me and then laughed. Her laughter was seldom an expression
of joy or good humor. Her laughter said things such as: see, I

knew that would happen, or, trust me, the world's a dirty place.

One time, her laughter was spontaneous. I was walking across the yard towards the house and she was standing, framed by the window, looking out at me. For a terrible second I had the feeling that I was looking into a mirror and seeing my own reflection in her face and so I didn't watch where I was going. I stepped on a rake that had been left lying and it sprung up and bonked me between the eyes. My mother began to laugh outright, a deep belly laugh. When I came into the house she was still laughing. And I learned that the way to make her happy was to hurt yourself.

The bus driver swung the baggage door closed. Mika hid the remainder of her laughter behind a pink glove. Just as I was turning away, stinging and angry, she touched my arm. "What would you like me to bring you from the city?"

And I said, "Candied almonds."

When she came home that night, she had them with her and when I opened up the bag, the sight of those lilac, pink, yellow and white candies affected me strangely. I sat cross-legged on the couch with the bag in my lap and played with the seed-shaped candies. The texture of them was like that of a very fine toadstool, pebbly and cool to the touch. They made my heart ache. In the same way my mother pinched her babies to express affection, in the same way my berserk hormones made me want to laugh and cry simultaneously or dream beneath musk-scented sheets of caressing and being caressed, and then recoiling in anger and hitting out when someone tried to touch me—I wanted to crush the candied almonds underfoot. I couldn't help but think about the images that the mystery novel had evoked, and about the possibility of some demented gray person in Eaton's candy department slipping a few poisoned almonds into the candy bin. And so I shared my gift, offered the candies up to my mother and to my sisters instead of eating them myself. While they sucked, I watched for the signs, the deep pain in the stomach, the sudden clutching and pitching forward, their expressions when they became aware of their own finality.

The smell of the cologne in the drugstore that day was like that act. It was power, it was anger and knowing something that no one else knew. And so I bought a bottle.

I took my purchase to the clerk. She rang it up on the cash register and slipped the cologne into a bag. Then she looked at me as though she'd only just seen me. "Have you been home for lunch yet?" she asked. She searched my face with a prying, knowing look. She was over forty years old and so I'd never bothered to remember her name. I knew her only by her breasts. They were enormous. The boys called her Tits Wiggle. I handed her the money. "No, I haven't, why?" What's it to you? Drop off, eh? Flake off, peel off, bug off, take a flying leap.

"It's not for me to say," the clerk said. "You'd just better get going. Go straight home."

I left the drugstore slowly, so as not to let her know that I was concerned. But as soon as I was clear of the window and her sight, I began to run. I knew something terrible must have happened if she wouldn't say what it was. And when I got home, I found out my grandfather Thiessen had died.

"Guess what," I said to Claudette. "My grandfather kicked the bucket during the night."

"Yeah, so I heard. That's tough."

"He was eighty-one years old; it was no surprise."

We'd met at the Scratching Chicken Hotel cafe during the noon break. My mother was away, sitting with my grandmother. Claudette didn't take her lunch to school as most of the farm kids did. Claudette wasn't farm. She'd been expelled from the convent school at Grande Pointe where she lived with her parents who owned Gagnon Chevy-Olds garage. I'd never been to Grande Pointe, but the kids said if you didn't speak French, no one would talk to you. I always ate my own lunch at home and then rode my bike downtown so that I could sit with Claudette while she ate hers. She was talkative, flashy and demonstrative, traits that I then attributed to her French-Canadian identity only because I didn't see these traits in my mother or my grandparents, who were not French, but Mennonite, a fact that I detested. Being Mennonite was like having acne. It was shameful, dreary. No one invited you out. How to be French, I didn't know. My father was seldom home and when he was, showed no interest or energy, I didn't know which, in perpetuating any of his own traditions.

"I had a cat once," Claudette said. "She was my cat for twelve years. Slept on my bed every night. When she passed off, I really felt bad. I 'ad her since I was a kid." She nudged me with her elbow. "You'll be okay. H'it takes time."

We'd all buried animals. I remembered my dog, Laddie, a collie stray. My grandfather had persuaded my mother to let me keep him. He used to take my hand in his mouth and walk me to school. Claudette's sympathetic nudge unsettled me. I squashed a drinking straw flat, rolled it into a ball and flicked it across the counter into the chocolate bars. "I had my grandfather since I was a kid too," I said.

"I guess, eh?" Claudette said and snickered. "I like you, you're bad." She pushed her plate of chips aside and ran her fingers through her thick black hair which she wore short and which met at the back of her head like a feathered duck's tail. She had tiny features and large eyes. We sat side by side with our arms resting on the counter. I was tanned deeply, a dusty dark brown, and she was very fair. I was the only Lafreniere to have black hair and I felt special, set apart. Today, people mistake me for Jewish or Italian.

"I guess he died of old age, eh?"

"Cancer. I think. I kind of lost touch."

"Jeez. Tough. I guess you'll miss him."

I didn't feel one thing or another. My face was a little numb as though I'd just been to the dentist, that was all. I shrugged. "He was sick for a long time. The only thing I really remember about him was that he ate a lot of sunflower seeds.

Every pocket, full of seeds, and he'd spit the shells out through his mustache into his hand. His hands were always moist. I didn't like it."

"No kidding." Claudette had grown tired of the topic. She played with the silver cross at her neck and her features had a painful bored expression. Coffee gurgled down from the tops of the coffee makers into the glass urns below. The waitress came over and began to clean up the dishes.

"Let's cut," Claudette said. "This place stinks."

We walked down Main Street, passed by the corner where we should have turned to go to school. "What's up?" I asked, surprised.

"On the day your grandfather died, you shouldn't have to go to school," Claudette said. "My parents, they went into the city for parts today. We can have the place for ourselves."

We cut school that afternoon. We walked, instead, to the outskirts of Agassiz and stuck out our thumbs. Two rides and we were at Grande Pointe. The town was a disappointment. I was looking forward to something more than the jumbled collection of buildings and houses on either side of the wide dirt street that cut away from the main highway and rejoined it a mile later. I wanted more than street signs written in French. Gagnon Chevy-Olds was the newest-looking building on the street. As we drew near, I saw an old man sitting on a painted chair.

"Who's that?"

"It's just my father's uncle," Claudette said. "My father lets him hang around the garage. He's got nothing better to do. Don't worry, he won't say anything about us being here. Half the time he doesn't know what day it is."

He wore a straw hat and gray wool pants and a white shirt, unbuttoned at the neck. The kind my father wore around the house. He beckoned to Claudette and began speaking to her softly, haltingly, in French. His wide face was calm, gentle, no will to harm in it. If someone said to him, tomorrow the world will end, he would reply, so be it.

Claudette leaned over him. "Speak English," she said loudly. "Can't you see I've got company? This is Lureen Lafreniere. She's a girl from school."

He looked at me, took off his straw hat and rested it on his knee. My mouth tingled. If I smiled, my face would be forever frozen in that position. I thought I'd recognized that gesture, the wide sweeping of his hand. He spoke again, and to me his voice was like the sound of newspapers being swept along the street by the wind.

"He thinks he knows your old man," Claudette said.

"Oh yeah?" My heart lifted.

"Wants to know if you're Prosper's daughter," she laughed. "Prosper Lafreniere was an old hermit, older than him. He died last year. I told you, the old guy's cuckoo." She made a winding motion at her temple.

"Tell him that my father's the barber at Agassiz. His name is Maurice. He used to play the fiddle."

She told him. I held my breath. I needed to know something of who I hoped I was.

"I don't remember your father. Was he of this place?"

"Told you, screws loose. Come on, forget it," Claudette said and began to walk away.

The old man lifted his hat, waved it at me. "Adios to youse girls," he said and laughed. I liked him and wished that Claudette hadn't spoken to him with so little respect.

I followed Claudette between two buildings to the back of the garage. There were sounds of hammering coming from the garage. Through windows in a door, I could see bright splashes of sparks from a welder. Claudette stood on her toes so that she could see inside. "Good," she said. "Jimmy's working today."

"Who?"

"Jimmy Nabess. He works on and off for my father. He's cute." She winked. "Maybe later, I'll invite him to come up."

We went up a flight of stairs. She unlocked the door, stepped inside. A gold crucifix hung above the door. She led me through a small kitchen into the living room. A trestle table rested along one wall; along another, pine bookshelves with knick-knacks on them, a highback wooden bench, and beside the bench a pine couch with burlap cushions. A spinning wheel sat in the corner by the window. Above the couch, there were dark paintings of a fort and Indians huddled around a fire, tepees in the background. Another painting: a cobblestone street leading to an old church and tall European-looking buildings with narrow windows, lining the street.

"Nice," I said.

"You think so? I don't. I think it's crap. My mother had a vacation in Quebec and came back with it. It's like living in a coffin," she said. "Be back in a sec." She went into the kitchen. A moment later she stuck her head around the corner. "Do you like your beer warm or cold? I keep a case under my bed if you want a warm one."

I took her love for beer as being part of her French identity and so I said I'd love a warm beer. I went over to the front window and looked out over the town. There was more to Grande Pointe than I'd first seen. I could see the peaks of houses across the river, where the town unfolded in neat rows among lime-green groves of maple trees. It looked like Agassiz, no different. The same muddy river that divided Grande Pointe ran along the edge of Agassiz as well and the same flotsam on that river, the bloated bodies of cows, broken trees, tin cans, passed through their town as it did ours. Claudette came back with the beer.

I watched as she tipped the bottle, there was a gurgling, and one quarter of the beer was gone. "They put beer in babies' bottles, the French," my mother said once, referring to my father's relatives. "So that they can go out to dances, they take the kids with them, fill their bottles with beer so the kids will fall asleep in the car, and they can have all the fun they want."

"And so, what's wrong with that?" Maurice said.

The Day My Grandfather Died

And she said, "If they could only see, realize, the damage they're doing to their children."

I tipped my bottle, parted my lips the way Claudette had, but the beer didn't flow down my throat. It foamed, backed up into my nose, stinging. My eyes watered. Claudette laughed and brought me a Kleenex. I asked for a glass and drank the first beer and talked about the other kids at school, some of the boys in our class; and I was surprised that the boys I had gone through elementary school with and now high school, and who I thought were disgusting, she thought attractive. I liked the homestead old feeling of her rough, wooden living room and she wanted a modern one like mine. A feeling of disillusionment was setting in along with a slight light-headedness. Claudette yawned, looked at her watch. "Be back . in a sec," she said once again. "I'm going to talk to Jimmy. Help yourself to another beer."

I went into Claudette's bedroom. There were clothes scattered about on the bed and cosmetics over the top of her dresser. I looked into the mirror. "Goodness, who is she?" Mika had said once when I was changing, my features rearranging themselves weekly during puberty, giving me at last a broad face, a too-thick nose and deepset eyes, too small; I tried to do tricks with cosmetics but it didn't help.

"She doesn't even look like a Lafreniere," Mika said and it was true. Several times I'd seen my father's brothers, and they were both short and fat and small-featured. I pulled my hair up and away, held it into a ponytail, tight, so that my eyes became slanted. Sometimes I thought I was Oriental, or Eskimo. I saw Claudette's blue bottle of Evening in Paris cologne. I dabbed some behind my ears and then took another beer out from under her bed.

"And this," Claudette said, entering the bedroom suddenly, "is my friend Lureen, the one I told you about?" She introduced me to Jimmy Nabess. Jimmy was Indian. He was short and slender; his hair, almost shoulder-length, was caught back behind his ears. He wore a baseball cap, a satin-looking

blue jacket with his name on one shoulder, and dusty blue
jeans.

"Hi ya," he said. His expression said that he didn't care if I
lived or died.

"I told him we're having a party, and he wanted to come
too. Hurry up and finish that beer. Parties are more fun if
you're drunk."

For the next hour, we drank beer steadily, almost
dutifully, as Claudette worked hard to fill each awkward
silence, the trailing off of conversation. Jimmy and I sat side
by side on the couch. I grew quieter and quieter because I
sensed his dislike for me. Finally, despairing, Claudette said
that what we needed was some music and went to her
bedroom to get her records. Jimmy moved forward on the
couch as though he were about to follow her and then
changed his mind, took off his jacket and began squeezing
bottle caps. I noted that our arms were almost the same color.

"You from Grande Pointe?" I asked.

"Uhuh."

I didn't know if this meant yes or no. "It seems like an
okay place."

"It's the same like any place."

"Nabess," I said. "Is that French?"

"No."

I didn't want to ask him what it was. "Lafreniere is
French. My father speaks French."

He shrugged impatiently. "So what's the big deal? Lots of
people talk French. Claudette," he called. "I'm dry."

"Coming, coming," Claudette said and put a record on the
player. She clapped her hands and began to do the twist. The
beer had made her face flushed, her eyes shine. "Hey come
on," she said. "Let's dance."

"I hafta get back to work. Your old man will be the first
one to kick my ass if I don't."

"Just one," she said.

They danced for a full hour. I watched for awhile. They

were caught up in their dancing, in each other. Occasionally Claudette would suggest that he ask me to dance, but only half-heartedly, and when she turned the record over, she went back to him. I got up from the couch. The room tilted. I walked over to the window. I saw the old man; he was crossing the street slowly. He walked, choosing each step as though it were his last. He stood in front of the cafe, shielded his eyes and looked in the window, searching for someone. Then he began walking down the street to the corner.

I willed his faltering steps, each rising and falling of his feet. He belonged in the picture above the couch, an old man walking along a cobblestone street. It seemed to me that he was no ordinary person, but larger. I wanted to walk beside him with my arm under his and claim him as my ancestor. I leaned with my forehead against the glass and the cool windowpane felt good against my stiff face. My breath was reflected back to me. I smelled sour beer and something else, the Evening in Paris cologne.

The smell of the cologne reminded me of fruit cake, almond paste and my grandparents standing with a tray loaded with chunks of dark fruit cake at their fiftieth wedding anniversary. Grandma wore a loose-fitting white dress made of some light material that did not show her large body, but hid it so instead of looking fat and awkward, she seemed to float. She wore gold leaves in her white hair and so as they approached me, I thought she was a vision, a fairy godmother who had the power to grant wishes. And I would have asked her to take away my aches and pains. I was never without sore limbs, "growing pains," my mother called them, and an uneasy stomach. I did not think they were growing pains. I felt that my bones were going to crack and splinter because of some inner pressure. I would have asked my grandmother to make me feel happiness. But she frowned at the tray of cake my grandfather carried and said, "Nah, Papa, look at what you've done. You've cut far too much cake. It will only be wasted." And the fairy vision vanished.

"Give it to the children, then," he said. And it came to me how their conversations always seemed to center on food, the growing of it, the preparing of it and the eating. That was all that mattered. To me, their lives had been narrow and confining; even here, now, at a celebration, they were unable to step across the limits and celebrate. I was angry and so I said, "Don't waste the food on us kids, feed it to the bloody pigs instead."

The old man had reached the corner. He seemed to hesitate and then he turned sharply to the left and began crossing a bridge which spanned the same river that flowed past my grandparents' cottage. I could see that river through the leaves of the vine arbor where I was sent as punishment, to reflect in solitude upon what I'd said about feeding good food to the pigs. Two words my grandfather forbade us to use because he said we didn't know their meanings: starve and hate. I knew my words had cut him deeply. There were several boys playing along the river bank trying to skip stones and I forgot about what it was I should be thinking as I watched and wished I were down there to show them how to do it and at the same time, make them feel stupid. Grandfather came in and sat down beside me. He didn't speak for a long time and then asked, "Why are you always so angry?"

"I guess I was born that way. I can't help it. I couldn't help being born."

"Not so, not so," he said. "God made a much brighter girl."

His way of speaking irritated me. "If you say so, then it must be true."

He pulled at my chin in an attempt to have me look at him. His hand smelled of sunflower seeds. His pale blue eyes were moist with sorrow. I couldn't explain my anger. I thought I was a freak, I didn't belong because I was totally different from every other member of that family.

"People make me mad," I said.

"I'm sorry for you, then. Because you become their slave when you let them make you angry. Being angry doesn't change anything. You can never change what people say and do. The only thing you can change in this world is your reaction to what they say and do. You're hurting yourself by being angry. Look here," he said. He took his penknife from his pocket. He cut a V into a vine leaf, lightly, barely perceptible. "When you come for German lessons on Saturday, I'll show you what anger does."

The following Saturday, the scar in the leaf had become deep and brown and the leaf had grown, but was misshapen. "That's what you're doing with your life," he said. "With your anger you make marks in it that will never go away."

He left me to think on this. I thought. I thought he was minimizing what I was feeling with cheap tricks with a penknife. I went into the garden. I picked up the hoe. I chopped and hacked until I had cut down all of his sunflowers.

I turned from the window, feeling morose and angry at the same time for Claudette's lack of attention to me. And for the first time I wondered, how was I going to get home?

"My mother will kill me," I said. "I think I'd better head for home."

Claudette danced over to me, stuck her fingers into my chest and pushed me backwards towards the couch without missing a beat of the music. "You can't go yet. Jimmy wants to have a dance with you."

She brought me another beer and put on a record. It was a slow song. She put her arms around Jimmy's neck, he put his hands around her waist and his leg between hers and they moved in time to the music.

I belched loudly. My stomach was swollen and felt full. I was in a haze, stupefied, and so I lay down. Through half-closed eyes, I saw Jimmy place his hand on Claudette's breast, his hand, brown, against her pale blue sweater and I thought, he shouldn't do that, he's squashing the pom-poms on her poodles. "Oh no," Claudette said in response to something Jimmy had whispered in her ear, "not with her here."

My stomach heaved and the room swung violently. I had heard that if you're drunk and the room moves, lie with one foot resting on the floor and the motion will stop. I tried that and closed my eyes. It didn't work. I smelled something thickly sweet, it was the Evening in Paris cologne and it made my stomach even queasier. Claudette laughed drunkenly. Jimmy maneuvered her across the floor towards the bedroom door with his pelvis. He backed her up against the wall and kissed her, his back to me now, his head going around and around and the room turning with it. My stomach revolted.

I bolted from the couch, stumbled past them into the bathroom and retched over the toilet. My whole head was numb now. The same thing had happened when my dog Laddie got hit by a car. My mother had demanded a response of grief from me. "Cry," she said and they all stood waiting, my sisters and my mother, waiting for me to cry. "You loved that dog," she said, "why don't you cry?" And I would not cry because I knew that she did not say it out of a feeling for me, but out of the necessity to be proven right, so she could say, "I told you, the world's a dirty place." My refusal to cry had cut its mark into me. And here I was, my grandfather had died and I was a piece of wood, numb in the head, unable to express what I should be feeling for an old man who had really cared about me.

"For God's sake," Claudette said. "Vomit and get it over with."

I tried, I strained.

"Shove your finger down your throat."

I stuck my finger into my throat, gagged, but nothing happened.

"Let me help," Claudette said. She stood behind me, wrapped her arms around my stomach and squeezed suddenly and hard. The flood of vomit, everything I had eaten, drank, whooshed forth, splattering the toilet seat. Once I began, I couldn't stop. I heaved and upchucked until there was nothing to come but green bile.

Claudette brought me water to drink, slapped me on my back as though I had just achieved something great. "Way to go," she said. "You'll feel better now. Whenever I drink too much, I just stick my finger down my throat and then I can keep on going."

"I'm not keeping on going," I said. "I'm going home. My grandfather is dead."

"So?"

I put my head into Claudette's pom-poms. My face began to fall apart, piece by piece. My mouth trembled and I couldn't make it stop. I began to weep. "An old man is an old man, right? It doesn't matter what nationality, they're all the same. He was old and he was mine and he died."

"Christ," Claudette said and pushed me away. "I hate sloppy drunks."

But I didn't mind. I didn't care what anyone would say.

12 / Journey to the Lake

Maurice was in the basement when Truda came home for the weekend and her call had jarred him from his deep reverie. He looked about like a person awaking from a dream. He stood in the center of the laundry room with a .22 rifle in his hands. Quickly, he put the rifle back into the rack on the wall. The automatic washer clunked into gear and began its final spin cycle. "Hello," Truda called down the stairs, "anybody home?" Their first words, all of his children, upon entering the house had always been the question, "Anybody home?" What did they think? Were they worried that everyone had vanished?

"Down here," Maurice called. He picked up the basket of wet laundry and went up to meet her. He smiled at the sight of Truda's large chunky body filling the doorway at the top of the stairs. He saw in her gray eyes the affection she had for him, magnified several times by the thick lenses of her glasses. She was plain, this daughter. Nothing pretty about Truda, but good and solid. He was almost sorry that she wasn't going to marry Brian, sorry for Brian that he'd missed out on Truda.

"Fancy meeting you here," Maurice said. "If I'd known you were coming, I'd have baked a cake." He set the basket down, hugged her tightly.

"Working overtime, I see," Truda said.

"A woman's work is never done," Maurice said. "I'm doing a few chores for the old lady. She had to work late tonight. Big wedding tomorrow. Just let me get this here out on the line and I'll rustle up a bite to eat."

"It's okay," Truda said. She shed her knapsack and set it on the floor. "I ate before I got on the bus."

"Well, I had a good supper too," Maurice said and thumped his stomach. "But that don't stop me from eating again." He'd gained more weight, he could feel it in the pressure against his belt buckle. Standing for any length of time made his abdominal muscles ache. But what the hell, he told himself, if a man can't eat, may as well shoot himself.

"Sit yourself down," he said. "Make yourself homelier, I won't be long." And he went out into the back yard to hang clothes on the line.

The basket of clothing bounced against his stomach as he carried it through the garden to the back yard where the clothes-lines were strung between two trees. He stumbled and wet laundry slid down from the top of the pile onto the dirt. He swore, picked it up and shook it. He set the basket of laundry down on the hull of his nearly finished boat. He was breathing heavily; the effort of carrying the basket up the stairs and across the yard made his heartbeat rise. He felt the lack of oxygen in his cramped calf muscles. His body had become awkward, did not respond the way it should. He dropped things, walked into walls, felt like a drunk man. He leaned against the boat and rested until his breathing became even.

Night was falling in the garden. He heard the sound of the town coming alive for a Friday evening. He no longer felt the pull of the town, though. He preferred now to do his drinking alone. He closed his eyes to the dots and bright flashes of light that danced in the air in front of him and saw old Henry Roy, lying in the narrow cot in the hotel room that had been his home, flesh falling away from his bones slowly. He saw the picture of a man locked inside a body that had given out on him; a living death. He shuddered and opened his eyes. What would be worse? He pulled the trigger and felt the hot path of metal through the roof of his mouth. The choice was his.

"What time do you think Mom will be home?" Truda asked.

"Eh?"

"Here, let me," Truda said and took the basket of laundry from him.

He felt foolish. She'd found him standing with his mouth open, staring into the neighboring yard. He was aware of her hard look and conscious of his stomach, a ripe pumpkin straining the buttons on his shirt. His hair was still thick and black, but he was getting old. He talked to himself, for instance, aloud. He blurted out parts of sentences in French, inexplicably, to no one in particular. " *Je ne sais pas* . . . ," he often said. He was unsettled by this because he had always thought he knew what was necessary to know.

Truda flicked a towel and hung it on the line. "I picked up the papers for you," she said. "I thought we might get started on them tonight."

Papers. What papers? "Oh, I see."

"You managed to get a copy of your birth certificate then?"

"Ah, what papers might that be?"

She turned and looked at him, a frown creasing the skin above her nose. "Your application for the old age security. We talked about it last weekend. Mom told me to pick the papers up for you."

He was irritated, first that he'd forgotten and then at Mika, for taking care of his business. "What did she want to go and do that for?" he asked. "It's a waste of time. I don't need old age security. I got security, I've got my work."

"What about after, when you can't work?"

He'd never allowed himself to think seriously about that. He knew he would have to quit eventually in some far-off time. He'd spend his days fishing, golfing or reading, although he did none of those things presently.

"I'll die with my boots on," he said. "They'll carry me out of the shop, feet first. Then I'll be pushing up the daisies. I don't need security." He saw old man Roy's eyes, the terrible lucidity in them, a fly crawling across an unshaven cheek, a hand frozen against a blanket, the short-circuiting of the brain freezing his body.

Two hundred and thirty-five pounds, the doctor whistled. Cholesterol count out of sight. What are you going to do about it? What happened to the diet? With proper drugs and weight loss, you never know. What would you do? Maurice asked. If you were me? The doctor walked away from the examining table. If I were in the shape you're in, I think I'd kill myself.

"You're going to be sixty-five this year," Truda said. "You're entitled to the pension."

"Let them give it to those that need it." Sometimes he felt as though he was building a monument.

"You've paid taxes all these years, why shouldn't you collect now? Look at it as being a kind of a refund."

A refund for living? Money given back to you, just before you died, as a kind of reward? Maurice sensed Truda's frustration and he softened. He realized that it was her attempt to look after him, provide for him. There was a time when he'd thought Truda was more flawed than the other children, the way she had stayed behind after they'd scattered and gone their separate ways. He knew her deep fear of being alone. "I guess that's one way of looking at it," he said. "I could just bank it, save it for my old age." He laughed.

"Lord," she said. "Use it to finish this boat. Hanging clothes around this beast is not the easiest. No wonder Mom complains. Do you think it'll be finished soon?"

The others had all stopped asking that question; even Mika had more or less resigned herself to the idea that he might never finish it, that the boat, overturned on two saw-horses at the back of the yard, would become a permanent fixture. He wished Truda would stop asking as well. He ran his hand down the spine of the craft. "By cracky," he said. "All it needs now is the last gel coat and it'll be finished. Put an Evinrude on back of this baby and you won't catch me this summer, no siree. It'll be finished by the centennial celebrations."

He waited until Truda had finished hanging the clothes

and they went back into the house. Truda set her knapsack on the kitchen table and took out a bottle of whiskey. Maurice was surprised. Truda drank?

"Do you mind?" she asked.

"Not so long as you pour one for me too," he said, and got two jelly jars down from the cupboard. Mika's shelves were lined with expensive glassware but Maurice still preferred the heavy squat shape of the jelly jar. He tried to be casual. He sensed that something was wrong. He'd been aware of all his children's problems coming inevitably in one shape or another over the years, and never without feeling guilty, of somehow being responsible. Because of this, he had never interfered with what Mika did when it came to the children.

Truda poured the drinks and Maurice made two thick corned beef sandwiches. Despite having eaten a large meal, he found that he had an appetite. He began to fill Truda in on the latest family news, retelling events he'd told her last weekend. And then something new, as though he'd only just remembered.

"They're going to change the name of this street. The street we live on. For the town's hundredth anniversary. What do you think it'll be?"

"Let me guess," Truda said. "They're going to name the street Rue Montreal, or Diefenbaker Place."

"Lafreniere," Maurice said. He swilled the rye about in his glass before tipping it up and finishing it. The heat of it in his stomach felt good.

"Well, hey, that's great. Can you believe it?"

"I haven't told your mother yet," Maurice said. "It's no big deal." He saw the moisture in Truda's eyes.

"When did this all come about?"

"At Christmas. Just before, I think. They told me their plans."

"I think it's a big deal. Imagine, Lafreniere Street after my old man."

"Not exactly after me," Maurice said. He poured himself

another drink. "According to the history of this place, a Lafreniere was one of three names on the original incorporation of Agassiz as a town. They looked it up. It's in the records. But shoot, I don't mind. I'll take what I can get. Lafreniere's a good name." He chuckled softly. His father had no relatives; at least that's what he'd been told all those years when they'd lived as a family in the house, no, don't call it a house. It was more like a shack.

" *Je ne sais pas*," Maurice said. Whether any of this matters or not. But pictures from his past kept rearing up and he was compelled to look at them against his will and there he was again, only thirteen years old, walking through the bush, stopping to look at a pocket watch.

Seven o'clock. It didn't matter. All he had was time. Soon he'd be swaddled in a damp blanket of cool air and, coming with nightfall, a chilling frost and he had nowhere to sleep, not yet. He'd raided the house once again for warmer clothing. There were weeds pushing through the cracks in the shack behind the house and he thought of his parents in the cemetery, only three weeks and already the weeds were growing upon their mounds of earth. He found nothing left behind in the house. Everything had been taken. The windows were broken, not even the smell of his family remained, just the overpowering smell of wood rotting. But in the rafters of the shack was his father's .22 and a box of shells wrapped in heavy wax paper. He cut away from the house knowing he would never go back to it. He walked unseeing, a sleepwalker adrift in the real world. Heard a voice again today, he told himself, recording as in a journal. It was like I was being followed; it was like a hand reaching to touch me. He stopped, looked over his shoulder. Nothing but the leaves flipping gently, their thousand different autumn colors in the waning light. He blew his nose between his fingers. His hands smelled smoky to him, like the smell of a wild rabbit he'd snared that day.

Journey to the Lake

Maurice sat staring, unblinking, into the jelly jar. Truda sloshed more whiskey into it.

"Cheers," she said and lifted her glass.

"Here's mud in your eyes."

"Okay, so when does this happen?" Truda asked. "When does this glorious name change take place?"

"Next month, during the homecoming. They're planning to have a boat regatta and a street dance."

"That only gives you a month to finish the boat," Truda said.

"It'll be ready. Old Man River is going to show those buggers what a boat really is. Take me a ride to the lake and back."

There was the sound of tires on gravel as Mika arrived home from work. They both gulped the remainder of their drinks and then laughed self-consciously over the fact that Mika still had this effect on them so that even now they felt guilty, had the urge to hide things rather than confront her. Maurice put the bottle into the cupboard.

Mika entered the kitchen carrying several packages. "Oh, you did come out," Mika said when she saw Truda. "Good, I've brought enough chicken and chips for three."

Maurice saw Truda about to protest and winked at her. "You don't say, chicken," he said. "That'll sure hit the old spot."

Mika unpacked the boxes of chicken and chips and set plates on the table. She switched the radio on and sat down to eat with them. Gospel music filled the room.

> *I come to the garden alone,*
> *While the dew is still on the roses,*
> *And the voice I hear, falling on my ear,*
> *The Son of God discloses,*
> *And He walks with me . . .*

The intimacy Maurice had felt changed instantly to something heavy and thick.

"I was hoping you'd make it out," Mika said. "I sure could use a hand. Roxanne Penner is getting married tomorrow, four bridesmaids' bouquets to be put together before two. Heard from Brian these days?" she asked Truda.

Maurice saw the blood rise in Truda's cheeks. She'd broken the news several weeks ago. Truda had decided to go to university instead of Flin Flon where Brian had been transferred as branch manager of a bank.

Mika chewed at a chicken wing. "I still don't think he'll wait four years," she said.

"I don't expect him to."

Mika pushed her plate aside. "What are you saying now?" she asked. "That you've changed your mind?" She reached for Truda's hand. "Where's your ring?"

"I've decided that I can't do both. I can't live in Flin Flon and go to university at the same time."

"That's ridiculous," Mika said. "You have to get married. You've practically lived with him for a year. I had to get married and so you have to, too."

Maurice was astonished at Mika's remark. Their eyes met. Mika leapt up from the table and began filling the sink with water. "What I meant to say was, we can't always do what we want," she said. "If your Dad and I had always done what we wanted, where would we be now?"

Far away, Maurice thought. With a bow plowing the waves clean through. Out of the twisting shallow river into the clearer blue waters of the giant lake. The desire to do this had been strong, a ballooning pocket on the mainstream of his life. But, what will be, will be, he'd often told himself. It kept him from making decisions. He took what came.

> . . . and He talks with me
> and He tells me I am his own,

and the voice I hear falling on my ear,
none other, has ever known.

The women's voices and the nasal tones of the gospel singers grated, like stone against stone. He'd like to pull the plug and stop that damned depressing poor excuse for music.

"Education is fine and good," Mika said, "but small comfort on a cold night."

Maurice saw defiance coupled with fear in Truda's face. He got up and turned the radio down so low that the music was hardly audible.

"Mind your own business," Maurice said. "Can't you see the girl's made up her mind?"

Mika's jaw dropped. Maurice reached around her, took out the whiskey and plunked it down in the middle of the table. "Want a shot?" he asked Truda. She shook her head.

"Now, isn't that a thing for a father to say in front of his child," Mika said.

"To thine own self be true," Maurice said. "Look, what we say is neither here nor there," he said to Truda. "You know going to art school is what you want, what you can do, so go and do it."

"It's not art school," Truda said. "Fine Arts."

"Whatever." He poured whiskey into his glass. His hand shook.

Mika unbuttoned her suit jacket. She slipped it over the back of her chair. "That's a selfish way of thinking," she said. "You going to stay up all night?" she asked, not giving him the opportunity to defend himself. She looked pointedly at his glass of whiskey.

"As long as I want to," he said.

"Well, that would be nice," Mika said. "But I've got to get up early if I'm going to get that wedding done on time." She left the room.

"She was up at five this morning." Maurice said. "She works hard." He toyed with his glass, breathed deeply, fighting off depression. He was aware of Truda watching him too closely. "Let's get some real music going here," he said, forcing himself to sound jovial. "It's Friday night, after all. What we need in this here house is some toe-tapping music."

He went into the living room. The floor seemed to tilt beneath his feet and he stumbled against a chair. He put on a Don Messer record. "Now that's more like it," he said and yanked gently on Truda's hair as he passed by her chair. She had slumped down into it, and played with her glass in a listless way, as though she was tired, had no energy.

"Oh, I don't know," Truda said.

"What don't you know?"

"What we'd, what I'd ever do if you weren't here. This place . . . it wouldn't be. . . . " She couldn't finish.

He was touched and pleased. "You'd go on, same as everyone else. But where would I be going? Shoot, I may get the boat in the river, but that's about all."

Truda reached for her knapsack, undid the buckles and withdrew a ceramic plate and two clay figures and set them on the table in front of him. "What do you think of these?" she asked.

"Where did you get them?"

"I made them."

"You don't say?" Maurice fingered the clay models. He picked one up. It was the figure of a small child, a young girl carrying a basket, crudely done, but the head and features looked realistic enough. "This looks like the real McCoy," he said.

Truda held up the plate. A bird divided the plate in half with its wing-span, one side green, the other blue, the bird stark white. "You couldn't tell the difference between that and one in a store," Maurice said. "This art school, do you think you'll make much money when you're finished?" He didn't think many people would want the things she made, even if she could make enough of them.

"I'm having second thoughts," Truda said. "It was an idea. The instructor seemed to think I had talent."

"Sure you do. It's plain to see," Maurice said.

"But maybe Brian is right. I could pursue pottery as a hobby. He said he'd buy a kiln."

"What do you want to do?" Maurice asked.

Truda played with a honey-colored braid that was draped across her shoulder and hung in a thick rope across her breast. She grinned sheepishly. "Both."

"But you can't do both."

"I know. I have to make a decision. God, I hate making decisions," Truda said loudly, stretching suddenly, and then she got up from the table.

"Let's get to work." She spread papers out on the table.

"What have you got there?"

"The forms. You know, for the old age security?"

He was confused. He couldn't remember what it was they'd said out by the clothes-line. Something about a birth certificate. "Old age security. And what does that secure for me? Old age?" He was not going to fill in any bloody forms.

"A monthly income," she said. "So that you can retire."

"I'm not ready to retire."

She sighed. "Well I am. If Mom wants me to help with that wedding tomorrow, I'd better retire *tout de suite*. We'll work on this tomorrow."

Maurice cleaned the table off, set their glasses into the sink. He switched the light off and stood for a moment at the kitchen window, looking out at the garden and the dark shape of his unfinished boat. It would never float. Put an Evinrude on back of that baby and she would sink to the muddy bottom. He hadn't interpreted the instructions right. The diagrams hadn't shown how many layers of cloth or coatings of resin to apply. But even if he'd been able to understand, the boat wouldn't have been a success. He wasn't a builder. The kitchen window he'd installed was crooked. All through the house where his hand had been, doors did not close properly, carpet was set down askew, walls didn't line up. He was a failure.

He turned from the window and went into the basement to take the last load of clothes from the washer. The house was still. Above him he could hear Truda in the faint cracking of floorboards as she prepared for bed. He set the basket down at the foot of the stairs. He took the rifle down from its rack and sat down on the stairs with the gun across his knees. He shouldn't have said that, Maurice told himself, thinking of the doctor's words. That was not professional. He shouldn't have said that. And then he thought that he should write it down, the words the doctor had said in his office, so that they would know it hadn't been his idea entirely. He set the rifle aside, searched through his shirt pocket for a pencil. In the furnace room was a box of things kept for the visiting grandchildren, chalk and a chalk board. He took down a half-bottle of scotch from the top shelf, uncapped it and drank deeply. He found the chalk, went back to sit on the stairs.

He felt light-headed. When he lifted his hand to write, he saw two hands. I, Maurice Ovide Lafreniere . . . he would write his statement on the wall. When he thought of Henry Roy and his full year of dying, he knew what he should do. To thine own self be true. Take his own good advice. I, he willed his fingers to write, but they wouldn't do as he wanted. Instead, he saw a jagged thick vertical chalk line on the cement wall. The chalk snapped. Truda was home. She would still be awake, hear the noise of the gun. He didn't want her to be the one to find him.

He lay beside Mika in bed. No moonlight shone in the window and it was totally dark in the room. He lay looking up at the ceiling, seeing nothing. To thine own self be true. Who had said that? Phrases, sentences, words that he'd picked out of the air all these years, formed by others. He had used them over and over without really knowing in what context they'd been said. He'd used words to build an image, not to express himself. Well, it's too late to start now, he told himself. To be, or not to be? To sail a boat, or not to sail a boat? No sail. Put an Evinrude on back of that baby and you won't catch me this summer. He closed his eyes, opened them again. He sensed that hand reaching to touch him lightly between the shoulder blades. He tried to find some shape to the room in the darkness. He had always been one to stalk a noise down in the night and call to it, who's there? Who's there? Through the window and pressed against the sky, he saw the bent shapes of branches reaching in the violet sky and he felt locked behind the windowpane, looking out, unable to move, feeling a hand about to touch him in the center, near his heart.

His breath quickened and heat spread across his body. Oh God, he said, and Holy Mother, Jesus Christ. He began to run. He ran along a worn path, familiar to him, running, running. He caught sight of something buff-colored off to one side of the path. He stopped dead, caught it up to himself knowing instantly what it was. It was his mother's moccasin, red beads, torn, bedraggled, pitched out of the house by unfeeling people. He clutched it to his breast and his grief rose in his throat. The smell of the soft leather was like his hands, like the smell of wild rabbit. Suddenly, a pinpointing of light pierced his head, a camera shutter opening and closing, and the bubble of his desire broke free and floated out into mainstream. Tears ran down the sides of his face into the pillow.

"Mika." He felt her beside him, warm. He willed his leg to move into hers, to wake her. It was pinned to the bed. He was wrapped tightly by fear, unable to move. He began to fight against it. Move, he instructed his arm and struggled to lift it off his chest. Sweat ran down his forehead. He felt the presence of something, someone standing beside the bed, watching his struggle, waiting for him to give up. Move, he told his legs and strained against the blankets. He saw the soft glow of light in the hallway as Truda opened and closed her bedroom door.

"Truda." He heard footsteps going down the stairs. He fought to raise his head. His tongue was locked in his head.

"Maurice Ovide Lafreniere, is that you, or isn't that you?"

"It's me," Maurice said. Twigs snapped. He turned. It was his uncle, Old Man Desmarais.

"I've been looking all over for you," the old man said.

"Is it you then, who's been following me?"

Desmarais swept the navy toque from his head, spit into the bush. "You're a hard one to track." he said.

"What do you want?"

"I've come to take you to your people."

At last. Maurice felt the wind inside him die. His heart grew calm, slow. He clasped the old man's shoulders.

"Father, Father," Truda called. "Can you hear me?"

There were sounds about his head, a swarm of mosquitoes, humming. He slapped at them.

"Mr. Lafreniere, can you hear us?"

He should tell Truda, don't worry, you won't be alone. Do what you need to do. "Go away," he said in French. "I want to go home."

"What is he saying?" Mika cried.

Maurice felt the break coming. He felt the heavy earth slide downward as the dike gave way. "How will we get there?"

"Water, of course," the old man said.

"Of course. The river."

The canoe was waiting. Maurice stepped down into it, felt it rock gently. He knelt in the bow facing the river and picked up the paddle.

"You must speak English," Mika said. "We can't understand you."

"Father," Truda cried. "Oh Brian, he's slipping away. I can feel it."

The canoe rocked sharply as Desmarais pushed off and they floated out from the shadows into the dazzling light of sun on water. Maurice dipped the paddle and pulled gently. They moved forward silently. Behind him, he heard a harsh cry. It was the call of the blue herons. He turned and saw them, hundreds, rising from the water, necks pulled in tightly, iridescent beads dropping from their blue wings. Maurice felt the air moving as hundreds of wings fanned.

"Grab hold," Desmarais said. Maurice dropped his paddle. He saw it slipping away in the water and thought to reach for it. He would turn around, speak to them all one last time.

"No, no," Desmarais said. "We'll lose the birds. Grab hold quickly."

"But I—" I didn't fill in the forms.

"Now."

Now. Maurice reached, caught hold of a scaly, rough bird leg. Blue wings fanned about his head, struggled against his weight. He felt the bird's mighty strength in his hands. It faltered, climbed, and then he was skimming across the top of the water, weightless, free, upstream on the river, through its loops and curls out, out to the broad mouth where the color of the water beneath him changed and the muddy silt settled to the bottom and there stretched before him the endless blue of the giant lake.

13 / There Is No Shoreline

A name in a newspaper. Menace to Society. Betty has been
kneeling on the floor in the youngest child's bedroom,
wrapping onion soup bowls and earthenware mugs into
newspaper and placing them into a large trunk that sits on the
braided oval mat in the center of the upstairs bedroom. The
items are new. They are surprises to be discovered when the
youngest unpacks. It's a tradition. All her children expected,
looked for the surprises. There are many shipping labels on
the trunk. Labels of places she has only read about in
newspapers or in the meager pleading letters she's received
from each traveling child. She reads the newspaper. Menace
to Society. It's the name the judge has bestowed upon a man.
It's like an ax splitting wood, she thinks, and is curious. Her
long pale fingers unwrap the paper carefully, iron it flat against
the rug. It seems that she gets all of her news this way, down
on the floor as she is slipping a sheet of newspaper beneath
the cat's dish or lining the bottom of a boot tray, or else when
she is packing or unpacking the paraphernalia that her four
grown children have acquired and carted in and back out of
the house on their many excursions into adulthood. It seems,
too, that the news she reads on the floor among the bits of
dried cat food or muddied shoes is more surprising, more
interesting. Menace to Society. Then she reads the man's real
name. It catches, like a hook meeting an eye, bringing two
pieces of fabric together. She has that kind of memory. She
thinks that it's compensation for her lack of travel, her
inability to go forward, this instant recalling of the past. It's a
trick that she doesn't understand or even want. She can be
walking through a crowded store or driving home from the
supermarket and a smell or a sound or a name read in a
newspaper will suddenly put her back inside a time. And she

can reach out and touch the sides of that time, hear the
voices of it, the music, she can smell the air.

She is behind the counter in the drugstore, refilling the
slots with cigarettes and feeling the blister on her heel
brought about by a pair of new red shoes. She silently curses
her friend, Del, for persuading her to spend the money on
them. The bell above the door jangles. She turns. A man
approaches the counter and scans the cigarette slots. Smoke
from his cigarette curls up into his heavy locks of blond hair.
It appears as though his hair has been shellacked into place
into a studied careless arrangement across his forehead. He
wears the type of white T-shirt that her father wears beneath
his barbering shirts, but that men are beginning to wear now
with blue jeans.
"Players Plain."
She slides the package from its slot and hands it to him.
His knuckles are cracked and rough-looking with black grease
imbedded in the chapped skin. A mechanic. His hands are
like Frank's hands. I could never let hands like that make love
to me, she tells herself. She wouldn't be able to stomach the
smell of waterless hand cleaner or oily rags, or the smell of
heavily greased hair on the pillow beside her. If she did, it
would be against her will. She has vowed: never again, against
her will.

The man rolls the change across the counter and then
goes over to the pay phone, walking with a slightly bow-legged
swagger. Betty kneels, slides open the counter door and begins
to rearrange the giftware inside. Two pale eyes meet her own
through the glass casing. A child's mouth, pressed against the
glass, resembles a snail climbing up the inside of a jar. Saliva
dribbles down the showcase. Except for the pale eyes, the
child is an exact replica of the man.

"Hey, come on, I've just cleaned that," Betty says.

His eyes shift sideways towards the man at the pay phone,
looking for protection, but the tongue remains on the glass.

Bribe him. She takes a two-penny sucker from the can on top of the counter, comes around the showcase and holds it out before him. His mouth pops loose from the glass, a grubby hand snakes forward and the sucker is gone. He wears a faded Mickey Mouse T-shirt, overalls which button at the legs and crotch, but the buttons have pulled loose and the overalls hang open like a skirt, exposing his ballooning plastic pants beneath. He scratches at his arms. Betty notices the bites on his arms. Some are the size of nickels, others of pimples.

She turns from the sight quickly. She doesn't need to feel sorry for him. So she goes over to the coffee bar instead and slips off the offending red shoes and feels sorry for herself. They cost twenty-five dollars. She has two jobs now. During the day she works as a filing clerk in the basement of the city hospital, next to the room where they conduct post-mortems on corpses. Evenings and Saturdays she continues to work at the drugstore. She's sorry she purchased the shoes because she means to save every penny she can. It's important for survival. She wants to move out, away from this city, away from her past and from Frank, who has given up on his dream to become a country western singer and is now a machinist for a bus manufacturing company. This thick-lipped and heavy-lidded Frank who looks slightly Mexican is filled with excruciating desire to screw and make a family.

The child follows Betty to the coffee bar. He stares at her stocking feet. Just then, Rose, a middle-aged woman who runs the coffee bar, comes up from the basement, red-faced and puffing slightly from the stairs. "Well, well," she says. "Look who's here. If it isn't Mickey Mouse."

The child pulls the sucker from his mouth and replies indignantly, "Me Rocky, not Mickey Mouse."

"I should have known. You have big muscles. No wonder they call you Rocky."

The child's father hangs up the receiver. He swaggers over to the child and scoops him up awkwardly against his chest. "He's called Rocky after Rock Hudson."

Rose plows forward the way fat people think they're entitled to. "I should have known. He's a handsome little devil. Just like his dad. I'll bet his mom spoils him rotten."

"He doesn't have a mother."

"Oh." Rose's expression is one of instant extreme concern. It makes Betty uncomfortable. Rose glances at the child quickly, leans across the counter and whispers dramatically, "What happened?"

The man meets her halfway across the counter. A smile forms on his blunt features. "She left me for a Harley-Davidson. What are you doing after work? I need a babysitter."

"Comedian," Rose says when the door closes behind them. She has offered concern and been scorned. "I'd of left him too. And did you see that kid? He was crawling with Lord knows what. I've never seen a kid so dirty. If there was one thing about my own, they were always clean. Not dressed in the best, but clean. There's no excuse for dirty."

Rose wears green or navy stretch pants with elastic waistbands to accommodate her fluctuating size, and loose flowered blouses to hide her pot belly. She smells of underarm deodorant. Betty doesn't mind that Rose takes pride in being ordinary, a carbon copy of most of the middle-aged women in the neighborhood. But what she minds is that Rose lacks imagination. And people without an imagination can't see beyond their own experiences. She has not made the error of confiding in Rose.

Betty thinks that women talking about their children all sound the same. She goes back to the cigarette counter. She is anxious to arrange her counters, wipe the casing once again, count up the cash and be gone. She's to meet Del and the two of them will go to a travel agent's office to look at travel brochures. Betty doesn't know where she's going to travel to. She just knows she's leaving. Del, whose parents are in the armed services and who has lived all over the world, has the

knowledge she needs. She leaves the drugstore. Her
destination is a small park that fronts on Portage Avenue.

The day she began going to the park, Rose had been
angry with her. "Why start hanging around that place?" Rose
had asked. "What's the big attraction?"

Betty couldn't explain that Rose's company was beginning
to make her feel claustrophobic. "It's outside, that's the big
attraction. And I'm only going to eat lunch there; in my
books, that's not hanging around."

"I can think of better places," Rose said. "You never know
what could happen."

Betty was weary, anxious to have something happen. City
people exaggerated. Betty doubted that there was real violence
in the park because when she sat out on the veranda at night
smoking a last cigarette, she listened to the kids who hung out
there. Theirs was a phony bravado. They made her smile, they
were so innocent.

"You sound like my mother," Betty said, knowing how to
appease Rose. To Rose, life was a series of jobs that had to be
done and Betty was one of those jobs. Even the recent
adjustment to widowhood had been a chore Rose had tackled
with determination. Rose had convinced Mr. Garvey to hire
Betty, Against His Better Judgment. Experience had shown
him that teenaged girls were unreliable, he said. They never
worked as hard as they could and left shortly after the first
paycheck or steady boyfriend. But even though Betty had
proven otherwise, Rose still worried that any deviation from
the established routine might be an indication that Betty was
slipping and going the way of all the young women that they
had hired and then Mr. Garvey would be able to say, I told
you so.

Rose dropped a sandwich and coffee into a paper bag with
the same resolute efficiency with which she ran the coffee bar
in Garvey's Drugs. "Listen here," Rose said. "I know what I'm

talking about. Don't forget, there was a stabbing in that park only last weekend."

"A stabbing, hah. Someone cut their hand. The newspaper said it was self-inflicted, a game of some kind."

"Some game. They called an ambulance, you call that a game? I'll bet the city picked up the tab too. Let them bleed, I say. Play with matches, expect to get burned."

"Just like Home Sweet Home." Betty took the bag from Rose. "Look at it this way, I'm giving you something real to worry about for a whole hour."

"Get out of my sight," Rose said. "As if I haven't got enough."

Despite Rose's anger, she went to the park. She entered the quiet greenness and immediately it was cooler. There was a large rock garden in the center of the park with castor bean plants in the middle of it. Her mother had attempted a rock garden once, but her mother was impulsive and hadn't thought it through first or planned it because she'd arranged the garden beneath a tree and nothing would grow in the shade. Gravel paths wound through the park from the four entrances and came together in the rock garden. Betty wiped dust from the bench before she sat down. She faced Arlington Street, the street where she lived. The sun tilted slightly in the west and made the houses on the street look more distinct. The houses had sharp edges, black shutters against white siding. Geraniums in windowboxes, motionless in the heat, were red splashes against the white houses. The house where she'd lived the past five months had an enormous graceful veranda which sloped down over her window in the front of the house like a gray umbrella. She realized with a start that the house was an attractive one, probably one of the nicer houses on the street. When she walked across that shiny, gray-painted veranda, passed between the white fake pillars and descended the wide jute-carpeted stairs, she saw her surroundings as though they were part of a photograph, a picture in a magazine.

Nothing seemed real to her. I am getting up and going to work, she recited. When she walked the two blocks to the drugstore, she counted the number of steps it took to get there. I am going home from work, she recited. She took her dinner from the oven where it was kept warm for her and ate it in her room. She was the only woman boarder. She heard the voices of the other boarders in the dining room as they played their daily cribbage games with the landlord. They talked about baseball scores and women. Or else she sat on her bed with her hands in her lap and watched the kids who ruled the park. They were her age. They wrestled each other to the ground and spat at people who walked by on the sidewalk. When she went to bed in the room at the front of the house beneath the gray veranda roof, she sometimes heard scrapings against the side of the house and saw shadows at the window. Or she heard water running in the toilet upstairs when someone forgot to jiggle the handle. She heard occasionally the sound of glass breaking in the night or a leather strap meeting flesh when the landlord pounded sense into the landlady. Nothing about the last five months seemed real to Betty. But she was beginning to wake up and her desire to get out and away from the drugstore was indication of it.

There was the crunch of wheels against the gravel path. A woman came around the rock garden pushing a stroller with a small child in it. She hesitated for a moment, framed by the tall red brick building which dominated the skyline behind her. When she saw Betty on the bench, she started towards her. The baby was fat and wore just a diaper and plastic pants. He leaned back into the stroller and looked dazed by the heat, asleep with his eyes open. As they grew closer, he looked at Betty, but without expression, as though she were part of the bench.

The feeling that made Betty want to eat lunch in the park also made her want to try to make something happen in the baby's face. She leaned towards the child and smiled. The baby's eyes flickered briefly and then he poked listlessly at the plastic balls attached to the front of the stroller. The woman came alongside Betty and stopped, interpreting the smile as an invitation to visit. She was tall and stringy. She wore a red elastic tank top that squashed her small breasts flat. Her legs and arms were tanned, but a puffy bulge of white stomach squeezed overtop her jean shorts.

"Sure is hot," the woman said.

"Hotter than yesterday," Betty said. She'd learned how to small talk from listening to Mr. Garvey and Rose over lunch, and the customers thought she was mature for seventeen because she could engage them in pleasant but meaningless chatter.

"And here it is, the end of August. You'd think we'd be getting some relief by now," the woman said.

"The forecast is for more of this tomorrow."

"Wouldn't you know it?" the woman said with a look of mock despair. "I'm in an apartment. Top floor and no air conditioning. Tigger's got the worst heat rash."

"Who?"

She laughed and motioned to the baby. "It's what we call him," she said. "His real name is Brian, but I don't think he knows it. We used to have a cat named Tigger." She pushed the stroller back and forth on the gravel path with short movements. The child's head jerked forward and backwards into the canvas stroller. Stupid broad, Betty said silently, feeling that careless motion, feeling sudden anger.

"It was a tabby cat. A gray tabby, you know the kind," the woman said. "They look like tigers? I really liked it. We had to take it with us when we went camping in the Whiteshell last year and it got away on me."

"That's too bad," Betty said. She was sorry that she'd smiled at the baby.

"It ran into the bush the first day we got there. You know what happened to it? It went wild," the woman said, not waiting for an answer. "Apparently cats do this. Dogs don't, but the camp warden said it happens all the time with cats.

Then the wardens have to hunt the cats down in late fall and shoot them," she said with a certain smug satisfaction.

They use them for target practice, I'll bet, Betty told herself. "That's terrible."

"Oh, you don't need to feel sorry for them," the woman said. "They're wild and I mean wild. You can't come near them. It's a kindness really to shoot them because they'd just freeze to death when winter came. Anyway, I'm looking for another one. And when I saw you sitting here, I thought I'd come over and see if you might know of someone who's giving kittens away."

"No I don't, sorry."

"Tigger here needs a pet, don't you sweetie?" She squatted in front of the stroller and prodded the flaccid child in the chest in an attempt to make him smile.

Betty saw the skin on the inside of the woman's thighs as she squatted. It was darker, as though it was permanently stained. The insides of her own legs were not like that. Brown pubic hair curled outwards from the woman's denim shorts. Her tanned hand rested on the stroller and Betty saw that she wore a wide gold band. The woman was married then and could know who the baby's father was. More and more Betty wondered who the father of her own baby might be.

"Who was it?" Mika, Betty's mother, had asked. She wanted to know, hoping, Betty realized, to pressure them into marriage.

"I don't know," Betty said. It was true. She didn't know. It could have been the tall blue-eyed man, the one who was training to be an RCMP. She'd first seen him sitting in the vestibule of the hotel when she passed by the window. She knew what the men who sat there watching women pass by were like, the bets they made, the words they used: bitch, cunt, whore. But when the patrol car pulled alongside her one night and the young one laughingly threatened to arrest her for wearing a tight sweater, she laughed too, because they were in uniform and she disassociated them from the hotel men. They offered to give her a lift home and she accepted, anticipating with mild glee Mika's frantic reaction about what the neighbors would think when they saw her. But the men didn't take her straight home. They took her instead into the country to an abandoned farmhouse. The young one led her into the house and told her to lie down and then she understood. All she felt was anger at her own stupidity and saw this as the penalty to be paid for it. He entered her while the older man stood watch in the doorway. She saw the moon resting upon his shoulder. Sometimes when she was on a bus or sitting on the veranda smoking, she would think about this and cry out involuntarily. When people stared at her strangely she'd realize that she'd let the interior pass through to the exterior and had exclaimed loudly and so she would count to herself, the number of stairs in a building, the seconds it took for a light to change from red to green, to prevent it from happening. But more and more she was letting herself think and when she counted the days, months, she was certain that it had been the RCMP man who had gotten her pregnant.

"Well, if you do hear of someone who is giving away a kitten, could you let me know?" the woman said. "I'll give you my number."

"You can if you want to, but I don't know many people in the city. I'm new here."

"Oh, too bad, Tigger should have a pet. Shouldn't you Tigger, eh? What do you say?" She tickled his armpit fiercely. "Come on, what do you say?"

Betty saw his head wobble slightly on its thin stem-like neck. He squirmed. Then Betty saw his mouth crinkle, move into a wide smile that did not reach into his eyes. What choice did he have but to smile? The woman is stupid, she told herself.

"How old is he?" Betty asked.

"Thirteen months in October." The woman got up, brushed a strand of hair from her forehead and surveyed the park with dark nervous eyes. "I don't know what I'll do once he starts walking. What this park needs is a wading pool for the little kids. A playground. This place has become such a hangout."

"That's bullshit," Betty said. "Everyone says that, but I live right across from here and I've never had any trouble."

The woman turned the stroller around sharply and began to walk back in the direction that she'd come. "And I wonder why," she said over her shoulder. "I just wonder why."

Betty watched as the woman lifted the stroller from the gravel path onto the sidewalk. Behind them, the tall red brick building jutted up from among the houses conspicuously and Betty counted floors, the fifth, the window on the corner. That had been her room, where she'd spent the winter and spring behind the glass looking down at the streets. Her baby had been a boy too. He'd been a big child, a coke and chocolate bar baby, the nurse had said. She thought he'd break her pelvic bones when he came. It's like menstrual cramps, Mika had said as she bent over the bread pan, her fists working the dough throughout their conversation, only it's a hundred times worse.

"I'm sorry," Betty said. She watched as Mika's fist plunged into the swollen bread dough. It fizzled and sank. No calamity or illness interfered with Mika's work.

"You're sorry," Mika said. "Good." There was perspiration in the fine hair above her top lip. The cords in her neck were strung tightly. "But what will that change, tell me?" She took the knife, sliced the dough into two and then once again. She held up a piece of it and formed a loaf. "It's not a mass or a tumor, you know. If you cut it, it will bleed."

"What do you want me to do?"

"Give it up. It's the sensible thing to do." She plopped the loaf into the greased pan and began to form the second.

"But what if I want to keep it?"

"You? Keep it? What do you know about children?"

"What did you know?"

"Listen," Mika said. "It's going to hurt. Like menstrual

cramps, only a hundred times worse; as it should. But if you keep the baby, the trouble only begins. Children are a constant pain." She wiped her eyes on her sleeve. She led Betty into the bedroom and gathered several limp cotton smocks from the back of the closet and pushed them down into a shopping bag in a furtive way as though they were shameful depressing items. "Be sensible. Don't ruin your life," she said. "Give it up."

"I don't know," Betty said.

"Well, do what you want, but don't bring it home to me," Mika said.

Mika had never used the word baby. So when the nurse placed the baby into the crook of Betty's arm, she was surprised at its warmth and heaviness and the soft curve of its reddish-blond head beneath her hand.

The feeling that came to her, that had made her want to eat lunch in the park, vanished. The sandwich Rose had made tasted like cardboard. She got up from the bench, counted the number of strokes it took to brush crumbs from her lap. She felt as though she carried an egg around inside her. An egg with a crack in it, starting from the top and going down to the bottom. It would split open.

Betty meets Del in the park and the two young women walk down Arlington Street to Portage Avenue where they'll catch a bus downtown. The park has become the center for their friendship. They go there often to sit and listen to the city. Occasionally, they talk with the boys who also gather there. And often, through a series of body movements, a secret language with one of the young men, Del sends messages, and like a tawny urgent cat, she sidles into the shaded back portion of the park to some boy's blanket. But not Betty. She has learned her lesson and nothing interferes with her goal to flee this city as soon as possible. The means to do this take shape in the metal tea can in the bottom bureau drawer.

As they near Portage Avenue, Betty becomes aware of a car moving alongside them, slowly. She turns to look. It's the man from the drugstore and his scruffy child. He salutes the women in a showy manner, stops the car and rolls down the window.

"You girls look like you could use a lift. Going far?"

A thousand miles, Betty thinks.

"That depends," Del says. She flashes a golden dimpled smile. "He's cute," she whispers.

"Cute like a snake."

"Depends on what?" he asks.

"Who owns the kid?"

"He's mine, but I'm not married, if that's what's stopping you."

"What can go wrong with a kid along?" Del asks and they get into the car.

They drive around the city for two hours, a listless aimless way. His name is Dave Reimer, they learn. He is a single parent. He does not say to them, I am a single parent. He is reluctant, almost ashamed to speak about it at any length. She took off, is all he says. But Del has an easy way of talking about intimate or personal things that is not in keeping with the times and once people get over their initial shock, they respond to her. Dave tells her Rocky's mother left when he was a year old. With some guy on a motorcycle. The sympathy in Del's green eyes is innocent and genuine.

At the end of the two hours, Del has joined Dave in the front seat and Rocky has climbed over into the back seat and bounces on the seat beside Betty, showing no signs of being tired although it's ten o'clock. They cross the river several times. It seems to Betty that they've been driving in circles. When Dave crosses the river once again, this time it's over an older rusting bridge, and they enter what appears to be the old section of Winnipeg. The street they travel on ends in the river. The lights of city center across the river bank are reflected back in the dark water. At the last moment, Dave swings the car to the right and they bump along a rutted dirt road. He turns off his headlights. Ahead, at the end of the road beside the dark still river, is a tall building. It looms up at them suddenly, white like the billowing sails of some ancient ship.

"Time to put the kid away," Dave says. He turns off the engine.

"Where are we?" Del is nervous, uncertain.

Dave motions to the tall building. "It's home. Rocky and me live here." It's an abandoned grain elevator.

They pass through the black slit of the sliding door and Dave pushes it closed. He switches on his flashlight. The circle of light flickers, barely dents the dark interior. The building smells dankly of urine, wood, gunny sacks and something else. Betty doesn't know what.

"Here." Dave guides them up a little step. The floor suddenly sways beneath their feet. Betty reaches wildly, finds a railing and hangs on. "It's just the lift," Dave says. Then she hears the squeal of metal, the squeaking protest of wood beneath her feet. Pulleys clank. The smell of rope is strong. She's being drawn upwards. The air grows warmer and smells faintly of straw. She still doesn't believe he lives here. The lift carries them up and up and then it stops.

"This is it," Dave says. He carries Rocky in his arms and shines the light for them. The light touches a small room. Betty catches sight of a rumpled bed and then clothing hanging on pegs. Dave sets Rocky down and squats. He strikes a match. It flickers and then a glow spreads outwards from the camper's lantern on the floor. He moves across planks that bow beneath his weight, kneels once again and another lantern sputters, hisses and spreads its light. Betty looks about the room. There's a narrow cot in one corner, a gray sleeping bag on the floor beside it. Nails hold clothing on the wall and the floor is spread with what looks and smells like dirty laundry. Dave shuffles through it, moves it from his path as he crosses the room. A cardboard box beside the cot is filled to

overflowing with toys. On the other side of the room a large
wooden spool is used as a table. She's seen the spools in the
ditches along the highways. They hold hydro or telephone
wire. The spool is scattered with pop and beer bottles, some
paperback books and a carton of cookies.

Del stands transfixed. Then suddenly for some reason, she
takes it upon herself to take charge of Rocky. She croons over
him and pulls his Mickey Mouse T-shirt off over his head.
"Look at his curly eyelashes. They're so long. Isn't he cute?"

Betty studies the child's face and wonders what it is she's
missed. She feels nothing but impatience to be away from this
place. She crosses the planks and goes over to Dave. He
squats, adjusting the flame in the lantern. Her footsteps are
suddenly hollow. Dave holds up the lantern. She sees the foot
of black space on either side of the planks. Her skin crawls.
"God."

Dave grins. "Isn't that something?" He searches behind
him on the floor, holds up a pop bottle and then lets it drop
into the black space. Seconds later, Betty hears the dull thud
of it hitting the earthen floor below.

"That goes down into the grain bins. I keep boards over it
all the time. There're ladders going down to the bottom,
though. If I couldn't use the lift, I could climb down."

A grain elevator. In the center of the city. The air is
thick and stifling hot. "What about Rocky? Aren't you worried
that he'll fall?"

"I thought of that," Dave says. He crosses back over the
planks and gathers up Rocky, who is naked now except for his
sagging plastic pants. Dave takes a leather harness down from
a nail on the wall and slips Rocky's arms into the harness. He
buckles it in the back. Rocky doesn't struggle or seem to
mind. He carries Rocky to the bed and puts him into it.
There's a rope lying on the floor, looped about the leg of the
cot. He picks up the rope and snaps it to the fastener on the
back of the harness.

"Houdini couldn't get out of that one." He reaches

beneath the cot and pulls out a box of beer. He opens three and motions the way to them back across the planks. A tiny window is nailed over with sacking at the far end of the room. Below the window on the floor are cushions from a discarded couch. Dave motions for them to sit down. Betty thinks of bugs and the bites on Rocky's arms and is reluctant. But Del sits down immediately, seeming not to notice the smell or the heat.

"Why don't you open a window? God, it's hot," Betty says.

Dave sits down beside Del. "Can't. The mosquitoes are hell."

She's impatient to be gone. He's brought them both here for a reason. She's anxious to get it over with. "Why do you live here? It's a shitty place for a kid to live."

"I live here because I love it, right?"

"Come and sit down," Del says. "We didn't have anything better to do anyway."

Betty does so reluctantly. Dave motions towards the child who is sleeping, curled and asleep so suddenly. "Children's Aid is looking for him. They want to put him into a foster home."

"How come?" Del asks.

"Because. They say I can't look after him properly. When Rocky's mother took off, my mother babysat for me. But she's working now herself. She can't do it anymore."

Betty can hear the wind. It has always been there, but as she thinks about what he's just said, she becomes aware of the wind in the rafters, swaying the whole building so that it cracks and snaps above and below, all around them. It's as though they are moving with it across some ocean in the middle of the prairie. Grain elevators, the sailing ships of Lake Agassiz. The idea intrigues her. Or, it's the ghostly sound of the carts, she imagines, the historic freighters of the prairies, that echoes in the rafters of the elevators.

She hears another sound. It comes from beneath them.

"What's that?"

"Rodents."

"Rodents. You mean mice?"

"Rats."

"So. What do you do then?" Del asks quickly, seeming not to want to think: rats. She forms the question that Betty has wanted to form, has thrown away instead to the listening of the wind and imaginings.

"What can I do? I leave him here."

Betty gets up, showing disgust and impatience. "What can you do? Quit working. Collect unemployment insurance. Go on welfare. Something."

"Hah. Very funny. Think I haven't thought of that? They don't give men welfare so they can stay home with their kids."

Betty wants to reach up and tear the burlap from the tiny window, to feel the fresh air. Dave pushes past her. He gets another warm beer from the box beneath the cot and comes back to sit beside Del. He searches about in his hip pocket, slips a snapshot from his wallet. He holds it up to Betty first. It's a picture of a young girl who squints into the sun, holding a bundle of blankets in her arms. Betty sees herself in the picture. They have both abandoned their sons; the fate of her own child is less clear, perhaps he is the child of a mother who bangs his head against the stroller when walking gravel paths in the park. To a baby, what mother it has doesn't matter as long as someone feeds it and holds it close. It's later that it matters.

"We went steady for a year before she got pregnant."

Del refuses to look. "What does Rocky do? When you're at work, what does he do?"

"He sleeps most of the time. That's why I keep him up late. Then I come by and see him at noon. Change his diapers. The longest part is the afternoon. He's not tired then. It gets hot."

Del looks frightened. She stares at the sleeping child. "That's awful. I think that's the saddest thing I've ever heard."

"I just don't know what else to do. We won't be able to stay here in winter. We'll freeze," Dave says.

There Is No Shoreline

"Well, you're going to have to think of something," Betty says, making it clear that she thinks it's his problem.

"Are either one of you interested in babysitting for free?"

Del and Betty are silent. They don't speak of Rocky again and when the three of them leave, Betty hears the child breathing gently and sees the rising and falling of the gray sleeping bag against his chest. She feels stricken. As though she personally is abandoning him, setting him adrift in the bowels of the creaking ship, and there is no shoreline.

The following day, Del comes to work with Betty and sits at the coffee bar chatting with Rose whom she adores. Each time someone comes into the drugstore she turns to look and so when Dave and Rocky arrive, Betty isn't surprised. Del leaves the drugstore with them and Betty doesn't see them again until she's finished work and walks into her room. They are there, the three of them, wrestling on her bed.

Dave gets up immediately, swooping Rocky from Del's stomach where he has been bouncing against her knees. They are play-acting, Betty realizes. They are engrossed in each others' giggles and stupid horseplay. They think they're a happy family. As though a family is just that: play slaps and tickles to make one feel happy.

Dave and Rocky leave quickly. Del leans against the bureau looking guilty. "We had no place to go," she says.

Betty straightens the spread on the bed and hates herself for doing so. She's becoming old, tidy, like her mother. She is becoming what she is. "You might have asked."

"I will next time. Sorry."

Betty is irritated that they've seen her strewn clothing and begins to fold things. She pulls open her bottom drawer on the pretense of putting the clothing into it so that she can check the metal tea can without being conspicuous. It appears to be untouched. She will open an account in the bank. No sense taking chances with her future.

Del winds and unwinds a strand of golden hair that has

pulled loose from her ponytail. "I'm moving in with Dave," she says with unaccustomed shyness.

"Congrats. Dave has his instant mother."

"So? So, what's wrong with that?"

"You want that? Don't you know that's what he's been looking for, for someone to come and be a free babysitter? Someone who will care for him and his kid?"

"He's no different than any other man," Del says. "It's just that the kid is born already. That's the only difference. Anyway, what's wrong with wanting to look after a man and kids?"

Nothing. Betty has to admit that. Nothing. Someone at this moment is looking after her own child. She wants to cry.

"We were wondering. All we need is a little money. Enough for the first month's rent and groceries. We could swing it then. Do you think you could?" Her gaze strays to the bottom drawer.

Betty freezes. "No bloody way. Forget it."

"It's okay. I have other options."

But Betty knows she doesn't.

The matter of the money becomes a point of tension between them. But even though Del sees Dave often, she still comes occasionally to talk to Betty. She sits with one leg slung over the railing of the veranda or in the park with her knees gathered to her chin, breaking smoke rings with her slender fingers. But their friendship is not the same. Betty has decided to move to Vancouver. She feels guilty though, for being the cause of the friction, and so when Del comes over one evening and asks to borrow a sundress, she complies with too much eagerness, lavishing accessories unasked upon Del. She is inside, dressing when Dave comes to pick her up. Instead of waiting in the car as he usually does, he comes to the house and leans against the railing of the veranda where Betty sits on the steps. As though he's just remembered something important, he pulls an envelope from his shirt pocket and hands it up to Betty.

"It's Rocky's birthday card."

Betty opens it. Happy Birthday Rocky, written in a spread, breathless sort of handwriting. There are x's and o's at the bottom of it. Paper-kissed kid. Painless mothering, she thinks, and then flinches slightly.

"I think it means something," he says, "don't you? I mean, would she have bothered to send it if she didn't care?"

It didn't cost anything to agree. "Probably not," Betty says and hands him back the card.

Rocky toots the car horn and Dave shakes his fist. "Kids," he says, as though she should know what it means to say, kids.

"I don't know," Dave says. "Sometimes I think that if she saw him, she'd want to come back. It's the only reason I've kept him. What do you think?"

Del comes across the veranda and the question goes unanswered. She looks beautiful, her tanned shoulders framed by the straps of the white sundress, her gold earhoops bobbing as she walks, accentuating her square jaw. She sees Rocky in the car and her wide smile vanishes.

"I thought you were getting a sitter?"

Dave shrugs, holds his hands up to indicate his helplessness. "I tried but I just couldn't get anyone."

"But we've never been anywhere without him."

Betty wants to laugh. She wants to say, see? But then she thinks of Frank. Frank who knows all about her and still persists. This could be them, wanting to go out, needing a babysitter. She feels guilty for wanting to laugh. "You wanted to go out? I'll babysit Rocky," she says.

Dave drops them off at the elevator. Betty waits for him to leave and then tears the burlap from the window. She holds Rocky up to it. Together they watch a man peeing in the Red River. Children, she supposes they're his, play at the river's edge. They wave willow branches in the air, dip them into the water. She becomes heartsick suddenly; it's like a gush of salt water in the back of the throat, for her brothers and sisters.

"I've done the sensible thing," she'd said. "It's over. You can send Dad in to get me. I'm calling from a drugstore on Arlington Street."

"The sensible thing would have been not to get pregnant in the first place," Mika said. "Now what?"

"I could always go back to school." Rose was listening in, wiping the counter top carefully, staying in one spot too long. Betty turned her back to the counter.

"You wouldn't fit in. You'd be the butt of every joke."

"I could get a job."

"There aren't any jobs in Agassiz."

"What do you want me to do then?" Her sweater was damp, her breasts were oozing milk.

"The sensible thing to do would be to stay in the city and get yourself a job. Start over again. But you're welcome to come home on weekends, if you like."

The man zips up and continues to walk along the river bank. The children follow like birds lifting and swarming and settling back down over some muddied object left lying. Across the river, water sprinklers swish dust from the sidewalks and cool dark stains spread out beneath the trees. The odor of exhaust from the traffic is trapped by the thick foliage along the river bank. Above the city, neon lights color the sky pink. Betty has never felt violence in the streets of the city. But she knows that it's there. It's there in the houses and apartments on Arlington Street, where everything is carefully laid down behind clearly defined borders of picket fences and hedges and the panes of glass in the windows. She holds Rocky and makes another vow. Not in my house, she says, never in my house.

She rummages through the box of toys and finds a tattered *Golden Book*. She attempts to read to the child, but he keeps sliding from her lap, wants once again to be lifted to the window to watch the children play.

She blows up a beach ball and for a time he is happy. She

waits for him to become tired and when his eyes grow heavy and his coordination sluggish, she's relieved.

She sits beneath the open window on the cushions in the gathering darkness and waits for Dave to return. She has the flashlight by her side should Rocky awaken. She listens to the sounds of the building. She feels the building sway. She puts her hands to its floor boards. She feels the vibration. Wood snaps. Overhead, rafters groan as dry wood rubs against dry wood. She imagines wind filling a canvas sail. Then the hair on her arms rises. The other sound. She reaches for the flashlight, flicks the switch with trembling fingers, sweeps the light across the floor in the direction of the scuffling sound. She sees the thick gray tail disappear into the shadows.

She leaps from the cushions. She shines the light across Rocky. There's another swift shadowy movement from beneath his bed towards her feet. She screams and kicks out at it. It swerves and scurries behind the cushions where she has been sitting.

Rocky begins to cry. He sits up in bed. He wraps both hands around the rope that holds him there. He rocks back and forth, his voice is a monotone wailing, an eerie chanting that she knows is not right for a child. The sound of it is worse than the sight of the rats. She pushes aside her own terror. She gathers the child to her. She places the flashlight on the cot to chase away the shadows and she sings to him lullabies that have sprung up from some deep underground stream.

The following day she gives all her money to Dave.

"Thanks," he says, "I'll never forget this."

The next day he is gone. He takes the money and Rocky and vanishes. Del waits several days and then joins her parents in Toronto. Betty never sees any of them again.

"What, not finished packing yet?"

It's a question put to Betty by the youngest child. The one she's packing for, the one she's played Brahms and Bach to and hung delicate-sounding chimes above the crib for; the youngest is leaving home. She stands on the braided oval mat with two large parcels clutched against her small breasts. Her questioning eyes are Frank's brown eyes, surprised, but good-naturedly puzzled by her mother's dreaming. Frank calls Betty a rare bird and has given her what she's needed. All Betty had when she married Frank was the new red shoes. He makes jokes about that now.

Somewhere, a child grew up without me, she wishes to tell the youngest. He has as much to do with shaping your existence here as have the first settlers, the women who cranked out their years in a one-room sod house, the Indians who hunted these plains for buffalo, or the Mennonite farmers. But she won't say it. She will, instead, move the memory out across an ancient lake and leave it there to find its rest among the glaciers.

14 / The Bride Doll

"A pretty wedding was solemnized," Virginia Colpitts read. "Pink and white peonies and blue delphinium in white baskets were placed on the altar and satin bows designated pews reserved for the guests."

Virginia and I lay out on a blanket in her back yard. We had always lived on the same street. First she had lived at the top of the street in an unpainted, unsteady house which had not survived the last flooding of the river, and then at the bottom of the street, in a bright new bungalow.

We lay in the shadow of a red barn, seeking shelter from the hot dry wind, and read accounts of weddings, placing ourselves inside the church as honored guests. I was smitten by the descriptions of veils, seed pearls and lily-point sleeves. I imagined satin to be as iridescent as moths' wings, shiny and silvery. I gleaned notices of weddings from the columns in the *Agassiz Herald* and then on Saturdays, Virginia and I waited outside to catch a glimpse of the newly married couple as they came from the church, looking over-starched with self-consciousness. Where once the couple had been as close as Siamese twins, they stood apart, awkward in their new state. I imagined doves fluttering above their heads.

Even though I had been taught not to pray for tangible things as that was a mark of selfishness (a waste of God's valuable time when one considered the numberless starving children), I prayed fervently for a bride doll.

"Why do you want one?" my mother asked.

"Because," was all I could say as I lay in the gutted bedroom where wall boards had been pulled loose and moist wood shavings tumbled free in order to dry. Wet shavings would swell and cause a fire, my father said.

Instead of praying for bride dolls, it was better to confess

sins, my mother said, and then to try to make right the
wrongs we did. And what about the crusts of bread I'd hidden
behind furniture because I didn't want to eat them? I was told
to think of those poor starving children and so that night I
crawled beneath the bed and fished a crust of bread out from a
corner and I ate it. Stinging pain sent me into my parents'
room where, to their horror, my mouth lit up with the
phosphorus glow of rat poison.

When I imagine myself as I was then, I see a slightly
chubby person with legs as stocky as tree trunks, standing
solidly in the middle of a tangled, confused yard. About me,
in the ruined furniture and rotting lumber, is the reminder of
chaos, an event which had turned our lives topsy turvey. But I
can't remember the actual flooding of the river, I can only
recall the immediate years after it, being warned not to touch
any of the debris, to wash my hands thoroughly before meals,
of things like diphtheria and having one's jaw locked shut. But
the worst was the tearing down and re-building of our house.

When I look at photographs from around that time, I am
usually wearing a white dress. The thick lenses of my glasses
are heavy and they slide down my nose as I frown to keep
them in place while I am forever peering out through the
heavy blond bangs of my over-grown butch cut. A shoemaker's
children need shoes, my mother said, a butcher's, meat. And
we were always in need of a haircut. In most group
photographs, I am either turned right around or looking off at
something to the side of me. I was a sheet of jelly then, a
hectograph, the old copier teachers used to prepare our work.
They wrote on the gelatin with an indelible pencil (it was
poison, we were warned not to chew on it). As the year
progressed, the faint ghosts of past tests, the damp outlines of
art work, criss-crossed, becoming a road map of the whole
year.

Virginia never tanned or was affected by the sun in any
way but my legs and face grew prickly and red in the hot
wind. While we lay out there on the blanket, I wished I could

climb above it, up where the vapor trails of jet planes arched into the sun, away from the whining of the electric saw and the hollow thud of a hammer echoing in the trees in the park as across a field, Mr. Pankratz finished building his new house.

Pankratz, the packrat, we'd named him because he'd built the house almost entirely from scrap. He'd paid little for the land because it bordered the edge of town and would be on the wrong side of the dike once it was in place. My father had branded him a "plain damned fool," but I didn't think he was that harmless. I walked in wide circles around the man to escape his clammy, pale hands which were forever reaching to pat my arm or the top of my head. In spring, my father said, water would back up from the river into the first and then the second park, flow across the road and completely surround Mr. Pankratz's house. So the man had built it up, had hauled in fill to raise the foundation as high as the level of the last flood. As a result, the house looked down over the whole town, the park, the bridge which spanned the Red River and the highway climbing to meet St. Mary's Road as it wound past Horseshoe Lake.

When Mr. Pankratz came to build our kitchen cupboards, my mother asked him why he had chosen to live there. "It must be terrible for mosquitoes," she said. And the park was a strange place in spring with oak trees standing in water, reflected back over and over. Once the water subsided, the ground remained soft and overnight, flesh-white toadstools, spongy and tall, sprung up from dampness. Virginia and I played down there. We told no one. The park floor was littered with flood-contaminated stock from the drugstore and off-limits. We played wedding. We collected toadstools and laid them out on wild rhubarb leaves for the wedding feast. Do you take this man as your lawful wedded husband? I asked. Do you take this woman to be your awful wife? Virginia would say, laughing, spoiling the ceremony. To her it was a game, the same as playing Dale Evans and Roy Rogers.

Mr. Pankratz removed his painter's cap and ran his hand

across his smooth bald head when my mother asked him why he chose to build his house on the outskirts of town. He took his pencil out from behind his ear, squinted and said, "The town is for families. What would an old bachelor like me want in town?"

He's worse than an old woman, my mother complained because Mr. Pankratz liked to tell stories while he built the cupboards. He liked his new house, he told us. Know what he liked about it the most? My brothers and sisters and I were sitting on the floor around galvanized wash tubs, washing mud from my mother's canning sealers. I could see my mother's shoulders bunch with irritation. "I wouldn't know," she said.

"The indoor toilet," he said and set aside the board he was about to cut, freeing his hands to illustrate some point in the story with a bunched fist or a sweeping motion. He had been thinking that morning when he got up, what a good thing it was that he no longer needed to worry about digging another pit for the outhouse. The indoor toilet in his new house was the best thing. When he'd lived on the farm, of all the chores, he'd hated moving the outhouse most. When the lime had been dumped into the pit too often the ground all around the outhouse became spongy. He was afraid that someday he would step off the narrow plank and sink up to his knees. Then it would be up to him to dig another hole, move the outhouse onto it and fill in the other.

"The job came to me, everytime," he complained. "I always did all the dirty work. Take David for instance," Mr. Pankratz said in a wounded voice to remind us of his sacrifice, how he had taken his sister's boy so she could be free to marry and move away to British Columbia and not have to live with the tragedy of David, who had stopped growing the day they discovered him up-ended in a water-filled rain barrel. "My sister has written only twice this year," he whined. "And I don't think she will even come to the wedding."

Throughout all the hammering and the sporadic whine of the electric saw, David sat on a chair outside, leaning against

the house, blond head bent over his lap as he chipped and
coaxed oddly shaped animals from blocks of wood his uncle
had discarded. All the while, he smiled at something we
couldn't see. When he walked, he seemed to feel his way
along, as though he traveled through a dream.

"The bride chose a waltz-length dress, featuring a
cummerbund and a lace bolero," Virginia read from the
Agassiz Herald. What was waltz length? I wondered as I
watched David's intense carving and Mr. Pankratz's struggle
with a sheet of chalk board. Drywall, it is called now, but we
called it chalk board because when it crumbled we salvaged
pieces to draw our hopscotch on the sidewalks. Mr. Pankratz's
house was new, but looked old. The roof had come from many
roofs, the windows from the old school. And the style of it
was like all the other old houses in Agassiz, like the one I
lived in, a tall, two-story house, windows arranged
unimaginatively, two up and two down.

"You are welcome to come to the wedding of Lena Harms
to David Pankratz, July 12, at 2 pm," the note read. There was
no posting an announcement in the *Agassiz Herald* for this
wedding. The announcement came in the form of a note
delivered by a small child, which we were instructed to pass
on from door to door. When my mother finished laughing, she
let me read it. "Feel free to invite a friend. Come and bring
your own refreshments," it said. The wording of the note had
been the bride's mother's idea, Mr. Pankratz explained, his
weathered cheeks flaring red. "She says in Paraguay, at a
wedding, the whole village comes. For this reason, I thought it
best we hold the affair at my place."

I had been inside the Harmses' house with Virginia when
she went to collect for the newspaper and I agreed. The family
had come from Paraguay the previous year. There had been
gossip about the father and the family having been sent from
the Mennonite colony because of something he'd done. They
lived in a bricksiding cottage which had been badly flooded.
You can't trust bricksiding, my father said. It doesn't let

moisture escape and a house can look perfectly sound from the outside but be rotten to the core. The Harmses' house had three rooms for fourteen people. Along the walls, boxes filled with clothing were stacked one on top of another. The women of the town had collected the clothing when the family had disembarked at the train station in the dead of winter wearing only thin muslin. Each day, the children pulled what they would wear from the boxes. All around us in the cramped kitchen were children. They sat on the table, squatted on the floor, babies lay on a cot beside the stove, all dark-eyed, dark-skinned. One swung down from the top of the door and stared at us with lively eyes, eyes like the eldest, Lena's, the color of black walnut. Dirty faces peered in at us through the window. When we'd come into the yard, we'd noticed a gas-powered washing.machine standing idle and Lena bending over a pile of clothing on the ground. A kettle boiled on a hot plate.

No understand, no understand, the woman said in broken English. She pushed her feet into a pair of man's plaid slippers and took the kettle from the hot plate. We followed her outside with most of the children. Lena stood beside the washing machine on one foot, scratching at the back of her leg with the other. She was taller than her mother, slender, a strong nose, not the fleshy little ball of a nose that her mother possessed. For two days she'd sat behind me in school in a desk that was too small for her so that she had to turn sideways in it and her tanned, sandaled foot bobbed up and down in the center of the aisle. Turn around, the teacher warned me when I couldn't stop staring. Lena's heavy black braids trailed down from her shoulders and lay against her full breasts. At recess, the boys turned rope for her so she could jump and they could watch her breasts bouncing beneath the paisley print dress. But she never knew. She skipped and laughed and you could tell she thought she was one of us.

Despite all the children, the jumble of clothing, I remember that the house was clean and the woman herself

The Bride Doll   187

radiated the pleasant odor of oranges. Virginia and I explained why we had come. The woman and girl spoke to each other in Spanish. The mother frowned. No money, she explained. No money for anything. Not for gasoline. My husband, he take for his car, she said, ducking her head in a shy manner. She shouted to the children in Spanish and they came running with a pail. Gasoline, gasoline, they cried in high musical voices as they went from door to door.

But if the wording of the wedding letter had been the mother's idea, the marriage itself had been Mr. Pankratz's. He'd been walking down in the second park on the west side of the bridge where the trees were dense and it was cooler, he said. He'd looked up and saw David and the girl walking along the bridge. Why did she come every evening to lean on his fence and call for David? he wondered and had followed them, he told my mother, because he worried about David getting lost. And as he saw how she held David's hand, and how willingly he followed, the idea had come streaking down and "hit me like a bolt of lightning. Too soon oldt, too late schmart," he said. "I'm not getting any younger," he told my mother. "David needs someone to watch out for him."

"But is she able?" my mother asked. She shook her hands free of soap suds, slipped her wedding band back on and sat down for once, to listen. I wondered what her wedding dress had looked like. When I asked, she put me off, saying that it was not a regular dress, but pretty, and had buttons at the shoulder. There was no photograph of my parents' wedding in the album, although all her relatives were there in their matrimonial finery. There was only one photograph of them together and it was a surprising picture. My mother sat on my father's knee, bare legs exposed and on her feet, tiny pointed-toed shoes with bows. Her hair was longer than I ever remember her wearing it. She had swept it up behind one ear and the other side swung forward, a dark wedge against her white skin. A dark-haired Marlene Dietrich. She raised a glass to the person behind the camera. My father rested his chin on her shoulder and laughed. What was the occasion? I wondered. She didn't remember. A party of some sort. It was before, she searched for the words, before, she said. Before the flooding of the river? No, no, long before that. It was before I became a better person, she said without explaining.

"The mother says that in Paraguay they teach girls in school all things a woman should know," Mr. Pankratz said.

"Be that as it may," my mother said. "There's more to it than cooking and cleaning. She looks so young. She doesn't look any older than thirteen or fourteen."

"Sixteen," Mr. Pankratz said. The air was thick with sawdust and the warm smell of wood. A two-by-four thundered to the floor. "It's a good bargain for the girl to get her out of that place," Mr. Pankratz said. "And the mother sees it as well. It'll be one less mouth for her to feed."

My mother sighed. "Well, they will make a nice couple," she said. "Lena is a good-looking girl."

"He only wants someone to wash his dirty socks," she said when Mr. Pankratz had gone.

Virginia folded the newspaper and held it against her chest. The sun transformed dry patches on her arms into silvery scales. Virginia and I were best friends. She had psoriasis and I, the coke-bottle eye glasses. "Dolores uses Kotex now," Virginia said. She scratched at her arms and blinked in the sunlight. Her eyes were always red-rimmed and sore-looking.

I didn't want to know what Kotex was but she took me inside the house which smelled sharply of aging varnish and cough medicine, a smell I thought came with their old house, but the odor had followed them here. Charlie Colpitts would walk a mile to get out of work, people said of Virginia's father and I associated the smell of the house with sloth. Mrs. Colpitts was a nurse at the hospital. She had scooped babies up from between legs, washed backs and bottoms and poked into bed pans and so people knew enough to leave the Colpittses alone. Mrs. Colpitts, Verna, was a short, sharp-featured woman with hair as stiff and unmanageable as Virginia's and Dolores's. She was the possessor of special knowledge. When I told her what my mother had said about Mr. Pankratz wanting someone to wash his socks, her face snapped to attention. His socks worsht, she said. Huh. As long as that's all he wants.

Virginia and I stood in Dolores's closet, examining a Kotex pad. "She puts it between her legs," Virginia explained. I resisted the explanation. I did not want to envision anything blotted or stained beneath satin skirts. "No, no," Virginia said. "They plan for that. They count the days so it won't happen."

The day of the wedding my mother sent me to Mr. Pankratz's house with a batch of buns. The sun had risen above the horizon which, beyond the shock of twisted oak trees in the park, was the stark horizontal line of St. Mary's Road. Above Horseshoe Lake, a veil of mist would be lifting and in the shallow ditches, ivory clouds of yarrow bobbed in a green sea. The bittersweet scent of a prickly rose bush growing thickly among the rusting shell of a car made my throat ache. As I walked, I remembered the same road muddy and slick after the flood and the sudden sound of rushing water stopping me dead. There, inches before my feet, the road fell away into a large hole. I stood mesmerized, watching with horror the yellow water roaring and tumbling beneath the road, carrying rocks and debris along with it. A temporary underground stream, my father explained but it didn't diminish the feeling I had of a world surging beneath my feet and I about to be swallowed and swept along underground with it.

I pictured my destination. I imagined that Mr. Pankratz had knocked lightly on the groom's door as he passed into the kitchen and heard the immediate, anxious reply of the bedsprings and then footsteps as David followed him into the kitchen. It was one of the "dirty jobs" Mr. Pankratz had explained to my mother, teaching David not to arise in the morning until he knocked. One winter David had wandered away from the house in his night clothes and suffered frost bite. I imagined the two men bent in silence over their breakfast plates, eating quickly, almost furtively, but as I entered the yard, I heard voices and came upon them behind the house on their hands and knees, weeding the garden.

"Already, visitors," Mr. Pankratz greeted me, scrambling to his feet. The glint of metal in the seat of his pants caught my eye. Once Mr. Pankratz had been crawling across a roof and split the seam in his trousers and he had used a length of stove-pipe wire to hold it together. Wired for sound, people joked. Old Pankratz doesn't want to miss a thing. Would the bride be required to mend his pants? From the park came the sudden scolding of a squirrel. Startled upright by the sound, David listened, a weed still clenched in his fist.

"Look who's here," Mr. Pankratz said to David, touching him to draw his attention. "Look what she brought." But David never looked at any of us directly. He seemed to be in another place, the place where his animal carvings took shape. From a fir tree at the back of the yard came the coo of a mourning dove. The sound was right for that time of day while the air was still cool and the dew had not yet been burned off by the sun. The sound was like gently moving air, like my mother's sigh.

I wondered what the bride was doing at that very moment. Mr. Pankratz had given the mother money to buy a dress, he'd said, so she would look half-decent. Was she awaking, stretching and yawning and seeing the dress, did her heart beat faster?

"Tell your Momma, thank you," Mr. Pankratz said. As he took the buns from me, his cool hands brushed against mine and I stepped back quickly, feeling in my mind his sticky touch on my arm. "Hurry, hurry," he said sharply to David as he carried the still-warm buns into the house. "They aren't going to be able to make their bachelor jokes about my garden today."

From across the field came the sound of Virginia's india

The Bride Doll   191

rubber ball smacking against the cement and calling me to play.

The sun was hot and high in the sky, casting short, sharp shadows in the dirt of the yard when Virginia, Mrs. Colpitts and I crossed the field to the wedding. Mrs. Colpitts had allowed us to paint our nails for the occasion and I admired the poppy-red splashes on my hands. My mother, several of my sisters and brothers, and a few other women were already there. My father would not close down his barber shop to come. The only time he had ever closed his shop was when my oldest sister insisted on getting married on a Saturday, and then it was only for half a day. Mr. Pankratz and David had changed from their work clothes into white shirts and black pants. They sat on a makeshift bench, leaning against the house, waiting. And then, as though people had agreed to arrive at the same time, a line of cars traveled down the dirt road, slowly and almost silently. The brittle call of a crow down in the park grated at our silent expectancy. People came walking, carrying dishes and pans of food. Mr. Pankratz nodded his greeting to each one. The women, with quiet efficiency, began setting the food out on the table which Mr. Pankratz had made of plyboard and sawhorses. We strolled about the yard waiting for the arrival of the bride. Mr. Pankratz mopped his ruddy face and squinted at us from behind his handkerchief. Sit still, my mother cautioned. I sat on a chair and thought the people were like chickens, the way they glanced at David from the sides of their faces, advancing towards him so far, as though they might peck him on the leg, and then veering away quickly at the last moment. The way they craned their necks to peer down the road to see if the bride was coming. David whittled at a piece of wood, seeming not to notice any of us.

And then suddenly, everyone fell silent. Even the smallest ones paused in their restless games to see what was happening. My throat began to tighten. The crow flapped up from the trees in the park, laughing loudly as two smaller birds cried and darted about its head. At the top of the road, we could hear a flutter of sound, a light tinny clamor and then, growing louder, it became the voices of children singing. We all stood up. Down the road they came, the entire Harms family, barefoot children jumping around Lena in circles singing, "She's a bride, she's a bride. Lena is a bride." The older ones carried smaller ones on their hips. The parents each carried a bundle. Closer and closer they came, dancing and laughing and shouting in Spanish. My dress stuck to my back. My heart twisted at the sight of the bride and the pink flowers in her arms. Everyone stood motionless, staring, as single file, the family crossed the plank that spanned the ditch. David pulled at Mr. Pankratz's arm and smiled suddenly. "Lena," he said. "It's Lena."

"What the hell," Mr. Pankratz swore softly. "She didn't buy the girl a dress."

On Lena's blue-black head, attached with many pins, was an ivory lace curtain. Her dress appeared to be a bedsheet gathered at the waist with a man's necktie. The flowers were plastic and coated with dust. People moved aside to let the family pass through into the yard, carrying with them the smell of dust and heat and oranges. The mother stood before the groom, foxtail fur wound tightly about her neck. Above it, perspiration beaded her wide mottled face.

"I bring her to you," she said and dropped the bundle at his feet.

Mr. Pankratz stepped forward, his white hands on Lena's dark skin as he drew her towards him and led her over to David's side.

The father stood before them, grinning and nodding his approval. His dark hair, slicked straight back, shone with oil. "How you say. Good luck?" He looked to see if anyone appreciated his humor.

Lena's bold smile revealed large, straight teeth. She turned and spoke to two girls behind her who scrambled about

The Bride Doll   193

arranging the curtain veil until it fanned out across the grass like a frayed fish tail.

I heard a sharp intake of breath. "Pity the poor thing." I thought I heard my mother's voice.

"Well, he's a better person than I to take the both of them on," a man said.

About me, I saw the evidence of laughter withheld in the flickering of muscles around mouths. Tears welled and spurted behind my glasses. "She's beautiful," I heard myself say. "The bride is beautiful."

Mr. Pankratz cleared his throat noisily. The women began to nod. "Yes of course, isn't she lovely?" someone said quickly.

"More than that. Every bride is lovely, but Truda is right, she is beautiful," my mother said as I ran from the yard crying.

"Well missy, what was that scene all about?" my mother asked.

She removed her hat and set it down on top of the china cupboard. The cupboard stood in the center of the dining room instead of its usual place against the wall beside the chimney. The linoleum had been ripped up from the floor, revealing the rippled floorboards beneath. Light filtering through the curtains made the air seem granular and gray. I imagined I could see molecules dancing in front of me. My mother had gone visiting after the wedding. As she set her hat down, a splash of gold sunlight rested on her cheek.

"A curtain," my mother said, not waiting for my reply. "Imagine. I think it was one of the things I sent over there." The floor boards groaned suddenly beneath our feet. A crack zigzagged up the wall behind her head. She frowned uneasily. My father had come home and gone into the basement to work. For weeks he'd been jacking the house up in an attempt to level the floors. Easy does it, he said. And little by little, the warped, twisted house was being straightened. The house groaned and china plates shivered in the cabinet. A chunk of plaster broke loose from the ceiling and scattered on the floor. "Oh Lord," my mother said. I was about to turn from the sight of it when my mother's hands flew up in front of her face. She shrieked. The china cupboard wobbled forward, dishes sliding together. Her shriek rose above the sound of shattering china as the cupboard crashed to the floor.

My father came running and stood in the doorway, red-faced and panting. "Is everything all right?" he asked.

My mother folded up and crumpled to her knees. "Is everything all right?" she cried. "Look, look at what you've done," she said and raising her hands to the cracked walls, the crumbling ceiling, she began to cry.

My father stepped forward and then flung the crowbar he'd been carrying across the room. "It was an accident, for God's sake, Mika," he said. "It's only dishes. I thought it was something serious."

My mother's voice cracked. "But it was all I had," she said. "It was all I had left."

My brothers and sisters stood gaping. I left the house. My mother's cries were as birds' wings churning the air about my head as I ran down the road. Breathless and chilled, I leaned against the red barn, my back warmed by heat trapped in the weathered boards. I waited until the china scraps were gathered and scattered into the garden and the cabinet thrown on top of the heap of rubble in the back of the yard. I waited beside the red barn until I saw them later on, before my sister came calling and searching for me. The wedding couple walked among the trees in the park in their wedding clothes, two pale ghosts moving among the purple shadows, a flutter of silver and white. The following day, in the heat of high noon, they stood beside the road, waist-deep in the bobbing yarrow, holding hands, and smiled at me. Another evening, I saw them out by Horseshoe Lake while thunder rolled over the cattails and the air hung thick with the scent of a storm. And one night as I watched from a window in my tall narrow house, the groom held the bride's veil high as they walked up and down the streets of town and no one laughed. Below them in the flood-littered park, for a fractured second, among the toadstools a lady slipper glowed, singly and silent.

15 / Falling in Love

I get off the bus and I stand beside the highway at Jordon Siding, wondering what to do now. I've come to a dead end. Stopped by the reality of a churned-up landscape. For shitsake, as Larry, the past-love-of-my-life, would say. Today, in late June, while the fields around me are growing towards harvest, I am empty. I'm split in two. One part of me can think, what are you going to do? And the other is off somewhere, wandering through empty rooms, bumping into dusty furniture, hoping that this may be a dream. And that Larry is still here.

"I'm sorry you didn't know, ah," the bus driver searches for the correct word. Am I Miss or Ma'am? He pushes his cap back onto his chunky, sandy head and glances down and then away from my breasts which nudge out against Larry's denim shirt. No, I'm not wearing a bra. His glance is at once shifty and closed as though he, too, is guilty of betraying me. And immediately, I'm glad that at least I have not made the mistake of being pregnant. Grateful that I never gave in to those odd flashes of desire to make love without a contraceptive, to play a kind of roulette game with sex.

"Didn't they tell you when you bought the ticket that the road was under construction?" the bus driver asks. His eyes take in the shoebox I carry beneath my arm, tied closed with butcher string, air holes punched in it so Satan can breathe. A going-away present from Larry, a black rabbit. He has taken off, Larry has, has flown the coop and left me with the rabbit and one measly shirt to remind me of him. Larry, I'm remembering you in the briny smell of armpits.

I remember this morning, the acne-faced girl in the coffee shop at the bus depot in Manitou saying something about having to go to Winnipeg and then back south to get to

Agassiz. But my mind wasn't paying attention. I was aware
instead of her squinty mean eyes enjoying the lapsed state of
my affair. Larry Cooper is wild, I'd been warned, and he's
lazier than a pet coon. And I told myself that they were just
jealous. There are no callipers wide enough to measure the
scoured sides of my stupidity. This year, I have learned
something about the eternal combustion engine, about love.

Before me, where I should be making my connection with
another Grey Goose bus that will carry me thirty miles east
across farming country to Agassiz and back into the bosom of
my family, the road is a muddy upheaval of rocks, slippery clay
and top-soil. Under destruction. The whole world is under
destruction. Larry used the word 'dead-end'. And so he has
turned the other way, headed down the highway to Montreal
to work in his brother-in-law's car rental business.

If you love someone, let him go, Larry's mother said. And
if he comes back, he's yours. Whatever you do, don't take this
thing personal, okay? Larry's like that. Every spring, he takes
off. Spring fever, it's in his blood, she said. And then she
evicted me.

"You'd better get back on the bus and make your
connection in Winnipeg," the driver says and it's clear from
his tone that he's decided I'm a Miss which gives him certain
authority. I'm aware of faces in the windows looking out at
me, slight amusement at my predicament. I see in the window
my greasy black hair tied up into a pony tail, Larry's shirt, my
jeans held at the waist with safety pins because I have lost ten
pounds. My luggage is an Eaton's shopping bag.

When I woke up and discovered Larry missing, I didn't
worry at first because he often went out riding before dawn.
He liked to be alone in the early morning. Larry liked to
watch the sun rise. He's out ripping off truck parts, you mean,
his mother said, raising an artfully plucked eyebrow and
flicking cigarette ashes into her coffee cup. But she didn't
know Larry the way I thought I did. He would come back to
me, crawl beneath the sheets, hairy limbs still cool from the

early morning air, breath minty and sweet, and he would wind himself around me and describe the color of the sun on a barn roof, or the distinct clatter of a tractor starting up. On such a morning, he brought Satan to me because he said its shiny black coat, its constant nibbling reminded him of me. On such a morning, he came home and invented a gadget that cooked wieners electrically. He stuck wires into each end of the wiener, plugged it into the wall and instant, cooked wiener. Another morning, he was inspired to try to build a more effective water pump.

I lay in bed waiting for Larry, looking up at the new ceiling tiles overhead. His mother let us live rent-free in those three rooms above the butcher shop if we fixed the caved-in ceiling. I liked the suite the way it was when we first moved in, sawdust and shavings ankle-deep on the floor, ceiling slats dangling free, the lone lightbulb suspended by a single twined wire. It was early Canadian Catastrophe. It reminded me that when I met Larry, I was sitting in the hotel cafe in Agassiz, between jobs, waiting for the world to end. For a year, I'd had the feeling that a bomb was going to drop and that would be the end of us all. For this reason, I left school. I was filling in time, waiting, and then Larry walked in and I thought that if the bomb fell that day, I'd rather be dead with him than anyone else.

But Larry wouldn't live with a caved-in ceiling and when he'd fixed that, he enameled the kitchen counters black. And the paint never quite dried and if we let a dish stand on it overnight, it became permanently stuck there. And then I went crazy and hand-stitched curtains for the windows in the front room. Larry nailed Christmas tree lights onto the wall above the couch and we made love in their multi-colored glow. We made love every single day for six months.

I waited for Larry to return and listened at the same time to the rats thumping about in the butcher shop below, dragging bones from the bone box. (I never minded the rats, I figured they worked hard for what they got.) Above me, near the ceiling, a shaft of light came through the small window, spotlighting Larry's note taped to the closet door. I knew before reading it that Larry had left me. I have this built-in premonition for bad news. As I reached for the note, I could smell Larry, like alkali, dry, metallic, in the palms of my hands. And scattered in the sheets were his c-shaped blond pubic hairs. I read the note and it was as though a thick, black, woolen hood had fallen suddenly into place over my head.

Two days later, Larry's mother dropped by. She told me to get out of bed. She wanted her sheets back. She had me clean out the fridge. I have brought along the left-overs of our relationship in the shopping bag. Lettuce for Satan, a dimpled, wilted grapefruit and one beer. And resentment, which is a thick sludge clogging my chest. If Larry, by some miracle, showed up now, I would jump on his skinny back, grab hold of his blond hair and wrestle him to the ground. I would stomp on his adam's apple.

"Forget it," I say to the bus driver. "I'm not going all the way to Winnipeg. Just forget it."

He laughs. "I don't see what choice you have." He puts his sunglasses back on and I can see myself in them. And it seems to me that he, along with everyone else, conspires against me. That I have never had a choice.

"You looked at my ticket when I got on. Why didn't you say something?"

"I thought you knew."

I pick up the shopping bag and begin to walk away. "Well, I didn't. And I'm not spending three bloody hours on the bus. So, I guess I'll walk."

He blocks my way. "Whoa, Agassiz is thirty miles away. And it's going to be one hot day." He scans the cloudless sky.

Larry, you creep. This is all your fault. "What's it to you whether I walk or ride?"

The driver's thick neck flares red. He steps aside. "Right.

It's no skin off my nose. If you want to walk thirty miles in the blazing sun, go ahead. It's a free country."

The bus roars down the highway, leaving me in a billow of hot sharp-smelling smoke. The sound of the engine grows fainter and then I'm alone, facing that churned-up muddy road where no vehicle could ever pass. Thirty bloody miles. God-damn you, Larry. I hear a meadowlark trilling and then a squealing rhythmic sound of metal on metal. It comes from a BA gas sign swinging back and forth above two rusting gas bowsers that stand in front of a dilapidated wood-frame building. Jordon Siding garage and store. Eureka. A telephone. I will call home and say, guess what? No, I'll say, it's your prodigal daughter, to get them thinking along charitable lines. I have seen the light. But all that is another issue, one I don't have the energy to think about. Plants fill the dusty store window and off to one side, a tiny yard, freshly laundered clothes flutter from a clothesline.

I enter the dim interior and feel surrounded. The atmosphere is dreary, relentlessly claustrophobic. It's a typical country store and yet it reminds me of old things, of fly-specked calendars, lambs and young girls in straw hats smiling with cherry-painted lips, innocent smiles. And me pulling a toboggan through the streets of Agassiz each New Year, collecting calendars, trekking through the fragile blue sphere of a winter night that seemed to embrace all ages so that as I bumped along ice and snow I thought, years ago, someone like me was doing this, may still be doing this. But at the same time, I felt the world dangling like a bauble about to shatter on the floor. I went to the garages, grocery stores, the bank. I needed many calendars because during the coming year each time a month ended, I wrote messages on the backs of the spent time and hid the messages in the garden, in flower pots, beneath stones, for people from another world to discover when I would be gone. A fly buzzes suddenly against the window, trapped between the foliage of the plants and the glass. Beyond, a counter, glass casing, but there's nothing inside it but shelf-lining, old newspapers.

"Hello, anyone here?" I call in the direction of the back rooms behind the varnished counter where I imagine potatoes boil in a pot, a child sleeps on a blanket on the floor while its mother ignores my voice, sits in an over-stuffed chair (the type Larry and I inherited with our suite, an olive green, scratchy velour couch and chair), reading a magazine. What is she reading? I wonder. I look about me. No telephone in sight.

Outside once again, I face that bleak landscape and begin walking in the direction of Agassiz. I face the sun and walk off to the side of the road, following the deep imprint left behind by one of the monstrous yellow machines that sits idle in the field beyond. Why aren't there any men on the machines? Why aren't they working today? I begin to feel uneasy. The sounds of the countryside rise up and Satan thumps violently against his box in answer. Around me stretch broad fields dotted with clumps of trees. In the distance a neat row of elms, planted as a windbreak, shade a small farmhouse and outbuildings. Overhead, the flat cloudless sky, no perspective, I cannot gauge distance. It's as though this is a calendar picture of a landscape and I have somehow entered it. Except for yellow grasshoppers sprinting up before my feet and the tireless hovering of flies above the ditches, there is no movement anywhere. I turn around. The garage is still the same distance. I can turn back and wait for a car and hitch a ride to Winnipeg. I could go back to Manitou. But it seems to me that I have been set in this direction, that it's inevitable. I walk for an hour. Satan continues to struggle. I stop to rest, lift the lid off the box a crack and push wilted lettuce through to him. I sit down, take Larry's note from my shirt pocket and unfold it on my knee.

Dear Lureen,
  I'm sorry if you got your hopes up. Like the song goes, you always hurt the one you love, the one you shouldn't hurt

at all. That's life. But this town is a dead-end. You know
what I mean. I think I'll take my sister up on her offer.

You are okay. Don't think I'm leaving because of you. I
know you will get over me. Anyway, if it works out, I'll send
you some money. I might send you enough to come to
Montreal. I'll see. It just depends.

You can have Satan. I don't trust my mother to look
after him anyway. Once, she forgot to feed my goldfish and
they all turned belly-up. Notice, I am leaving you my denim
shirt because you liked it so much.

Tell the old lady not to get in a sweat.

Luv U,

Larry.

Whatever you do, Larry's mother said when he introduced
us, don't get married. A cigarette dangled from one corner of
her mouth and she squinted at me hard through the blue
smoke. She was blond like Larry and I thought that at one
time she must have been beautiful, you could see flashes of it
sometimes when she wasn't being sarcastic. I'm only telling
you for your own good, she said later when Larry was out of
the room. He's like his father. Lazier than a pet coon.

Larry was not lazy. He could pull the head off a motor,
ream out the cylinders, do a ring and valve job in two days
flat. I'd tell him I wanted to go to the dance at Rock Lake and
he'd rebuild the transmission that afternoon so we could go.
He opened the housing, called me down the stairs to come
and see the giant cogs, how the gears were supposed to mesh.
And I couldn't help think that the combustion engine is a
joke, or at least a hoax perpetuated on man to keep him busy
tinkering so he can't think about what's really happening.
Wheels moving wheels, moving pulleys, moving more metal
and so much motion for so little effect, arms, lifters, valves,
wheezing breathers, springs, filters, cylinders, shoes, things
pressing against other things, grinding, particles of chewed-up
metal sifting into other important parts. God, it was

overwhelming. Faulty timing, a coughing, farting engine, a rotten swaying front end, screeching wheelbearings, all these problems Larry and I faced and overcame in six months.

Okay Larry, I said, wanting to say, this is silly. There has got to be a much simpler way than the eternal combustion engine.

Internal, internal combustion engine, he said, and anyway, you are paid not to think, but to do. So, okay, I played the game. I soaked bolts and other metal shapes in my dishpan, brushed them down with Varsol, removed grease with a paring knife, had them looking like new. I learned how to install brushes in a generator. I took it apart in my lap. I thought the copper wires were beautiful. And then, that what I was doing was important. That maybe I'd like to have a part in the running of the internal combustion machine. And the next time Larry complained about having to wash his feet with his socks on, maybe I'd let him ride bareback for awhile. Maybe the two of us could open a garage?

Larry flicked the end of my nose with a greasy finger and said no way would he put in four years getting his papers just to satisfy some government-hired jerk who had never taken apart anything more complicated than a Zippo lighter.

And always, we made it to the dance on time. That night, we'd be cruising down the highway, eating up the miles to Rock Lake, radio turned up full volume, Larry driving with two fingers and reaching with his other hand for me, naked beneath my sundress. And the gears would be meshing and the motor singing, the timing tuned just right and the radio playing all our favorite hits. And Larry would squeeze my breast and say, hey, honey bunch. Remind me to slow down long before we get to the corner, okay? I got no brakes.

Ancient history. Ancient bloody history. I rest my head against my knees and I don't want to cry, Larry's not worth it, but I do. And then I take the lid off the shoebox and I pet Satan for a few moments and then I carry him to the side of the road and drop him into the tall grass. He scurries away without a backward glance.

Do you think it's true, Larry said, turning away from me to examine his naked physique in the mirror, that a large ass means a short sex life? That's what my mother told me.

And I spent the next two hours convincing him that she was wrong and that he had the neatest, hardest, turned-in buttocks I had ever seen. Bullshit. I wish for Larry an extremely short sex life. May he never have sex again. I pick up the shopping bag, swing it back and forth a couple of times and let loose. It flies across the ditch and whacks against the telephone pole. Screw yourself Larry. Stick your scrawny dink in your ear.

Free now, I walk faster, arms swinging, following the fishbone tire pattern pressed into the yellow clay. I will go to Winnipeg, look for work. Or I will go to bed and stay there. Or I could go back to school. And then I hear a sound, the sound of a motor geared down low—Larry? My heart leaps. I wouldn't put it past him. Larry can do anything. Even materialize out of thin air. I look up. There on the crest of the muddy graded mound is a pale blue car, the bullet-nosed shape of a '51 Studebaker. It slithers sideways first one way and then the other. It stops, starts, makes its way slowly towards me. I see a man behind the wheel, copper-red hair, a brushcut. Not Larry. The car comes to a stop and the man opens the door. I measure the distance to the farmhouse beyond. Could I outrun him? He unfolds from the seat. He's match-like, tall and thin. He stands up, shakes creases from his gray slacks, tiptoes across the ruts in shiny brown penny loafers and I begin to relax, he looks harmless. He stretches out a long pale hand to me, it looks fragile, like worn porcelain. I keep my hands behind my back. He doesn't seem to mind and folds his, one overtop the other across his stomach. He tilts back slightly on his heels and smiles down at me. "Well, well. Bless you. This is the day that the Lord hath made. Let's just take a moment to rejoice in it." He breathes deeply. "Thank you, Jesus."

God. A Pentecostal fanatic. One of the holy rollers.

"I saw you coming down from the corner and I said to myself, 'Now there's the reason God had for waking you up this morning.' " He lifts his hand suddenly, pokes a long finger into his red hair and scratches.

A grasshopper leaps up between us and lands on the roof of the car. I can see a resemblance between the insect and the man: long limbs, angles, ball-bearing shaped eyes.

"So, you're stranded then," he says.

"I didn't know about this." I indicate the upturned road.

"No matter," he says. He flutters his flimsy hand in my direction and catches himself on the chin in the process. I begin to like him. His smile is wide, lights up his steel gray eyes. "Everything works out for the good in the end. For those that trust in Him. Where are you hoping to get to?"

Life, I want to say. I am hoping to get through life, but I don't think I will. "Agassiz."

"Agassiz. Well, well. The heavenly Father has given me business just outside of Agassiz. I can get you close to it. Closer than this. Didn't I say everything would work out?"

He leads the way around to the passenger side, opens the door and suddenly I feel awkward. Larry would let me crawl through the window before he'd think to open a door for me. The car is like new inside. The seats are covered in clear plastic. A sheet of plastic lies on the floor. On the dash is what looks to be a deck of playing cards but the box says, "Thought for Today." Clipped to the sun visor is another card that reads, "I am a Flying Farmer."

He turns the car around in stages and soon we are bumping down the road, mud scraping against the bottom of the car. Despite the good condition of the car, there's a slight ticking and I want to tell him that he ought to watch the valves but I don't think it would be polite. I look over my shoulder and sure enough, tell-tale blue smoke billows from the exhaust. He's a clumsy driver, shifts gears too soon, strains the engine, rides the clutch. And then the tires grab hold of a groove of deep ruts and he speeds up, letting the car find its own path.

"So, what's your story?" he asks after awhile.

"Story?"

"Sure. The Lord sends me lots of people. I know when someone has a story."

And so I begin the way I always do, with the question that makes people frown or shrug or walk away. "Have you ever thought that at this very moment, someone may be pressing a button and that the world may come to an end? And we'll all be instant cooked wieners?"

He laughs. "Now why would I want to waste my time thinking about that? I couldn't live with those negative thoughts hanging over my head all the time. I know that He is able to keep me against that day. Whatever a man thinks, that's what he is. And I think about all the good things we've got." He thumps the wheel for emphasis, sticks his head out the window. "Look around you, this country is *beaudyfull*. Good crops this year. The fields are white unto the harvest. Thank you, Jesus." He begins to hum to himself as we slither down the road. Then he sucks something loose from his teeth. "Cooked wieners, my, my. That just won't happen. Know how I know? Because I wouldn't be here right now if that was true. The Lord would have returned already if it was the end of the world and I wouldn't be here. I'd be with Him."

I know the story. I have been brought up on this. Graves opening, the rapture of the saints. People reaching towards a shining light. Whenever I heard the story, I would imagine grabbing hold of a tree on the way up so I could stay behind. "How do you know that's true?"

He laughs once again. "And how do you know that it isn't? It takes more faith to believe that it isn't true than to believe that it is. Know why? Because of hope. Man is born with hope right in him and you've got to go against the grain not to believe. Now tell me, what's the story behind the story? What brings you here today, to this place, this time?"

And suddenly, my tongue takes off and I tell him everything, about being young and hiding pieces of paper from the calendar that say, Whoever finds this, my name was Lureen Lafreniere, I lived in Agassiz, Manitoba. This month, when I was running, I slipped and fell and cut my hand on a sharp piece of ice. Five stitches.

"For awhile, I stopped doing this, I thought it was a silly thing to do. But it came back to me, the feeling, so strong, that I couldn't sit still in school. I had to get up and move, just do something, because I felt that something terrible was going to happen that would prevent me from . . . from. . . ."

"From doing all the things you want to do even though you aren't even sure what it is you want to do."

"Yes."

"There's nothing new under the sun. I've heard that one before."

"Yes, but just when man says, nothing is new, everything is the same as yesterday, then comes the end. Therefore, watch and wait."

He smiles and his smile makes me smile. "You know your scripture. Bless you sister."

And then I tell him how I met Larry, about the past six months, about the feeling of impending doom leaving me. I talk to him as though I have known him for years and he doesn't ever interrupt, just says, "whoops" and "bless you" when we hit large clumps of mud. I talk non-stop, as though this man were sent for just this reason. And when I finish, he doesn't answer for a long time, just squints near-sightedly at the road and I think that I have made a mistake. I hold my breath and wait for his sermon. The Thou Shalt Nots.

"You love him," he says finally and puts a long, slender, cool hand overtop mine.

"Yeah." I realize this is true. That I am in love with Larry.

While waiting for the world to end, I have fallen in love. I fell for Larry Cooper. I'm falling.

"Well, well. Love is great. Love is wonderful. The Lord knew what He was doing when He created Adam and Eve."

I wipe my eyes on Larry's denim shirt.

"That fella of yours will come back. You can be sure of that."

"He will?"

He squeezes my hand. "Believe it and it will happen. Tell yourself, Larry's coming back."

Shit. The power of positive thinking crap. "Larry's pretty stubborn, you don't know him like I do."

"Shh. I understand. You know Larry and you may be right. But that's only one side of it. Listen, this is my story. Long time ago, I was in a bad accident. A plane crash. I went down in the bush in northern Manitoba. I thought I was finished. I walked in circles for two days with a broken collarbone. When I came upon the plane the second time, I cried. Broke right down. And then a verse from the Bible came to me. It was, 'not by might, nor by power, but by my spirit.' It was the Lord telling me to trust Him. So I knelt in the bush and I prayed and I said, 'Okay God. I'm lost. I can't find the way myself. I've already tried. And I'm tired and I'm injured and so I have no choice. I'm going to trust you. Show me the way.' And I opened my eyes, got up, started walking and I hadn't walked more than five minutes and there in front of me was a road. A paved road. So you see, from my side of it, I was finished. There was nothing I could do. But from God's side, He had only just begun. And God knows Larry better than you do."

I want to say, I know how that happened. Often, when you try too hard, the answer escapes you. You have to give up and then the inner mind brings the answer to the surface. There wasn't anything supernatural about your experience. It happens all the time. I bite my tongue.

"That's very nice," I say.

He turns to me in astonishment. "Nice? I tell you about my wonderful experience, how the Lord delivered me and you say, 'that's nice'? It was more than nice, sister. It was a frigging miracle."

Would an angel swear? I ponder the question later that evening as I lie in bed in the front bedroom of my house in Agassiz. He dropped me off three miles from town, near the elevators, and when I turned to tell him, as a favor, that he'd better get the valves checked, the car had vanished. And I was shocked. I sat down beside the road to think about it. I rubbed my stiff calf muscles, my feet burned as though I had walked a great distance. And I came to the conclusion that I had imagined meeting that man. The mind can do that. It was a way of coping with the situation I was in. But the question intrigues me. Would an angel swear? And was that swearing? I have always imagined swearing to mean to swear on something, to have to prove in some way the fact that you are telling the truth. The error of not being trustworthy.

The reception I received from my family was surprising. My mother was strangely tender, as though I had fallen ill with a fever. My younger brothers and sisters regarded me as someone who had come from a long way away, a distant relative, and they were guarded and shy. "Are you expecting?" my mother asked while the two of us changed the linen on the bed in the front bedroom. And I said no, but that I wished I was. She flicked the sheet and smoothed it straight. "No you don't," she said. "You just think you do, but you really don't."

As I lie in bed, the sounds around me are all familiar. The town siren blares out the ten o'clock curfew. The curtains on the window are the same ones I've had since I can remember. But I pull the sheet up around me and I feel like a guest, a visitor in the home I grew up in. How will I ever be able to sleep without Larry?

I remember our first date. Larry showing off, climbing up on a snowplow in the municipal yards, starting it and ripping through the chainlink fence before he could figure out how to stop it. And later, driving eighty miles to Manitou to crawl across the roof of the butcher shop, breaking a window to get into the suite. Still wearing our parkas, it was bitterly cold, I gave up my virginity while our breath hung in clouds of frost in the air above us and the beer we'd bought popped the caps and climbed up in frosty towers from the bottles. Afterward, teeth chattering, we chewed frozen malt and Larry warmed my hands in his armpits.

The memory climbs up the back of my throat, finds its way into my eyes, leaks down the sides of my face into the pillow. Okay God. I'll give you this one chance. This miracle involves another person, his own stubborn will. I clench my teeth. I feel as though I am levitating off the bed. This is it. Thanks for bringing Larry back to me.

I sigh. I'm calm. Tension seeps from me as I lie in the room where I have first thought of love and making it happen. And I hear the breeze in the trees outside the window. I have hidden many particles of time beneath their branches. I see the faint glow of the town. And if I got up, I would see the green watertower and the siren on it that orders the movement of my town. I would see the skating rink, my father coming down from the corner on his way home from the Hotel, to the news that Lureen's back home. And then I hear it, a jangle of keys that stiffens my spine, sends my heart jumping. Then a cough. I'm rigid, listening. A whistle. I leap down the bed, pull aside the curtains and below I see him, his narrow pale face turned up to the window, Larry in his white windbreaker, collar turned up, the glow of his cigarette.

"Larry?"

"For shitsake. What's keeping you?" he asks.

And I run barefoot down the stairs, through the rooms, out the front door and then Larry catches me by the wrist and pulls me to him, wraps me around his skinny shivering body.

"Blew a rod at Thunder Bay," he says. "I couldn't fix it."

Liar. "I'm sorry," I say. He kisses me. His mouth is chilly

Falling in Love

and warm at the same time. I wedge my tongue between his shivering lips.

He pulls away. "I caught a ride with a real weirdo. He offered me fifty bucks if I'd jerk him off. So I said to hell with it and I took the first bus going west."

"Hey honey bunch," I whisper into his neck, "let's go to the park. We can talk tomorrow."

"The park, what for?" But I can feel him growing hard against my stomach. "I haven't got anything on me. You know." His tongue answers mine and it's like the faint fluttering of a moth.

I link my arm through his and lead him in the direction I want to go. "Oh, by the way, I let the rabbit loose."

He stops walking, frowns. "What did you go and do that for?"

"Well, he was heavy, Larry. I suppose you never thought of that. And there I was, thirty miles from nowhere. I had to walk because the bloody road was under construction, so what was I supposed to do?"

"You've got all the brains," Larry says. "Why ask me?"

And we walk arm in arm down the road, Larry and me going to the park.

16 / Niagara Falls

In January, Henry J. Zacharias had his first stroke.

It was late afternoon, around four o'clock, when Elizabeth began the eleven-mile drive from the hospital in Reinfeld to their farm, a trip she would make over and over. "I keep a close watch on that heart of mine," Johnny Cash sang as she traveled down the long stretch of road that connected the town with the highway. She switched off the radio. Music didn't seem right at a time like this. She drove cautiously, holding onto the wheel too tightly, fearing an accident. It was at times like these, when your nerves were stretched too tight, that things went wrong. She passed by the feed mill and slowed down as she approached Ellis's Greenhouses. Should she stop and let him know about Henry, that she wouldn't be able to come in for the seeding? No. He would wonder how she could even think about such things.

The thump of tires against the pavement felt rhythmic and sure, but the point at which she aimed seemed fixed and unreachable as the horizon which sometimes in winter disappeared so that she couldn't tell, where was sky, where was land? She was vaguely aware of a cluster of brown trees in the middle of a field, huddled together in a bank of snow like old women at a funeral, long shadows, their skirts blotting out the wash of pastel sky-colors reflected all about in the hard snow. Minutes later (how many, five, fifteen?) she passed by her lane, past the buildings all yellow with green trim that distinguished Henry J. Zacharias's farm from the others; from Henry P. Zacharias (no relation), who was called Hank by his neighbors and whose farm was twice the size of theirs and stretched all the way to Roland.

Realizing her error, she braked quickly, felt the wheels skid on ice. She held her breath to contain her rising panic, steering into the skid instinctively, thinking, already I have gotten myself into trouble, felt the vehicle swing out of the slide, pass center and fishtail sharply. Today she couldn't go off the road, not today because then Hank P. would have to come with his tractor to pull her out and (one thing for certain) she didn't want to have to ask him for anything, but the wheels caught at buried gravel and the car steadied. She breathed a prayer of relief. She backed the car slowly toward the lane. The driveway had disappeared. She searched through the windshield for some sign of it, a track that would guide her safely into the yard, but the combination of waning light and fresh snow had erased all traces of it. The house itself appeared abandoned, the windows dark mirrors reflecting the setting sun. She was cut off from her house. She got out of the car and walked down the lane. The fluffy snow, ankle-deep, bit at her bare skin. She hadn't stopped to put boots on this morning when she saw Henry fall. She'd run from the house not thinking, just oh God, oh God. One minute he was walking, strong, and the next, like a bird crashing into the window, he faltered, his arms flailing, looking for something to hold on to, and he was down, a brilliant red plaid heap in the snow. Fresh snow covered the spot near the mailbox where he'd fallen. She walked back to the car and followed her footprints into the lane, passed them by, and then braver, drove by faith into the circle of her yard.

She waited in the car until she'd stopped shaking and then went into the house. She stamped snow from her feet and walked across the kitchen, her steps sluggish, as though she waded through water, to the calendar which hung beside the telephone. "Arrive Niagara Falls, 8 am," she'd written on it that morning. Only a week away from their first vacation, an anniversary present from their only son, John, and his wife, Sharon. She picked up the pencil and wrote, "Henry goes to the hospital." Her spidery, odd-shaped letters ran off the square into the next date. Henry was there in Reinfeld in the hospital and she was here, at the farm. The floor cracked suddenly as though someone just entered the room. Phone John's place, she told herself, see if they're back from the city yet. But she didn't pick up the receiver. She knew too much. She'd seen the doctor thump hard with the heel of his palm against Henry's breastbone to try to rouse him. She knew his illness would take up many squares on the calendar. Inside his head, a large field had been marked off. She'd stood beside his bed and watched him fall deeper into sleep. Where are you? she'd asked him silently, and then, where am I? Was she the one who had fallen asleep today?

"I'll give the money for the train tickets back to John," she'd told Henry at the hospital. She meant to say, don't you worry now. She was surprised when he responded. He moved his hand across the blanket towards her own.

"Seed," he said. "John should be spending money for seed, not trips." His voice came from a great distance. And she thought again, it is a dream. I'll open my eyes and be in my room upstairs.

She held his curled fingers lightly between her large hands. "I'll tell him you said so." Their son wasn't a farmer. He owned a large implement dealership in Reinfeld. Henry was confused, or was he saying, tell John to look after things?

"John spends entirely too much money," Henry said, and Elizabeth thought that maybe his illness wasn't so bad after all, if he could still think to speak out against John. But several hours later, Henry grew too weak to talk and he sank into sleep.

Elizabeth turned from the telephone. The bad news would keep for a while. She read the words she'd written on the calendar. She picked up the pencil which dangled from its string and in tiny, controlled letters she wrote, "All day it snowed." She would train herself to live alone.

She switched on the stove and filled the kettle with water. The mantle clock in the dining room chimed the hour. She went into the room and turned on the light as though that would lessen the effect of the clock's counting. All around the

walls on varnished shelves was her collection of china plates. She didn't like china, but it was what other women did. John and Sharon were delighted. They never knew what to buy for her and so they bought a plate from each place they visited. She had a plate with a picture of the Niagara Falls on it. When she'd seen John's slides of the falls, they made her feel like the bonging of the clock made her feel, off balance and clutching the air about her. "Horseshoe Falls," the plate was inscribed, "160 feet high, 2,950 feet wide, 500,000 tons of water a minute," which to her was the same as saying, "every second a baby is born." It was unfathomable.

But it wasn't these plates she'd come searching for, but for something older, something that came from a different time. She found it on the shelf in the china cupboard, the porcelain cup and saucer that had come from Russia. Her mother had brought it with her and had written down that she was to have it when she married. She felt its smoothness against the thick calluses of her palms and took the cup into the kitchen. She filled it with hot water and sat down at the table and pressed its fluted edge to her lips. She looked out the window. The moon had risen and beneath it stretched the winter-blue curve of Henry's fields. Before she'd begun to work in the greenhouses, she'd preferred winter. She'd never been able to face the stark bleakness of Henry's fields without feeling numbed by the ugliness. She hated how she'd battled daily the wind that swept in under windowsills, covering everything with gritty black silt. Her headaches used to come with those high winds. She preferred the depression that the immense stillness of winter carried because in winter, it was clean. She massaged her chest where an odd ache had begun to form and thought about who she should telephone. She should really try to get hold of John just in case he had come home from the city a day earlier than expected and heard about his father. And then she realized that if that happened, he would call her. She didn't have the energy to call John and face the questions he would ask, not letting her finish saying what she'd formed in her mind. Should she call Mika? No, her sister seemed to enjoy hearing bad news and would grab hold of the information and make it seem worse than it really was. Irma. Irma worked in the greenhouses with her. Better to call Irma because Irma understood. She was married to a cranky, bitter man who had lost his legs. And she, eyelids heavy with the thought of it, was married to Henry who today had entered his own place. She had lost his mind.

Elizabeth opened her eyes, realized it was morning and was amazed that she'd slept so soundly. The first thing she saw was Henry's boots on the carpet across the room, beside his bed, and she remembered a week ago, Henry walking three miles to Hank P.'s place. To keep him talking in the barn long enough until the polls closed to prevent Hank P., who was Liberal, from casting his vote. What did you talk about for such a long time? she'd asked, her heart doing its familiar flip flop each time he'd come back from talking with Hank P. We talked about God, and what He means to me, Henry said.

Everything is lawful, Henry often said, but not everything is good and so they were one of few left in the farming area around Reinfeld who didn't have the tell-tale television antenna on top of their roof. Occasionally, she drove into town and watched Ed Sullivan at Irma's place. She had never been able to match Henry's goodness, she thought, as her eyes met his Bible lying on the table beside his bed. She went into what used to be John's bedroom, her sewing room, and stood looking for a moment at the dress pattern spread across the worktable, pieces cut in half lengthwise so that she could add tissue, enlarge the pattern to fit. Yes, that's how it is, she told herself, eating and drinking and never thinking that tomorrow it could all end. She felt guilty immediately. I'm beginning to sound more and more like Mika, she chastened herself, it's a stroke, he could come out of it yet. Above her worktable, the window where she'd been standing when it had happened. She dressed and went downstairs and erased the vacation plans from the calendar. She didn't allow herself to ask how she felt about this. What had happened had happened. It wasn't Henry's fault that she would never get to see the falls. She had nothing to complain about when it came to Henry. She often said to Irma with a clear heart that she had no complaints at all.

Except for the farm, Irma reminded her when she'd said, Henry is all right, I have no complaints. Henry was seventy-two, she forty-seven. Most men his age had already built their retirement houses in Reinfeld, erected fake windmills in their back yards, wishing wells in the front yards, constructed sturdy fences and died. But neither one of them had wanted that. Henry secretly hoped that John would still take up the farm and she, when Mr. Ellis had confided in her his intention to sell, that they would sell the farm and buy the greenhouses. And so when Irma reminded her, "except for the farm," the frustration and desperation of past years was as fresh and tart as an unripe apple. The farm wasn't hers to sell. Do, don't ask, Irma said once. Just tell. Irma's husband had no legs, she didn't need to ask for anything, she thought, as she plaited her long auburn hair. She watched herself do this, saw her awkward fingers fumbling with the tiny pins, her face, rounder; she'd been gaining weight. The mirror told her what she still didn't feel completely: you are here, real, alive, and Henry is the one asleep.

Before she telephoned John, she called the hospital and asked, how is he? The same, the nurse said. He spent a quiet night. Henry was too quiet. His falling was like a feather resting among feathers. She telephoned John and gave him the news and arranged to meet him at the hospital. When she hung up some of the tension that had gathered in her shoulder blades fled. She picked up the pencil and wrote, "My first day alone" and beneath that, "Phone Mr. Ellis soon."

In mid-February, as Elizabeth turned off from the highway onto the road that led to Reinfeld, the sun sparkled on crusty snow and on rooftops and she thought Reinfeld looked like a Christmas card picture of Bethlehem shining with the blue tinge of a pointing star, making it special, set apart, unlike the other towns that hugged the American border. The highway didn't pass through Reinfeld's center, splitting it in two. It wasn't necessary to string gaudy lights above the street or to have a sign that said, "Welcome to Reinfeld." Its borders were symmetrical, the streets, predictable, and the sameness in the decoration of the houses made her feel that nothing would ever change. She drove towards the hospital thinking that despite everything, she was content.

She walked into Henry's room. He looked at her, blinked several times and said, "Chicks. Have you ordered the chicks yet?"

"What?" Elizabeth asked, startled. Her own dream-like state had diminished and she had reconciled herself to his, that it was permanent. His place had become real. The walls were green. His cubicle had a tall, narrow window that looked out over the town of Reinfeld. A brass radiator beneath it. Beside his bed, a wooden one-drawer chest, painted brown. Above it, a mirror. Henry, in a wheelchair, staring down at the curled fingers in his lap, a towel tied beneath his arms to hold him upright. Henry's white legs, thinner, dangling uselessly as the attendant lifted him in and out of bed. Because she was strong and healthy, Henry's place seemed confined. But she knew the effort it took for him just to breathe and so she knew that for him, it was the right size. But now, his voice a whisper, but his voice, saying to her, "Chicks, have you ordered the chicks yet?"

She'd called Mr. Ellis and had gone back to work transplanting tomatoes and her life had become routine. She was confident enough to try variations to the old pattern, sleeping in past seven o'clock, staying up later at night, continuing the nightly ritual of drinking hot water from the porcelain cup that had come from Russia.

"He spoke to me," Elizabeth said to the nurse. She'd run from the room, grabbed hold of the first person she came upon.

"Oh, he speaks often," the nurse said. "Especially during the night. He talks about an accident. We feel that he hears things."

"Things, what things?" Accident and chicks. Her face grew flushed.

"Oh, the other patients, their radios."

They should have told her. Prepared her for the time when he would begin to ask questions. How did it happen? Did I fall? And then, what about Hank P.? How did that one happen?

"And that's not all," the nurse said as she followed Elizabeth back into Henry's room. "We have a surprise for you. Show your wife what you can do," she said to Henry and for the first time, Elizabeth noticed the metal bar hanging above his bed.

Henry reached up, his whole arm trembling, and curled his fingers about the bar. He began to pull himself upright.

Elizabeth slapped her hands against her cheeks in astonishment. "Isn't that wonderful?" the nurse said.

Yes, but it's only an arm, she told herself later as she sat beside his bed knitting a sweater which she planned to send to her sister for the youngest baby. It's only an arm. When she considered how far he was from walking and even then they weren't sure about his right side. "Henry," she said loudly several moments later as he lay panting from exertion. His hearing has not been affected, the doctor had told her, there was no need to yell, but she couldn't help it. It seemed that because he couldn't talk above a whisper, he couldn't hear either. "I have been wanting to talk to you about the farm." Her metal needles clicked out a frantic pace. "I was thinking, the way prices are that now would be a good time to sell."

He didn't respond. She set the knitting aside and went over to his bed. He stared at the ceiling. She sat down on the edge of the bed. Spittle ran from one corner of his drooping mouth. She snatched up a tissue, began to dab at it. "Think of it," she said gently. "Everything considered, we should get rid of the land."

He pulled away. "No," he said, and then louder, "I forbid you to do that." He began to thrash his head from side to side on the pillow. She held his cheeks between her hands, felt the faint flutter of his muscles as he tried to free himself. She felt ashamed, unworthy.

"Henry, please, be still." His head was fragile, as fragile as an ancient porcelain cup that would shatter if you flicked it hard with your knuckle.

"It's all right," she said. "We don't need to talk about it yet." She had dreamed of him one night, that she carried him out and away from the hospital. I'll care for you, she'd said. I'll look after you, make you well. And here she was, upsetting him. He grew still. She patted him lightly on the cheek and felt that peculiar ache rise in her chest. The farm, it wasn't hers to sell. She took up her knitting once again. "The way your exercises are going," she said, "you will be up and around the yard by spring."

He blinked rapidly. "Phone Hank P.," he said harshly. "Tell him I'll lease the land. One year only."

Elizabeth dropped a stitch, squinted and raced to pick it up before the whole sweater unraveled. "I'll tell him," she said.

"He's not being very realistic," John said. "Expecting anyone would even want to lease the land for one year. Especially a guy like Hank P."

Especially Hank P., Elizabeth thought. He would be the one to do it. "You're a fine one to talk about being realistic," she said and laughed. When he was small he would butt his head against her stomach, his crib, the walls, in order to make things happen. In the early grades in school, teachers said that he threw himself on the floor and banged his head when he didn't make one hundred percent on a test.

"But he's not thinking," John said, choosing to ignore her gentle teasing.

Elizabeth shushed him. "He's your father." And John was his son. There were indelible marks other than his short stocky frame, his bullishness. John was deeply religious like Henry, in an unbending, fierce way that made her feel defensive and inadequate. And yet, father and son had never worked well together.

"You have to realize why your father wants to hang on. What has he got?" A bed, a chair, a window in a shoebox of a room.

John got up from the kitchen table and put his arm around her shoulders. "And what about you?" he asked. "Shouldn't we be thinking about you as well?" If she stood up, she would be a foot taller than he. All his caresses came when she was sitting. She leaned back in the chair and let her head rest against his chest. For the first time since Henry had fallen in the snow, she felt like weeping. He kneaded her shoulders, demonstrative in a way she'd taught him. The way Henry might have been if someone had shown him how. She'd kept house for Henry a full year without realizing that he cared for her. Not until he fired the hired man for making jokes about her size.

She saw the look of annoyance pass across his face. "I'd keep the business in Reinfeld as well," he said. "And open another one in Morden. Because business is good. Now's the time to do it."

"Father always said you spend too much money." She pulled her hands free and began to clear away the dishes.

She expected an outburst, but John got up and began to help her. He scraped food from plates. Sharon had taken a day to go shopping in the city and he'd come for supper.

"We're positive we should do this," John said quietly as he set dishes down into the sink. "We've prayed long and hard and we're sure that this is what God wants us to do, too."

"Well then, that's good. Do it." She was conscious of her voice sounding tight and strained.

He cleared his throat noisily and spit phlegm into the garbage can, just as Henry used to do. "I'll need money to do it," he said. "I've got too much tied up in machinery right now to go to the bank."

"How much money?" Henry had five thousand dollars in their savings account. She had a little from working in the greenhouse.

"Twenty-five thousand."

"So much? I don't have that much money."

"I know," John said and she knew now the reason for his quietness. He was worried. She felt the knot of braids pull at the back of her head. She ran water into the sink, began stacking dishes down into the soapy water.

"What then?" she asked, fearful, her old sickness bumping there beneath her breastbone, dreading his answer.

"Sharon's father has agreed to lend us part of it. I could sell Dad's machinery," he said. "I could get a good price for it."

Henry's acreage was small, a little over one section, that was all. What kind of a price would she get without the machinery?

"Mama," John said, using his old name for her, a form of endearment. "He'll never work again. I thought you realized that."

It was true. And Mr. Ellis could up and sell the greenhouse before Henry realized it. "And what would I do?" she asked. "If something happened to your father, what would I do in town? Work in the shop?"

"You wouldn't need to work," he said. "If things go as well as they have so far, you wouldn't need to work anymore. Sharon and I would see to that. I think it's a good investment for you. We'd be partners, the three of us, you, me and the Lord."

"How could you refuse such a generous offer?" Irma asked the following day. They carried wooden flats in from the yard

and stacked them against the wall in the greenhouse. The
time was right to begin transplanting, culling the spindly
seedlings and transferring the stronger ones to the flats where
they would grow thick and straight. Now is the time to do it,
John had said. Now is the time, she repeated over and over
while she worked.

"What do you mean?" Elizabeth asked, offended by Irma's
tone of voice. Irma Muller is an old woman who tries to look
young, John had once said, because the woman colored her
hair blond and used cosmetics. Elizabeth had not reminded
him that she and Irma were the same age.

"Well kid, how could you refuse a partnership with God,
tell me? He's got you over a barrel, that one. Smart."

Elizabeth knew what it must look like to Irma, but she
was certain John was sincere. "He's my son," she said. "If a son
can't come to his mother, then who should he go to?" She
said this to slight Irma, who let her only daughter Marlene
run free like a stray dog.

Irma let a bundle of flats drop to the ground with a great
clatter. "Why doesn't he go to his father?" she asked. "No, he
knows better," she said and lifted her little finger. "He's got
you right there."

Elizabeth was hanging her overalls in the back porch after
work when she saw Hank P.'s truck pull into the yard. She
was about to call into the house, Henry, you'd better come,
Hank P. is here, and then quickly step out of sight, but. . . .
She folded her arms across her chest. She would speak to him
on her own. Had Henry somehow gotten a message to him?

Hank stood with the door open neither inside nor out. He
seemed uncertain whether he should enter. "How is Mr.
Zacharias today?" he asked. His red sideburns grew thick and
curly half-way down the sides of his face, making it seem
broader than it was. She noticed a button missing from his
shirt and his bare stomach, curly fine hairs. So he didn't wear
an undershirt in winter either, not like Henry who wore one
summer and winter, day and night. Her eyes met his. He was

almost as tall as she was. It made her uneasy to stand eye to
eye with a man.

"He's the same," she said.

"I'm sorry to hear that," he said, as nice and polite as if
someone listened behind the door. He stood turning his cap in
his hands, which were sprinkled with cinnamon-colored
freckles (young-looking hands cupping a large white breast).
His hair, red, against her own dark hair. That old man, he
can't be of much use for you. Was he truly sorry? For her, or
for Henry? She knew what he'd gone through when his Anna
died with cancer.

"I've come to see you about the cultivator," Hank said.
"Mr. Zacharais said last fall, if I fixed it I could use it."

She nodded.

"So, I thought you should know. I'll be working in the
machine shed until it's done." He turned in the doorway and
put his cap back on.

He was being so polite. "Wait, Henry wanted me
to . . . ," Elizabeth began.

He removed his cap once again and waited.

"Henry said to, he sends his regards," she said and looked
away. Blood rushed to her face. I have never made love to
anyone other than my husband, she'd told Irma, so that she
could taste the memory of him rushing against her. She had
written on the calendar, "Today while I was digging among
the garbage heap for mushrooms, I found a leper in lovely
clothes of hard knotted flesh." Henry had read it, asked her
what it meant. It's just an idea that came to me, she said.
That's all. Did Hank think she was remembering that
afternoon half-way between Winnipeg and Reinfeld? The day
she'd gone to get the chicks. "I'm not here most afternoons,"
she said to cover her confusion. "But feel free to come in and
help yourself to coffee. I'll leave it on the stove."

He stared at her longer than was necessary to thank her.
He closed the door behind him and she stood rooted, confused
and angry with herself because she had not given him Henry's

message, because she had blushed so readily and now, after all these years, what did he think?

In March, the doctor intercepted Elizabeth as she was about to enter Henry's room. "I'm sorry," he said flatly, "but Mr. Zacharias has contracted pneumonia." It seemed like a strange way of putting it, as though Henry had an obligation to take on this new disease.

Her chest ached as she watched Henry's straining to breathe. Tubes dripped medicine into his veins. A nurse came in and pushed a rubber hose into his throat, switched on a machine and sucked up his mucus. Elizabeth gagged. But when it was over, Henry could breathe easier and so she was grateful to the nurse and smiled at her, stepping out of her path quickly to show she was anxious not to be a nuisance.

Today, she would have told him about the snowstorm, how Hank P. had plowed their lane so she could come to the hospital. "Snow as high as my waist in the lane," she had written. But such news was of no use to poor Henry. He struggled to speak. "What is it?" she asked, dreading some message, some final command, some last question about chicks and accidents.

"Ruining the land," Henry said.

Her heart constricted. "Who is ruining the land?" Had he heard somehow that she hadn't leased it yet?

His mouth, encrusted with fever blisters, moved painfully slow. "Communists."

Her shoulders sagged with immense relief. She watched the slow drip, drip of medicine into the glass tube for several minutes and then left.

Elizabeth felt the sides of March press in on her as she listened daily to Henry's feverish ranting. The septic tank froze and she didn't call John. John was too busy with his own life and besides, she really was undecided about the money. She hated to picture them praying every day, or the thought that she really might be the answer to their money problems. She called a company in town to come with their heat lamps

and torches to thaw out the septic tank, but they weren't in
any rush and so in the meantime, she squatted amid the trees
beside the granaries and threw her dishwater onto the yard
and bathed at Irma's house in town until it was fixed.

Henry seemed never better, never worse. They took away
his exercise bar. He was gaunt and appeared bitter over this
new setback. She felt responsible. As though she'd caused it to
happen by talking of selling off the land. Since she'd decided
not to carry Henry's message to Hank P., she couldn't look
fully into her husband's eyes, brilliant with the remnant of his
fever, but off to one side. The evasion and the sameness of her
life depressed her. March weighed heavily and it was on such
a day that she arrived for work to find the "For Sale" sign
pushed down into the ground beside the greenhouse. She
stared at it, telling herself, this is what you get. This is what
happens when you even think such selfish things. She backed
the car out and drove home.

When she opened the back door, she saw rubber boots on
the mat. She reached up to hang her coveralls and saw Hank's
parka. She felt the strangeness of its presence pass through her
hands as she hung her clothes beside his. When she stepped
into the kitchen he was working with his tools at the sink.
The faucet lay in pieces on the counter.

"I thought seeing as how I had my tools with me, I might
as well fix it," he said without turning around.

That was what he'd said that summer, pulling alongside
her car, offering to fix the tire. "You needn't have gone to so
much trouble. John would have fixed it for me." Then
knowing she sounded ungrateful, she thanked him, feeling the
blood rushing to her face once again.

There was nothing she could do without coming too close
to him and so she poured a cup of coffee and watched him
work. He was across the room and yet it seemed as though he
was there beside her. Bending his red head across her chest,
his hand cupping her breast, tongue circling her nipple. Soon
he was finished and washing his hands, and she was lying

across the seat in the car, thinking, so this is what it's like with another man. She had to tell herself over and over to remember that she'd been disappointed that it hadn't been all that different. He wiped his hands on her good dishtowel and squatted to pack his tools into the toolbox. She noticed the straining of the muscles in his thighs against the fabric of his pants. She stared down at the bottom of the porcelain cup. She used to imagine what it would be like with another man and when she'd glanced down at him poised above her, she'd been amazed at how similar he was to Henry, she thought he'd be bigger, stronger looking. Maybe if she had let herself go more it would have been different, she told herself. Let him touch her all over and smell her the way he wanted to. He stood beside the door ready to leave.

"It's fixed," he said.

"Thank you." She smiled.

"I've also finished work on the cultivator today," he said. "Tell Mr. Zacharias it's working."

"I will." He acted as though someone were looking over his shoulder.

He hesitated. His expression changed. He seemed to be nourishing a cunning thought. "Has Mr. Zacharias ever said what he plans to do?" He spoke with a gesture, indicating with his freckled, sure hands (between her legs forcing them open) the wide expanse of Henry's fields. "We, some of the neighbors, would do the seeding for him. If that's his wish."

"I plan to sell," Elizabeth said.

His thick eyebrows shot up, he recovered and his face became expressionless.

"Would you be interested?" she asked.

Again their eyes met and she saw something else flicker in his eyes, a look of unsureness. She was surprised and then faintly exhilarated by the thought, I have made him feel uneasy.

"I might be."

As the door closed behind him, Elizabeth lifted the cup

and pressed its edge against her teeth. Her breath was hot inside the cup and moisture clung to the fine dark hairs above her lip. She watched Hank's truck turn the corner at the end of the lane. I plan to sell, she'd said, as though it was her farm to sell. And saying it made it seem real. I am tired of carrying people around on my back, she'll tell Irma, who will crow and say, well it's about time. She got up from the table and wrote on the calendar, "Make an appointment with the hairdresser."

In the middle of April, Henry had another stroke. "Henry has another bout, quite bad," Elizabeth wrote, the terse calmness of the words denying the turmoil inside. She stayed with him all day now, leaving only to get a bite to eat at a restaurant in town. She stood at the narrow, tall window beside his bed and noticed it was finally spring. Moist warm air rushed into the room overtop the gentle hiss of the radiator. Below in the parking lot, people arriving to visit, wearing light coats, sweaters and also below, Hank P.'s truck.

She emptied the basin of water into the sink beside Henry's bed with shaking hands and turned to face Hank, who had come into the room without making a sound. He nodded to her. His eyes took in Henry's shell-like body, the tubes in his nose, the bag at the foot of the bed that collected his wastes.

"I heard he was worse. I'm sorry," Hank said in a kind way that made her remember that his wife had suffered. Hank was different than the Hank who had laughed while she'd rammed her car into his car, because he wouldn't let her pass, making her angry in a way she never thought anyone could. She was about to thank him but saw that his voice had lied. The same smug expression was there, uncovered, and his desire for her, controlled, he would wait until she couldn't wait. He was passing his lust for her across the inert form of her Henry.

"If you need anything at all," he said. "I'll come."

She nodded. "John can come, too."

Henry sighed deeply and they were diverted to him, to the bed. His chest moved gently up and down and the blankets with it. His sternness was pinched out like a candle; had it ever been real, or had it been a covering? she wondered. Henry hadn't asked her for anything and he had shared all with her. He was a feather now, falling among feathers.

Hours later as Elizabeth came back from eating lunch, the nurse met her at the door of the hospital and said, "Mr. Zacharias has just died." Then they took her to his room and left her alone with him. She pulled out the drawer and dropped his comb and brush into the plastic net bag she carried in her purse. She collected his partial plate from the cardboard container. She thought she might cry. It was the time for it. She looked around the cubicle for one last time. Henry's final giving out had already been absorbed by the breath of others. She imagined the lane, his residue fading even now beneath the melting snow. It was all done now: his slippers, housecoat, the partial plate. She set the bag down. There was one last thing she wanted to do. She gathered Henry in her arms and carried him over to the window. He was lighter than a child. "See, out there," she said. "It's spring."

When she passed through the large glass doors, she was surprised to discover that it had been raining. "First rain today," she would write on the calendar. She'd signed the papers to release Henry's body to the undertakers with a steady hand. No, she'd said, I don't need to wait for my son to come. But I'll wait. She walked towards his car on the parking lot. A door slammed shut as Sharon came running towards her. It's all right, she'll tell them. I'm all right. She would go to see the falls. She would hold onto the railing or she would let herself go. Whatever she did, she would do willingly.

17 / Moonlight Sonata

August 17, 1960. Above me, a moist burlap blanket descended over the shoebox of the town where I lived until the sky was in place, draped in heavy folds and turned beneath the horizon. There were four of us sitting in front of the Hotel on Main Street that Saturday night, waiting. We were always waiting for something to happen, some event which would ease our tension-filled boredom.

Around us, pressed into the inky sky, were the blue cut-out shapes of buildings, windows lit, squares of hard yellow light dividing the shadows on the sidewalk where we sat on our haunches, leaning against the stucco wall. Moths skittered across the surface of the night, a blizzard in the lights above the doorways, the streetlights, drawing my eyes to their center until I, too, had that feeling of swarming, of coming to the light.

I remember on the corner, a telephone booth. Someone had kicked through the glass door and inside it, smelling of beer, a swaying man embraced the telephone to keep from falling. I recalled reading a survey in the newspaper on how forty-two percent of women polled said they were discontented. The main problems, they said, were their mates' selfishness, drinking, and bad house habits. I knew the man in the telephone booth and thought he was probably guilty of all three. And that if they had done a survey in Agassiz alone the percentage probably would have been much higher because all around, like the sickly sweet smell of a ripening garden, discontent hovered.

Strung across Main Street, colored lights and several burned-out bulbs combined to create a chain of dots and dashes. Coded messages. Get out, they said. Go away now before you can't. The warm pavement bit my haunches as I sat

beside Gail and watched the horseplay of the two boys,
Wayne and Scott, tearing at each other, karate-like chops,
fake blows to the stomach.

—flea brain !

—hiyah !

—pissuparope you sonofabitch

—oh yeah? oh yeah?

I see the same boys now, younger though, in almost every
school-yard I pass by. Their shouted obscenities are more vivid
but the intent the same. I see the boys kneeing one another,
grabbing at each other's crotches. The fake blows. The not so
fake blows. I remember my son, the oldest, coming home from
kindergarten the first day with a bloody nose. They played pile
on the rabbit, he said. And I was the rabbit. When they
played football, he was the ball. He was small for his age,
thin, loved to cut and paste and when my students came for
their piano lessons, he wrapped his blanket about himself and
curled up on the floor and listened. Now he drives around
with them on the weekend, the ball carriers, screaming
"faggot" at homosexuals on Memorial Boulevard. But, oh, I
know his baroque behavior well, the tensions lurking beneath
his eyelids, the complexity of his bones. Frank, his father,
understands other things. He understands the drinking, the
speeding tickets. He hosed the boy down in the shower,
toweled him dry, laughed at him as he retched his first drunk
into the toilet. But the drugs Frank doesn't understand. And
like me, he lies in bed while the boy is out, perplexed and
silent. The air in the room is heavy with our thoughts and I
remember that.

The air was close that night, my chest ached then, too,
with the fullness of it. It made me want to stretch and gulp
for more. I think I knew I would be leaving Agassiz soon and
so I was making an effort to record the place. Like the soil of
my valley, thick and black and sticky for days after a rain so
that it spatters pant legs and has to be chipped or brushed
free, I wanted the memory of that place to cling to me. I

wanted to remember the heat of it, the discontent, the feeling of living in a shoebox.

Gail sat beside me on the sidewalk. She was short, blond, always crossed her arms over her large breasts. I saw her in a shopping mall recently, so terribly middle-aged and sagging at every point that I was shocked and saddened. Do you see that woman, I asked my daughter, the one standing at the checkout? We used to be in the same grade at school, I said. God, she said, shocked, and then looked at me with new eyes, appraising, and then reluctant admiration. No kidding, she said. God.

Gail nudged me. "Look who's coming." She always spoke as though everything was a secret, drawing attention with a flick of her head and speaking from one corner of her mouth. "Jeez," she said, "what do you think?"

Herman Schultz, or Torch, we'd named him, walked towards us bent forward at the waist as though he trudged uphill. Hands plunged deep into the pockets of his made-over pants, he muttered to himself, a frown half-hidden in the clump of damp curls at his forehead. When he saw us he stopped suddenly and reared up like a prairie dog giving warning.

Wayne held Scott fast in an armlock. "Torchy, baby," he said, his face red with exertion. "How's it hanging?"

"Wait up," Torch said and began to run towards us.

"Do we look like we're going someplace?" Wayne asked.

"Aw, come on," Scott pleaded and Wayne released him. Scott was tall and thin and looked as though he'd been chipped from wood with a fine chisel.

Herman shook his finger at us, and his eyes, the color of cracked blue pottery, shone with suppressed rage. "Okay. Okay. What did you go and do with him this time?" he asked.

Scott straightened slowly, massaging his shoulder. "I give up. What did we do with who this time?"

Frustration gleamed in Torch's eyes. "You know damned well. My dog." On his pale doughy cheeks was the faint glint of red whiskers, but his voice never changed from its soft feminine tone. It would always have pleading at its base. He carried food around in his pants pockets to lure stray dogs home to the two-room, bricksiding house where he lived with his mother, a tall, tired-looking, prematurely white-haired woman who saw all dogs as being wild dogs, and the men who sat on the Post Office steps during the day as being wild men. She worried about Torch being kidnapped. So she waited for early evening to send Herman downtown to fetch what replies she received from the dictated letters she sent, urgent enquiries into the whereabouts of her German soldier husband missing in Russia during the war.

"Search me," Scott said. "You tell me. Why can't we leave your mutt alone?"

Wayne stepped forward. He raised his arms above his head. "Tell you what, honky jerk. Any animal you can find, you can have."

"Here's your big chance," Gail said. "He wants you to feel him up. Grab it."

"There's nothing to grab," I said, falling for it, allowing myself to be drawn into the 'let's degrade Wayne' routine.

But Wayne was a deviate. He knew he didn't belong with us. Why had he chosen us, the fallen, instead of the "in crowd," those who left the first of every July to go to the lakes? The ones who fornicated on sandy beaches while their parents played bridge and drank gin slush out on their patios. They arrived back the Labor Day weekend, reputations intact, while ours had been bandied about, imagined. My sins under the microscope, blown up out of proportion. Wayne hadn't been born in Agassiz. He'd come five years ago. His father had a position of importance in the town. He knew he could do better.

"Aw bug off. All of you cocksuckers," Herman said. When his mother reached out and touched his golden head, he said, aw, bug off. When he soared like a bird from a fourth floor balcony, breaking his back, he said, leave me alone. I read about it in the newspaper. A party. Drinking. None of us had been trained to drink and so we drank excessively and I imagined Torch had as well, pushing them back, feeling the release and the words to express himself. I saw him lying on his back on the pavement below, looking up through his cracked-blue pottery eyes at the ring of legs around him. Leave me alone. Bug off.

Unlike the others, I'd met Herman's strange mother, who used to do housework once a week for my mother and who would tie her white hair up into a kerchief because she was afraid of getting spiders caught in it. She told stories about the war. About fleeing a burning city with Herman on her back and how she worried and worried, her bony fingers arranging and rearranging the doilies on table tops, about his being affected by the bombs, the concussion of air slamming about his fragile ears. For behold, she said, the Lord came forth out of his place and came down and trod upon the high places of the earth and his shoes were flames of fire. It didn't matter where you ran, she said. There was the fire and the noise and Herman never cried. Never cried. Herman had in his staring eyes the smoke and the fire, she'd said. Somewhere, his father is. Somewhere he will hear about us. And that will be that.

Mrs. Schultz made Herman a birthday party once. My mother forced me to go because she wanted to know, what was this strange woman's house like? Was it true, did she only have one bed in the house? There were none of the usual birthday games, but one that Mrs. Schultz in an attempt at gaiety earnestly showed us, a kind of seven-up game with an orange which she released quickly and let run down her arm and then flicked up into the air with a jerk of her biceps, saying, hup, hup, each time she did it. But the effort had been lost on most at the party. They giggled behind hands. Herman was downcast. He kicked at the leg of the table. "What is it, my wonderful child?" she asked.

"Bug off," Herman said and Mrs. Schultz covered her face in her hands.

I stayed behind when the others left quickly and silently. I
scraped sticky un-cooked cake from plates into a paper bag.
Outside, Herman played hide and seek with two dogs that had
followed him home. I saw his checkered shirt flash past a
window. He circled the house silently, outwitting the animals
who ducked and sniffed at the ground, seeking him out. I
heard his laughter, an hysterical, high-pitched staccato as the
dogs leapt and licked and bounded around him. Mrs. Schultz
sat on a wooden bench in the kitchen beside the woodstove,
her hands at her face. "My wonderful child," she said and
rocked. Then she began to pull at her white hair, at her long
thin nose. Our eyes met. She sighed and folded her hands
across her knees. "I tried to make a party for him so he would
feel like other children," she said, her voice barely a whisper.

"It was a nice party. The cake it—it was a delicious cake. I
liked the icing."

"But they didn't eat." She raised her hands, palms up,
towards the table.

I continued to clear away the rubble. How had it come to
be my accepted responsibility, this cleaning up after people?
Putting salve on hurt feelings. "It was too soon after dinner," I
said. "They weren't hungry yet." I remember my mother
standing over my sick-bed after the doctor had left. She had
scrubbed and rearranged the room before she'd called for him.
Stripped the bed and put on the best linen. Well? she asked,
her voice sharp in my fever-wracked head. Did he notice the
pillow slips? Through the eyes of my sickness she appeared
before me wavery and translucent. He asked me who did the
wonderful needlework, I heard myself say, the words sluggish
on my thick tongue. He liked the roses on the border.

Mrs. Schultz knelt suddenly, knee joints snapping loudly
as her floral crepe dress cascaded down from her bony rump in
graceful folds against the splintered floorboards. The muscles
in her arm tightened as she drew a record player out from
beneath the bench. It was the type of player we had in school,
a brown net front, one speaker, a handle beneath the hinged

Moonlight Sonata

lid. Where had she got it? Had it been payment from someone for the housework she'd done? Then, I imagined her carrying it, trudging through bombed-out streets with Herman on her back, the record player thumping and banging against her legs. The turntable rasped softly. Dishes rattled in the cupboard as Herman crashed into the side of the house, careening beneath the raw energy of the dogs. She gasped and pressed her knuckles against her teeth. "They will bite him," she said. She stared at the window.

"They won't bite him," I said and continued to clean away the mess of the failed party. The cake was not cooked, I'd tell my mother. It was awful. The pink icing was sticky and gooey and I wouldn't be surprised if we all got sick.

The turntable spun around and around. Mrs. Schultz sighed deeply as she placed the arm on the record, sat down, leaned against the wall, and reached for a basket on the floor. She shook free a large doily and began to crochet. I expected to hear the twangy strains of a gospel quartette and steeled myself against it. "The heaven is his throne, the earth his footstool and where is the place of my rest?" she said to no one as the speakers crackled loudly.

From the disk came thin, clear notes, a piano being stroked, sure and precise. The melody began to unfold. I listened, my mouth suddenly stiff and shaking. The music was not a lullaby, but something else that made me stand still, my breasts leaning into it. My fingers began moving on their own across the table top, tracing the graceful cadences, the rising and falling of it. I sat down, slid, I should say because my knees had given way, to the floor. I leaned against the kitchen wall. "Ahh," Mrs. Schultz said, as her nimble fingers ducked and jerked white threads into lacy scallops. The melody flowered and rose and with it the feeling of a door opening up inside me, sunlight and dew. I closed my eyes until the last note faded and the grinding, dull sound of the turntable and the rasp of Mrs. Schultz's weeping circled the room. Outside, the dogs yelped and exclaimed their joy. She has two beds, I would tell my mother, who had sent me on this mission. A lie.

"Make like the birds and flock off," Wayne said to Torch that night, strutting towards him, flapping his arms up and down.

"You're full of bird shit," Torch said, his frustration breaking loose and rolling down his cheeks into his red whiskers.

—hahahahaha

—may the bird of paradise fly up your nose

—we care, right?

—right

"Okay. Okay for you then," Herman said and wrung his hands.

"Aw, come on." Scott slung a bony arm around Herman's neck. He fished into his pocket and brought out a packet of matches. "Here, it's on me. Have a ball. It's Saturday night."

Herman shook loose, "You're all crazy," he said. He shoved his hands into his pockets and walked away, head down, muttering loudly.

"He'll find the dog," Wayne said. "Eventually."

Gail sighed. I knew what she was feeling. All summer we'd gone in circles, one foot on center for luck, for safety, and then veering off, we ripped aimlessly through the cemeteries already growing in our minds. Above the telephone booth, in the glow of the streetlight, tiny wings thrummed and bodies pinged against the hot glass. The ache in my chest had grown sharper and I stood up to stretch and draw more air into my lungs.

The beer parlor door opened and Wayne's father stepped outside. With him came a blast of hot air, an explosion of hoarse babble. He seemed stunned for a moment and then, seeing us, came over to where we sat. I had never known anyone's father to be so old. He was shorter than Wayne, stooped at the shoulders, and his complexion as gray as his hair.

Moonlight Sonata

"And so, what are you young people up to tonight?" he asked and smiled but his smile didn't reach his eyes.

—hello Mr. Thompson

—hi

—greetings and hallucinations

"How's that?"

—just kidding, sir

"Nothing much," Wayne said. "As usual."

The man leaned against a car to steady himself and took out his wallet. "You young people should be doing something," he said. "Not just driving around." He held out twenty dollars. "Here, it's my treat. Why don't you go to Winnipeg, take in a movie or something?" His hands shook.

—wow

—gee, thanks

"The prick," Wayne said as he backed the car from the curb. "The old lady's away at the lake. I'll bet the bugger's on his way to St. Jean to saw off a hunk."

We didn't talk for several minutes. Scott's father had taken off one day, leaving behind a short dark woman with immense sad eyes and two children. Gail's mother was in a mental institution. We had an unspoken agreement never to talk about our homes.

"Where we going?" Scott asked, breaking the silence.

"To the cemetery," I said. "To untie Torch's dog."

"Aw, come on," Wayne said. "It'll give Torch something to do."

We entered the cemetery traveling down a narrow gravel pathway to the very back. I asked my grandparents to forgive our trespassing. Earlier, the ants had done their task of removing the sticky seal from the hard, round peony knobs and the bushes had flowered hugely and now the petals, like flecks of rust, spotted the ground all around. The muggy air held the scent of pine and the spent flowers.

We got out of the car and walked to the far corner. My stomach caved in at the sight of Torch's small spotted dog hanging from the fence, tongue lolling grotesquely. It had jumped over the iron railing that enclosed the grave, seeking freedom.

Frank lies on his back, staring at the ceiling. The light from the streetlamp divides his face in two, light and shadow. Touch me. I would take him inside me and stop thinking, only we both know we would get started and every slight noise, a car passing, a footstep on the pavement outside, would leave us rigid and tense, listening. Twice during the night, I heard a telephone ringing, pulling me up out of my dreams and I have stood in the middle of the living room clutching at my nightgown, facing a silent telephone. Mom, I'm not coming home. Thought I would let you know. His words slurred or too quiet. Don't ask me where I am. I listen intensely for background noise, for clues, but always, only the hollow sound of his voice. I hate the cars, his drinking, but I prefer it to his solitary wandering through a dream world. The glowing red digital numbers on the bedside table illuminate the thick dark hairs on Frank's arm. He has never told me that I worry too much.

"Did I know that was going to happen?" Wayne asked.
"The dog was retarded," Scott said. "Just like Torch. Forget it."
He turned the car radio up full volume. The voice of Buddy Holly singing, "That'll be the day," enveloped us. I gathered myself up into the corner of the back seat and felt the thump of tires in my spine, the sweet smell of evergreen car deodorizer, and thought, oh, oh. Turn it off. Because it seemed that every time something bad happened to me, that song was playing. Like the time we fishtailed off an icy highway and rolled into the ditch. After the sounds of metal tearing and glass shattering and the tools left lying on the floor of the car had ceased their clanging and bouncing and the choking dust had settled, I pulled myself out from beneath

Moonlight Sonata

the dash to the thin jerky melody of "Oh, that'll be the day."
We counted the cost to the beat of the music, Gail's missing
nose, one shattered leg, a crescent scar on my shin from a tire
wrench.

"We should have buried it or something," Gail said. "Then
he wouldn't find out. He'd think it ran away and would forget
about it." She was morose and quiet. We'd been drinking for
an hour, speeding down the highway, directionless, the
purpose to keep moving because a parked car drew attention.
The alcohol hadn't worked for me the way it usually did,
giving me a rush of exhilaration, elastic vocal cords so that I
could imitate Brenda Lee or Johnny Cash and go off
screaming or singing at the moon until they had to chase me
down, sit on me and drag me home. We'd driven for several
hours, going south from Grande Pointe towards the border
and then west and were heading back towards Agassiz, about a
mile out when we rounded a curve in the road. Ahead, the
heavy clouds reflected the flickering glow of a fire. As we drew
closer, the fire became many fires dotting a field.

"Jeez," Gail leaned forward and grabbed Wayne by the
shoulder. The dancing light of the flames cast her eyes into
deep shadows. When they'd grafted skin onto her nose, they
took it from some hairy part of her body and so the tip of it
was covered in fuzz like a peach. "Stop the car," she said.
"That's my old man's hay."

"I've always wanted to do this," Wayne said and turned
down a road choked with weeds. Thick, acrid smoke rolled up
from the stubble. We moved slowly through the thick smoke
and felt the press of heat against the windows. Gail rolled
down her window and the car filled with smoke, stinging our
eyes and throats.

"For Christ's sake," Wayne complained.

"Look." She pointed. Among the dotted fires a fire, held
high, zig-zagged across the field. I knew who it was even
before Wayne turned the wheel sharply and the headlights
caught Herman's white face. He turned and ran from us, still

carrying the torch, his too-large pants flapping around his
ankles, slowing him down.

"Stupid bugger," Gail said as Torch ran towards a small
shed. "There's gas in there."

Wayne and Scott leapt from the car and began chasing
him. Herman saw them coming, flung the torch aside and
veered off into the smoke.

"Stupid bugger," Gail said once again as Wayne and Scott
came back to the car. "Wait until I tell my dad about this."

"Shutup," Scott said. "And drink your beer."

Later that night, we gathered together in the basement of
Wayne's house where his father had built a damp and airless
rumpus room. We didn't talk about Torch or his dog. Earlier
the sky had opened and a great rushing downpour had flooded
the streets of Agassiz, making driving impossible. We could
still hear water running in the tiles beneath the concrete
floor. Four people sat in the center of the room in various
stages of nudity, their bodies slick with perspiration. The only
light came from two candles where the four sat, playing strip
poker. There were ten of us altogether. When we'd come back
into Agassiz, we'd come upon a carload of kids from Grande
Pointe, who had spent the night drinking in a tavern in South
Dakota and were sitting out the cloud-burst in the Hotel cafe.
The windows in the basement were closed tight and the air
contained the smell of our bodies, of damp hair, sex, of smoke
and beer. I sat on a plastic couch and watched the players
through an alcoholic haze. I saw Herman's white face, the
terror, the despair. I sang, "Oh, that'll be the day." It seemed
to me that the card-players' heads had become disconnected
from their bodies and floated loosely above their shoulders.

—can it Lafreniere
—up yours
—I wish
—someone shut her up

Gail sat on Scott's lap on the couch beside me. Scott
buried his nose in her fluffy pink sweater. A curly-haired boy

Moonlight Sonata

from Grande Pointe came and sat down beside me. He slid his hand beneath my sweater and I wound my arms about his neck, seeing his black curly head between my legs, his shoulders white beneath the moonlight and my back cushioned by the springy damp earth beneath the trees.

—stupid cupid you're a real mean guy

—count me out

—straight flush

A cry arose in the room as Wayne flung down his hand, stood up and removed his shorts.

—sexy

—far out

The curly-haired boy sucked at my neck. "Let's go into the other room," he whispered in my ear. "For old time's sake."

My stomach churned and the air pressed down on the top of my head. A going-away present. I stood up and the room tilted crazily. "Sure," I said. "Why not? I'll be right back."

I went upstairs, through a hallway, past the bathroom and stood in front of a bedroom door. Mr. Thompson lay on the bed on his back, mouth open, snoring loudly, dentures beside him. I watched the gray hair on his chest rise and fall for several moments. I thought of nudging him, waking him up and sending him down the stairs. But he was too far gone. Too old. He didn't lie there waiting for Wayne to come home and in the end, what good does it do? Those of us who do, end up knowing too much, having too much to carry around and examine and pull apart during the night. Mom, don't try to find me. The telephone calls. The hunting down. The driving miles through the night on strange roads. Roads leading to more roads and a stranger at a door opening into a room where his naked, frail body sprawls across a bed. Frank's silence, his terse face. Damned drugs, he says.

I found my way to the back door and stepped free from the tightly cloistered air out into a dripping cool night. I was leaving them behind. I had had enough. But I didn't know yet what I was going to go to. I began to walk away from the town, down the road that led to the river, past Mrs. Schultz's house. As I passed by, she came to the window and cupped her eyes, peering out at me. She beckoned. Come, come, I heard her voice from behind the glass. She opened the back door. Her white hair hung in wet strands against her neck. She twisted her fingers and plucked at her dress. "You are a good child," she said. "You can tell me where my Herman is?" The rasping sound of the record player filled the silence between us.

"He'll be home soon," I said. "You only have to wait."

Relief lifted years from her face. She began to tremble. She sat down on the bench and clasped her hands. "Thank you my God," she said. Her throat convulsed as she swallowed hard. She smiled. "Sit, sit." Beside her on the bench was a tall stack of records. She slid one out from near the middle and set it on the player. As the strains of violin music rose up between us, I sat down on the floor to listen. She reached and pulled the light chain and moonlight loomed in squares on the splintered floor. "It's God," she whispered. "He's here. Listen to the music, it's his resting place." I closed my eyes and listened and imagined that I could hear him walking along mountain tops. When the record had finished playing, she put on another and then another, until at last, she put on that record I'd first heard and the music I had carried around with me all that time leapt inside me in recognition. I hummed along, played the notes out in my lap. As the music rose to its stirring climax, we heard a dry sound, the swish of grass against pant legs. Mrs. Schultz reared up, hand to her mouth. Floorboards creaked as Herman entered the kitchen. Smoke and heat clung to his clothing. "What is it?" she asked.

"Mama," Herman said and rushed across the room towards her, falling to his knees in front of her. "Mama," he cried and pressed his face into her lap.

She leaned back and sighed, stroking his heavy curls, pulling at them gently. "My wonderful child," she said. "I was so worried, so worried."

The red, squarish digital numbers fade, numbers lurking behind numbers, outlines of the time spent waiting and still, he doesn't come home. Soon gray light will filter through the window, a dull wash pocked by the sounds of birds rousing themselves, calling out in expectancy, faith, that the sun will rise once again.

18 / Ladies of the House

Max's telephone call came at a time when I'd been thinking about Malva. Waiting, that's all I ever do, I remember her saying in the high, affected, little-girl voice she reserved for Big Max, Max's father.

I was in the basement, sorting baby clothes. I'm not a collector. If Larry, my old man, sets the newspaper aside to yawn or scratch, I whip it away to wrap potato peelings. The kids' drawings last only two days on the refrigerator door. They've learned not to mind. But after sorting through the baby clothes, I couldn't bring myself to do anything with them. I repacked the booties and bonnets, the burp-stained nighties, yellow, white and green. I never allowed pink or blue and laugh when I remember my youngest, my little girl, who had been bulky and bald and had the scowl of a midget wrestler. The neighborhood thought she was a boy at first and Polish men would stop us in the street to pinch her cheeks and say, "Strong like an ox. Make Daddy proud."

More and more while I tie shoelaces and fish apple cores from beneath beds, I think of the different women I have met and scorned. And lately, I've been remembering the summer of Malva and so I shouldn't have been surprised when Max phoned, even though seven years have passed and I thought he was in Vancouver. I used to wonder if it was my thinking about people that made them contact me like that. Was I a sender and everyone else a receiver? Once I wrote it down, the number of times in a day I thought of a person seconds before they telephoned and it was six. Now this doesn't surprise me.

In the basement sorting the clothes, I thought of Malva, her large steaming presence and the small house in East Kildonan where she lived with her five kids. She was never without rings of dampness beneath her arms, reaching to her waist sometimes, or the Kleenex tucked into the sleeve of her dress to dab perspiration and melting cosmetics from her face. When the phone rang, I had gone upstairs to defend the refrigerator against the kids. "Is the lady of the house in?" Max asked and I thought, great, just what I need, a week of free dancing lessons while the kids clean me out.

"Remember me?" Max said. "Max and company?"

Sure I remembered. I chased the kids outside and sat down on the floor in the hallway to talk. Max said he just couldn't picture it, me being married and all. "And all." I didn't ask what he meant, "and all." "I thought you said you hated kids," he said and I wanted to tell him to get out of my life but instead told him everyone hates kids when they're fifteen. "Not me," he said. "I was always crazy about my brother Buzzy, you know that." While we talked I imagined that he closed his eyes at the other end of the telephone, trying to picture me a mother. That he stood in a dingy hotel lobby or in a space as large as a closet that smelled of dirty socks and a rumpled bed and was remembering me, how I looked seven years ago, pared down to my bare essentials on that beach in Lake Winnipeg, face too thin, no hips to speak of. I was like one of those dolls whose limbs are connected by wires and elastic, threatening to spring apart any moment.

I wanted to tell him I'm okay now. Being a mother has smartened me up. If, for instance, when my kids grow up, they decide to take off with someone like him, I will know it right off and threaten to break their kneecaps, as Bobbie, who lives across from me, is fond of saying. I'd wring their necks. This is a rounder, smarter version of me, I wanted to tell him. As in v-e-r-s-i-o-n, not virgin. (My goal once was to be a virgin for life. I was keeping myself for myself. How Malva laughed!)

Now I skim my energy off by the spoonful, to keep doing so many different things at once, like the way I kept my eye on the front window while Max talked, watching my kids zip through their rash beginnings. If they suspected I was still on the telephone, they would swing from tree to tree like monkeys. I keep my ear tuned to their sounds as well, and can detect the slightest quiver of fear, pain, or the silence that means they are plotting to overthrow the neighborhood. And then I stop whatever I'm doing and go to them because I'm not one of those mothers who scream from windows and doors. You can hear the others, this is a neighborhood of screamers, especially Bobbie. And they always frame their challenges the same way. If you don't, they say, then I will. I imagine their kids grinning while kneeling among the garbage cans, rolling the threats in their untrustworthy palms, deciding if they should gamble. And then Bobbie has to follow through, come galloping across the street with her sawed-off broom handle. If I say they will get hit, Bobbie says often, they will get hit. At least she's consistent. The others just yell louder and louder as the day goes on.

No, because I've been going to the library and reading up, I'm one of those who think there is merit in squatting in the dirt with the kids and explaining things. I require that they stamp in rain puddles. I wonder with a nagging fear, what if the books are wrong? Will my kids someday accuse me of not being enough of a parent, of not waving broom handles? On this, Larry, my husband, has no opinion. Don't ask me, Larry says, because he feels he has had a bad example for a mother. It was she who advised me against pink and blue and buys the kind of presents that, if you didn't know her, would make you think she'd made a mistake with the name tags. For instance, last Christmas she bought our boy an EasyBake Oven, the girl a twelve-piece socket set and Larry an electric train.

So what did Max picture? I wondered. Me with a child at each breast and a halo around my head? I could never picture myself married either, or with kids. I told him it happened all the time. I slept through my first pregnancy and dreamed of a fat salmon curling and swerving about inside. But the second I felt my baby's head, wet between my legs, and saw his tiny, pale testicles, I decided to get serious. Although, I suppose, no one would ever admit to not being serious about parenthood. Even the man I read about who sat on his new baby twice in the same week because he kept forgetting where he put it said he took his job as a father seriously. I work harder at being a mother than I do at being Larry's wife. Children are interesting. I told Max I had two kids, a dog, a cat, a goldfish and a husband, Larry. And when I said it, listing it like that, I was amazed that so much had attached itself to me in such a short time. My oldest will be in kindergarten in fall. The next year, the youngest. And then what? Larry has put his foot down. No more kids.

Max asked when all this had taken place, wanting to find himself in it somewhere, I suppose, his voice taking on the tone of someone who had come across a worm in the creamed corn. It happened gradually, I said. It had taken six and a half years. It's strange, I said, what happens to time. Once, summer was eternity. Now, six years have just skidded past, bumped and piled up onto each other, becoming a lump of chicken pox, cuts, bruises, of forgetting Larry's features when he's not home, not noticing how he smells when he is. Everything is mixed together. Standing at the window last night, waiting for Larry, I remembered what Malva said when she waited for Max and his father to finish packing the night they left to go back to Vancouver. She was showing me the photographs, a stack of them, Malva tall and slim, in her cheerleader skirt, on the volley-ball team, Malva at CGIT camp in the summer.

"Those were the best years of my life," she said. "A bunch of us made a bonfire on the beach and stayed up all night."

"What about the mosquitoes?" I asked. "Didn't you get chewed to bits?"

"Mosquitoes," Malva said. "There weren't any."

"But they didn't have repellent way back then, did they?" I said, but Malva, being the type you had to hit over the head to insult, didn't notice.

"If there were mosquitoes at camp, I would have

remembered," she said. "And there weren't. We stayed out all night and not one bite."

"But it's strange," I said to Max, "what happens to time when you can do that, look at old photographs like that and remember dates and events and people's names and the nice things but forget about mosquitoes and can't remember what the present month is or where you went yesterday."

"Well I can," Max said. "There's nothing wrong with my memory. And you sure changed your mind in a hurry, if you know what I mean."

"No, I don't."

"Well, for someone who said they wanted to be a virgin."

I gave him a point for remembering. I felt I should apologize. He was remembering that wild night on the beach, both of us burrowed down into the damp, warm sand. Too much wine that time, I'd been too relaxed, searching for the Big and Little Dippers, lying there content to let the night cartwheel across my eyes. And before I knew it, Max was drawing snakes on my bare belly, saying, guess which finger did it? And suddenly he was on top of me, a slippery little eel trying to wiggle his way up inside. But, thank God, he'd drunk too much, too, and his weak tiny prick collapsed. When I think of my own kids on a beach getting stoned, I get sad. And then I quickly put the sadness away because it won't happen. I have everything planned. Too many kids have been ruined by a failure of planning. Sorry, sorry, Max said after I bucked him off and sent him flying. He threw the left-over wine into the lake. Wait until you meet Doris, my mother, Max had said, yelling over the sound of the waves. She'll straighten you out, he said, his face shining with purpose, as though I were a knot he intended to pick loose.

"Where are you now?" I asked Max, feeling safe because even if he was in a phone booth on the corner, I could plead my kids and say I couldn't get away to meet him. I couldn't picture him anywhere except in a confined space, a car, in the cluttered house trailer on a parking lot where he'd lived with his father that summer.

"I'm at Malva's," he said as though I should know. That was why I'd been sorting through baby clothes and thinking about Malva. They, no doubt, had been talking about me.

"How is old Malva, anyway?" I asked, feeling guilty suddenly as though I'd betrayed something.

"Completely gray," he said. "Or else she's stopped dyeing her hair. I promised Dad I'd drop in on her and say hello. Crazy, eh?"

Sending a son around to say hello to an ex-lover was crazy. Why did he do it then? To gloat? "Are your parents still together?"

"It wasn't so great in the beginning," Max said. "In fact, the old bugger took off again. On the train. I caught up with him in Regina and brought him back. But now, you wouldn't believe it. Both of them go to the Baptist Church regular. Dad even quit the booze. Mom can't quit grinning. But how about you? You happy?"

"I'm doing okay."

"I'm okay, you're okay. That's the name of a book," he said, sounding young, like the Max I'd met seven long years ago with his father in Agassiz.

"Good-day," Big Max, Max's father, said to my mother in spring. He was being polite. He was containing himself, being serious and toned down because he sensed my mother would not approve otherwise. "Well, hello sweetheart," he said to Malva several weeks later and won her heart. I love the ladies, he said often. I love helping them out.

He stood at the screen door at the back porch, looking in at me and my mother where we stood washing clothes, both of us startled by his sudden appearance. His belly was patchy with tic-tac-toe patterns of white threads that my mother used to mend tears in the screen where the little kids had poked their fingers through. She mended, they poked and so on.

There were two families in my family, the older group of children who were labeled the "big kids." And the younger group, the "little kids," who I didn't know very well by choice, just saw as skinny or chubby forms running here and there, crying, pestering. I realized early that it was dangerous to pay the little kids much attention because they tended to grab hold and get hopeful and follow you around.

Once I asked my mother, seriously, because I wanted to know, had she really wanted all of us? And so I asked her why she had so many kids. Didn't you believe in birth control? I asked. For two seconds her face underwent a series of emotions. I could see her struggle not to hit me. I realized I had phrased the question wrong. And then her chest caved in as her shoulders dropped forward. Nothing worked, she said.

That was another thing, her chest. I disliked how it hung down beneath her dress, shapeless, like two floppy pears. I thought if she'd hitch herself up properly, like other women, that maybe she wouldn't be alone so often at night. I listed my complaints to her. She didn't raise kids right. When you're up to your ass in alligators it's hard to remember that your purpose is to drain the swamp. I thought my position, my bird's eye view, would be welcomed and so I told her, you're doing it wrong. Kids are a vacuum. Whatever's around will rush in and fill the space. So you just can't take things away from them without giving them something to take its place. But she resisted all my advice with a scornful sneer.

All along, I wanted to know why Max's father was called Big Max, but didn't ask until it was almost too late. He was shorter than his son, as wide as he was tall, which didn't make him seem big to me, but soft and ineffective as a rubber ball with a hole in it. He was partially bald, red-faced and had quick, small eyes.

"Is the lady of the house in?" Big Max asked.

My mother put her hand to her mouth, remembering the treacherous, loose teeth. Her dentures needed relining. She kept putting it off, saving every extra cent to send one of the talented little kids into the city each week to study the trumpet. I am banking on the boys, my mother said often, because you girls just go and get yourself pregnant. Years ago, she had cried and spit blood into the slop bucket because they couldn't afford to have her teeth fixed, only pulled all at once and false ones put in place. For weeks she seemed to be all teeth, two rows of gleaming porcelain in her bruised face. She wouldn't go anywhere. She stared at her reflection in the mirror and moaned. But now, a hand was sufficient to cover the embarrassment of teeth dropping down unexpectedly, revealing a pink moist space for all to see. My father played bingo at the Legion and had won an ironing board, a clock and last week, the jackpot. It was rolled up inside a tumbler in the cupboard, money to reline my mother's teeth.

"I am the lady of the house," she said from behind raw knuckles.

"Oh, I beg your pardon, Ma'am." He blushed. "But you don't look old enough. You two could be taken for sisters." I thought I would be sick.

My mother laughed, a short harsh bark as if to say, don't think I believe that malarky because I don't.

"Could I have a moment of your time?" he asked quickly and demonstrated how filthy the couch was by placing a handkerchief over the end of the vacuum cleaner hose and vacuuming to show the amount of dirt left behind even though she had just cleaned it.

"I had no idea," Mika said, cheeks flaming.

"That's quite all right, Ma'am," Big Max said. "It's not as bad as some I've seen. Let me tell you. The lady next door," he said and raised his eyebrows.

"Oh," Mika said.

"You wouldn't believe it." He handed her a card which said, "Max and Company. Specialists in At-Home Rug and Upholstery Cleaning."

"Oh, I don't know," my mother said. She held up the

circle of dirt as though it were a piece of soiled underwear. "I could do it myself. With a brush and soap suds."

"That's true. You could. But all you'd really be doing is grinding the dirt in deeper. We have special equipment which sucks it all away."

My mother frowned, wiped her hands on her dress and sat down on the piano bench. "How much?"

He told her.

"I'm sorry," she said, getting up quickly. "But I don't think I'll bother. The couch," she said, her words cut off suddenly as the teeth slid downwards.

Big Max wound the vacuum hose around his neck and picked up the machine. He looked tired. "That's quite all right," he said. "You're under no obligation whatsoever." He walked through the kitchen, the hose trailing and bumping along after him, into the back porch to the screen door. He set the machine down and took another handkerchief from his pocket and dabbed at his neck. "Say, I wonder. Could I bother you for a drink of water?" he asked. "It's been a long day."

Mika rushed to the kitchen sink to oblige. Big Max went to the top of the driveway, stuck his fingers into his mouth and whistled. Along came Max, pants too long and rumpled over his dusty shoes, his jacket, a polished cotton windbreaker, hung open, sleeves jammed to his elbows, buff collar turned up. He had a long, thin face and an expression of boredom which I later discovered was exhaustion from staying awake nights, trying to keep track of his father. Max wasn't handsome in the dark, pouty, thick-lipped way most girls required. He had dirty-blond hair and a fuzzy mole on one cheek. But the reddish fringe of a moustache made him interesting. Big Max introduced us, winking at me as he did so. He clapped Max on the shoulder. "Meet my right arm," he said. "No work to be had in Vancouver, so Max here says, there's money to be made in the east. And so here we are. I see you don't think there's anything wrong with putting the kids to work either," he said and motioned to me.

"Certainly not," Mika said. "I had to help out and so do they." She sat on the edge of the kitchen chair, feet hooked in the rungs, while they sipped at the water, being patient although I knew she was straining towards the sound of the washing machine, the load that should be rinsed and hung out to dry.

"The boy's lonesome for his mother," Big Max said quietly with sad eyes as he handed her his empty glass. Max's eyes met mine, wavered, and he looked up at the ceiling. I saw the flicker of his tongue in his cheek. "We're just trying to make enough to pay off a few bills and then head back home. "You know how it is," he said. "The wife's getting tired of waiting."

"Oh yes," Mika said. "Bills. I know." She glanced at Max and chewed her lip.

"I'd throw in the chair as well," Big Max said. "I'd do the chair and the couch for the same price I quoted. Only, don't tell the neighbor."

Mika hesitated. She looked up at the clock. She sighed and got up from the chair and went over to the cupboard. She turned her back to them as she counted out her teeth-relining money. "You may as well do all the chairs," she said, "the dining room ones as well."

"There you go, kids, your big chance." Big Max slid the car keys across the counter. "You're on your own this afternoon. See what you can do."

When Max and his father had finished cleaning Agassiz they moved on into Winnipeg. Big Max let Max have the car to drive out and pick me up. The summer was long and hot. I knew that I wouldn't be going back to school and so meeting Max was a diversion, a way to keep from thinking about what to do. I carried the vacuum hoses around my neck. I became their apprentice.

Max was sitting at the table doing the books. Even though we had cranked open all the windows in the trailer, it smelled of dirty socks and stale bread. The noise of traffic on Portage

Avenue was deafening. "And what are you going to do this
afternoon?" Max asked his father.

"What are you, a cop? I give you a chance to make some
extra money and you ask questions. I thought you were
broke."

Max threw aside his pencil. "We're broke. You and me.
And no wonder. I suppose you're going out with her this
afternoon?"

Big Max cleared his throat and drummed his nicotine-
stained fingers on the table. "What d'ya say, honey," he said,
winking and nudging me in the ribs. "Let's ditch this guy." He
smoothed his sparse hair which was gathered up from one side
of his head and slicked down over his bald spot. He looked at
his watch, got up and pulled aside the curtains. "She'll be
coming around the mountain," he sang.

"Get serious," Max said. "We promised Doris we'd send
her a hundred a week. Where's the money coming from this
week?"

"She'll be coming around the mountain when she comes."
He stopped singing. "We're just going to a movie, son. That's
all."

"And you're taking the whole works of them with you."

"Well, we couldn't get a sitter."

Max grew pinched around the mouth. "Christ. I'll bet
Buzzy hasn't been to a movie since we left."

"Great balls of fire," Big Max said as Malva opened the
trailer door and stepped up inside. "Speak of the devil."

"God," Malva said. She looked disappointed to see Max
and me there. "You saved my life. I'm just about beat." Malva
was a large, pink and white floral printed woman with jet
black hair which stuck out in all directions, white sandals and
a large woven handbag with multi-colored straw flowers. She
had an electric-pink cupid's bow running up and out of her
natural lipline and a pencilled beauty mark on her cheek. Bits
of her drooped now, a strap slid down one arm. I noticed a
run in her stocking.

"It just doesn't pay to dress up in hardware," Malva said in a high little voice. She crossed her thick leg and tucked the run out of sight.

Big Max grew perky and flushed and jauntily crooked his elbows at his sides as he hurried over to the refrigerator and took out two beers. "I told Malva to drop in after work and take a load off," he said.

"Load, is right," Max said, but his father appeared not to notice. His hand shook as he poured the beer into glasses and set them on the table.

"Why don't the two of you get off your bums? Go out and do something," Malva said. "I know if you were mine, I'd damned well make you."

I'd met Malva several Saturdays in a row. The only thing she could talk about well was her kids. That Cal, I don't know what I'm going to do with him besides kick his arse, she'd say. Do you think you could come around and have another talk with him? Or, Millie's being a regular pain lately, she'd say, and go on to describe something cute Millie had done, disguising her pride in complaints. Max would smoulder while his father made sympathetic noises and opened more and more beer until Malva would fall apart at the table, shrieking at his corny jokes, her grown-out permanent hanging down onto her forehead in sweaty black strands. Once when Big Max went to the bathroom, I said to Malva, "Why don't you go home where you belong and look after your kids?"

Her face twisted and crumpled and she began to cry silently, wiping her eyes with the back of her hand, removing the painted-on beauty mark. "You," she said and glared at me through swollen eyes and a puff of smoke, "don't know what it's like."

Like the run in her stocking, Malva was flawed, as far as I was concerned. Play with matches, get burned. Jump off a roof, suffer gravity, I'd learned. It was the law of consequences. And Malva had broken the law. She was a divorcee. "You don't know what it's like," was no excuse. If you can't stand

the heat, don't go into the kitchen in the first place, I
reasoned and although I disliked my mother's clenched-jaw
approach to life, I was still proud of her because she had not
broken any of the laws. She had not run away from us or
taken a lover. She had played it straight.

"I'll drop you and her off," Max said, scooping up the keys
from the table top.

Malva and Big Max looked at each other over their beer
glasses. Big Max set his down, licked foam from his top lip.

"It's okay," Big Max said. "We've got time to spare. We
thought we'd take a cab on over to the house."

"Cabs cost money," Max said.

We dropped them off in front of Malva's house. From
every corner of the yard, kids came running, clutching and
grabbing at Malva's dress, her purse.

"The most they'll be able to do with that bunch around is
rub varicose veins under the table," I told Max as we drove
away. "Don't worry."

Minutes later, Max and I cruised a likely looking street,
one shaded by an arch of elm trees and graceful, sweeping
birches nodding from front lawns. We chose a less imposing
house, one without the clipped, precise look of the others,
where the birch was overgrown, pushing against the front
window and shutting out the light. There were weeds among
the flowers. As we rang the doorbell, I had the feeling we
were being watched. The chimes echoed inside and
immediately the door was opened by someone who looked like
the wife of a United Church minister. She stood in a cave of
a hallway, above her, a dazzling chandelier, around her, dark
walnut walls. In contrast, she was a pastel person in her pale
blue dress and hair. She wore a soft painless look on her long
face, which matched her dress, uncreased, unflinchingly
serene. She would not say shit if she had it in her mouth,
Max said later. Oh dear, she might say, or my, my.

Max explained we were working our way through college.

"Yes, yes," she nodded. "I think that's just wonderful," she said, not waiting for him to finish his whole line. "I have had three in university, and I know how difficult it must be for you young people. Wonderful," she said in a voice I couldn't imagine ever being raised, "that you young people are willing to work like this. I do admire your industriousnesh," she slurred when Max went out to the car to get the cleaning equipment.

"She's bombed," I whispered when Max came back. As we wound our way through more walnut hallways, she strained to appear steady, picking her way among the solid furniture as though she walked across a creek on stones.

"I apologize for the mess," she said as we entered the living room, but there was no mess. The furniture was arranged predictably around the edges of an oriental carpet. Judging from the dust on the table tops and the plumped cushions on the furniture, I felt that it had been a long time since the room had been a real mess.

She wobbled slightly and leaned against a chair. "This is the one that could use cleaning," she said, indicating a royal blue love seat. "Do you think you could manage it?"

Max gave her an estimate. "I think that's very reasonable," she said and I could see him kicking himself. "But before you begin, I think I shall pop into the kitchen and get us all something nice and cold. It's a warm day. Do you young people like iced tea?" she asked and smiled at the wall beside my head.

"Amazing," Max said when she'd left the room. "A quiet drunk. I've never met one before."

She returned with a tray and three glasses. Max seemed mesmerized and became serious and quiet, getting her to talk so he could catch her in a slur. An hour later, we were still drinking iced tea and refusing stale fig newtons. I unpacked the equipment but Max ignored me. He asked for more tea. The woman grew talkative, lively, and two spots of color rose in her cheeks. She took Max to the fireplace and showed him photographs on the mantle, naming and placing each person.

I began to vacuum and so they moved on into the dining room to continue their conversation away from the noise. Max took out his wallet and showed her pictures of Doris and Buzzy. And so I went on ahead and mixed the cleaning solution and poured it into the machine. I foamed down the love seat and began working the suds in. My hands turned brilliant royal blue.

"Shit," Max whispered, "didn't you test it first?"

I shrugged. That was always Big Max's job, to make sure the fabric was color-fast.

He groaned. "Get it off, fast. I'll keep her talking."

"Isn't it rather uneven, blotchy?" the woman asked when I'd finished.

Max explained the way his father would. That was how velvet was. It's the nap, he said. The problem of the nap. It would look entirely normal when dry. She seemed satisfied. She blinked in the sunlight as we said goodbye at the door. "You are very fortunate," she said to me, "to be going to university. I made certain mine went. But do they appreciate it?" she asked. She hung onto Max's arm. Her voice had risen.

Max shrugged loose and smiled as he backed down the stairs. "I certainly do, Ma'am," he said. "I appreciate every single thing. Hurry," he said to me, "the old dame's going to fall apart."

We stepped into the house trailer hours later to the startling sight of the kitchen nook folded down into its bed, rumpled blankets, beer bottles, a pizza box and crumpled Kleenex. The impression left behind in the blankets of two sweating bodies.

"I guess they did more than rub varicose veins."

"Shut up." Max's tense face looked bruised beneath the eyes. His skin took on a sour odor. He went about the trailer kicking doors, clearing away the evidence of his father's tryst, going further than he needed to, washing dirty socks in the sink, cleaning out the cupboards and discarding rotting food.

And then he went to the payphone on the corner and called his mother in Vancouver.

"Malva's a pig," Max said, slapping a card down in front of me.

"Malva's a pig," I said because he was in no mood for disagreements.

"How could he do this? To my mother?" He snapped several more cards down. "If you could've heard her. She was crying."

I arranged my hand. To me there was nothing sad about adult problems. It was entertaining to watch grown people make shambles of their lives. It was like poking a wounded caterpillar with a stick and watching it curl into itself. "Why don't you do something about it?" I asked.

Do something, my mother had pleaded, finally coming to me for advice one day. He's taken off, she said, and he says he's not coming back.

Who, Dad? I asked because the idea was silly. She was silly for believing it. Where would he go?

Places, she said. He has places. Where do you think he goes every night? She stood at the buffet, looking out through the lace curtains towards Main Street. She was crying. I was impatient to be out and gone. It was Saturday night. It was then that I told her, no wonder. Look at yourself. Do yourself up, why don't you? Fix your hair, put on some makeup. Don't be such a drag, I said. And maybe he would stay home with you.

"Like what, do what?" Max asked.

"Think," I said and played my first card.

"Guess what," Max said the next day when the coins had clanged down into the box. I heard traffic sounds, he was calling me from the phone booth on the corner. "The Thing has asked me to baby-sit so they can go out pubbing." Plastic banners above the used car lot flapped in the wind, sounding like waves on a large lake.

"And one of the kids is going to get sick while they're out."

"They are?"

"And you'll have to call the pub and tell them to come home."

And so began a summer of sabotaged dates, faked emergencies in Vancouver, hatched by Max and his mother and me from the telephone booth on the corner, the conference room for our war games. Malva and Big Max never had a chance. I saw him deflate slowly. When he was with Malva he was jumpy. They got on each other's nerves. The climax came one night when Big Max had too much to drink and Max slipped out and arranged for his mother to call Malva's house, something she'd never done before, and he persuaded his father to talk to Buzzy who was sick again. And Buzzy started sobbing and saying, come back Daddy, and Big Max began to cry as well and then Malva began wailing in the kitchen about not wanting to hurt children and then Doris got on the line and began to cry and several minutes later, Big Max was promising to leave for Vancouver that same night.

"You would not believe what happened to my parents," I think Max said. "They're like two love birds." Maybe I made that up.

"Good, I'm glad. I love happy endings."

"Not only that," Max said. "Our business took right off when we got back to Vancouver. We have five cleaning vans now. As a matter of fact, I'm in Winnipeg to see if I can interest anyone in a franchise."

Through my front window, I saw smoke curling up from the city, the brewery chimney. We live close to Larry's work. He's a body man. Would I like to get my hands on that body, he jokes when a stacked woman walks by. He works in an autobody shop several blocks away. It's his own. Around us, different odors compete for my attention, the garbage incinerators, the brewery, a potato chip factory. The faint wail of a siren threads its way along my nerve endings and I listen for the kids.

"Congratulations."

"Yeah, well. I didn't call to brag, eh?" He grew quiet. "It's just that I promised myself years ago that if I was ever back in Manitoba, I'd give you a call. You never answered any of my letters. I'd like to know how come. I've been wondering all this time. How come you took off? Was it because of me?"

We might as well do something while we wait, Malva had said after she had finished crying and washed her face and patted swollen eyes. She colored in the beauty mark and the cupid's bow. She set a box down on the table between us. She blew dust from the lid and began to sort through the contents. "And what do you think you'll end up doing in Vancouver?" she asked, her voice tinged with sarcasm.

"I'll probably get a job," I said, "not that it's any of your business."

"I'll bet. My guess is that you'll get more than a job. My guess is that you'll get pregnant."

"Guess again. You hope, you mean. Misery loves company. We're not all stupid, you know."

"Hah." Malva spread snapshots across the table. "What makes you think you're any different?"

And I told her about my plan to remain a virgin for life.

"Hoo hoo," Malva said when she'd finished laughing. She wiped her eyes on a corner of her blouse. "Then you'd better become a nun. Because I, for one, will not hold my breath otherwise."

Max came and stood in the doorway for a moment, a wide grin, hoses wrapped around his neck. "So how's it going, girls?" he asked.

"Don't you girl me, you little runt," Malva said. The door slammed shut.

"You can't blame him for wanting his parents back together," I said.

"Fools will rush in."

"Just because you couldn't hang onto yours."

Malva leapt up, knocking the chair backwards. She raised her hand. "You brat," her husky voice rasped from too much smoke. "You ignoramus. If you were mine, I'd slap you silly."

I got up. "Just try."

She stuck her finger into my chest. "Sit down." She began to rummage through the box. She held up a large photograph. "Meet my Ex. The one I couldn't hang on to."

I was surprised. He was handsome.

"Know why I couldn't hold onto him?"

I shrugged.

She lit another cigarette and sat down at the table. "Simple. I told him I was pregnant. I'm pregnant, I said to him. And he asked me, how did it happen? And I said, sorry, must have been something I ate. My diaphragm slipped," she explained. "Did I have any control over that? And he said *he* was up the creek. *He* was up the creek. That's the absolute pits, he said. Most people say shits, but not him. Not my Ex." Her hands shook. She set the picture down. "He was the kind of a guy who talked and looked nice, better than most. Better than Big Max. That's why I went for him. I am perturbed, he'd say before he'd hit one of the kids. So, he said he'd look into the matter. And to make a long story short, that's what he did."

"Did what?"

"Found some guy who would do an abortion."

I felt sick to my stomach and sorry I'd started the whole thing.

She ground out her cigarette in the ashtray and blew smoke in my face. "And I said no way. And so, a week or so later, he says to me, okay dear. I'm sorry, but you've given me no choice. And after we made love, he left me."

Big Max had come into the room silently and stood behind her chair, wrapping his arms around her neck and rocking her as he talked. He kissed the top of her frowsy head. "Isn't she something?" he said. "My Malva. Who would have thought I'd been lucky enough to find someone like her. Isn't she gorgeous?" He pressed his face against her head. "Oh, Babe," he said. "I'm sorry I have to go. Really sorry."

Malva began to cry. "Go away," she said to me. "Just go away."

"The car's ready to go," Max said loudly from the doorway. I took him by the arm and led him outside.

He chewed his knuckles as, through the windows, we watched their movement from the kitchen into the back bedroom.

"Just like Dad," Max said bitterly as the light in the bedroom blinked out. "He always has to have one for the road."

An hour later, we headed down the highway. Big Max took the first driving shift and Max climbed into the back seat and slept.

"She'll be coming around the mountain when she comes," Big Max sang. I watched the flash of telephone poles, the wires rising and falling but the vanishing point remaining fixed in the headlights. Insects splashed against the windshield. I tried not to think of the time passing and the distance between myself, Agassiz and my family growing wider and wider. I had no plan. I had no idea what I would do when I got to Vancouver. Big Max swore as a large insect exploded on the glass in front of his face.

"Why do they call you Big Max?" I asked to create an opening for conversation, to keep from thinking about the highway, the dark miles flashing past in the telephone poles.

"Who, what?" he asked and laughed. "Oh, that. It's a family joke." He patted my knee. "Listen," he said, lowering his voice. He jerked his head towards the back seat. "The kid's told me. You know. About you and him? Well, just want you to know. This is Big Max," he said and cradled his crotch with his hand. "If it turns out the kid's no good, you know where I am."

And so the first place we stopped for gas I said I had to use the can and I kept on going.

"I just got cold feet," I said to Max on the telephone. "That's all."

"You're sure?"

"What else? I was pretty young to be leaving home."

"Yeah. I know. But all these years, I was kind of thinking, you know. That maybe it was me." His voice wavered.

"Oh no, no. Absolutely had nothing to do with you. I got cold feet. I told you."

"I'm glad," he said, sounding bright and cheerful once again. "Anyway, you should try me now. Now that I've had all these years of experience."

"Thanks, but I think I'll pass," I said and laughed. We talked for a bit more and then I said I heard the kids and had to go.

I hung up the telephone and went out to them and mended a hole in their plastic wading pool. Then I took a package of chops from the freezer and put it into cold water to defrost because I can never remember to do it first thing in the morning. I had a full hour before I needed to think about cooking and so I went into the basement to finish stripping down a piece of furniture. We may as well do something while we wait, Malva said. I see others in the neighborhood, a neighborhood of screamers and, like me, watchers at the window, shadows behind lace curtains, silhouettes against a hall light, leaning with our elbows on the sill, all over the city, in Vancouver, watching for the mailman so that we can get the good and the bad news and get on with the day. Watching for our kids to be free from school so we can get past the chore of supper and put them to bed. Waiting for late husbands so that we can get on with our arguments, our inflictions, and then reach for one another beneath the blankets, touch feet and whisper about the mail, the children. Wait for another day. And as I worked and worked, scraping away the sharp-smelling paint remover and uncovering the pale, unevenly grained wood beneath, I thought of my mother. That I should write her a letter. But I didn't know what I would say. I thought of Malva. I think about myself. When both kids are in school, what will I do?

19 / Dreaming of Jeannie

Bobbie stands in front of the steamed-up mirror in the bathroom, curling her eyelashes. Every night for the last month now, while she slings beer downtown, Wayne sits with his nose in that damned Physics book, neglecting Jason. Slinging beer, she says when she's making a point, but really, she seldom serves beer because she works at the Town and Country where everyone drinks Rusty Nails and Golden Cadillacs.

"Help, help," Jason says suddenly and makes a gargling noise. He's sitting on the toilet seat, watching her get ready for work. He squeezes his throat and sticks out his tongue. "Help, I'm being swallowed by a boa constrictor," he says. He's learned the song at the "Y" day camp and she wishes he hadn't. It's warm inside a snake, he says. You can see right through the skin.

A blob of blue mascara clings to her eyelash. "Go bug your Dad. I can't concentrate." The setting sun glances off the aluminum siding of the house next door into the bathroom window and through the plastic shower curtain, casting a rosy pall on the wall behind her. Reflected in the mirror are the new swan plaques she bought at Woolco. Above the tub, iridescent blue and mauve plaster of paris fish swim in a school. The mottled pink soap dish, tissue holder and toothbrush rack all match. She loves their marbled effect and wedgewood-type design. Finally, she's getting the house the way she wants it. From the kitchen comes the sound of pages being turned. She doesn't know why Wayne bothers to study Physics. He is studying to write the provincial exam in the end of June. Wayne, she thinks as she plucks the mascara loose, is so thick-headed he would probably get more out of the book if he put it under his pillow and slept on it every night.

"The snake is up to my neck," Jason gasps and then begins coughing.

"Stop that. You want to get bug-eyes permanently?"

"What's bug-eyes?" Jason asks, beginning what she knows will be a slough of questions designed to get her attention.

"Wayne," she calls, "isn't it time for Jeannie?"

Wayne flips through pages. She thinks she hears the sound of lead on paper. *What does this mean?* he writes in the margins of the Physics book. Good question. She opened the book once. Closed it. Not my bag, she told him. I never had a head for Science or Math. The teacher used to send me to the blackboard for target practice. The book smells strange, like something pressed too long with a hot iron. She follows Jason to the kitchen. Wayne stares at the wall, chewing the end of his pencil.

"Isn't it time for 'I Dream of Jeannie'?" she asks. "You haven't watched it all week." She would give anything to have a figure like Barbara Eden's. Wayne says he doesn't care as long as her boobs don't get any bigger than his hand. But she wouldn't mind. She read somewhere in a magazine how when Barbara Eden was pregnant she worked right up until the baby was born and no one could tell a thing because they disguised it with clothes and camera angles.

Wayne glances up at her and shuts the book. He squeezes around to the end of the breakfast nook and reaches across to the fridge, opening it. "I thought you were going to Eaton's before work," he says, his head still inside the fridge. Like his brother, Ronnie, Wayne has never gone in for sideburns or long hair but has begun to wear blue jeans because Ronnie does. But he wears them all wrong. He buys the pants too large so they bag in the seat and he rolls up the bottoms. Wayne likes flood pants and back pockets bulging like tumors with his wallet, his fold-up brush and comb. He sits there on the end of the bench, size thirteen brown oxfords planted on the floor with his head in the fridge. There is no room in the kitchen for both of them if they stand. So someone must sit at the breakfast nook under the window if they both want to be in the kitchen.

"I am going to Eaton's, why?"

"Dressed like that?" He backs from the fridge and gestures with the Coke in his hand.

"Course not. What do you think? I'm going to wear a coat, silly. How do I look?" She swings on her heel, doing a full circle for him, and notes the mixture of pride and uneasiness in his face. The elastic fish-net stockings bite the soles of her feet as she turns. The pleated mini-skirt brushes against her thighs.

"Same as always, bow tie's crooked," he says. He reaches across the cupboard and pulls open the cutlery drawer, searching for an opener. "You want a ride down?" He sets the Coke on the table and takes a brown envelope from the drawer. Bobbie holds her breath.

"I wouldn't mind. But come right back because Jason should get to bed early tonight."

"Forget it. Jason and me are going to the drive-in for a change. Aren't we, big boy?" Jason isn't big, but undersized for his age and scrawny like she is. Loose change rattles across the table. "Hey." Wayne shakes the envelope, looks inside it. "There was thirty bucks in here this morning."

"I needed a few things," Bobbie says.

"Great." Wayne crosses his arms against his chest. The veins in them swell. But he never uses his size against her. Wayne is the type who does things in secret to get back rather than outright stamping around. He keeps things inside and would let air out of a tire instead, like he did to the Italian at work, four flat tires because the guy kept hogging all the gravy jobs on the assembly line. Or, she thinks, he might decide to quit looking after Jason while she works and then what will she do?

She follows Jason out to the car, hooking the gate behind

her. The sun, suspended above the skyline, is a fiery balloon. From the garbage incinerators on Logan, the odor of rotting food mixes with a sharp metallic smell as it curls upwards. She waits for Wayne in the car.

Jason leans over into the front seat. "Honk the horn," he says and presses it. Bobbie smacks his arm.

"If I wanted the damned horn honked, I would have done it myself," she says. Jason curls up into the back seat and pushes his fingers into his mouth. "I'm telling Dad," he says.

"Go ahead. And I'll give you to the Eskimos and they'll feed you to their dogs."

Jason yells and kicks the back of the seat. Thank God for work, she tells herself. "Watch it," she warns.

Wayne comes from the house with his jacket slung over his arm. He slides in beside her. "You forgot your book," she says and laughs. "You could read on the way."

He backs the car from the driveway. "Whereabouts do you want to be dropped?" he asks as he swings out into the traffic.

"A straight line is the shortest distance between two points." She leans her head into his arm. "That's about all I ever learned." The muscles in his arm relax. He slides his arm around her shoulders and she knows that before she leaves the car, he'll press himself against her, or wedge his tongue between her teeth in case she meets a handsome man at work.

"I was thinking," Wayne says, "that maybe I should have taken a course in Physics. It's probably easier than just reading. That's what Ronnie did."

Ronnie is Wayne's older brother. He went back to school last year and finished pre-med. Bobbie is pissed off at Ronnie. Just because he has taken one Psychology course, he thinks he's an expert on kids and says they're doing everything wrong with Jason.

"Gotcha!" Jason says and lunges. He squeezes her neck. "I'm a boa constrictor."

"I'll constrict you," Bobbie says and pries his sticky hands free.

"Get off the pot, Jason," Wayne says. "We have had it up to here with your snake business."

Bobbie stands in front of Eaton's. Jason's feet wave as he scrambles into the front seat beside Wayne. Be good, Bobbie warned him when she got out of the car. You be good, Wayne said, and don't take any wooden nickels. Love ya, he said at last, leaving her standing there on the sidewalk feeling the full dead weight of his "love ya."

She moves through the flow of people on the sidewalk in front of Eaton's and pushes her way inside to the sudden onslaught of colors. She wants to check out the bath mats and toilet seat covers and she remembers seeing in a magazine a container for a spare roll of toilet paper that you can set out on a shelf or toilet tank. She passes by the cosmetic counters and a large poster that says *Hollywood!* She angles her way through a crowd of women who gather around a counter. *Gerrard of Hollywood*, the poster says, with, lower down, a photograph of a girl and the name, *Twiggy*. A gray-haired woman sits on a stool while a tall blond man smoothes lotions onto her face. The man turns. Holy cow. Clint Eastwood, she thinks. Once she saw Bobbie Hull, the hockey star, in Sporting Goods autographing hockey sticks. And it was the same thing. He looked bigger than he did on TV. He had one foot on a chair with the hockey stick across his knee as he autographed it for a sales clerk, who chewed her thumbnail while she waited. Bobbie circled around behind the skates and watched. Jason was too young for a hockey stick and she wasn't sure what team Bobbie Hull played for so she stayed hidden behind the skates. The way he carried himself, the easy way he smiled as he handed the woman the stick said he knew he deserved special attention. If she were Barbara Eden, she would have walked right up to him and introduced herself, no sweat.

Clint Eastwood says something funny and the women laugh. Bobbie is disappointed. It's not really him. She can tell by the voice. Immediately she notices he is not quite as

Dreaming of Jeannie

handsome and a lot shorter. He demonstrates the *Twiggy* look in cosmetics for the women. Bobbie thinks the gray-haired woman is making a complete ass of herself. It doesn't take long, the saleslady tells her when she asks. "He's a fast worker," she says and winks. "Less than twenty minutes."

"I do many movie stars," Gerrard says later as he hands Bobbie a cotton ball with facial cleanser so she can remove her make-up. But he doesn't say which ones. Does he do Barbara Eden? she would like to ask, but doesn't want to look ignorant like the gray-haired woman did. He's taken her rain-and-shine and hung it on the back of the stool and seems not to have noticed her fish-net stockings, go-go boots and mini-skirt. She's glad that the plastic cape he drapes around her covers her knees. She takes the cotton ball from him, wanting to touch the curly hairs on the back of his hand. A gold chain glints in the hair on his chest. The sight of it hits her behind the eyes, spreads down and settles in her breasts. He is not a fumbler, no throat-clearing before he speaks, no nervous scratching of his chin. He moves quickly.

"This *Twiggy* look is definitely for you," he says. Her heart bangs blood into her neck and cheeks. "We could do a modified look if you like or you could go for the full look."

"There's a pretty girl," she hears someone say in passing and she flushes. Everyone is staring at her. How was Barbara Eden discovered? she wonders. "I'll have the full look," she says through the tight knot in her throat. His hand is cool as he spreads cream across her forehead.

Is her skin comparable to movie stars' skin? Is he thinking what a surprise it is to find someone like her in Winnipeg? She can't tell anything from his hands. He shows her how to find the line of her cheekbones which are high and prominent, he says. Delicate bone structure, Dresden complexion, he explains to the women as he works. Dresden is in Germany, she has learned from selling Avon and counseling her customers on what colors suit certain complexions. Germany, where her father came from after the war. Only her father is not a delicate person, but a hard slaughterhouse man. With her face tilted up she can see the curve of her nose in the mirror. Broken nose, he doesn't say. Notice the chipped eye tooth and the false front teeth, he doesn't say that either. His fingers are cool as he spreads color across her cheeks, down her nose, and she imagines the curved bone straightening beneath his touch while his breath, orange scented, falls around her face like petals of a flower and she will lick them up and swallow them one after another and a tree will spring up inside her.

Too soon, he's finished. She wants to protest. He tilts the mirror so she can see. "Do you like it?"

God. She doesn't know. The person who stares back looks stricken, like she has all the problems of the world squatting on her head. A refugee.

"You see the effect I've created with white? It makes your eyes seem twice as large," he explains. "I have enhanced what you already have, that's all."

He has brushed on three different colors of eye shadow and painted eyelashes beneath her eyes almost half-way down her cheeks. But it's the false eyelashes that make her look weird. Two pairs, layered with mascara, and each time she blinks they tickle the hairs in her eyebrows. "I like it," she says.

He smiles and it makes the lie worthwhile. She folds her right hand overtop the left to hide her rings. What will she do if he asks her to meet him afterwards?

He bends near to unfasten the clip at her neck and she wants to push her face into his thick blond hair. "How old are you?" he asks.

"Twenty-three."

"You really should be using moisturizer," he says. "So many people think that face creams are for older women. But in this climate, everyone needs protection." He holds up a bottle of pink lotion. "This is very light. Your face doesn't feel greasy, does it?"

She shakes her head. No.

He removes the cape. "You're a beautiful woman," he says. "Your greatest asset is your skin."

Everything she wants to say stops in her throat. A woman. A beautiful woman. "Let me help you, Miss," the sales clerk comes into focus and hands Bobbie her purse. She collects her coat from the back of the stool. She takes her time. She longs for him to say more.

"Over here dear." The clerk motions towards the counter and Bobbie, vaguely aware of the admiring glances of the people who part to let her through, hears the gentle, low voice of Clint Eastwood telling a woman that this *Twiggy* look is definitely her.

Sixty frigging dollars' worth of creams in frosted bottles with statues of naked women for caps. On her charge card.

"And so he wanted someone to model this *Twiggy* thing for him," Bobbie says to Lana while she waits to cash out her tabs, "and so I said, what the hell, it's free."

She pulls off her boots and puts her aching feet up on a chair. Every last bit of the light-hearted atmosphere of the lounge has been crushed out and the room is like one huge smouldering ashtray. The final show begins in the cabaret upstairs and rock music blares through the plate glass wall above them.

"Sodom and Gomorrah up there." Lana works during the day at an exclusive golf club and met Billy Graham there. He gave her a special invitation to attend his Crusade. She acts as though she met a real star and keeps the invitation on her mirror in the change room. As she sets the machine down, her skirt moves up, revealing a button clipped into her fish-net stocking. Stamp Out Reality, the button says.

"Some guy gave it to me if I'd let him pin it on," Lana says when she asks. "I thought my kids would like it."

Jesus is Coming Again, Stamp Out Reality, Zap Them All

With Love, Peace, Follow the River Inside Yourself and Then Out Again. Everywhere she turns there are signs and buttons and scrawlings on buildings written by people who seem to be moving to some urge that she doesn't understand. What is reality that it needs stamping out? We are worm food, she tells Lana who spouts the life after death thing all the time since she's been to the Crusade for Christ. Bobbie has been to the nuisance grounds enough times to know that we are worm food and that's all.

Except for one hippy-type at the bar, the room is empty. Bobbie watches the bartender wipe the counter in front of the lone drinker for the third time. It's all linger and relax, she thinks, but once the last call is in the kitty, bingo. Lana finishes with the adding machine and Bobbie begins to add up her tabs. Music crashes down on them as the cabaret door opens. "Look who you see when you haven't got a gun," Bobbie says. Ronnie, Wayne's brother, comes down the stairs followed by another man. He squints in the light, sees her and waves.

"My favorite sister-in-law," Ronnie says as he lurches over, bends and kisses her on the neck. "Looking good," he says and stares at the front of her blouse. Two fried eggs, Ronnie says about his wife's boobs. Poor Carol, she is almost six feet tall and has nothing in the top story at all. Bobbie always makes a point of dressing up whenever they go to Ronnie and Carol's. "Looking real good," he says.

"I'll drink to that," his drunk friend says.

"What are you doing here?" she asks, meaning without Carol. She mixes the right amount of friendliness and business in her voice. She knows from working in this place when somebody is coming on. As far as she's concerned, the smart-ass university types are the worst kind. Like the guy who was studying Political Science who smoked a pipe and spent a week staring at her and then asked if she'd go home with him. He wanted to study her great organizational abilities. Hah.

Dreaming of Jeannie

She was blond but not dumb. She's sure as hell glad Wayne doesn't go out drinking with his brother.

"I'm celebrating," Ronnie says and leans against the table. He slings his checkered sports jacket over his shoulder. He's smaller than Wayne and not as good looking.

"What this time?" she asks.

"I've chosen my orifice," he says. "I've been accepted into dental college."

Bobbie thinks of Wayne sitting at the breakfast nook, pretending to read the Physics book, and what this will do to him. Then she remembers that she didn't have a chance to look at the toilet seat and tank covers in Eaton's. She is about to say something when Ronnie lurches off, his friend trailing behind.

She slouches into a plush high-back chair as she waits downstairs in the main foyer for the taxi to come. The dining-room waitresses also sit there in silence, a row of white shoes, sensible crepe-soled oxfords and her own black patent boots with the three-inch heels. The door opens. Wayne stands beneath the crystal chandelier, nervous and looking out of place in his rolled-up jeans. But she notices he's shined his shoes.

"Where's Jason?" she asks. When he comes unexpectedly like this, she thinks he's checking up on her.

"In bed," he says. Even his voice seems out of place. "It's only a ten-minute drive."

"'Night, Bobbie, straight home now," Teddy, the bouncer-doorman, smiles as they pass beneath the canopy.

"You seem quite friendly with him," Wayne says as they get into the car.

"I'm friendly with lots of people at work," Bobbie says. "They like me."

Wayne is silent as he backs from the parking spot. "Friendly to a point," she says. "I know how far to go." The headlights of their car sweep across the parking lot, capturing Ronnie for an instant as he walks across their path.

"Well, well, well," Wayne says and grins. "What have we here?" He flicks off the headlights. They watch as Ronnie walks over to a dark-haired woman who leans against a silver Barracuda. He slides his arm around her waist and steers her inside the car.

"It's none of our business," Bobbie says and feels strangely let down. Wayne should have been a cop, the way he delights in finding someone doing something wrong.

"Well, well," Wayne says. "Get that. A classy broad with a new car." He smiles as they begin the drive home.

His whiskers are prickly against her fingers as she makes him look at her. "What do you think of my eyes?" she asks. You are a beautiful woman, Clint Eastwood said, his crinkly blue eyes staring straight into her own.

Wayne squeezes her kneecap, making her jump. "Your eyes are like two pools," he says. "Cess pools."

She pushes his hand away. When he parks the car, she jumps from it before it's completely stopped and hurries into the house. Jason's door is closed. Wayne forgot to leave a light on for him. She bends over Jason and arranges his blankets. She smoothes hair from his forehead and smells the sharp dusty odor of it. She frowns. That damned Wayne. He hasn't bathed Jason again. When she goes out into the kitchen he doesn't even look up, but chews his pencil and stares blankly at the Physics book in front of him.

"Yes, master," Jeannie says in living color and blinks her eyes. Bobbie has tried all afternoon to do her eyes slanted like Jeannie's. She wishes she could find Harem pants. Even though Wayne is late and she's keeping supper hot, she laughs as Major Nelson winds up on the ceiling. Jeannie has a good sense of humor. Jason curls on the couch beside her, sucking his thumb. She's glad she happened to go past the Radio Shack and saw the TV sale. She only had to put ten percent down. She would really like to get a stereo, too. The living room has got a long way to go before she will be satisfied.

Dreaming of Jeannie

Jeannie disappears into her bottle and Major Nelson falls to the door. Next is the Brady Bunch which she hates. She gets up and goes to the kitchen to look at the clock. The Physics test has been finished for two hours now. Wayne's being late means either it went okay or it didn't. All day she wondered how he would do. She leans against the refrigerator and tries to stretch the tension from her shoulder blades. The kitchen is stuffy and smells of burnt eggs. A good soaking before she goes to work will ease some of the tension or she will never last the night.

She sprinkles rose-scented bath crystals into the bathtub and watches the water turn deep red. She thinks of the slaughterhouse, cement basins and maroon pools buzzing with flies. She swishes the red water and sees the slash of a knife, pigs hanging upside down, blood splashing to the door. A calf raises its head, eyes bulging as the wind escapes from the hole in its neck. In the nuisance grounds outside, a rock sends the rats running.

She lays back in the warm water and tries to enjoy her bathroom. It's almost perfect. On top of the puffy pink tank cover is a rose bowl with plastic pink and white roses inside. A white poodle conceals the spare roll of toilet paper. What if Wayne is with Ronnie? she wonders. Another woman? She sinks down into the water so that just her face is above the surface, surrounded by the popping sound of pink bubbles. Get real, she tells herself as she pictures Wayne with his blue jeans rolled up past his ankles, his size thirteen feet looking like duck feet. The only man in the room with a brush cut. The popping bubbles irritate her. As she sits up, the tension between her shoulder blades increases.

She slams cupboard doors when she takes dishes down from the shelves and smacks them into place on the breakfast nook. "Supper's ready," Bobbie calls. "Come and get it."

"Aww, I'm watching the Brady Bunch," Jason says even though the program is over and she knows he's just watching commercials.

"I'm warning you. Come now, or it's no supper at all."

He leans with his elbows on the table and scowls as she dishes up his supper. "Where's Dad?" he asks.

"Who knows? Eat."

"I hate scrambled eggs," he says. "Boa constrictors don't eat eggs." He shoves them to one side of his plate, stabs a piece of egg with his fork and dips it in ketchup. He draws a Happy Face on the bottom of his plate.

Very creative, she tells herself. Like the loonies on TV, painting one another's bodies. He'll get on well in this world, she thinks as she dials Ronnie's number. It's several minutes before she can bring herself to ask Carol if she's seen or heard from Wayne. "It's just that I have to go to work," she says, "or I wouldn't care. Some of the Blue Bombers have been coming in since spring training started and I hate to miss, because they're always good for a laugh."

"Really," Carol says with such undisguised envy that Bobbie feels sorry for her, because she is so tall and boobless and clued-out about Ronnie going around with other women.

That damned Wayne, Bobbie thinks as she hangs up. Not to call or anything. She telephones the Town and Country to let them know she won't be in. Jason laughs as she enters the kitchen. He has drawn Happy Faces all over the table with ketchup.

"You think that's funny?" Bobbie asks. "Let me show you what's funny." She sets his plate down on the door. "You act like a pig, I treat you like one. Get down there and eat."

Jason stares at her and then at the dish.

"Now."

"Where's Dad?" he asks.

"Now."

He slides out from behind the breakfast nook and edges past her. He stands in front of the dish. "I don't got a fork," he says.

"Pigs don't need forks. Eat."

His pulse jumps in his neck like a mouse caught in a glass jar. "I'm not hungry."

"Eat," she screams.

Bobbie sits on the couch in her housecoat, eating popcorn and drinking strawberry *Kool-Aid*, waiting for Wayne to come home. It's still too early to call Lana and ask her how things went at work. There is nothing but news on TV. She tries to read her book, *How To Win Friends and Influence People*. Learn to appreciate, the book says, and be interested in the other person. This is going to be hard, she tells herself, because Wayne is a boring person. But she wants him to be interested in her. And so first she has to be interested in him, the book says.

She hears the metallic rattle of keys and then his key turns in the lock. Her heart jumps. She sets the book aside and arranges herself on the couch so it will look as though she has been curled up watching TV and not waiting. She hears a thump as something is dropped heavily on the kitchen table. The Physics book. He walks past the couch, not looking at her. The smell of smoke and beer lingers. "How did it go?" she asks.

"Wouldn't you like to know?" he says. The toilet seat thuds against the tank. From the sounds of his stream he has had to go for a long time. Tomorrow, she will have to wash it off the door and the wall behind the toilet. He flushes the toilet and goes into the bedroom. She hears the bed springs squeak, his shoes clunk to the door. She waits several minutes and then turns off the TV before climbing into bed beside him in the dark to find his back turned to her. She slips her hands inside his shorts and rubs the gooseflesh from his skin. He's icy cold. He moves close to her.

"How did it go?"

He rolls over onto his back. She strokes the inside of his hairy thigh up into his moist crevice, across his flat, hard abdomen. She squeezes his spongy penis.

"It didn't," he says.

She puts her head on his shoulder, touches the cords in his neck with her lips and tastes bitter salt. The cords tighten and jerk. Oh shit, she thinks, he's crying. The bed moves with the convulsing of his stomach muscles. She boosts herself up onto an elbow and touches his face. He's laughing.

"What?" she asks and pulls his hair. "What, what?"

"Woo," he says and wipes his eyes. "Just like old times."

She holds the creases of his grin between her hands as she shakes his head. "Tell me, for pete's sake."

"The exam. They caught me cheating."

"Wayne," she says in mock horror and jumps on him. She straddles him and sweeps her nightgown over her head and flings it over the side of the bed. "I think that's terrible." His penis climbs up his belly.

"I knew the answers," he says as his mouth finds her breast. "Honest, I did. I don't know what got into me." He stops laughing, rolls onto her. She feels the pebbly surface of his pimply back beneath her fingers.

"Great," she says. "Some example you are for a father."

"How was Jason today?" he asks.

"Okay, okay," she whispers. "Don't wake him."

He giggles. "They caught me looking at the answers of the guy beside me." His beer-tinged breath is in her hair. She opens her legs to him. It's on the tip of her tongue to ask him, what do you think of my Jeannie eyes?

"Wayne," she says instead. "Forget Physics. You don't need it anyway. As far as I'm concerned, I've got the pick of the litter."

"Well, what can I say," he says.

20 / Spring Cleaning

They were sitting in the kitchen, Lureen Cooper and Marlene Paquet, waiting for their friend, Bobbie, to arrive with a bottle of rum. Marlene had chased the kids out into the chilly spring to play beneath the heavy clouds and telephone wires slung low from rugged cross-bars and glass condensors. They were enclosed in the kitchen which smelled of pine disinfectant, chlorine bleach. Their wash rags lay in a heap in the sink, shredded and torn. Around them on the gleaming enameled walls were dull rectangles of oxidized paint where pictures once hung. Just hang the pictures back up in the same place, Lureen had advised. But Marlene thought she would paint over the spots tomorrow.

Lureen watched as Marlene rolled cigarettes for them with prunish-wrinkled fingers. "What do you think, should I invite Bernice and her old man to the party?" Marlene asked as she handed Lureen a too-thick cigarette which would split its seams.

"It's your party," Lureen said. What she really wanted to talk about with Marlene, while they waited for Bobbie to return with the bottle of rum, was what she would cook for Easter.

"Sure, it's okay for Claude to say invite them," Marlene said. She flicked tobacco from her tongue. "But guess who's going to have to put up with Bernice coming over every day? Claude? Because you know as well as I do, once she gets her foot in, it'll be game over." Lureen listened with growing impatience. She admitted that this Bernice and Mike thing was puzzling but she was tired of discussing it.

"Well, this is it," Lureen said, mimicking Bernice, who implied she knew everything there was to know and waited patiently for them to realize it. Well, this is it, Bernice said with a slight smile on her anemic bony face as she examined a speck of dirt beneath her fingernail and chewed it loose. Lureen understood the look Bobbie and Marlene gave each other when Bernice said that. They wanted to smack Bernice across the mouth. Marlene joked that Bernice was such a terrible housekeeper that when Mike went to pee in the sink, there were always dishes in it. Bobbie had dubbed Bernice, "The Creature From the Black Lagoon," because Bernice's large ears stuck through her thin dark hair and she stored her bottom dentures in a junk drawer in the kitchen. Lureen suggested that Bernice's smugness was ignorance.

Sounds of shooting and dying erupted suddenly from the living room. They had left the television set turned on for the kids who all day wandered out the front door and in the back every few moments. They had rid the closets and cupboards of the things that tended to collect during the winter, the mismatched socks and empty sanitary napkin boxes. Now that the spring cleaning was complete, they wanted to enjoy their rum in peace and so they made a plate of sandwiches, set it out on the back stoop and hooked the door. From the window, Lureen had a perfect view of a block of sagging garages, battered garbage cans or sometimes Bernice, bent over and clutching her grapefruit-sized stomach as though she was afraid it would fall out, picking her way into their bitch and brag afternoon. I bleed like a stuck pig, every month, Bernice explained her swollen stomach, her constant anemia. They can't do nothing about it.

"Ever notice how Good Friday is always like this?" Lureen asked because she wanted to stop talking about Bernice. She referred to the smoke-colored sky, water dripping from the eaves. "It's always so gloomy."

"Hah. You just think so because the kids are home," Marlene said. She sent a cloud of smoke up towards the ceiling and frowned. "Dammit. Will you look at that? I think we missed a spot." She got up and dabbed at the door frame. "You're wrong," she said. "It's not always gloomy. It was sunny last year. I remember because I took the kids out to Aunt Sally's Farm at the zoo. Claude was away. As usual," she said and threw the rag back into the sink.

Marlene Paquet was not French, but a Mennonite. Lureen Cooper wasn't English. She hated it when people thought she was. One of the things she disliked about being a Cooper was their lack of customs. Just ham for Easter, she had complained to Marlene, that's all. Dull and boring. There were no colored eggs or Paska bread with icing letters spelling out, "He is Risen."

One of the kids began pounding at the door and then kicked sharply.

"Jesus." Marlene jumped up and went out into the back yard to settle an argument. The kids, five of them, were a collusion of bicycles and wagons. They gathered around her. Bobbie's boy had seized the opportunity of her absence to act up.

"You're not my mother," he said to Marlene. "You can't make me."

"Sheesh, kill him," Marlene said when she came back inside. "What's keeping her, anyway?" Reward yourself, Bobbie said. It's the only way I can force myself to do this crap, meaning the walls and ceilings. They smoked their cigarettes and waited for her to return. Lureen felt ground-out like the weather because Larry, her husband, was also away, as usual. He was away building a business. Well so long, he'd said to her one day. You won't be seeing much of me for awhile because I'm going to be busy building a business. Those were not his exact words but she liked to work things down to one basic line. And for once, she'd told them, Larry kept his word. She hadn't seen much of him since then, but telephoned him every afternoon to ask how it was going. She imagined him building the business, brick by brick, with a "Leggo" kit. Larry inquired, how was it going with the kids? Be sure Jamie stays away from the models, he said, referring to his electric train in the basement. And make sure they eat right and wear their mitts. Tell them this and that, he said and she felt like a telephone answering service. She enticed him into long conversations about the kids. She recited pieces of information which she read in the newspaper. She asked him questions. Who really shot JFK? she asked. And why do you think all those women went and jumped from bridges when Marilyn Monroe died? Even though Larry was just around the corner, she sometimes thought it was as though he'd gone to China for the week and stumbled in every Saturday afternoon suffering from jet-lag. Yellow-faced and surly, he greeted her as though he had a mouth full of broken glass. He curled into a ball in the center of the bed and slept until Sunday afternoon. While Larry built his business, she categorized and labeled and thought and dusted furniture with stained underpants.

"She's here. Finally," Marlene said as the front door slammed shut. "What in hell kept you?" she called.

But it was not Bobbie. Bernice tiptoed into the kitchen from the living room in her fuzzy bedroom slippers, walking as though she were avoiding puddles. She pulled her sweater around her sunken chest.

The kids had betrayed them, Lureen thought. Yeah, she's home, they probably said. She's not doing nothing.

"It's me," Bernice said and stepped onto the braided mat. She shook one foot and then the other like a rain-soaked cat. She surveyed the room with her deep-set eyes, in search of betrayal, exclusion.

"I don't usually use the front door," Marlene said. "Usually I have the couch in front of it." Marlene's husband, Claude, was a traveling salesman for a tool company. While he was away, she washed walls and arranged furniture. She arranged it according to the seasons, around the flow of cool air in summer and away from icy winter drafts that coated wall sockets with frost.

"I didn't come the back way because I was across the street, at the store," Bernice said. "I wasn't busy and so I thought I'd drop by. So what have you guys been up to?"

"Working our butts off doing spring cleaning," Marlene said. "Love your timing. We just finished."

Bernice crossed her arms over her chest and surveyed the room. "Smells like a soap factory in here," she said. "You sure wouldn't catch me doing no spring cleaning."

"Must be nice," Marlene said. She ground out her cigarette and lit up another.

"I clean," Bernice said. "But I do it bit by bit. When Mike's off, he gives me a hand with the big jobs."

"Good for Mike."

Lureen had been thinking about the folly of their work binge while washing walls. Although she would never come out and say it, she thought Marlene's Mennonite background had not been entirely done away with when it came to the housecleaning thing. She had been thinking of writing an article for *Chatelaine* on how not to have to do spring cleaning. How they were being foolish and driven and shouldn't worry if grease from cooking coated the set of good dishes on the top shelf. Wash them as you need them, she was going to say. Or do as she did, cover them in Saran. Come Easter, she would drag Larry out of bed, whip the Saran off the good dishes and serve up his ham on clean pink thistle and pussy willow plates. But it ticked her off that someone like Bernice might have caught on.

"Anyway," Lureen said loudly. "As we were saying. This guy I'm reading, Velikovsky, makes a lot of sense."

"Uum," Marlene said. "As you were saying." She contained her smile in the tiny muscle which jumped beneath the mole beside her lip.

"I mean, when you think about it, that bit in the Bible about the Red Sea parting."

"God. The Red Sea. I never think of it."

"But you would if you could make sense out of it and I think a cosmic event happening just at the same time as the sea parted is the answer. It's the same thing as the quick-frozen mammoths. A possible explanation."

Bernice shook loose her slippers and inched towards a kitchen chair. They ignored her.

"I always figured it had to be something other than the ice age that caused the mammoths to be frozen instantly. Some of them even had buttercups in their mouths."

Bernice parked her sharp rump on one corner of the chair and leaned forward with her elbow on her knee. "Well this is it," she said.

"What is it?" Marlene asked.

"What she said," Bernice said. "A cosmic event. It had to be." Because her bottom teeth were missing, Bernice's jaw jutted forward unnaturally. Lureen thought she wasn't so much a creature from a lagoon. In her stretch black ski pants, she resembled a daddylong-legged spider.

"Coffee?" Marlene asked abruptly. "Or don't you have time? I don't want to force you."

Bernice picked at a cuticle. I quit wearing my teeth because they hurt, she said once. If Mike doesn't like it, then to heck with him is what I say. She crossed her legs and swung her foot. "Mike's off today," she said and smiled. "It's his turn to look after the kids."

Lureen walked home from Marlene's feeling light-headed because of the rum. Pressed against the fence around her yard was the litter of winter uncovered, newspapers, wrappers of all sorts coated in a powdery dust. She disliked this dreary in-between season after the snow had melted, exposing the grit and garbage which was also entangled in the chokecherry bush. The bush was the only nice thing about her yard. She wondered how it came to grow there against the fence. She had looked it up in a book, chokecherry, and learned the fruit was used in pemmican after being pounded into mush. She read many books, biographies, television-repair manuals, child-rearing books, cereal boxes. She was proud of herself. She understood the language of the Bible and Shakespeare and income tax forms. She knew the women resented her books because once Marlene had asked her, what are you trying to prove, anyway? Sometimes, she wondered if they talked about her in the same way they did Bernice. She carried the frozen farm chicken Marlene had given to her because she complained to them over their rum about having to cook ham once again for Easter. You can have your Paska bread, Marlene said. There's just too much else that goes along with it. Customs give your kids something to be depressed about when they grow up, she said. But when Lureen looked at her children running around the yard, she felt a pang of doubt. That maybe she was cheating them by not teaching them about Easter. She missed the smell of the bread baking, the toadstool-shaped loaves crawling up and out of their cans and collars of wax paper. She missed the Easter baskets. Her sisters took turns making them, decorating them in mustard yellow and purple crepe paper. Even now, her mother was probably rolling colored eggs across newspapers to dry and planning Easter baskets for the youngest ones still at home and for the grandchildren who would be there for Sunday dinner. Only now, her mother shaped the nests from Rice Krispie cake and the grass was dyed coconut and so everything, the baskets included, was edible.

"I'm sorry," Larry said when she telephoned him. "But there's no way I can take the weekend off." The sound of the air compressor chugged and clanked in the background. Her chest tightened with the sound of his voice. When he came home, just the sight of him getting out of the car jumped forward to meet something in the center of her eye. Even though he often looked frowsy, rips in jeans, every new shirt initiated with a smear of grease, buttons yanked loose or tears snagged where he had brushed against sharp pieces of metal, still, she was captured by the sight of his thick, yellow, too-long hair, the methodical slowness of his movement across the yard to the house.

"I promised this guy I'd have his car ready to go by the weekend and I'm way behind. I'll have to stay here until it's finished." He sounded as though he had a cold. He was allergic to something he used in the shop.

"Come on, it's Easter weekend."

"So?"

"Well, we should do something."

"Why?"

"For the kids. It's a holiday and most people do something on a holiday."

"They'll survive. I have to do what I have to do."

She felt anger rising. "What you want to do, you mean."

He ignored her. "So, what's new?"

"Not a hell of a lot. I'm reading a book."

"What's it about?"

"Oh, this guy. He claims that the oil and gas deposits actually came from the sky. From the tail of a comet that passed close to the earth." Saying it made it sound silly. When she'd read it, she felt it made sense. Now she didn't know.

"Oh. Science fiction?"

"Kind of."

"Say." He hesitated for a moment. "What kind of do is Marlene having anyway?"

"The usual. Neighborhood people. She said to come around eight."

"I don't think I'm going to make it," Larry said. "You'll have to go without me."

Lureen resisted the impulse to throw the telephone against the wall. "That's just great."

"I'm sorry, but I just got to get this car done."

Now that the kids were in school and had to be in bed early, Lureen missed not being able to go down to the garage to sit and drink Cokes and watch him when he had to work late. She missed crawling around the inside of the cars, pulling loose torn headliners, side panels, helping him make it new. He whistled when she was there and told jokes or else they worked without speaking, finding their rhythm in the country western music he listened to. She missed the satisfaction of seeing pieces fitting together, the jars of nuts and bolts whose placement in the metal jumble Larry had memorized or knew instinctively.

Because she and Larry had moved seven times in six years she arranged furniture once and it stayed that way until the next move. Although they had moved frequently, they had not moved far. From one small town to another. Larry changes his jobs as often as other people change their socks, was what she told the women, but it was no longer true. They had not moved for two years. And she no longer helped put together the metal puzzle. Now she had to think about things like spring cleaning and cooking ham for Easter.

"This is quite a nice place you've got here," Mike said at Marlene's party.

"Get him," Marlene whispered and nudged Lureen in the ribs. They had seen Bernice's husband only from a distance before. He had come to the party dressed in a suit and tie. He was tall and very blond and did not look like a mailman. Lureen thought there was something young and earnest in the stiff wave above his forehead, his glossy shoes. He had sprayed them with *Amway Shoe Glow*, he explained when Claude commented on the glassy look of them.

"They're the same shoes he wears on the route every day," Bernice said. "He's nuts to spray them because his feet can't breathe."

"And you wouldn't enjoy it very much if they did," Mike said without a trace of annoyance.

Lureen thought of the contrast, Marlene's hand-made, pinchpleated drapes and the gray blanket Bernice had nailed up to her front window. When you sit at her table, don't lean forward, Marlene had warned. There's so much crap on it, you'll never get your arms loose. Marlene stood in the doorway watching as Mike admired the furniture Claude pointed out, their new raisin-colored frieze couch with its glittering silver threads, the color television set with remote control. Marlene had opened up the gateleg table and covered it with a linen cloth and set out food. Lureen knew Marlene was looking for signs of envy or dissatisfaction. "Hey, is what you do legal?" Mike asked Claude. "This is terrific," his good-natured smile never wavering.

"Oh, Marlene's a real work-horse," Bernice said and told them how early in the morning she had seen sheets on Marlene's clothesline.

Mike shook his head and sat down beside Bernice on the couch. He put his arm around her shoulders. "Sure can't say that about you, can we mother?" he said.

Bernice laughed. "You wouldn't catch me doing anything at that hour. Not until I've had at least a pot of coffee."

Which Mike probably made and brought to her bedside, Lureen thought. Marlene raised her eyebrows. Mike was an enigma, Lureen realized. He had stepped over some line. Last winter he made a skating rink for the kids in the neighborhood and skated with them. Carried their own around on his shoulders. On his days off he hung out the laundry, did the shopping, painted cupboards. I'll bet he's a fruit or pervert of some kind, Bobbie had said and while they laughed, nevertheless, they watched from the window for evidence and found none.

Bernice wore the same black baggy sweater she had on yesterday and the fuzzy slippers. Marlene wore a long black skirt and a peach satiny blouse knotted at the waist. She had gathered her auburn hair up into a French twist. Lureen wore her only dress, pink, of some nubby material which she bought in Eaton's. It was a good thing they weren't going home for Easter she decided, because another of her family's customs was that everyone bought or sewed a new dress for each religious holiday. Claude, who she could tell had been drinking long before they arrived, began to talk to Mike about hockey. Lureen didn't know any of the men well. They had an unspoken agreement that if a husband came home unexpectedly, they all left immediately. They spent their time

discussing the men's likes, dislikes, comparing. They spring-cleaned, read, kept the kids quiet on Saturday mornings and stayed attractive. Except for Bernice.

Lureen found a corner and nursed her second drink. Several other couples arrived and each time the door opened she thought of Larry. Above the kitchen door, a crucifix and the Christ were impaled in agony, an insect specimen under glass for their inspection. Lureen realized, as she listened to the jokes, the laughter, that her mother would disapprove if she knew that Lureen had gone to a party on Easter weekend. Of the crucifix, her mother would say, that's the problem. The Catholics leave him hanging. Lureen's mother, who was a Mennonite like Marlene, didn't believe in crucifixes being hung anywhere, but she had a plaque in the kitchen that one of the kids made at a summer camp and decorated with pine cones and macaroni which said, "By Grace Are Ye Saved." Which means, her mother said, that you don't deserve it. Claude's sardonic laughter grated on her ears. He had told the same joke three parties in a row now. When Claude got drunk he would take out his dentures and drop them down into his drink so no one would take it when he went to the bathroom.

"Hi guys, better late than never," Bobbie said as she stepped into the room and all conversation was suspended. Wayne had picked Bobbie up at work and she hadn't bothered to go home and change but had come to the party in a black, pleated mini-skirt, fish-net stockings and go-go boots. She pulled her head-scarf free and her platinum hair fanned out across her back. "Did I miss anything?"

"This is Mike," Bernice said.

"Well, what a surprise," Bobbie said and shot a look at Lureen which said, is she kidding?

Claude jumped up. "What are you drinking?"

"I'll help myself," she said in her throaty voice. "I'm not crippled."

"I can see that."

Lureen felt the bald hunger in the men's eyes as Bobbie left the room and for a moment, she resented her.

Only Mike seemed unaffected, and Wayne, Bobbie's husband, who was dark and silent. When he sat down, he crossed his legs and folded his arms across his broad chest. "Once a Month Wayne," Bobbie complained about their sexual activity during their bitch and brag afternoons. Lureen thought Wayne was the perfect example of a man who would go berserk and shoot his family on a quiet Sunday afternoon and everyone would be surprised. He was a polite man who kept to himself, they would say when interviewed.

"That's a real nice outfit," Mike said.

"I couldn't see myself in a get-up like that," Bernice said.

"I guess not." Claude laughed loudly.

"Get Bernice," they heard Bobbie tell Marlene in the kitchen, "her idea of dressing up is to wear pantyhose under her ski pants."

Bernice swung her leg up and down, up and down. Mike leaned forward and said something. She shrugged his arm from her shoulder. "You don't have to say that," she said, "I know what I look like."

Bobbie came back into the room and handed Wayne his drink. She hesitated and then went over to the couch and squeezed in beside Mike. "I've been serving drinks all night," she said. "What's one more?" She smiled at Mike and put her hand on his arm. "I guess you would know all about sore feet," she said.

Wayne shifted in his chair and cleared his throat. Bernice smiled at him and continued to swing her foot up and down. "Know why you wouldn't catch me in a get-up like that?" she asked and everyone stopped talking to listen.

"Some people care what they look like," Wayne said.

"Nope," she said, "it's because I'm made like Phyllis Diller. My legs don't go up that far."

The guy's obviously retarded, had been Bobbie's sullen

comment when the women had washed up the dishes following the party. Lureen pulled the pink dress over her head and threw it onto the bed. Retarded. Clueless, all of them, wanting to hide behind such a statement. She'd wanted to explain it to them, the matter of grace. It's grace, she should have said. Bernice has grace. She stood still, listening as a car passed in the lane. Although it was almost midnight, Larry was still not home. She stood looking out the window for a moment at the row of houses behind the fences, in front of them the telephone poles and the lines that connected her to Larry. She liked the telephone poles. They reminded her of gardens and woodpeckers telegraphing messages between the lines of time-splintered wood. She imagined her mother's street, silent and white beneath the moon. Her mother was crawling about on her hands and knees or reaching for a suitable hiding place for the Easter baskets. She saw the frosted Paska bread, lined up on the table, one for everyone. She wiped her eyes on her underslip. She stood in the hallway and listened to the quiet sound of her children breathing. And then she went into the kitchen and put the chicken back into the freezer. She took out the ham. Tomorrow, she would try something new with it. Marlene had suggested, stick it full of cloves and baste it with beer.

21 / Toronto Street

Truda sat out on the veranda facing Toronto Street and watched the Chinese student in the apartment block across the street as he, narrow and thin, bent over his books studying. He'd been sitting motionless for an hour. His shoulders looked pale and impotent beneath the overhead light. All his strength lay beneath the stroke of his blue-black hair, a thick wing across his forehead. At the top of the apartment block, the fifth floor, the setting sun banded the brick face in brilliant ochre. On the second floor where the student bent over his books, deep shadows had mounted the wall during the hour as she'd sat and watched and the student had moved only once, to turn on the light.

In her ears, the dreary rhythm of the long bus ride into Winnipeg echoed like waves caught in a conch shell and when she closed her eyes, the highway rose before her in flashing white lines. She leaned back into the dusty wicker chair and gave in to her weariness. She would be able to sit as the student did, motionless for hours, and not think about anything. Not think about Brian. Or that she had just rented this dismal, damp house on Toronto Street with its strange smell. Not very clever, Brian would say.

The wicker chair cracked sharply as she pulled her dress straight. Polyester, blue-gray to match her eyes, no ironing required. When she'd dressed, she'd chosen the outfit carefully. But as she'd knotted the scarf at her throat, the ever-present scarf which was supposed to bring the eye up to her wide friendly face and away from her spreading bottom, she felt sick. How color-coordinated and safe she was! No loose ends. She worked at appearing to be self-possessed, perhaps a hint of sex in the way she wore her hair, silver-tipped and carefree. Her hair, a slight flickering aberration in the total look, the

Total Woman, the Banker's Wife uniform. I don't care how much it costs, she'd often said to the girls at the Kinette meetings. It's important to me, the way I feel about myself, whether my hair looks good or not. Her careful preparations embarrassed her now. Since she'd got off the bus, she felt diminished, almost invisible. If she'd arrived stark naked it wouldn't have made any difference.

She had managed to pry loose several windows in the veranda and a breeze lifted and swept down the narrow alley between the apartment block and the Bronzing Company across the street. The breeze sucked heat from her skin as she rocked in the previous tenant's wicker chair and watched the Chinese student. She wanted to stay in the veranda awhile before confronting the night. The previous tenant hadn't used the veranda, she could judge that from the absence of odors. In the house, the air, heavy with the smell of pipe smoke, stale food and mildew, had as its base something else, a tinge of ammonia; bitterness, she concluded. In the veranda, the odor of street dust and the dry scent of newspapers stacked all along one wall made her feel safe. Neutral ground. The weariness lifted. She reached for the overnight bag on the floor. Her fingers found the Tupperware containers of fruit, vegetables and hard-boiled eggs. She arranged the containers on the floor and unwrapped several pieces of buttered bread. She had prepared the food in her own kitchen, furtively, not because she needed to be secretive, Brian had known she was leaving, but because she felt guilty about being able to think of food. It was like the time Brian had the accident with the saw and she'd come home from work and read his message to meet him at the hospital. When she saw the splatters, the amount of blood in the sink, she knew the accident had been serious and so she'd made herself a sandwich because she knew she wouldn't feel like eating once she got there.

As shadows mounted the brick wall across the street, it seemed to Truda that the sound of traffic on Notre Dame Avenue had risen and funneled now into Toronto Street, echoing dully beneath the arch of trees, sounding like rushing water. When she got off the bus on Ellice Avenue that afternoon, her impression of Toronto Street had been one of gaiety, colorful houses, vivid shades of yellow, lime green and pink, window-boxes and a truck tire painted white with geraniums growing in the center of it. There were children, bare-chested, clad in sagging diapers or blue jean cutoffs, astride bicycles, lolling in strollers or squatting, and fingers prying stones loose from cracks in the sidewalk. She wanted to kneel beside them to touch their dusty heads. I can live here, she'd told herself, feeling hopeful and lighthearted, the same way she'd felt about the house Brian had built. The extra bedrooms for their children. She imagined herself in a brightly colored skirt. A peasant skirt. Did they still sell them? She would let her hair grow once again to its natural length, down between her shoulder blades. She would buy cookies and be a cookie-at-the-door person because children liked her.

A grocery store on the corner leaned precariously to one side, several broken windows. Where would she buy food, she'd wondered, if she didn't have a car? Unless she bought one of those fold-down carts she'd seen other women use. Older women who shopped wearing funny out-dated hats concealing their loneliness beneath circles of pink rouge or pious or overly friendly mannerisms, or the others, the stooped sour ones with heavy scarves knotted tightly beneath chins, stealthily counting out change from their plastic change purses.

She'd memorized the advertisement. Two bedrooms, it said, a veranda, lots of light. She had pictured a place with clean, broad windows curtainless because she fancied the implications of a curtainless window, of an ivy growing up the casement. In Winnipeg people don't know their neighbors. People are unfriendly. You won't be able to go out alone at night, Brian said, not because he was trying to dissuade her but to give her the facts. Always the facts. Truda thought differently. There would be welcome freedom in anonymity.

She had imagined high white ceilings in the house and pottery cradling plants all along broad sills. Not this low-slung cottage with its one long room, two cramped bedrooms exposed off it, the bathroom off the kitchen; not sanitary. But what had helped her decide to take it was the round oak dining table. The table was an antique, the house, old. She distrusted the formal comfort of new houses. The comfort that sapped energy in the end, the form: the predictable arrangement of floral and flocked furniture, the white sheers on bay windows, the heavy valance and drapery, the seascape above the couch, breakers curled and forever suspended in their crash against the rocks.

The sudden blaring of a car horn punctuated the echoing rush of traffic, startling her. She looked up. The Chinese student flicked through pages in a book. Newspapers flipped up suddenly, rifled by the breeze which had risen quickly, swooped down between the buildings into the veranda. Truda swung around to face the door behind her, expecting to see something, someone standing there. I'll take the house, she'd said to the voice on the telephone because of the falling night, the old house. He was confined to a wheelchair, the slightly nasal voice stated. He was pretty old. Clean up the place and I'll throw in a month's free rent. Had he ever bothered? Truda wondered as she hung up the telephone. From the looks of the place, no. The voice had promised to come around one day to meet her and haul away the junk from the basement.

Look kid, get used to it, Truda told herself and pressed her hand against her chest to try to still the thrashing. Get used to it. She had read articles on being alone, on separating. She had done the test. Imagined herself eating alone, sleeping alone, shopping alone. She had prepared, even though this wasn't a real separation, but a temporary thing. A chance for her to find out if she wanted to go back to school, Brian said to their friends.

But even though she wanted to confront the aloneness,

she was flooded with relief at the sight of two people, a man and a woman bathed in a slice of light as they stepped out from the house next door. She sat up straighter to make herself more visible. The people became dark forms as they stooped and sat down on the top step. From their hands came the tinkle of ice against glass. The small, compact woman leaned her coppery head towards the man and spoke intimately in the husky voice of someone who smoked too much. Truda's loins leapt with desire at the man's low murmur, his laughing reply. She had seen the woman earlier, during the afternoon when she'd walked around the block, trying to come to a decision about the house. The sunburned woman had come from the house wearing a scanty bikini. Their eyes met. Hello, Truda had said. Can you tell me where a person would buy groceries? she was going to ask. Or where is the nearest bank? The woman turned from her and went back into the house, leaving her feeling foolish and slighted. She searched the street to see if anyone had seen. Above, trees met in a canopy of green, the color changing in the movement of hot air. Across the street, two children straddled bicycles, their faces shimmering and changing shape in the dappled shadows as they stared back at her.

Use it or lose it, Truda had read. She put her hand between her legs to try to still the ache. A woman should have sex twice a week, at least. That will keep her young and vibrant. Keep her from drying out. The couple leaned forward, elbows on knees, voices low, the man's interrupted as he drew on his cigarette. Around her, darkness sifted from the corners of the veranda, a fine powdery blackness which would soon cover her. Her foot searched for and found the overnight bag. It was all she had. The rest of her things she'd packed in two boxes and sent on ahead on the transfer. She had only to call when she got in to have them delivered, the man in the transfer office had promised, but she had called several times and there was no answer. Should she believe the bored voice on the telephone, the landlord, that he would ever appear?

Above the apartment block the translucent sky, still water radiating a sun about to slip into its surface.

She folded the Saran wrap carefully and pushed it down into the side pocket of the overnight bag. The Chinese student reached up suddenly, long and hard, stretching his thin arms. Truda felt her own tension flee. So he was alive then, not just an image imposed on a window. Other windows in the apartment block were lit up now, but there were still many dark ones as well. Vacant? She wondered if she'd been in too much of a rush. She should have inquired about vacancies across the street. She had nothing in writing, just the voice telling her where the keys were, in the rafters of the garage, and where to mail post-dated checks. Always get everything in writing. Dumb, dumb. The breeze lifted once again, and the metal ring on the window shade tapped sharply against glass. A sudden grating sound of metal against cement jarred and the comfortable heaviness fled. Jolted upright, Truda clutched the arms of the chair and listened. The sound came from the back of the house. Heart thudding, she watched as the Chinese student reached for another book and began to turn its pages. The couple leaned into each other, the woman's quiet laughter, low and harsh, aggravated. Truda forced herself to get up. She walked to the door. The couple touched glasses and the ice rattled sharply.

As Truda entered the living room, a string trailed across her neck and she slapped out at it. All through the house strings were attached to light chains, to sticks, and tied to drawers and cupboard doors in the kitchen, in both of the bedrooms. Beneath her feet, she felt the indentation in the broadloom, the wheelchair tire marks. She followed the marks through the long narrow room into the kitchen. She crossed over to the window, about to pull the shade, but the sight of a dime-sized circle of streetlight resting on the kitchen table stopped her. A hole in the blind. She sat down on the chair beside the window. The hole was eye-level. A peephole? She imagined someone brittle and thin, a bag of dried chicken

bones in a heap of rumpled clothing, as hunched and bitter as
the smell in the house, leaning towards the window. Damp air
streamed up from the basement doorway, fern fronds uncurled
wetly against her neck. She put her eye to the hole. Outside
in the yard, illuminated by the blue glare of the streetlamp,
two children bent over a garbage can. She watched. Were
they the same ones she'd seen earlier during her walk beneath
the arch of trees? Deliberately and silently, they up-ended the
garbage can and shook its contents across the grass.

The blind flapped noisily at the top of the window. That's
it, she told herself as she watched the children flee. That's it,
she said as she marched through the house, pulled strings and
rolled up identical peep-holes. From the houses on both sides,
blocks of light were flung down into the long narrow room.
Somewhere a baby cried and water ran into a bathtub. That's
it, she said, not knowing what she meant, just that some
action was necessary now, some vague resolution to keep from
going backwards. To keep from calling Brian. She strode into
the veranda. The couple next door had gone into the house.
The Chinese student was still hunched over his work, his chin
cupped in the palm of his hand. She gathered up several
newspapers, carried them into the front bedroom and spread
them out over the mattress. She chose the room because there
were no grooves in the carpet and the window faced the
apartment block. She stripped free her A-line dress, her
Banker's Wife uniform. She peeled down her girdle, felt the
sudden release of pressure. As she stepped free from it, her
fingers automatically searched for the indentation marks the
girdle pressed into her white flesh, the criss-cross angry lines
that took forever to fade. She had the map of the world in
stretch marks on her stomach, her buttocks. But she hadn't
earned them the usual way, the accepted way. She searched
through the overnight bag and found her nightgown. It fell in
graceful, generous folds around her body. It had never failed
her yet, the bag. Wherever she had gone with Brian, to
Mexico, to Hawaii, she took along a change of underwear in

it, her cosmetics and the pill. (The pill she had left behind this time because she was repulsed by her menstrual odor, that unnatural chemical smell.) And she had not been caught in a bind when her bags had been delayed or lost as her boxes were, somewhere in a dark corner of a shipping depot.

She lay down on the narrow cot, the newspaper crackling sharply, causing her heartbeat to rise. She closed her eyes. Why had she continued to take the pill? she wondered. Habit. No more tampons. She anticipated the thick heavy flow, warm against her body. At better times, lying beside Brian in their queen-sized bed, she hadn't been able to sleep this easily, she thought. It was amazing, she could actually feel herself drifting towards tomorrow while still connected with the night and the city, its threads of sounds winding and unwinding gently about her fingers. The baby crying, why was the baby crying? she wondered.

A baby. Crying. The muscles in her stomach contracted sharply, yanking her upright. Listening. She'd heard something. A cry. She swung her legs over the side of the cot and sat on its edge, bathed in the light from the window. Perspiration trickled down between her breasts. The barn-like taste of boiled eggs clung to her tongue. She swallowed and felt that little click of hysteria in the back of her throat. Wait, she told herself. Think. You could have been dreaming. It could have been, what? The coppery-haired woman drenched in sweat, moving beneath her husband's body, arching to his minnow swimming up the canal. The cry, she'd heard it before. While sitting on the beach in Hawaii with Brian, she'd heard that cry rising above the sounds of water and the multitude of voices blending together in the heat, the whine of power boats. It sent a shock through her body, sent her scrambling awkwardly to her feet to shade her eyes and search the water. What is it? Brian had asked, peering up at her from the crook of his arm. I don't know, I don't know, she said. Maybe someone was drowning. She looked for activity around the lifeguard station. She paced the beach, the cry echoing in her breastbone. Sit down for God's sake, Brian said. People are staring at you. What should I do? she asked. Would you rather I not go to the beach at all? What she camouflaged with scarves and A-line dresses overflowed on the beach. Don't be silly, Brian said, flicking her bottom with a towel. I like getting back a good return on my investment.

Truda sat on the edge of the cot, fighting the desire to get dressed, to walk to the telephone booth on the corner. What would she say? That when she'd sat draped in towels beneath the over-sized straw hat, watching him playing tennis, she hadn't noticed the strange pleasure in his face when he introduced her as his wife? Pleasure at their surprise, the sudden covering up of astonishment. That when she'd stood at the window watching him as he walked down to the beach, his strong tanned back squarish and set, she'd suddenly realized that they would never have children. He never intended they would. All this waiting to build the house and a patio, to take the vacations had been a lie. She couldn't forgive him, not for that. During their perfect vacation, the second honeymoon, standing in her queen-sized bathing suit, she was quietly sorrowful, listening to something inside herself cracking open, a sluggish, deadening feeling creeping into its place.

Truda wiped her face on her nightgown, lay back, sighing. As her eyes grew accustomed to the light, she could make out the swirls and wing-like patterns on the wallpaper. Above the apartment block a nimbus cloud banked evenly across the sky. Was he homosexual? Had he taken a lover? There was never any hint of either. She couldn't see the Chinese student but she knew he was there in the window, thinking, reading, oblivious to the rising and falling sounds of traffic, the rattle of the blind in the veranda. A thud against the side of the house. The children. Were they returning to spread more garbage? Would they crawl through the basement window and creep up the narrow stairs and, goddammit. That's it. Truda got up swiftly, shed her nightgown and slipped back into her dress. She squeezed swollen bare feet into her sandals. Knees trembling, guided by the grooves in the broadloom, she groped her way through the darkness, out to the veranda. Before her, the Chinese student worked over his books. Look at me, she urged. Lift up your head for once. The door slammed shut behind her as she stepped out into the blue-black night. Look at me. The student wrote notes in a notebook.

Earlier, she'd seen a drugstore on a corner. Perhaps it would be open and inside there would be people. She began walking towards Notre Dame Avenue. As she turned the corner, fear prickled the hair on her arms. This was not the broad busy Avenue the way she'd remembered, but dark and narrow, heavy with the cloying smell of petunias, peonies. Overhead in the trees, shadows roiled, stirred by the wind. She'd taken a wrong turn. Move lawnchairs around and watch Truda get lost in her own back yard, Brian said.

Brian! Her breath came quick and shallow, making her feel lightheaded. Drunk. She turned and began walking in the opposite direction, ahead, a squat-shaped house and welcoming yellow light beating through all the windows.

She leaned against the fence and waited for her breathing to grow calmer. Someone is following me. A telephone. I have to use a telephone. Just as she was gaining courage, the door opened. Two short dark men walked down the sidewalk towards her. She stepped from the shadows. As though she were invisible, they brushed passed her, silent, somber. At the bus depot, too, she'd had the feeling of being invisible as she'd watched families gathering around huddles of luggage, talking, excited. Behind the men, holding the railing for support, an old woman's stiff arthritic movement as she came down the stairs.

"Pardon me. But I wonder, could I use the telephone?"

The woman's hands twisted and fluttered and white scales dropped from her fingers and floated to the grass. Petals. Her gnarled fingers plucked, tearing apart a large flower. As she drew closer Truda saw in her face a look that matched the anguished twisting of her fingers. Thick white eyebrows drew together across her sharp nose as she turned and glared. "Why are you here?" she hissed. "What has this got to do with you?"

The short dark men returned, stumbling as they approached the house. Between them, a glint of metal, and then the moon moved out from behind the clouds and Truda saw the tiny white coffin.

"I'm sorry." She turned and ran down the street. I'm sorry, I'm sorry. Freed of the girdle, her flesh jiggled and slapped against itself as she ran. She wound her arms around her belly to hold it still. She was a mound of jelly which strained her lungs as she ran, slowed her down, kept her from doing all the things other people did. Trapped her. What has this to do with you? Nothing. She would never have children. She would be content to be the Aunt, the bearer of gifts, the one who staged the baby showers. Never the bearer of a tiny white coffin.

She walked as in a trance, finding it easily, it was only just one turn around the corner, back to the house. She climbed the stairs into the veranda. As she passed through the doorway, the light string slid across her shoulder. God! she thought. A spider, a web, a hand, and grabbed at it, yanking the chain and flooding the veranda in white light.

The Chinese student lifted his head, flicked hair from his eyes. His bony shoulders bunched up sharply as he pushed his chair back, rose and came over to the window. The sudden bright light pained her eyes. She raised her hand to gesture to him, felt foolish and let it drop to her side. He leaned forward, resting his elbows on the sill, and stared across the distance between them, their eyes meeting beneath the canopy of silent elms.

Go to sleep, Truda instructed herself as the student raised himself and returned to his table. She turned out the light. But she knew sleep wouldn't come now. Not until she'd finished crying. Ahh, she said later, this is silly and smiled in the darkness. Tomorrow, she'd find a store and buy cleaning supplies, something to bleach away the stain of bitterness. She sat in the wicker chair and listened for the voice which would cry out again in the strange subdued house behind her. But as the minutes passed, all she heard was the traffic on Notre Dame Avenue, funneled into Toronto Street, rising and rising, a rhythmic swelling of traffic sounds, water rushing beneath trees and occasionally, the peppery sound of a motorcycle breaking the monotony of the rising hour.

22 / The Bird Dance

Dear Andy,

I am writing to you because I have no one else to write
to. I try and talk to my friends at school but they aren't
interested in other people's problems. And how many of them
do I help? They come to me all the time for cigarettes and
advice. I hate this school. I want out!! Sometimes I think it
would be interesting to plant a bomb here (just kidding).

You don't know what it's like to live at home right now.
You're lucky. Be glad you don't have to live here. I don't
think it's fair that I have to. Certain people are very ignorant
and I can hardly keep from hitting them when they come near
me.

Andy, this is why I'm writing. I want you to do
something, talk to Mom, because she listens to you. Dad Larry
(as he is *not* my father anymore!) is coming over here almost
every day. At first it was just to use the shower, right? And
then he started bringing along a bottle. One morning when I
got up, there he was asleep on the couch. I can't stand it. *He
goes into the fridge and eats our food without even asking!!*
Everything is fine until the minute he steps in the door. How
are you doing? he asks, pretending he is interested but all the
time with that sick-dog look in his eyes, trying to make us feel
sorry for him. What a suck. She falls for it and lets him in
and then magically, he produces a bottle (even though he is
supposed to be broke) and they get drunk while I sit and
watch TV. Sometimes he comes downstairs and watches with
me and asks a bunch of stupid questions about the program,
trying to make me talk. I see right through him. I can tell
what he's thinking. "I can't let him drive home drunk," Mom
says. It's just an excuse. I am thinking of calling the police
when he leaves here. It would pay him a lesson to get

arrested. Boy, what if I tried that? Wouldn't he scream if I started drinking!

Guess what? I'm in love. With Rick Savage. When Def Leppard comes here I'm going to meet him. It's meant to happen. Rick says he wants me with him in England. Brenda and me have planned how we'll let them know we're in the crowd. Mom won't like this *but* we're going to throw our panties on stage!! God, I pray every night that we'll be able to get tickets when they go on sale!

Andy, another thing. Mom says I *have to* stay in this school. Don't you think I should have the right to decide which school I'm going to?? She's in no shape to tell me anything right now. I'm looking after myself so why should I have to listen to her? Mom is a mess. I wish she'd get a job like normal people or at least go bowling or something like other mothers do. I know what she's thinking. She's afraid that she won't get another man. She thinks having Dad around is better than nothing. Last time we went to the bookstore, I found a book I wanted her to read. It was about why women feel that they are nothing without a man around. And she wouldn't buy it. She said it makes her disgusted to think that people make money writing that s—t. Write me and tell me what to do. I'm desperate.

Your adorable, attractive sister (eat your heart out).
Me.

Dear Andrea,

It's Autumn, today I noticed. I used to look forward to the seasons changing because at the house there always seemed to be something to compensate for the change. Each season had its blessings as in fall in the spatters of colors in the back yard reminding me of when you were all little and we did those things, the tooth brush dipped in poster paints, a piece of window screen, and splatters of paint outlining a leaf, giving shape to something invisible.

And in the winter, the sight of the houses across the

street, the colored lights strung along the eaves and rooftops coated all in snow, made me feel enclosed, at peace. You could tell which houses were insulated by the amount of snow on the roof. Insulation: the new status symbol in River Heights. And gradually, as energy consciousness spread, more and more rooftops were thick with snow all winter. Except ours of course.

If you can imagine, what attracted me to the house in the first place was sunlight. Your Dad and I had been looking to buy for several months and as soon as I walked into the house, I knew it was what I wanted. It was near the end of June and I was smitten by the sunlight on the hardwood floors. The woman had painted the walls a soft gold and the effect was, I don't know, after the traffic and sheer grit of Selkirk Avenue, it was restful, quiet. And so I didn't want to notice that the kitchen was too small, or the cracks in the basement walls. The strategy of boxes piled up in front of the cracks. I'm too easily influenced by sunlight. And then what did I do? Painted everything in the house pale blue and white to give the place an airy and cool feeling. In search of the ethereal, I lost the warmth. I bought that "Falling Leaf" poster, that depressing thing that lacked substance, all mushroom and mauve and beige, and wouldn't admit that I hated it. Your dad, being more of a calendar above the kitchen table type, a leaping trout or an antique car, didn't appreciate the poster. The basement, he planned to convert into a kind of beer garden. None of his ideas suited my shades of blue and white. He was right about the kitchen in the end, it was too small. I lost all interest in cooking.

Well, here in this new place, I don't know yet what compensations there will be for the hot and cold of the seasons or how many kids to expect for Halloween. These are important considerations. There is not much to learn from the apartment block behind me about the changes the seasons will bring. In the front, there are possibilities in the houses across the street. But there are no trees. I have noticed an abundance of trees on my walls since I've moved. It's happened unconsciously. The silk screen your friend did for me is on the wall in the bedroom. I bought a piece of batik at the Folk Festival for my workroom but when Dee started to pin all her Def Leppard and Bowie posters all over the walls down there, I decided to put it in the front window. It makes up in a small way for no trees on the front street.

Now that I've arranged the furniture and cupboards I have time to think. And I never thought that I would have to get used to living in another place. I'd hoped we'd make improvements to the house. Finish the basement. I had resigned myself to a lot of things by then, including the beer-garden approach to decorating. I wanted to enlarge the kitchen for when you kids got married and I would rediscover the joy of cooking. The only move I ever looked forward to was if by some miracle, we got our dream house beside the river. But eventually I gave up on that, too, although we continued the ritual, the driving around on Sundays searching for the perfect spot. When things began to go the way they did, I narrowed down my expectations even more, and all I wanted to do was just be able to hang onto the house we had. It was like peeling an apple down to its core.

Anyway, here I am, living in an apartment for the first time. It's a four-plex, but to me, an apartment nevertheless. It's different for you. You're just beginning, but I'm halfway through when it's supposed to be the time to grow little soft bellies of opulence or mild complacency. At least a bigger car. Or a few trips here and there, winter in Florida, etc., polyester pantsuits, stretchy to allow for the opulence. But not this, eh? I'm running three miles a day, flexibility exercises, in weight training for singlehood. Being flat broke without a job, starting over at forty. And it seems, too, that not only must I become used to being single, but all the other changes as well, the changes of the age, unfulfilled expectations. Things we were taught would happen as a matter of course if we followed the recipe.

The Bird Dance   313

How am I doing, you ask? I suspect Dee has written to you on the side. Is Dad still coming around to see me? Yes, he is. Dee is angry about that as well. But it's my choice, too, so don't be hard on him. I tell myself it's because I can't stand the thought of his being one of those people you read or hear about on the news. Like last week, on the radio, the police discovered the body of a man about 53 years old, burned to death in his car which was parked downtown somewhere. He lived in the car, it seems. Close to hooker city. Fell asleep in the back seat with a lit cigarette. I stood there crying my guts out over a man of no fixed address. Your Dad is sleeping down at the garage, but often I can't reach him there and so I don't really know where he is most of the time. I suppose after what we've been through that this seems strange to you, but I want to know is he sick, hungry? Do his pants need pressing? To keep on saying to you and Dee that you can't know what it's like to have been married twenty-three years and then suddenly to be single isn't enough. Let me try to explain.

Last spring. Around the time you left. You and I went for a walk and it was drizzling, icy and cold. I was hanging onto you, I think I was drunk. Anyway, both of us were in shock over something.

What was the situation that time? Situation, such a nice calm word. It seemed at that time every day held a fresh pain, coated in ice, magnified and distorted. I could examine the tiniest line in it but could not comprehend the whole of it. I think it was the day you broke a window. An unaccustomed raging, it left us numb to see your anger breaking loose like that. I hung onto you, my feet wouldn't work the way they were supposed to, I blamed it on the ice, and you were crying. I consoled you, said not to worry. I did a good job because soon you were telling me that I was courageous, patient, and wonderfully full of insight. We snapped the icicles free from the eaves. And then you left.

Once you left, your Dad began what seems to be his life's work in earnest, and strange people began to drop by at all

hours to drink with him. Where was Dee at that time? I don't
remember except for those cryptic notes left on my pillow.

"Dear Mom, check one box only. I hate it when people
try and teach me lessons. Life is not school. Do you promise
not to try and teach me lessons anymore? Yes____ No____ "

During this time, I'd come home from work at night or up
from the basement during the day and meet face to face either
the old man and his fat dog, or the man across the street who
worked the night shift, or that madman, Fritz. The others
were only a nuisance, Fritz frightened me. I was reading *The
Tin Drum* and it seemed that the book oozed and the house
contained some energy of it, bizarre, off-center, evil. I couldn't
sleep. I imagined the air above the bed fractured and about to
fall apart. I discovered gargoyles in the "Falling Leaf" poster. I
imagined the word "Kill" was woven into the drapes. I'd wake
up with cold sweats and pray like crazy or recite the 23rd
Psalm. What scared me about Fritz was his rheumy unfocused
eyes, the way he punctuated his stories with a fist slammed
into his palm. As in: "Yes sir (slam), I tell my wife, bend over
the kitchen table (slam) and I lift her skirts and boy, oh boy, I
give it to her like that (slam, slam). She not walking very
good after that." One morning I opened the basement door
and there he was, standing on the other side of it, breathing
heavily. It was a tense moment. That was when I decided to
move out.

Those men coming around to drink at all times of the day
were a kind of fraternity forming around your Dad once the
word got out that I was leaving him. They were consoling
him. Even the fat dog drank. Where was my support? You'd
fled. The counselor down at the Women's Bureau said in
essence, kick him in the balls, he'll respect you more for it. I
went to see a minister. He said he felt God was in the
business of saving people, not marriages. I think he meant
that I had better get out for my own good. I didn't expose my
kernel of fear, that it could prove to be your Dad's salvation. I
went home and added more things to your Dad's boxes, dishes,

towels, sheets, things which he now says just clutter up his life.

Now that all the pressure is off I don't seem to be as strong as I was. I'm fading, breaking out in disgusting pimples on my chin and forehead. I have a constant dull ache in the breastbone. I have begun to smoke a cigarette now and then. I wake up in the middle of the night and think about where I'll be at age sixty-five. And so when your Dad began coming around in the night, knocking on windows, I let him in, not because he was cold and drunk and tired. I let him crawl into bed with me and I warmed him and held him because it made me feel like a saint. I was flipping through the Book of Proverbs today and came across this nugget: "Bread of deceit is sweet to a man; but afterwards his mouth shall be filled with gravel."

I'm afraid Dee has had a bad start at school, many absences because of illness. I have trouble getting her up in the morning. Stomach aches and not much energy. She plays her guitar every day and rushes home with words to new songs which she writes down and puts to music and plays over and over until (thank God) the lady upstairs bangs on the ceiling. Which offends Dee mightily but spares me her wrath. We aren't used to this. I may have to move the piano to the basement as well so that when you come home at Christmas, you can sing Kate Bush and Ricki Lee Jones songs to your heart's content and no one will bang unless it's me, of course. That's why I gave Dee my workroom downstairs. I don't like her being so far away from me, but at least she can play the guitar and listen to her records without offending anyone. But in the meantime, I can only bring myself to use the skill saw while the lady upstairs is out. If I'm desperate, I use the hand saw, but it's so time-consuming.

How are your courses going? I hope you're settling in well and that you and Bev are hitting it off as you'd hoped. I plan to bundle up some blankets and the things you asked for and put them on the train. No word from Student Aid yet? Here's hoping.

Cheers,

Love you, Mom.

ATTENTION!!

Dear Mom,

Before you go to sleep *please read this with an open mind.* If there is anything you want to say after you read this, please write it down. It will keep us from yelling at each other.

Love, Dee xxxxoooo

Dear Mom,

It is so utterly ridiculous.

The demands that were put upon me in the past year were so intense that I *had to grow up fast.* I had *no one* to lean on because Andy was in Quebec, Jamie, where is Jamie may I ask? And you: sure as − −!! not you! I was busy watching you. You were always depressed, irritable and feeling sorry for yourself. I had no one to lean on. All my friends did not want to be dragged into anything that had to do with someone else's personal life. I am stuck in a school that I hate. The expectations, that I had no choice in responding to, would have been impossible for any other thirteen-year-old. Any other person my age would have complained and done just what Dad, Larry does, drink. You think it's impossible for a teenager to drown their problems in drinking, but it's not. I kept the secure mind that I was blessed with instead and I grew up. Sorry if it's inconvenient for you. But I had no choice.

Now I'm expected to be 13 again. Sorry, but it's impossible. The mental level I am set on is solid, here to stay, never to be 13 again. It has to be that way. There are still tons of obstacles to come. I must be, and am, ready for them with no interference whatsoever from anyone. Because the Lord in heaven knows that you aren't mentally stable for

The Bird Dance

anything else that anyone throws at you. I am what you could call an angel sent from heaven to be your protector.

Mom, you say that I have to spend time with him (ugh, Dad) because you can't bring me up on your own. I think it is about time you realized why you can't. It's because I'm too advanced for you and if you are (which you most definitely are) fifty times more advanced than that devil of a "father," just think how cramped I am with him. I, Mother dear, have been bringing myself along, quite efficiently I might add, for one to two years. I don't need any help now. Okay, I do admit I need some help in a few departments, but not as many as you submit yourself to. I do realize that growing up is caring for others and I promise I will absolutely start treating you more like a human being (which you are). *But stop seeing Dad!!* You don't know him like I do. Devil is mild. *He is using you!!* You can't make me spend time with him. Start yelling now.

Love, Dee xxxxoooo
ps/this is not a joke.

Hi Momsie!
Curses! I come home with a whole afternoon stretched ahead to study and what happens? I get two really good letters. So of course I have to take time out to write. I can never wait. I always have to pick up a pen right away.

What is this? Not rushing into anything with Dad? What is there to rush into? I thought you were getting yourself together at last. You were sounding better and better. I think you've always had lower expectations for yourself than I could see for you. I still see for you. Once you get yourself out of that mindset, I think it should be clear sailing. Well, on the track anyway. I do think you should have some regular counseling. You do have a lot of reinforcement of traditional ideas to overcome, twice as much as me, ideas/ideals that were drilled in from day one. Even I (having been born 20 years later than you) find myself slipping occasionally into the "once I have a nice man to take care of me . . . everything will be

just perfect. . . . " Keep busy. Glad to hear that you will be
having a booth at the craft show. How's the work going? You
must send me a photograph of your craft display. It sounds to
me that despite everything, you're beginning to enjoy your
new place.

Tonight Bev and I are off to our first symphony. She has
discovered several other Anglophones living in this block and
we're going to take them along. Lately, I have been listening
to classical music as I can study to it. Saturday night, I went
to a fabulous "spectacle," a new Quebecois singer named
Claude Dubois. There were over 16,000 people in a huge
arena. He put on a great show, but he is the "Americanite" of
the Quebecois, a lot of love songs and totally non-political. A
big difference from Gilles Vigneault, patron of separatism, who
is also loved here. I have to do a 15-minute oral presentation
and I'm going to do it on the difference between the two
artists and the attitudes they represent as reflected in their
audience. I sure do miss singing, gulp. It hurts when I think
about it. This is the first time in years that I haven't been in a
choir.

I'm comfortable here at Laval. I can walk into the
cafeteria and have a choice of people to sit with. It's very
relaxed. I'm doing a lot of reading, all in French, of course,
and am literally amazed at the fact that I can sit and read
French fluently without picking up the dictionary every two
minutes. Now it's every 15 minutes, which isn't bad. *En tous
cas (entica)* (anyways) I think I have got the idea across to you
that everything is all right here.

I have heard from Student Aid and I will have enough
money for the year. So don't worry. I'm going to look into the
possibility of a job with Parks Canada at Ft. Louisbourg this
summer in Cape Breton. It's the oldest fort in Canada. I'd
have to speak fluent French, dress in period costume and live
the same lifestyle as the first settlers did. What an experience
when you think of it. You'll be relieved, I'm sure. It'll be much
tamer than the year I spent up north and feathers in my hair

and all that. I feel so at home here that maybe I have discovered my true ancestors at last.

Had a great letter from Dee. Tell her thanks. She's such a sweetie. I miss her. Tell her I'll write soon and send photographs of my apartment. Hope you keep well, Mom. By the way, have you heard anything from that brother of mine?

Love, Andrea.

Hi!

C'est Moi. Your talented, highly intelligent, one of a kind sister (not kidding). What does a Rubic's cube and a guy have in common?? Answer:

THE MORE YOU PLAY WITH IT THE HARDER IT GETS! (TEE HEE).

Guess what? I was in Mary Scorer Books yesterday and found some poetry by Jim Morrison. I couldn't help it, I screamed and everyone thought I was crazy. Jim Morrison, Andy, he's so intelligent. Did you know that he isn't really dead? Everyone thinks so. But he isn't. He escaped from a life he didn't like. I just love his poem about we all live in the city. It makes me think of the zoo and the animals in cages. I think the city molds us. It binds us as one but there is no individuality. I can understand why Dad wants to build a house in the country. Andy, I think part of his problem is that he hates the city and likes to be able to have his freedom without people telling him what to do all the time. I told Mom this. She said I was right. That when she and Dad first moved into the city, he drove the truck up onto the boulevard and the police came by and gave him hell. That night, he lit a fire in the back lane to burn the packing boxes and someone called the fire department. Mom said he never forgot that. Maybe if he gets his place in the country he'll be my Dad again. But I don't know.

Andy, I love Dad. I remember when I was little and he put Jamie on his shoulders and then lifted me up onto Jamie's shoulders and we played basketball like that and I got to put the ball into the basket. Mom said we only did that once, so she could take a picture of the three of us pretending to be happy. I know she is wrong. She thinks she knows everything. Perfect memory. Jamie, Dad and I always played like that.

Guess what? Jamie phoned from Calgary. I was home alone and when the operator said it was him calling, I almost fainted. He's quit the rigs. He said he almost lost an arm. He sounded lonely and I felt like crying but I didn't want to make him feel worse. He thinks he might come home for Christmas. He said it would be nice for the whole family to be together again. And I know how he feels. I'm glad Dad is back.

But that is why I'm writing. I'm worried. I'm glad Mom and Dad are back together again, but I'm not sure. When Mom's away at a show, Dad goes out. He says he's going out just for a few minutes and then he's gone for five or six hours. Sometimes when he comes home I think I can smell you-know-what on his breath. Also. Here goes. I think Dad is going out with other women!! I saw him. He was coming out of the Plaza with a *bottle* and when he saw me, he looked guilty. He said he was picking it up for a friend who was sitting in the car waiting for him. A *woman*. When I asked who she was, he introduced her as "this is Debbie who is just a friend." But the woman looked surprised when he said I was his daughter and guilty, too. I said, "Does Mom know?" and he said, "There's no point in causing trouble. You know your mother."

I think I know what's going to happen. Mom and Dad are going to split again, very soon. Even if Dad is going out with other women, I love him. And I forgive him. But, what about Mom? She'll never be able to get a boyfriend. But why should I worry? As far as she's concerned, I might as well not be here. She doesn't pay attention to me anymore. It's just, Dee go to bed, Dee turn down the stereo, do your homework. She only wants to talk to him. She doesn't trust me. Every time I go out I have to fill in a questionnaire. I think she's afraid I might get into drugs or lose my big "V."

School is the same. Terrible. The Home Ec. teacher hates me. I broke a needle on the sewing machine and she got mad. I don't know how to thread it and I'm afraid to ask and then I do it wrong and it sews funny and she gets mad again. She thinks I'm making a mess of sewing to get on her nerves but I just can't do it. I hate sewing. I want to take electronics but they won't let me. I would rather take cooking. At least you get to eat your abortions.

The only thing I've got these days is Rick Savage. He says he can hardly wait until I'm finished school, although he doesn't like me going because when I'm at school I'm thinking about the kids I'm with, the dances coming up, my work, and I'm not thinking about him. I have promised him I definitely will not find a boyfriend. But he says that it's okay because he's dating girls in the meantime until I can get to England. I have just got to find a way to get there!! Mom says I should do some babysitting. But I hate kids! I will never in this life have kids. As soon as I can, I'm going to have a hysterectomy. Or stand in front of a microwave oven. I don't know what I'll do with Mom when I go to England. I'll have to take her with me.

I hope you're having a good time in Quebec. At least somebody is having a good time!

Please check one: Yes No

1. I think you should quit school and go to England
   now.   ___ ___
2. I think you should tell Mom about the Woman.   ___ ___
3. I think you should get someone to beat up the
   Home Ec. teacher.   ___ ___
4. I think if you ran away for two years it would
   really smarten Dad up.   ___ ___

ps/If you don't have Def Leppard on your Xmas list don't come home.

My Dear Daughter of the Light-Brown Hair,

Can you imagine, I awoke in the night to the sound of hundreds of low-flying geese migrating south. Hours and hours of geese passing overhead and I can still hear them. It gives me such a strange feeling, like the feeling I got when I stepped out of the car and walked across the piece of property that I think Dad and I will buy. It was a feeling of recognition, perhaps *déja vu*, of the sound meaning more than just a sign of winter. When I stood on that land it was like that, a spirit of recognition rolling across the fields and I had at the same time the impression of air swirling about the sun as in a Van Gogh painting. I'm not flipping out. I'm telling you that I met something, made a contact out there on the land. When you face west, there are miles and miles of fields and trees that are now just like an artist's brush strokes against a watery looking sky. East is the river hidden behind bushes and trees, which Dad says we will clear away so I will have my view of the river, that I may look upon it and listen to its silent flowing, and he will have a place to dock his boat. I know, I know. I'm letting myself get carried away by this whole business. I can't help it. I'm beginning to hope. We've even investigated various house plans. I prefer one that offers a solarium in the front hallway but I'm treading softly, holding my breath, not wanting to disturb or place even a flicker of dust before impetus. He wants to leave his job and build the house himself, but I believe I have him convinced that it would be better in terms of security if he stayed at work and we subcontracted. Besides, I don't want to wait ten years for a house!

About the Christmas craft show. There have been a few problems, namely I haven't been getting at the work. I don't know. The few pieces I sold at the Folk Festival are one thing, but a whole booth! I think I'm getting cold feet. Since your Dad moved back in, the old budget has been strained and I don't know if I'll be able to afford all the materials.

I did something impulsive today. I went to Carol Grass's

art exhibit and I bought two of her paintings. I couldn't help myself. I wanted to cry when I saw the show, it was such an emotional experience for me, the trapped wingless birds becoming women locked, caught inside tubes and uterus-shaped forms beneath the ground, but still dancing and balancing the moon in the palms of their hands. The colors are vivid, really don't go well with the rest of the room and I'm gradually whittling down my savings. But. I'm not going to worry. I think your Dad needs this chance to get himself straightened around financially and I guess I feel guilty about having had the past five years to work on my heritage boxes. I only hope he'll stay at his job and forget about starting up the garage again.

In your last letter I got the impression that you're having doubts about whether you should be studying languages or not. I thought you loved your courses. I thought you were excited about discovering and linking up with your ancestry and all that. And now you're contemplating music? Good grief. There's no money in music. And you say you aren't interested in teaching it, either. There will be so many opportunities for you if you stay with French. You could always do music on the side. Think about it. You shouldn't be discouraged about your "B's" and "C's." It's still early in the year.

One last word. Dee is a handful. Can you write to her? She can be such a shit and such a sweetheart. I feel sorry for your Dad right now as she treats him as though he were stupid, a necessary evil to be endured for my sake. We, poor aging parents, limp about like wounded birds supporting one another after one of her swooping attacks. Makes life interesting. As Maggie Muggins used to say (remember her?) I don't know what will happen tomorrow.

Cheers, Mom.

Dear Mom,

Where were you? You forgot to phone me yesterday. Is everything okay? I waited all day. I guess/hope that you were just preoccupied with the way things are going. I'm glad to hear that Dad has quit drinking and that the two of you are finally going for counseling but I still worry when I don't hear from you. How does Dee feel about everything? Knowing her, she's probably telling you all the time.

Thanks for your vote of confidence regarding the music. I can't believe it. You've been an example to me of someone who has made sacrifices in order to do what you really want to do. If parents only knew the kinds of influence they have, how it makes us feel when they say those things, they might think twice. How much money do you make on your heritage boxes?

I have been immersed in classical music lately and just going nuts. CBC plays gorgeous operas on Saturdays and every other day from dusk 'til dawn. And Mom, I'm half melting and half dying because I'm not singing these days. When I go to the piano rooms after I run, my voice is loose and supple and I sing at the top of my lungs. Bev and I still go to the symphony. It's not as good as the Winnipeg Symphony, but it's still nice to go. When I come to Winnipeg I want to take in as much good music as possible.

Sorry to hear about Dee's report card. Yikes. I hope she starts to work soon. Do you think she might be having too much time to herself down there in the basement room? I think she's the kind of person who should be kept busy. Why isn't she involved in any school activities?

I think you should try and keep the booth at the Craft Show. Garnet (remember him? He's one of Bev's Anglophone finds) thinks your work is unique. He's never heard of a heritage box. He would like you to design one for his parents' twenty-fifth. I didn't promise.

Let me know.

Andrea.

ps/I have signed up for seven courses next term. No sweat. Maybe just a bit. Grammar test on Wednesday. Time to study.

Garnet is coming over tonight and we're going to study together and listen to music. Did I tell you he plays the piano?

Hi Mom,

I shouldn't be writing. I should be reading but at times I find Quebecois Lit so stifling that I need a breath of fresh air. I was at Garnet's last night and read some of his collection of Al Purdy's poems. I just felt like crying, perhaps it was because they made me smell the Prairie and made me feel that I should be studying Western Canadian Literature and not this narcissistic Quebecois stuff. I am literally suffocating on it and the lectures affect me physically: I get a lump in my throat, my neck starts to ache, I have a nervous reaction every time the prof comes up with another cliche about these authors who are "omniscient, innovative, geniuses, giants, gods." I refuse to believe this is possible in a 17-year-old melancholic crazy child. I start to want to get out of here because it's so intro-introspective. These people have been spending 300 years trying to know themselves. It's like walking up a down escalator. Maybe it's just me. I want to hop on a plane for Europe or a third-world country just to be assured that there exists a world outside of Quebec. I don't know what I'd do if it wasn't for Garnet. We have so much in common.

I have been wandering around the apartment all day, thinking and doing little knicky-knacky things. The kitchen is my favorite room, so big and colorful, especially with my new Van Gogh poster and a big food collage I made. The room is white with the cupboard doors painted a rich, sea blue. And I'm feeling funny, wondering about myself and sex and relationships and ambition and body and spirit. Whew. What a mouthful. Perhaps it's just the wind.

I feel sad. I have been talking a lot and intensely with many people, written umpteen essays, got back into running and into (not sure if I'm happy or sad) a "relationship" with Garnet. He's been such a close intellectual and fun friend and I'm worrying that this is going to wreck our friendship. But mostly, I have mixed feelings about breaking my celibacy pact. I feel as though I've said goodbye to an old friend, that single independent me that I've finally grown to like. Why does it feel as though I have signed over my body and therefore my mind and soul with the act of sex? That's why I'm so sad. I don't want that. I'm afraid that it will destroy all my goals and ambition. That I've lost all my self-determination by crossing that line. And so then, I'm wondering, will I ever be able to be married or live with a man without being swallowed up completely? Even someone as open and understanding as Garnet from whom I receive immense comfort and friendship. I still feel sad.

Anyway, I've applied at the school of music. Garnet believes I've done the right thing. I can hear you groan. If I'm not accepted, I'll finish my degree. If I am, well, the economy is so rotten, the best place to be is in school anyway. I'm just giving you warning, that's all. This is my hope, to study music. I don't know where Garnet fits in in all of this.

Take care. Tell Dee I love her.

Love Andy.

Andy,

Ten days to the Def Leppard concert and no tickets yet!! Brenda said her Dad had bought the tickets and it turns out he decided he didn't want her to go to the concert and so he didn't buy the tickets. *And she didn't tell me!!* All the good seats are gone. Dad says he is going to try and get some but Dad is a *Pig* and I don't believe anything he says!! This can't be happening to me. God just can't let this happen. I will never speak to Brenda again. What a slut.

I'm writing this letter in detention. I accidently sewed my shirtsleeve to the apron I'm making. But that's not why I got the detention. The witch expected me to just sit there and take it while she screamed at me and called me stupid. So I pointed to myself and said, "See this? This is the face of someone who cares." It was worth it. I hate her. Some of the teachers are okay. I've been thinking lately that there's just so much pain in the world and we are all busy running towards it. Why do we do that? And then when our life is over we'll realize what we missed by always running to the pain. And we will be sorry.

Last weekend, Mom let me go to this girl's house for a sleepover (she wanted to get rid of me). Her name is Carla and she's new in school. Carla's mother wasn't home because it was her father's weekend to have her and he was supposed to supervise the sleepover but he never showed up. Carla phoned these guys who drive a car and they came over with beer. We got drunk. It was great. We laughed and ran around outside until two o'clock in the morning. One of the guys started smoking you-know-what and passing it around. I wanted to call Mom to come and get me but it was too late and so I said I was going over to the 7-Eleven for cigarettes and I walked around the neighborhood until about five o'clock and then I went home. Mom was still up. She was sitting on the couch listening to records, waiting for Dad to come home. I told her what had happened and she didn't yell. She said I should have telephoned but she was glad I came home. When she tried to get up off the couch, she couldn't. Mom was drunk. She tried to hide it by yawning and saying she was really tired, but I can always tell when she has too much to drink by the way she swings her arms around when she talks. I made her eat a bowl of Rice Krispies and helped her to bed. I poured the rest of her vodka into the sink and put the bottle back in the cupboard. Do you think it was God who sent me home to look after Mom? The next morning, she opened the cupboard door and took the bottle out, looked at it and threw it into the garbage, but didn't say anything. Then she starts to pull this Big Mother play and asks me a thousand questions about what I did last night!! I can't stand it.

I'm going to quit school. My marks aren't that great anyway. I'm not like Brenda who can read anything and remember it. I can't. I'm not like that. I can feel *Catcher in the*

Rye, but I can't tell you what it's about. I can understand people. That's why everyone comes to me for advice. I know what people are thinking. I know the future. I even know what people are going to say and do before they speak. I write things down when they come to me just so I can prove to myself that I didn't imagine it, that I really can know things before they happen. And a long time ago I predicted Mom and Dad would split again. And I predict another thing. Dad is going to move in with that Debbie. I had a dream about it. I dreamed he was sitting at a table in the kitchen with her and she said to him, "Now I understand why your wife couldn't live with you."

Are all men nerds? The boys in my class sure are. I see right through them, too. Will I always be able to do that? How can you fall in love with anyone if that's the case? Oh well, at least I will always have RICK SAVAGE. And I don't care what I have to do, anything. I'm going to get to the concert. He'll be looking for me.

It's destiny. If you don't hear from me in a long time, the next time, it'll be in an English accent!

Bye. Dee.

Greetings and Hallucinations!

(As they used to say in the 50s or 60s. Bad sign. I'm losing track of decades.)

Well, you did it. Glad to hear that you're glad to be going back to Laval and that the music department is also glad to have you. I can hardly wait to see what will happen now. Get into dedication and all kinds of things could go right or wrong. You could get fat or thin. But, as your Dad's mother used to say, "If you want to get drunk, get drunk, but don't inflict your hangover on me."

I've been to my counselor today (am I getting possessive about him?) and I'm in a strange mood because of it. I'll spare you the gory details. I'll not bash and bitch through my childhood, puberty, etc. I'm too old for that kind of nose-picking thing. I'll just say that he gave me instructions to set aside a certain amount of time each day to feel sorry for myself instead of doing it all the time and trying not to. Like Dee in the shower with a washcloth stuffed into her mouth so I won't hear her crying. I said to Dee, "If you hear me crying, don't worry because I have given myself permission to do that now," and she said, revealing inherent genes, "Just so long as you don't come crying to me!" (Just kidding, she said.)

I received your lovely, comforting letter and all the praise and encouragement which I will put on and wear like a glove for several weeks. Note the attempt at creativity. Which probably means I shouldn't be writing but working on my new design. I'm going to make my next box the shape of a house.

I can't explain how I'm doing or whether or not my sessions with the counselor are helping any. Right now they serve to demonstrate to me how stupid I am while I continue to do stupid things. How do you know when your husband has a lover?

1. He begins to study you when he thinks you're not watching.
2. He affects an aloofness, an absent-mindedness so that he can think of her.
3. He suddenly has a great deal of energy and enthusiasm and treats you with strained friendliness.
4. He can't concentrate and isn't interested in the kids' problems or else he over-reacts out of guilt.
5. He buys new underwear.

There. Take it and frame it.

I don't think this life-long feeling of being a fish out of water will ever leave me. It grows stronger. "They" tell me (the counselor is not a person but a collection of conclusions gained from hundreds of women who continue to do stupid things) that I'm feeling worthless, rejected and unloved. If that's the case, then let me tell you it's a weightless feeling, a blue and white room, a stepping down and the ground moving away. It's constantly looking for a container to give me some shape.

Last week while walking through Eaton's store in search of a perfect shower gift for someone I don't even like. I came upon a television set which was turned on. An advertisement for a K-Tel record was on. "Learn to do the bird dance," the voice said and people were actually doing it, flapping their elbows and pecking and they were smiling as though they had just died and gone to heaven. Were they paid to smile? Fat people, skinny people young and old dancing the bird dance and discovering a new lease on life. It made me feel sick. It made me feel as though I had also been doing that bloody bird dance for the past twenty years and was still doing it; in search of the perfect shower gift for someone I don't even like. Something for the couple to argue over in court two years down the road. And that I'm not going to be able to stop doing it. I looked for a place to jump from. I called Carol and asked her to meet me for lunch. I wanted to tell someone that I was thinking of jumping. But instead, we talked about sex, unfaithfulness (hers), guilt, and never about dying. Her glasses were a mirror and I could see myself, distraught but covering up, eating and listening to myself in her frenzied gulping conversation, she not saying what she wanted to say anymore than I. It could have been a scene in a Monty Python skit. And then I got my idea to build the next box in the shape of a house. But instead of squares for photographs and family momentos I would have eyes in the box different shapes, colors, staring out through the glass.

When I got home, I wrote my idea down and filed it and then laughed myself silly. On one hand I think of dying, on the other of collecting material. Like the man who once sat across from me in a cafeteria, bemoaning the state of affairs in the world, saying that life was not worth living and then worrying aloud whether or not the apple he was about to bite into had been washed.

The fly in the ointment, as my Dad used to say, the pebble in the shoe is that your father is doing so well. He can drink and, seemingly, handle it. He's started up the garage again and I understand, if I can believe him, he's making it work. He's living with that Debbie person who is very understanding and never asks questions and he is getting laid regularly. The bitterness is that men seem to be able to skate from relationship to relationship and never fall in. The counselor says that the main reason why there are more women at singles' affairs is that when a marriage begins to falter, a man goes out and lines someone up, so he has someone to go to when it breaks apart. If your Dad was miserable and unhappy, then I wouldn't feel quite as bad as I do.

I went to Agassiz last weekend to visit Grandma and while the men were out, she and Aunt Betty read "Dear Abby" columns to each other. They were searching for instances of men who in the end, "got theirs." Men who had in some way damaged their families and ended up dying lonely deaths, unloved, filled with regret (you know). They pounced and held up examples to the window to better trace the outline of the life behind the words, aha, serves him right, look at him suffer now. They were comforting themselves, perhaps me, with the idea that there is justice. I didn't say anything because they have only just begun to accept that perhaps some marriages should end. But that acceptance has to be based on someone being wronged and someone paying in the end. I didn't tell them that men burning up in cars, men of "no fixed address" are the exception, not the rule. Because we need to believe what we read in "Dear Abby," even though life demonstrates differently.

People say to me, Lureen, how come you don't date? I never see you with a man. I don't tell them about those singles' clubs, overweight Polish and Italian men in white shoes, stamping out their territory on the dance floor. It leaves me cold. Jamie says, come on Mom, you won't find a man in the yellow pages. I wish, he said, that you would have had as many men as Dad has had women since he's left. Jamie thinks to challenge me into action. But I say, shame on me. For sure that means I'm to be pitied, worthless, etc. What a piss-up. And where shall I find these men? Go out, they say, trample over the other women, stick my foot out and trip up a man. Buy a push-up bra. And I tell them forget it. It's too easy.

But it's been wonderful to have Jamie home. He's a real sweetheart to have around, although if he says "life begins at forty" one more time I will break his arm. He is calm and quiet and loving and caring and all that. And willing to listen. He fixes things, makes them work again. Does his own laundry. He lends Dee his records and they argue about what is good and bad music. He took her to the David Bowie concert and consequently I'm not hearing quite as much about Def Leppard, but too much of Bowie. Jamie has begun to draw once again. I think, like us, he will live.

Say hello to Garnet.

Cheers, Mom.

ps/ I have a job interview tomorrow. Don't hold your breath.

pps/ Dad just dropped by. He sends along his hello.

23 / Keepsakes

"It's like the old Eaton's mail order. You don't always get what you expect, kid." Mika hears one of her daughters speak in a dry, jesting tone. They're playing Scrabble in the living room, but as usual, doing more talking than anything else. Who said it? Betty? No, Betty doesn't joke as easily as the younger ones do. Amazing, she really can't tell who said it. Where once their voices and features were as varied as her teenaged granddaughters' (who have painted their eyelids purple, put on tight jeans and gone walking downtown. It nags at Mika that their mothers appear oblivious to the way the girls flaunt themselves), now there is a certain sameness, a flat safe look in her daughters' faces. She's noticed as well their readiness to agree, to paraphrase one another's ideas. When they'd gathered noisily around the breakfast table, she'd studied them, wanting to connect them with the things in the keepsake chest upstairs. Why did I bother to save all those things, she wonders, if in the end, they don't tell me anything?

The china cups rattle sharply as she sets them in place on the table. As if by magic, the dining room draperies slide open. Beyond, the bare branches of her pin cherry bush bend against the wind. The men, she thinks, will they be safe up there in this wind? The draperies slide shut just as suddenly. She discovers the culprit and leads him over to the living room door where he might catch sight of his mother. They have all come home for the weekend. She borrowed a rollaway cot and bunked the younger ones on the floor in the TV room. She'd heard them several times, up and prowling like cats about the house, into the refrigerator and the cupboards. She worried. What junk had they been watching on the late movie? Then, the child's croupy cough had kept her awake most of the night. She had listened for his parents to get up and go to him and when they didn't, she knew she would only lie there stiff and fearful over his ragged breathing and so she got up. While they'd slept all about her in the house, below in the TV room, she had dragged the chest from the closet and fulfilled the promise she'd made to herself, to get rid of things for once, to stop saving and divide what she had among them.

Laughter rises in the living room. "Remember," someone says, "how Dad would make us stand on a piece of brown paper and then trace our foot so he could order our shoes from Eaton's mail-order? I used to wonder what they must have thought when they got ten cut-outs of feet in the mail."

"You're kidding," the new daughter-in-law says. "What a great idea.

More laughter. Their exaggeration rankles. There were never ten at once, she thinks. Some of you had already left home, flown the coop, as your dad used to say all the time. The three girls.

"Can I do something?" The new daughter-in-law squints worriedly at Mika through her large tinted glasses.

"No, no," Mika says. "I'm just going to cut more ham and then I'm finished." Will there be enough? Should she heat up the cabbage rolls just in case?

"Remember the time Dad bought that whole box of shoes? A real bargain, eh. Or so he thought until he found out they were all for the left foot."

Not true. They were all different sizes.

But she lets them get away with it because they are off now and telling stories for the benefit of the new person, the daughter-in-law who hovers anxiously in the doorway, caught between their stories and needing to be of some help to Mika, who is setting out the lunch. Mika listens to these stories. Each time she learns something new. Previously, at these sporadic weekend gatherings when they first began to flock home all at once, never alone, they told their stories with urgency and stealth. Stories of betrayal, favoritism. Some had called her names. But she has noticed how lately, their stories have changed. They have become harmless and humorous, slanted to expose the teller's daring, or what they imagine to be unconventional childhoods.

"Yeah, yeah," Mika hears herself call out to them. "That was your dad all right. Anything that was a bargain, he bought. Whether we needed it or not."

"Cheaper by the dozen, he always said," Betty says. Betty's memory matches her own more closely than any of the others', Mika realizes. They remember the same things.

"He sounds like such a neat person," the new daughter-in-law says. "I wish I'd known him." Mika knows she looks for clues that will reveal to her the man she married. Let me tell you about James. I think he was the one who kept banging his head against the crib.

"What about the bells?" Betty's steady voice overcomes their laughter and talk. "What about the time we all tied bells to our boots and darn near drove the Sunday School teacher batty?"

Tell us about the braids, Mika urges, caught by Betty's soft voice and how they all stop to listen when she speaks. It gnawed at Mika when she'd discovered Betty's braids in the chest that she had never been able to ask why Betty had cut her hair off that day.

Arms outstretched for balance, the child lurches back into the dining room once again, seeking out the drapery pull. The unsteady gait of the toddler makes Mika cringe. She shudders, imagining his head bashing against the sharp corner of the buffet and a wedge-shaped cut opening up. I had one who used to walk off chairs, she has told them. I think it was Rudy. He had no sense. I would stand him on the table and he'd walk right off if I didn't stop him. "So, that's what happened to Rudy. He fell on his head. Now we know." They stole the story from her mouth. They don't recall Rudy doing that. But she does. She remembers Rudy walking off the shed roof.

Now, they would put a hockey helmet on such a one and let him go. Then, I had to tie him up. People thought I was being mean, but I had no choice. She feels vindicated now by Rudy's prudence, how he has listened to her and got an education and can afford to build a new house. On this windy, frost-threatening day, the men and the grandsons are off helping Rudy shingle the roof of his new house.

I had one who ate dirt. That's all right, Mrs. Pats said. She always looked for something good in everything. Every person has to eat a peck of dirt before they die, Mrs. Pats said. But Mika feared pin worms. When the children ran wild, twitched and squirmed, she would look and, sure enough, discover the lashing white threads inside them. It was an embarrassment for her to have to ask at the drugstore for the purple worm pills, to push them into ice-cream cones to entice the younger ones to take them. And so she made that one wear mittens. Which one was it? One of the girls. This one is different, Mrs. Pats said, stockings rolled down around thick blue ropes of varicose veins, huffing and puffing into the kitchen without knocking, the first one to inspect her new baby. The one who ate dirt. Where do such ideas come from, she'd wondered, about having to eat a peck of dirt? The idea was strange. It made her think of the story she'd been told about the woman in Russia who had been buried alive.

This baby has long limbs, Mrs. Pats said. Make sure you let her go four hours between feedings. Introduce solids early to prevent anemia. The heavy pewter salt and pepper shakers in the keepsake trunk were Mrs. Pats's wedding gift to her and the woman's right to visit every Saturday afternoon when the week's baking cooled on the counter tops and Mika took advantage of the warm kitchen to bathe the children, one by one. Mika loved the heaviness of the salt and pepper shakers and their soft, dull color. Once she had painted the walls in the living room a gray to match and Maurice had made jokes about it, had told all his customers down at the barber shop how his wife had decorated the house around a pair of salt and pepper shakers.

She'd never had one who would go four hours between feedings.

I had one who hated water. It took two of us to give him a bath. Sometimes Mrs. Pats would help me. He screamed and screamed and I didn't know what to do but to force him into the tub and hold him there while someone else washed him. Sometimes I had to hit him and the shape of my hand would be there on his seat, raised and red. That's not going to help any, Mrs. Pats said. But I didn't know what else to do.

I had one who, one day, came home from school or from wherever she had been. I didn't always know. They often said one thing and did another. Even Betty. And who, for no reason I know of, marched upstairs into my bedroom and took the scissors from the sewing box and cut off her hair. When I lifted up the pillbox hats in the chest, all those hats, shoes and purses Mrs. Pats was always passing along to me, as though I ever went anywhere, there under the hats, curled like two question marks, were Betty's braids. All I could think about when I saw them was the verse in the Bible about the sins of the parents being visited upon the children.

"I'm getting married," Betty had said. She had telephoned one day just when Mika was sitting at the table, thinking that Betty was doing so well at last, working at a good job and making something for herself. She had been thinking how lucky it was that Betty didn't have to do maid's work for the rich. Not like she and Elizabeth had done. Making so much and sending so much home and never anything left over for themselves. Being treated like dirt.

I'm getting married, she herself had written to her parents, and sent the message home with her sister Elizabeth.

Mika remembers. When Mrs. Pats had asked her what her plans were, she'd answered without thinking. "I don't have any plans," she'd said. "I'm not going to make a wedding for Betty and that's it."

Immediately, she'd wanted to swallow her tongue. She knew even as she'd said it that she would make a wedding. She watched her fingers plucking nervously at her skirt and winced at the sight of the garden dirt caught in the chapped skin. I won't make a wedding, she'd said and at the same time thinking she'd have to start wearing garden gloves to get her hands in shape for it. None of her children had inherited her broad hands or her stubby short fingers. All her children had long fingers, slim hands. Hands of a piano player, Maurice had said and went out and bought a piano which had sat silent ever since Betty had left home.

"If you don't make a wedding for Betty, then who will?" Mrs. Pats had asked, surprise flashing across her shiny face. Strands of her pewter-colored hair had pulled loose from the metal combs and trailed down both sides of her face. Her hair was now the color of the salt and pepper shakers. She sat on a chair on the veranda with her knees spread, cradling a bowl of peas in her lap. "It's traditional for the bride's parents to put on the wedding, you know."

Yes, I know. I know about tradition. I have been here long enough to have learned the English ways. I taught myself to read and write. And I'm going to make a wedding for Betty. Where they sat, a hedge of overgrown lilacs screened the veranda from Main Street. Across the street, three of her children played in the school yard, waiting for her. They were there between the branches of the lilac bushes, split into pieces like vivid moving jigsaw puzzles, lying on their stomachs on the swings, twisting the ropes and lifting off, flying and spinning wildly as the swing unwound. They didn't do the simplest things the usual way. Not her children. Like Betty, throwing over a good job and announcing out of the blue that she was going to marry this unknown Frank person.

"I met Frank in Winnipeg," Betty said. "I met him at a country western show. He's in a band and plays bass guitar. By the way, he's Mennonite."

"So, he's a Mennonite. What's that supposed to mean?"

"I thought you'd be pleased about that, at least. But it doesn't matter. We love each other. That's what matters."

And the vinegar had come flooding up her throat into her mouth. "My, my, isn't that wonderful," she heard herself say. The skin on her knuckles stretched taut as she clenched the receiver. "I hope you're not planning on wearing white."

Mika bends over the freezer, searching for the milk cartons filled with cabbage rolls. The child followed her down to the basement and she hears the bright tinkle of metal against glass. The child plays with Maurice's jars of nuts and bolts, shaking them up and down, making his own music. I had one who played the most beautiful music. I don't know how she did it. But she would listen to a song on the radio and then sit down and play it just as well, better even. Sometimes at night, she would come home and sit and play in the dark and I didn't mind. It made me want to cry the way she could play *Ebb Tide*.

His name is John Peters, she had written in the letter. Elizabeth will tell you all about him. He's one of the Peterses who once had the store in Reinfeld. He's thirty-one years old. But we agree, it doesn't matter because we love each other.

Father says no. This you must not do. Elizabeth, hands on hips to make herself look bigger. As if that's necessary! I'm to send you home, Elizabeth says. Mother, Father, they know nothing about this man. Father says he will find work for you at the hotel.

Elizabeth. Who does all the lifting and carrying in the house. Elizabeth, who is big and strong, does not carry her.

Mika cries and cries. She begs. She paces about the cramped room, fists clenched tightly. She stands in front of the mirror, heart crashing, but watches without feeling the determined slow movement of the scissors in her hands and jagged chunks of thick auburn hair dropping to the floor.

In the keepsake chest there are many letters. Things she can't pass along. Mika hugs the frozen milk cartons to her breasts as she walks up the stairs. What will she do with those letters? Letters from Elizabeth. The letters filled with recipes, accounts of jelly-making, preserving, butchering, requests for measurements so Elizabeth could sew dresses for the girls, knit mittens and socks and fashion coats from left-over clothing given to her that was otherwise of no use. They were always polite requests, her sister was never anything but polite. The biting tongue had passed her by. But as she'd re-read the letters, she could find condemnation there because she hated those blistering days in the kitchen with boilers steaming on the cookstove, hot syrup running down the sides of jelly jars, cucumbers stuffed squeaking and complaining into quart sealers. Because she had forgotten how to write in German.

In the letters there were hints of when would Mika learn to control herself. When would she take her sister's advice and begin to use the rhythm method, surely that would be acceptable to Maurice? How could she explain to Elizabeth that their life had no discernible pattern? That it wasn't a question of religion at all.

Among the left-overs there was a wrinkled photograph which looked as though someone had once crumpled it up tightly in a fist and then smoothed it straight once again. The photograph puzzled her. It was of a stone monument sitting in a dirt square. The picture had been taken in the village in Russia where she'd been born. She couldn't remember the place clearly, but remembered instead the stories her parents had told her. As she began to be absorbed by the day, her children, the stories grew pale until she could no longer remember any of them except the one her grandmother had told her, that strange frightening story about the woman they buried alive. She imagines a woman sitting on a chair with black skirts and a black shawl covering her white head. She's sitting there beside the monument, her jaw collapsed because her teeth are gone. Her hands are folded neatly in her lap and she is listening for the muffled sound of a woman's voice coming from the ground. It didn't happen that way. That's not the way the story goes. But she sees it in her mind, how the woman on the chair sits there listening and can't do anything about it.

"Why in the world shouldn't I wear white?" Betty had asked and Mika heard in Betty's voice the same smirkiness that always turned her mouth up at the corners whenever Mika tried to tell her anything. Usually, she would simply run from the room, or if she chose to listen, it would be with that silly, secretive smile in place. Mika wanted to slap the sound from her voice. She wanted to pinch and twist the smirk away and shout, wake up. Wake up, or you'll be sorry.

Born April 21st, a boy, eight pounds, seven ounces, Mika had written in her devotional book. My first grandchild. A darling baby boy. I never even saw him.

"Look," Betty said. "Just because I had a baby, that doesn't make me any different than anyone else I know. Including you. I can count, you know." For the first time, the smirkiness was not there. Her voice became blunt and hard.

Jolted, surprised, Mika felt her cheeks burn. "Well, so. So then you know. To wear white is a sin. I never did when I married your dad and I won't be a part of you doing it either."

Follow the light, Maurice had said, right to the end of the hallway. That's where I am, the door beside the light on the second floor. Those red lights pointed the way home, the exits. I don't know. I don't know, she said. It's up to you, he said, his voice deep and careful, coming from the bed behind her. Those red lights, it's as though they're pointing out something, something more than. . . . Pointing the way to what? he said into her neck. I've got something that's pointing, he said. He strummed her breast with his thick fingers.

"Remember how Dad could come home late and wake us all up? He'd be carrying ice-cream cones. And Mom would get so mad because he'd wake us all up and then we'd get all sticky with melting ice-cream. I think I would've killed Frank if he'd ever pulled a stunt like that. But we weren't complaining, then. Oh no," Betty says as Mika enters the living room, her arms laden with the things from the keepsake chest. The things she's been saving.

"Hey! Far out, Grandma. Let's see." The granddaughters have come back from downtown. How many boys have they met? Did they make promises to meet them later? Will they climb inside the boys' cars? They swarm around her as she sets the bundle down on the floor. Shrieks of high-pitched laughter as the granddaughters pounce and rummage through samples of art work, pages of arithmetic. "Boy Mom, were you ever dumb. Look at this. And you have the nerve to get on my case about school?"

A flash of light as the living room drapery slides open. The child has discovered another drapery pull. A piece of paper tumbles down the road in front of the house. Across the road, a carmel-colored German Shepherd paces up and down its run. The curtains close slowly. Mika frowns at the sight of greenish mucus trailing from the child's nose. She wishes the mother would put him to bed. From the kitchen, the smell of cabbage rolls sifts through the air. "Should I check on them?" the daughter-in-law asks, feeling left out as all of them, the daughters and granddaughters, ignore her as they laugh and compare samples of handwriting, the homemade birthday cards.

"What about these?" Mika asks and pulls the braids out from behind her apron. They dangle in the air in front of her face, thick coarse hair, heavy, not like Betty's hair is now. Betty's hair at age thirteen, her own handwriting bands the end of one. "What about the time you cut off your hair? Why did you do it?"

Betty looks up, startled. She gets up slowly and reaches. Mika pulls away. "What's the story behind these?"

"Yes, tell us, tell us," the granddaughters say.

"She probably believed in the hair fairy. Thought she'd put them under her pillow and cash in."

Laughter.

Betty's mouth shivers and her lips turn up into that

secretive smile. "I don't remember cutting off my braids," she says. "I think Dad did it. I think he got tired of listening to me complain about having to have my hair done every morning."

One of the granddaughters reaches, snatches the braids and holds them up to her ears. "Look at me, you guys. Look at me," she says. "I could make a Dolly Parton wig out of these."

And then they are all grabbing and examining the hair, passing it along and exclaiming over it.

Mika follows the smell of the cabbage rolls into the kitchen. Is it true? Did Maurice really cut off the braids? It was something he would do. In a fit of impatience, it would be just like him to cut the hair in one swift movement. I had one who ate chalk. No, it wasn't chalk. It was dirt. I had one who ate rat poison. A stupid child. We had to rush her to the doctor. Good thing he was only across the street. The twins. Once the twins got into some medicine. I think it was my phenobarb. Or was it painkillers? It wasn't my fault. I kept them up high, but one of the twins was a climber.

"Let me help you with something," the daughter-in-law pleads. She looks up at the clock. The voices from the living room have grown louder as the granddaughters join in.

"Hey, Mom. You used to tell me that if I stayed out in the rain I would melt. Remember? Well, I can remember being caught in a rain storm when I was a little kid and scared shit—"

"Uh uh," her mother warns.

"Being terrified."

The daughter-in-law sits down at the table. "I think it's really neat," she says, "that you had such a large family. It must have been fun when they were all little."

"Yes," Mika says and smiles because she can't think of anything else to say.

A flurry of moving limbs, the flash of purple eyeshadow, as one of the granddaughters enters the kitchen, pulls open cupboard doors. She is not one of Mika's favorite granddaughters. Mika thinks she tries too hard all the time to be different, not to fit in. "When do we eat?" she asks. "I'm starving."

Mika turns, catches sight of something flying past the window, a man? Sometimes she sees something similar, just as she turns, something flitting from room to room.

"We're waiting for the men," she says. She lifts the pan of cabbage rolls from the oven and sets them on the counter. More tomato juice. That will save them from drying out.

The granddaughter slouches down into the chair, pouting. "Waiting for the men? What for? Why should we have to wait?"

"Because," Mika says. "Because they'll be hungry from working so hard. And because I say so." Why does the mother let this one wear so much make-up? "Now, would you please be a good girl and go down to the basement and bring up a jar of tomato juice?"

Mika fingers the tattered photograph. She pulls it from her apron pocket and sets it on the table. She smoothes it with the palm of her hand. I had one who used to loosen the caps on my pear preserves so the syrup would ferment. She used to drink it, the fermented juice. The only way I found out was when she broke a jar and cut her hand. I think she still has the scar.

"What have you got there?" The daughter-in-law picks up the photograph, squints at it.

A monument. A rocket-shaped stone. Why would anyone want to take a picture of such a thing? And then not write on the back to say what it is. She sits down in the grand-daughter's place. "It's the strangest thing," Mika hears herself say, "but in Russia, they once buried a woman who wasn't dead."

Mika continues to tell the story, her voice gathering strength, rising up in the kitchen along with the smoky-sweet smell of ham, cooked cabbage. Heat radiates from the granddaughter's body as she sets the tomato juice down on the table. She will interrupt, Mika thinks, ask about food and when is it time for eating. But she is surprised when this one lingers, stands in the doorway fiddling with the strings of an apron dangling from a hook, stands there in the doorway, listening.

Born in Morris, Manitoba, Sandra Birdsell moved to
Winnipeg in 1967. She is also the author of a novel, *The
Missing Child* (Lester & Orpen Dennys, 1989), which won the
1990 W.H. Smith Award for a first novel. *Agassiz* was
published in Canada by Turnstone Press as *Agassiz Stories* in
1987. Birdsell is a scriptwriter, playwright, and filmmaker, who
has won numerous awards for her writing, including the
Gerald Lampert Award for new fiction, the National Magazine
Award for short fiction, and the Canadian Book Information
Centre's 45 Below Award.

Agassiz was typeset in Goudy Oldstyle
at Stanton Publication Services
and printed on acid-free Glatfelter Natural paper
by R.R. Donnelley & Sons Company.
Agassiz was designed and illustrated
by R.W. Scholes